WILL OF FIRE

A *Buried Goddess Saga* NOVEL

III

RHETT C.
BRUNO

JAIME
CASTLE

WILL OF FIRE

©2018 RHETT C. BRUNO & JAIME CASTLE

JOIN THE KING'S SHIELD

S ign up to the *free* and exclusive King's Shield Newsletter to receive early looks and new novels, peeks at conceptual art that breathes life into Pantego as well as exclusive access to short stories called "Legends of Pantego." Learn more about the characters and the world you love.

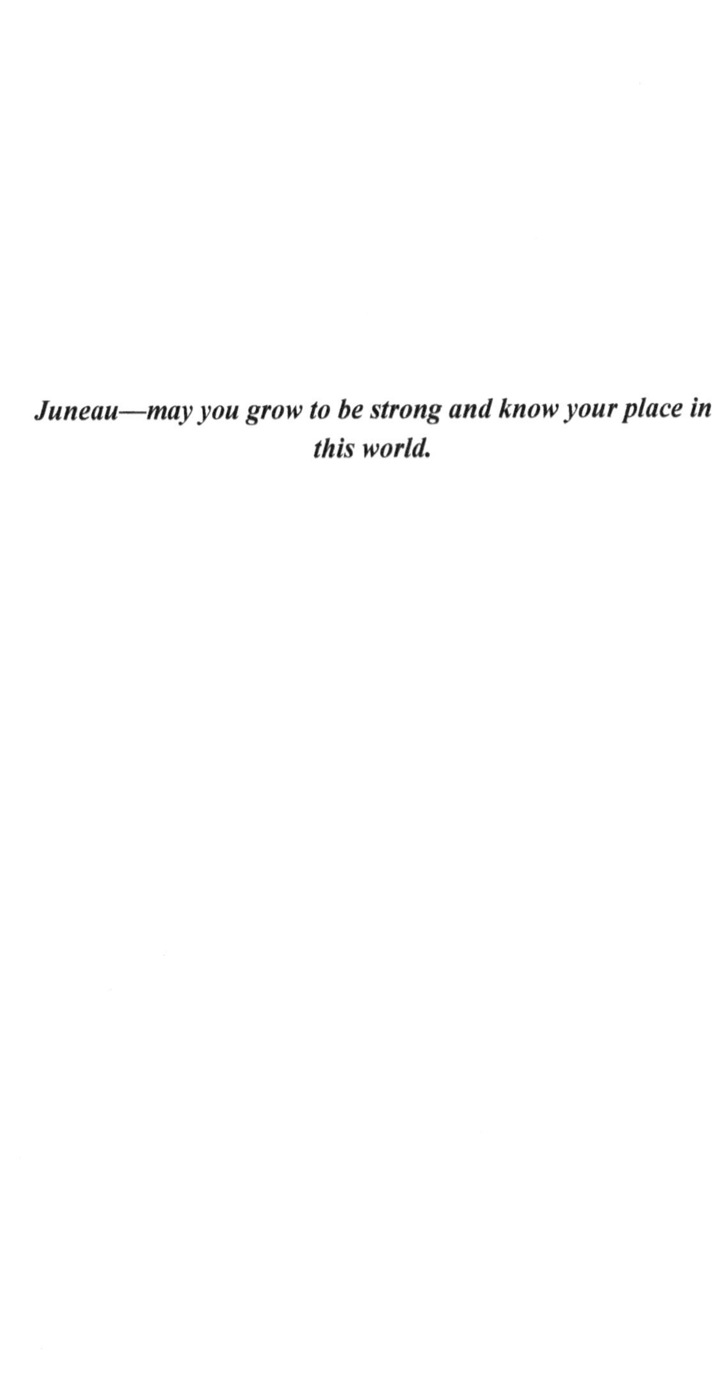

Juneau—may you grow to be strong and know your place in this world.

BROTLEBIR
BREKLIODAD
THE DRAGON'S TAIL
hornsheim
THE
GLASS KINGDOM
fettingboroough
YAOLIN CITY
PANPING
THE
BLACK SANDS
nahanab
saujibar
LATIAPUR
THE BOILING WATERS

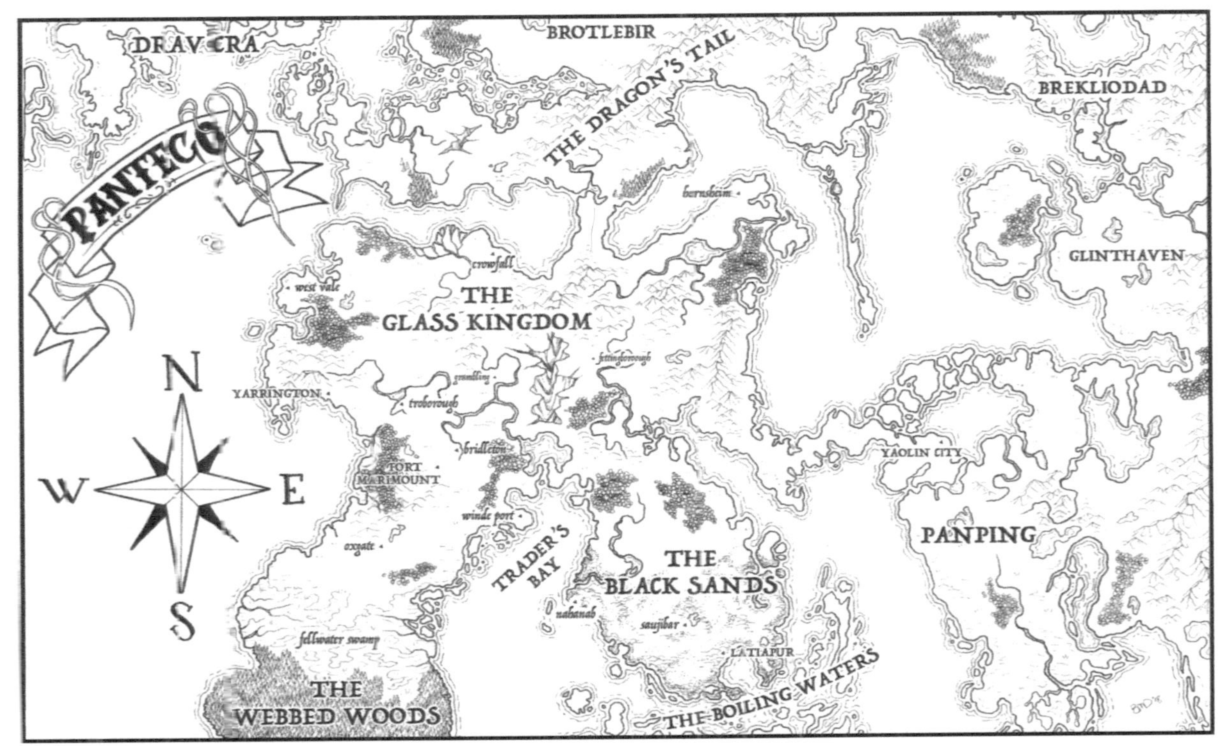

PANTEGO
DRAV CRA
BROTLEBIR
THE DRAGON'S TAIL
BREKLIODAD
berusheim
crowsfall
GLINTHAVEN
west vale
THE
GLASS KINGDOM
fittingborough
grandling
YARRINGTON
troborough
bridleton
YAOLIN CITY
N
W
E
S
FORT MARIMOUNT
winde port
PANPING
oxgate
TRADER'S BAY
THE
BLACK SANDS
nahanah
saujibar
LATIAPUR
fellwater swamp
THE BOILING WATERS
THE
WEBBED WOODS

PROLOGUE

Devlin Boremater stood before the altar in Fessix, just east of Crowfall. Beside him, blind Father Morningweg leaned wearily upon his cane, blessing the townsfolk as they entered. It was a small village settled along the water in the Northern Glass Kingdom. Like every day before and every day that would come, the sun rose, and a sliver of its light shot through a pinhole in the back wall, beaming directly through the Eye of Iam hanging above him. The light refracted through the glass, painting vibrant colors down the central aisle.

Devlin, the altar server, acted as the Father's eyes, watched as the flock filed in one by one to hear the morning sermon. It was the same as always in the sleepy town as the cold of winter set in upon an already frigid landscape. Devlin whispered each name to the father as men and women approached. Father Morningweg smiled at each of them and listened to the town gossip.

He never could help himself, even though Iam would disapprove.

Fishermen spoke of how the fish stopped biting as ice covered the Strait of Bautim. Most others complained about the deepening chill in the air. More than a few discussed the latest town scandal that Mistress Falhua had been unfaithful to her husband, the bailiff. A man, dressed in Yarrington fashion, said he'd heard whispers during the last feast at the Glass Castle. Apparently, King Liam had toppled from his chair and was rushed away. His wife, Queen Oleander, then had a public meltdown, slamming tableware against the wall until every noble in the Great Hall left.

Devlin wasn't sure he believed them. Although he wasn't yet a man and was an orphan without parents to take him to see the great city of Yarrington, he'd heard enough stories about the Queen from passers-through. The way they talked of her beauty, he couldn't imagine her suffering from fits of rage. Besides, rumors about Liam's declining health had been rampant for years, and High Priest Wren discredited them as stirs of dissension from enemies of the Crown.

"Welcome all," Father Morningweg said as the pews squeaked. Devlin took his own seat on the platform. "The light of Iam shines upon you this morning. Winter may be on its way, but that does not mean we let darkness set into our souls. Iam the all-knowing gave us this harsh season so we may learn to find the strength within to endure. So we might never grow soft in this, His world, and forget to count all the blessings he bestows. We are fortun—"

A shrill scream reverberated from somewhere outside, loud enough that all those who'd just sat down leaped up and studied the door. A woman burst through, face drained of all color, terrified.

"The Drav Cra—they—their ships emerged through the fog and cloud," she stuttered.

"You are sure?" the village bailiff questioned. The woman managed a nod, and the bailiff hastened to her. "Everyone stay here."

"Stay here?" a man protested. "Last time they slaughtered my cows."

"Better than your children, aye?" The bailiff stuck his head outside. A bell from the docks chimed. "Everyone in!" he bellowed. "The house of Iam is our protection. Come now!"

Stragglers—all those late to morning service—sprinted through the doors before they were slammed shut and locked. It was impossible to know if the entire village made it in.

"Is everyone here?" Father Morningweg asked.

"I... I think so," Devlin said, scanning the faces of the huddled crowd. His heart raced. He'd never been through a raid before, though he'd heard the horrifying tales parents told their children at night to frighten them.

"Are you sure, boy?"

"As best I can be," he said, putting on his bravest face.

"It is all right, my children," Morningweg said to the entire congregation. "What do we do when the devils come?"

"Shield ourselves with Iam's light," many of them replied in unison, Devlin amongst them.

"Good. Here, within these walls, we are shielded by the light of Holy Iam. The heathens come only for our food and supplies because they live in shadow without fortune. Let them have it. For His love protects us and they are like infants thrashing in the darkness."

The sound of ships cracking against the docks was loud enough to hear through the stone walls. Everyone winced, even Father Morningweg. Devlin felt the man's hand on his shoulder and immediately all fear dissipated. Although the father's touch might have calmed Devlin, the screams and whimpers of fear still coursed through the church.

The bailiff worked to restore peace, but there was really no saying if, with all the panic, someone had been left outside. Mothers and fathers searched through their crowd for their children, and when finding them, pulling them close. Others called out for family members or friends who may have arrived separately.

Outside, heavy footsteps rumbled like thunder. There was shouting in what Devlin imagined was Drav Crava. Father Morningweg hushed his flock and pointed them toward the Eye of Iam. With his fingers, he circled his eye sockets, empty after his vow of sightlessness, and whispered a silent prayer. Devlin did the same, then rose to stand next to the priest, grasping the man's forearm with both hands. The room grew eerily quiet save for the sniffles of small children.

Despite being locked, the thick, worn, wooden doors swung open. Dust and snow swirled, and through the fog stepped the savages. There were two in front. One had her face painted, half white at the bottom, half black on top with red around her eyes, so their fury shone. Bones and trinkets rattled from within a nest of raven-black hair. She was a warlock. If the tales Devlin had heard could be believed, they painted themselves to evoke fear. It worked. Devlin tightened his grip on the father's arm, and his heart thumped even faster. Beside her was a more refined man, garbed in a robe of crimson. His face didn't need paint, for a red birthmark stretched across his face into five points.

"It is okay, my son," Father Morningweg said. "Stand, therefore, and see the salvation of Iam."

"You do not belong here, heathens," the bailiff called, standing at the doors and in front of the people of Fessix. "Begone or the wrath of King Liam will befall you as it once did."

Before he could get out another word, the female warlock slashed his throat with a crude knife. Devlin flinched. The villagers gasped as the bailiff fell to his knees and the warlock climbed over him up onto one of the pews. She hopped from one to the next, glaring down at the innocent people.

"What happened?" the father whispered.

Devlin couldn't find any words.

"Silence." The birthmarked man calmly spoke as crying broke out once more. "It will all be over soon."

A group of hulking, fur-clad warriors strode into the room, axes and spears in hand. They shoved the people aside and made way for their apparent leader to stroll down the aisle. Devlin watched in horror, then looked up at Father Morningweg. The man's face remained stoic. All the talk of Drav Cra Raiders and how they were like walking demons on Pantego were true, but seeing the real thing was even worse.

When Devlin came into the service of the priest, he'd been told of the many raids the father had endured since the church sent him to serve the people of Fessix. He'd assured Devlin that the raiders always kept out of the church. As if though they worshiped the Buried Goddess, they feared what might happen should they anger Iam.

Not this time.

The villagers all watched in silent horror as the heathens passed. Parents held their children, covering their mouths to stifle the cries.

Devlin Boremater winced as the female warlock leaped down in front of him, then circled him. The sight of her eyes, bright against her black face paint, sent a shiver coursing down his spine.

"Drad Redstar," she said, addressing the birthmarked man before rattling off words in Drav Crava.

"My dearest Freydis," the man replied, gently stroking her cheek. "Their time will come soon enough."

He moved to shove by Father Morningweg toward the nave and the Eye of Iam, but the priest blocked him and spread his arms wide. "Please, there is nothing for you here."

Devlin hadn't noticed, but he'd been cowering behind the father, shaking.

"Out of my way, priest," the man named Redstar said, "or you will join your bailiff."

Father Morningweg kept his nerve for a few seconds longer, then shrunk out of the way, dragging Devlin with him. Redstar strolled by, ignoring Devlin. Instead, he turned and headed down the stairs of the crypt.

In the back of the church, a man panicked and ran for the door. He made it outside where a brown wolf, big as a horse, pounced on him. His screams could've curdled blood as the great beast dragged him out of view. More cries sounded.

"Nobody else move!" Father Morningweg shouted. He turned to Freydis. If the man had eyes, Devlin imagined he'd see fear there, too. "Please, take whatever you want. No others must die."

"But Father," she said, voice heavily accented. "Wouldn't we be doing a favor sending them to the Gate of Light?" A few of the Drav Cra raiders laughed.

"If it is our time, but I beg you." He fell to his knees. Devlin took the opportunity to shrink back behind the altar. "They have families, children who still need guidance."

"Relax, priest," Redstar said. He returned from the crypt carrying a broken shard of stone with unfinished, ancient artwork painted on it. From his studies, Devlin knew it was one of the few relics left over from the age of the God Feud. It had been stored in Fessix, kept in a sealed reliquary, in hopes of remaining hidden in an unremarkable town, but Redstar's hand was now bloody as if he'd somehow bashed through the thick glass.

"The tablet," Devlin squeaked before he could help himself.

Father Morningweg's head turned toward the sound, and Freydis' did too. Devlin crouched down further.

"How dare you touch that!" Father Morningweg snapped, drawing the warlock's attention. "That is a holy relic."

"Not to me." Redstar stopped in front of the father. "It is the final piece of a story. Ancient priests, men like you, broke this story to pieces and hid them around their land until they too forgot the truth." He tenderly ran his fingers across the engraving, wiping away a layer of dust. "It has taken a lifetime to gather, but this is the last."

Devlin watched with admiration as Father Morningweg found his nerve again, standing to block the Drav Cra's path once again. "I... I won't let you leave this church with it. You—you'll—have to kill me."

"Now what fun would that be?" He swiped his bloody hand through the air, and heathen magic sent Father Morningweg sailing into the wall.

"Father!" Devlin cried out, running toward him. Freydis smiled, then spat on them both.

Redstar grabbed Devlin and drew him in close, placing a knife against his neck.

"Leave him be, heathen!" Father Morningweg cried. "Kill me, but leave him be."

"How will any of you see the truth of the Dawning if I kill you now?" Redstar said. "I suppose you won't see much of anything though would you, priest?" He dragged the tip of his blade up Devlin's cheek. Devlin's body went stiff, petrified from fear.

Redstar lowered the blade and handed the piece of sacred stone to one of the raiders. In response, the man asked a question in Drav Crava.

"Freydis, burn the church and let them pray to the ashes," Redstar said. "Then, return to the north and prepare the clans. It's time I pay a visit to my sister. I shall summon you when the time comes."

"We await the death of the enemy," Freydis replied.

Redstar strolled out of the room, and his men followed

behind. Freydis then kneeled before Devlin and Father Morning-weg, and a sinister grin spread across her face. "Where is your god now?" she asked as she drew her crude knife, slid it across her palm and squeezed blood over their heads.

"You will help the priest see the truth that will come, boy," she said, standing.

Devlin shivered. He was crying now. He wasn't sure when it started, but he couldn't help it.

"But you will only need one eye for that." She placed her hand over one side of Devlin's face. Her skin was as hot as a roaring fire. Her fingers covered his eye and burned it, branding his skin. Devlin cried out, falling to the ground, clutching his eye.

"Now you are halfway to priesthood. You're welcome."

Father Morningweg wrapped his arms around Devlin and held him tight as she left. After a few moments, the townsfolk stirred and shrieked, and the acrid smell of smoke filled Devlin's nostrils.

I

THE KNIGHT

Torsten heard the rumble and watched the familiar streets of Yarrington bounce by through the bars of a prison carriage. His ankles and wrists were cuffed, chained to the floor as if he were any other prisoner of war. Others, most of them afhems or commanders of the Shesaitju, judging by the number of their elaborate tattoos, shared the carriage.

One of Afhem Muskigo's Serpent Guard sat across from him, mask removed to reveal a face too soft to belong to a grown man. Torsten wasn't sure why they kept him alive. Serpent Guards had no tongues and wouldn't be giving up any secrets.

Down at the end sat a wiry boy from the Glass heartland. He had the extreme misfortune to have been an assistant to Yuri Darkings before the traitor murdered Wardric Jolly and fled. Torsten could tell he knew nothing.

"Where are they taking us?" the boy asked as the carriage banked. His face was pressed against the bars, his body trembling.

"The Glass Castle, Shield barracks," Torsten answered. "Doesn't matter. There'll be bars either way."

"I swear… I didn't know what my master was plotting."

"I believe you. A week ago, that might have been enough."

The boy glanced at the white helm sitting between Torsten's legs, left there by Redstar as if part of some cruel joke. "But you're the Wearer of White," he said.

The gazes of all the captive Shesaitju snapped toward Torsten, bright with anger. As if he didn't have enough problems. Somehow, they'd made it the entire journey without his identity coming up. Without wearing his full suit of armor, the gray men had no way of knowing what the helmet signified. The Serpent Guard's hate-filled eyes opened and now fixed on Torsten's throat.

Torsten ignored them and raised his chained hands. "A week ago, that might have been enough, too."

"It's a mistake though, right?" the boy said. "Everyone always talks about how honorable you are. What they claim you did, it can't be—"

"It is," Torsten snapped. The boy shuddered, his whole body slammed back against the carriage wall. If any of the Shesaitju wanted to go for him, he wouldn't stop them. Countless times in his mind he'd replayed those moments after the battle, and every time the truth was evident.

He'd killed one of his own men.

After finding Wardric's body and accusing Redstar, Torsten publicly attacked the King's supposedly-reformed uncle, having to be restrained to keep from killing him. But that wasn't why he found himself chained up in a carriage. In his rage, Torsten threw a King's Shieldsman aside like a rag doll. The boy was just trying to keep Torsten in check, and for his efforts, his head hit a rock. Dead on impact.

Torsten deserved to be where he was. He was meant to lead an order whose sole purpose was to shield the followers of Iam from evil and darkness, and he'd failed them. Torsten didn't even know the fallen Shieldsman's name. He'd played so spectacularly into Redstar's hands that they were now the same thing. *Murderers.*

"I… I don't want to die…" the boy whimpered.

"If you are truthful," Torsten replied, "Iam will not let you."

"His light… it—is it gone?"

"Never."

The boy hung his head against the bars and began to weep. Torsten knew he was telling the truth. *Nobody is that good an actor—except perhaps Whitney Fie—Blisslayer.*

Torsten cursed himself for thinking of Whitney at a time like this, yet simultaneously wished the thief were there. He'd have known how to pick the locks holding Torsten in place, how to smooth-talk his way out of a mess of his own making.

Torsten recalled watching him flee Winde Port by ship after helping with the failed ambushing of Muskigo. The thief had no reason not to. He'd only helped in exchange for Torsten aiding in the search for Sora, and judging by how his blood mage friend burned down all of Merchants Row, she was in perfectly good health and in no need of aid. Whether she truly was touched by Iam, Torsten didn't know, but there was something special about her. He'd seen it in her eyes.

She'd stopped Redstar in the Webbed Woods, survived being captive to the Dom Nohzi, single-handedly ended Muskigo's brief occupation of Winde Port, and in doing it all, saved Torsten's life twice when he was supposed to be saving hers. The memory helped Torsten cling to the faith that Iam remained with him despite his failings. For whatever reason, He was working through her; using that same wicked magic Redstar used for evil to do good. To make light from darkness.

It has to be a sign.

And Torsten needed one.

Through the bars, he could see the faces of Yarrington citizens celebrating their victorious return. Afhcm Muskigo and his rebel army had been battered and forced to retreat. The price, in gold and lives, was grave, and his influence would continue to spread amongst the people of his conquered homeland. Much of the Glass army and their Drav Cra allies remained in Winde Port to prepare for an extended campaign into the Shesaitju lands to end the rebellion, but it was a victory nonetheless.

Only, the cheering citizens didn't praise the Glass soldiers or King's Shieldsmen who had died in the fighting. They celebrated Redstar. The man who'd 'summoned wind and flame to drive the gray men away.' And Redstar, in turn, heaped all credit upon Nesilia's shoulders, never mentioning once that the fire had sprung from Sora's hands. Torsten even wondered if the unnatural wind Redstar's magic appeared to be behind had actually been Sora's doing—Iam protecting Winde Port from invaders through her hand.

There was nobody to tell them it was all a lie. Even the King's Shieldsmen marching back with them remained silent as Redstar's name dripped from the crowd's lips. Thanks to Torsten, they had no leader to guide them, to show them that they were being deceived.

Torsten hadn't seen the masses in such jubilation since Liam's last war nearly a decade ago. Even the snow couldn't keep them indoors. Sure, mothers wept for those lost, but the victory had been swift and overwhelming. More fathers were left to embrace returning sons than expected. Priests of Iam thanked their God for success and prayed for the souls sacrificed in defense of the Kingdom of Glass. However, they weren't alone.

Men and women dressed in crimson, hooded robes, wearing white, expressionless masks with a single line of red running down from one eye-hole dotted the crowd. It was the garb worn by cultists to the Buried Goddess. Torsten had broken up plenty of rings in his day as a Shieldsman, rooting them out of basements in the city or caves beyond. Never had he seen them openly on the streets unless guards were chasing them.

Presently, nobody else even seemed to notice them. They blended in, and why wouldn't they? For riding at the front of this victorious army were the true followers of Nesilia, the Buried Goddess. They needn't hide behind masks. The warlocks and dradinengor chieftains of the Drav Cra, and their Arch Warlock, Redstar, uncle to a king he'd once cursed and tried to kill.

Torsten couldn't believe he hadn't seen Redstar's plot.

The carriage turned onto the Royal Avenue and drove along the walls of the castle. Only months ago, the Queen Mother, Oleander, thrown into a frenzy by the condition of her son, had lined that wall with the hanging dead for no reason good enough to excuse. Now, Glass soldiers and city guards stood along it, cheering and carousing.

Torsten knew that with Liam gone, the people, more than anything, were starved for a hero. A name to revere as they had him before he fell sick, before all these dark times of rebellions and broken faith. Redstar had given that to them. While Torsten failed to subdue Muskigo, Redstar had turned air and a spark of fire into a miracle victory.

Even if it wasn't true, Torsten didn't blame the people for believing it. He blamed himself. He was the one who refused to end Redstar's life in the Webbed Woods so that he could return him to Oleander as a gift and reclaim his title as Wearer. He was the one who thought respecting the commands of King Pi to be more important than striking down evil.

Selfish, foolish, murderer.

The carriage stopped. Yuri's assistant's crying grew louder as he realized what would come next. The Shesaitju stirred and tried to get a better look through the narrow openings. All but the Serpent Guard, still quietly staring.

The doors opened and the King's Shieldsman, Sir Nikserof,

appeared along with a few others. Lines of regret wracked his face.

"This is where you get off, Sir," he said as he stepped in, hand on his sword and ready for any of the Shesaitju to make a move.

"You don't have to call me that," Torsten said.

"You're still Wearer until the King says otherwise, Sir." He knelt in front of him and unlocked the chains on Torsten's ankles, then his wrists. "We won't have you appear before him chained up like a dog."

Torsten stretched out his limbs. He lay a hand on Nikserof's armored shoulder. "Thank you."

"Don't. I must believe it was an accident, Sir. Stress from the ambush, from nearly drowning and freezing to death. You should have been with a healer, not finding more bodies and trying to lead an army."

Torsten opened his mouth to respond, but nothing came out. He stared longingly upon the face of a good, loyal Shieldsman, a man who'd followed him into battle without question and barely made it out alive. Accident.... He couldn't say. In that moment, he saw red, and whoever got in his way would have met the same fate as that Shieldsman. Nikserof was just lucky he was behind him.

"All right, up you are." Nikserof lifted him. "And don't forget this." He shoved the white helm into Torsten's chest and then helped him toward the exit.

"W... what about us?" the boy at the back of the carriage asked.

"Quiet," Nikserof said. Torsten was surprised at his tone. It was kind but authoritative. He liked Nikserof and wished he'd known him better, like so many of the other Shieldsmen. The saddest part was that of all the Shieldsmen left alive, he knew Nikserof the best.

"I've got him," another Shieldsman bristled. Sir Austun

Mulliner yanked Torsten down as hard as he could. He'd been friends with the Shieldsman Torsten killed, so Torsten didn't blame the man for rough treatment.

He couldn't even bear to look Mulliner in the face. Instead, he watched Yuri's assistant's terrified eyes through the bars as the rolling prison rumbled away. There was no saying what would happen to him during an interrogation, but this much was clear: both were accused of being complicit in the death of a King's Shieldsman, and only the man responsible stood unchained before the castle.

"Ah, Sir Unger. I hope the ride wasn't overly dreadful." Redstar approached from behind him, flanked by Freydis. She was as menacing as ever, and still hadn't even bothered to wash the blood from her knotted hair after the battle. Redstar snapped at a few of his warriors, and they led a collared dire wolf toward the outer stables. He and his people, making themselves at home.

Torsten's insides began to boil just from the sound of him. "Let's just get this over with."

"You must understand, Torsten. This is not what I wanted."

"Oh, I think it's exactly what you wanted. The ear of the King. You're not different from Bliss, spinning your lies about your fallen goddess."

Redstar leaned in. "I spin nothing, old friend. This heart knows only truth."

Torsten's fists clenched, and his brow furrowed. He stared at the high doors of the castle, unwilling to look Redstar in the eyes. "Did you tell Uriah that before he died?"

"We didn't have a chance to speak. I did not kill your friend, and I didn't ask him to chase me. Regardless, in killing Bliss, we have already avenged his death. You should be thanking me."

Torsten finally whipped around to face him, and it took every bit of his willpower not to strangle the man. Freydis stepped between them, her hand on the hilt of her dagger. The fingernails of Torsten's free hand dug so hard into his palms they drew tiny arcs of blood. Somehow, he held back. He had no desire to make Redstar's case for him further, that he was an unhinged murderer incapable of donning the white helm.

"One day, your blood will stain my sword," Torsten said. "For now, our king awaits us."

Redstar laughed, clapped his hands. "I look forward to it." He walked on ahead, Freydis returning to his side. The doors swung open and in they went, foreigners and heathens. King's Shield-smen who'd remained behind stood on either side, features twisted by confusion.

"Sir, what is—"

"Just watch the doors," Torsten told them. "Everything is fine."

"Let's go," Austun Mulliner said from behind, giving Torsten a light shove.

"Enough, Sir Mulliner," Nikserof snapped as he caught up. "He's still your wearer."

Austun looked between Torsten and Nikserof, bit his lip, then marched off toward the Throne Room on his own.

Torsten drew a deep breath and continued through the soaring greeting hall. Vibrant colors painted the carved stone walls, and light filtered in through the grand, stained windows illustrating the history of the kingdom. The statue of Liam Nothhelm the Conqueror seemed like it was staring at him as he went by, stoic. He couldn't imagine how the great King would have looked upon him now. He'd trusted Torsten to be Wearer after Uriah passed, and look where he'd led them.

Redstar's grin stretched from ear to ear as they headed straight into the Throne Room. King Pi sat slumped on the Glass Throne, the Glass Crown sitting crooked upon his head, tangled in long hair. The Royal Council watched from behind. Among them was not one familiar face except Wren the Holy who'd gone pale at the sound of Freydis openly wearing her heathen trinkets in the Throne Room. He looked like he was going to faint.

Queen Oleander stood directly at Pi's side, gorgeous as ever. A long dress the color of a clear sky hugged her figure, stopping just above her ankles. Her silvery hair was pulled back into a braid that fell to her hips, accentuating her perfect jawline. Her cheeks were no longer red and puffy from crying as they'd been the last time Torsten saw her, tormented over dealing with her unpredictable son. Again, that trademark confidence Torsten knew so long oozed off her.

"Welcome, brother," Oleander announced. "And Sir Unger." Her glower fell upon Torsten and his heart sunk to his stomach. He'd instructed her before leaving for war to regain her son's trust, and judging by where she now stood and the demeanor she wore, her time in Yarrington had been fruitful. She, in turn, had tasked Torsten with eliminating Redstar, yet her traitorous brother strode down the hall alive and well, a bounce to his step.

"My lovely sister." Redstar strode up to the dais and swept his arms low into a bow. "I trust you've heard news of our glorious victory."

"Your victory over the Shesaitju was expected. Other developments, were not." She spoke to Redstar, but her heated glare never left Torsten.

Torsten reached Redstar's side and fell to a knee. "Your Graces," he whispered.

"Rise, Wearer," Pi groaned, still slumped and staring off to the side. "We need not waste time with formalities. There is much to address in the wake of what happened at Winde Port."

"Your Grace, if I may—"

"You may not." Pi's head finally turned to face Oleander. "Mother, inform them of what has transpired."

"Uh, Your Highness," Wren interrupted. He used a cane topped with the Eye of Iam and shuffled forward to reach Pi's ears. "Should this be discussed with them here?" He pointed to the warlock standing in the shadow of Redstar, then to the Drav Cra warriors standing at the entry to the room.

"His Holiness is right," Oleander said. "Please send your dog outside, brother."

"But of course." He murmured something in Drav Crava, and Freydis turned to leave, sneering at Torsten on her way out.

"How forgetful of me," Redstar said. "I wouldn't want to stain these hallowed halls."

"Thank you, Your Grace," Wren whispered to Pi.

"Step back and do not interrupt my son again," Oleander snapped. The lump bobbed in Wren's wrinkled throat as he slid backward. He traced where his eyes should have been with his fingers, then kissed the top of his cane.

"Go on, mother," Pi said.

"Of course, my precious boy." She took a step forward, swaying her hips as if to draw all the guards present into a trance. "It appears the betrayal of Yuri Darkings was more thorough than we'd ever expected. The chambers of Caleef Rakun were left unlocked before he departed for Winde Port. Many King's Shieldsmen were lost battling off his Serpent Guards, and Caleef Rakun was able to escape into the wilderness, alone."

Redstar cackled.

"You find that humorous, brother?" Oleander questioned.

"Not at all. It's just what I've come to expect when the King's Shield is placed in charge of something. You've really let the order go to waste, haven't you Sir Unger?"

"How dare you!" Torsten growled before being immediately silenced.

"Quiet," Pi ordered, low but authoritative. "I dispatched you to work together in ending this rebellion and clearly that has not happened."

"Not for lack of trying, nephew," Redstar said.

Torsten stepped forward and again fell to a knee. "Your Grace, this man tried to undercut me at every turn. I know you asked me to work with him in leading this army, but how could I trust him after everything he's done, with him questioning my every move?"

"Choose better moves," Redstar whispered.

Torsten rose and pointed to the Arch Warlock. "Do you see? This insufferable heathen stood in my way at every turn!"

"The army speaks of his heroics in retaking Winde Port whilst you fell into a trap laid by the traitor Darkings," Pi said. He leaned forward in the oversized throne. "Do you deny that?"

"I deny nothing. He would place all the credit at the feet of the Buried Goddess, but it was Iam who shed His light behind us. I felt it there, as we were surrounded by death, as I once felt it fighting beside your father."

"You would blame Iam for reducing half of Winde Port to ash?" Redstar asked.

"I would credit him for seeing this kingdom restored to its rightful glory!" Torsten approached Oleander and took her hands. She didn't fight it.

"My Queen, you know him," Torsten said, referring to Redstar. "You know what he is capable of. I know I failed you, but do not fall for this deception."

Her ruby lips parted, but no words came out. Torsten could see the flicker of doubt in her features, finally. That vulnerability she'd revealed before he set off for Winde Port when her son eschewed her.

"You do not appeal to her, knight," Pi said. "You appeal to me, and me alone."

"Watch out, Your Grace," Redstar said to the King. "He might try to bed you, too."

"How dare you!" Oleander snapped. Finally, her mask of composure slipped to the floor. She lunged at her brother, but

Torsten was there to intercept her. He refused to let another fall prey to the trickster.

"Is this not a hall for speaking truth?" Redstar demanded. "Do you not see the way he lusts for your mother, King Pi? I wouldn't be surprised if that were how he weaseled himself into the post of the Wearer after your father fell ill and Sir Davies died when it is widely spoken that the late Sir Jolly was far more qualified."

"He never wanted to wear the white helm," Torsten said.

"Or perhaps he wasn't as adept at fulfilling my sister's… baser needs when Liam couldn't."

"And how would you know?" Torsten said. "You were too busy fleeing to the Webbed Woods chasing monsters and cursing the Prince. Your current king!"

"Opening eyes is never easy."

"Quiet!" Pi thundered. His voice filled the hall, louder and with more timbre than any boy his age should be capable of. He stood upon the throne now, piercing golden eyes, so like his father's, fixed on Torsten.

"Sir Unger," he said, calculating. "I am blind to nothing that happens in these halls. Your attempted dalliance with my mother would be enough to have you hanged if I decide so, or if I was foolish enough to believe that it was not she who took the first step."

Oleander looked aghast, leaving Torsten unsure at how much headway she'd actually made in earning back the boy's trust.

"And Redstar," Pi continued, "if I am not mistaken it was you who advised I restore Yuri Darkings' position upon the council."

Redstar didn't miss a beat. "Alas, I am ashamed to admit that I overheard Torsten and Lord Darkings discussing that very arrangement while I was in the dungeon. I hoped to win your favor in improving your Royal Council."

"Is this true, Sir Unger?"

"I will not lie to you, Your Grace," Torsten said. "It was my intent. But nobody could've predicted Yuri's motives, even Redstar's Goddess. It was all our failures in allowing him back into power. So, use me. Send me to hunt down the Caleef and fix this."

"As you hunted Muskigo?" Redstar said.

Torsten sunk away from the dais.

"Your Grace," Redstar said, taking a few steps closer. "I believe we have wasted enough time pretending that our situation has not changed. The rebel army remains at large, and soon Muskigo will inspire more afhems to his cause whether we find the Caleef or not. The bulk of our armies remain in Winde Port preparing to march on the Shesaitju lands, but they are leaderless now. I sent a report of what the Wearer has done, and I believe it is time he is stripped of his command. Would you trust a man capable of coming so unhinged to bring justice to Muskigo, and restore order to your great kingdom?"

"Your Grace, I will make no excuses for what I have done, but this man is attempting to deceive you," Torsten said. "Do not forget that it was he who poisoned your mind and led you to leap from that window! It is only by the grace of Iam that you returned to us when Redstar would have seen the Nothhelm line ended."

"You speak of magic as if you understand it," Redstar said. "I did not curse the boy; I merely allowed him to see what the rest refuse to. The true power which watches over us. You claim I destroyed our king's mind, yet there he sits, alive and well. Stronger than ever. All thanks to me. For it was not Iam who brought him back, but the hand of my Lady."

"That is blasphemy!" Wren shouted. "Your Highness, I agree with the Wearer of White. Redstar may be your uncle, but from the moment he arrived in the capital a year ago, we have seen naught but suffering."

"Queen Mother," Torsten addressed Oleander. "Do you not

remember what he reduced your son to? How he had him rambling on about nonsense in the darkness?"

"Of course, I remember," Oleander replied, still diffident after her son's verbal attack.

"Then how could you, how could any of us listen to a word he says?"

"My uncle explained his intentions to me before I released him, Wearer," Pi said. "He helped me see in the only way he knew how and has already been pardoned. We are not here to discuss his place in my kingdom; we are here to discuss yours."

"Your Gra—"

"If I must ask one more time not to be interrupted, you will hang."

Silence filled the hall, thicker than any sound could.

"The truth, Sir Unger, is that you allowed Winde Port to be taken in the first place by ignoring Redstar's warning," Pi said. "You invited Yuri Darkings to Winde Port of your own accord. And you failed to eliminate Muskigo while Redstar was forced to take action and reclaim the city. And perhaps worst of all, you killed one of your own Shieldsmen in a blind rage directed at my uncle despite his heroics leading an army that was meant to be under your command. These are the reports I have received. Do you deny any of it?"

Torsten swallowed hard. He glanced back over his shoulder and saw his Shieldsmen. Not one of them spoke up in his defense, and only Nikserof's expression revealed the slightest grief. Sir Mulliner didn't smile, but his satisfaction at Torsten's facing of justice was evident.

"I do not," Torsten said, "but—"

"Stop." King Pi held up his hand. "You were sent to subdue Muskigo while he was removed from his people. Now he is back among them to stir the hornet's nest, and our coffers lack the gold to both go after him and repair Winde Port. You speak against my uncle, yet without him, we would be in a far worse situation. Winde Port would remain occupied, and Yuri Darkings likely still in his post ready to bury us."

"As I said, it is clear Sir Unger was unfit to inherit the helm from his predecessor," Redstar said. "We are lucky I was there to pick up the pieces."

Torsten lost what little restraint he possessed. He swung the white helm of his post into the side of Redstar's face. His birthmark split open at the cheek as he hit the ground. Torsten pounced onto him, punching him again and again. This time Redstar didn't use magic to fend him off. He merely cackled as Torsten struck him.

Sir Mulliner and other members of the King's Shield arrived to pull him off. It was the battlefield of Winde Port all over again, only now he was in front of the King, Queen Mother, and High Priest of Iam. All those important to him, present to see him acting like a wild beast.

Redstar crawled backward against the throne's dais. "Behold," he rasped, still cackling. He spat blood onto the marble. "Your Wearer, my King."

"He's using you!" Torsten shouted as he tried to break free. Sir Mulliner shoved him hard onto his chest and held him there. "He's using all of you, can't you see!"

Nobody could bear to watch. Wren prayed under his breath. The other worthless members of the Royal Council cowered. Even Oleander turned to the side and closed her eyes.

All but Pi. His unwavering stare remained on Torsten, the small boy who looked a giant upon his throne. "I see a man broken by his failings," he said. "In the name of Iam and the Glass Throne, I strip you of your position as both Wearer and Shieldsman. Your vows are nullified. And for the murder of Sir Havel Tralen, you will be imprisoned until I can think of what to do with you."

Sir Havel... Now he knew the name of the Shieldsman he'd murdered. He stopped fighting Sir Mulliner and stared toward the throne, eyes wet with tears. He didn't look to Pi or Wren, but to Oleander. The Queen Mother who'd hurt so many in the name of her son; the only person who might understand him.

"Please, Oleander," he said, imploring her by her own name. "You know me. I would never purposely bring harm to this kingdom. I am, as always, your loyal servant. But him?" He hadn't even the energy to point to Redstar. "He'll destroy us all."

Finally, Oleander half turned. He noticed the glint of a tear on her cheek, but she never moved enough to look Torsten in the eye.

She drew a deep breath. "The demands of my son, your King, are final," she said weakly. "You served this kingdom well during my husband's illness, and for that, you have my gratitude. I can offer no more."

Torsten felt like he'd been punched in the gut. "And what esteemed Shieldsman is to replace me?" he asked. He could hardly move, but he angled his restrained arm to point at Sir Nikserof who stood near the entry. "It may mean nothing, but Sir Nikserof's bravery in Winde Port was commendable."

Pi hopped down from the throne and began to pace. Now on the floor, it was clear how small and fragile he was, but he didn't walk like it. He moved with the swagger of a conqueror, shoulders high and proud like his father's always were.

"It is clear to me that the old ways are no longer working," Pi said. "I have been left with an unfit council, unable to complete a task as simple as having a crypt repaired on time. My father had no family to trust and had to see the worth in others, but I do. As of this moment, my uncle will be named my prime minister, closely overseeing the roles of all the Royal Council."

Murmurs broke out amongst the members behind the throne.

"And," Pi continued, louder as to quell the din, "he will assume the role of royal commander of my armies for the time being. We will install a new Wearer and generals who will honor and respect our alliance with the Drav Cra, and together, we will end all talk of rebellions."

The murmuring grew louder. Even Sir Mulliner and the other Shieldsman holding Torsten seemed confused. But Redstar remained lying on the marble wearing a bloody grin.

"Your Grace, the position of High Priest responds only to the will of Iam," Wren said. "I am his mouth and hand in Pantego. Your uncle is a servant to Nesilia, the Buried Goddess. I will not allow him to oversee our holy church."

"You will do as instructed!" Pi snapped. "It was my father's willingness to force our faith on others which leads now to an uprising. Redstar will have no control over the Church of Iam, worry not, but so long as he and his people are here, they are members of the Glass Kingdom. They will not be persecuted for speaking the name of a goddess whose magic helped save so many in Winde Port."

"You would allow these warlocks and blood mages to poison the ears of our people?"

"If Iam is the one true God," Pi answered, "then our people will not be shaken."

"This is an outrage." Wren stormed down from behind the throne and out of the room. Torsten had never seen the blind priest move so fast; he barely used his cane.

"Too long have we relied on old customs," Pi announced. "Under my father, the Glass Kingdom was a shining beacon in a dark world. Together, we can make it that again."

"Please, Your Grace!" Torsten shouted. "Think about what you're doing. He is her servant, not yours. He belongs to Nesilia, and she will bring ruin to us all."

"Yet Redstar tells me that Nesilia and Iam were of one flesh. That it was together, the God Feud was ended, not apart."

"He would say anything to gain more power. Don't do this."

"Ask yourself this, what if he's right? What if together, we can bring Pantego to greater heights than ever?"

"And we shall, Your Grace." Redstar stood, slowly climbed the glass stairs, and lay his hands upon the King's shoulders. "There is so much work to be done. Now, why don't you meet me in the Shield Hall and we can discuss our options."

"Yes, come Pi," Oleander said. "I can't bear to watch this any longer." She guided her son off the dais and toward the tower up to the private wing. She didn't even look back. Torsten had failed her, more than anyone else. He'd promised to bring Redstar down and instead allowed him to ascend to the side of the King.

Redstar stayed behind. He bent to pick up the bloodied helm of the Wearer of White. Then he raised it over his head and lowered it. It looked ridiculous without the rest of the armor, but he didn't seem to care. It was just a game to him, like everything else.

He regarded Torsten, still grinning. "You don't approve?" he asked. "Did it look better on Uriah?" He swiped his hand in front of his face, and for a moment his appearance changed to that of Torsten's mentor. The same face Redstar wore to trick him into helping him in the Webbed Woods. In a moment, his ugly, blemished façade returned but just seeing him mar the memory of Uriah again fueled Torsten.

"You won't get away with this!" He roared and thrashed, but Austun pushed down again.

"All right. Lock him up, Sir Mulliner." Redstar tapped on the helm. "That's an order."

Austun tried to get Torsten under control, but his massive body was too strong. A few more Shieldsmen jumped in to help.

"I have to handle everything," Redstar groaned. He brushed some blood off his face, then raised his palm. The Shieldsmen were yanked off Torsten by unseen magic; then the warlock flicked his wrist and Torsten slid all the way across the hall, striking the wall just beside Nikserof. Freydis stood beside him, a wicked grin smeared across her white-painted lips.

The Royal Council members, guards, and Shieldsmen remaining watched, utterly flabbergasted by the open use of blood magic in the Throne Room of the Glass Castle, a place blessed and occupied by the faithful to Iam for centuries. But Redstar didn't have to hide what he was anymore, and it was all thanks to Torsten.

II

THE MYSTIC

Sora hadn't left the captain's quarters of the Breklian corsair she and Whitney had stolen from Winde Port for a fortnight. She laid in a bed made of the softest material she'd ever felt, but she still couldn't sleep. Every time her eyes closed, visions of Whitney and that monster, Kazimir, danced through her mind. It was mental torture worse than any physical pain she could imagine enduring.

Her dwarven companion, Tum Tum, had long since given up on trying to stir her. The fact they hadn't sunk yet told her the dwarf knew the intricacies of sailing. It's not like she knew how, anyway.

As the ship rocked then dipped, her stomach rose into her throat, and she wondered if they'd already reached the Boiling Waters south of the Black Sands. The thought of stepping out into sunlight brought an overwhelming sense of panic. For a reason she couldn't put her finger on, she felt like anything more than darkness would be like screaming to the gods that she'd forgotten about Whitney.

She hadn't. She never would. And she couldn't forget how she'd…

What had she done? Was he dead, banished, evaporated like water on a hot day? All she knew was that one moment he and Kazimir were there, the next they'd vanished. She'd felt the energy of Elsewhere crackling in the area where they'd been. It made the blood coursing through her body tingle. Eventually, it dissipated, but not on Whitney's stolen half of the Glass Crown. She'd had to cover it with a blanket because every time she looked at it, she felt that same overwhelming sensation of Elsewhere seeking to work through her. If she touched it, her entire body, from her fingers to her neck, tensed.

Not for the first time, she rolled over and screamed into a pillow, beating it unmercifully with her fists. It always managed to make her feel a little bit better. But she knew what came next. Tears. Exhaustion. And finally, after her eyes were spent of the stuff, she'd drift off into nightmares.

Aquira heard her and squirmed up right beside her. The wyvern's body was like a furnace, and even though her scales were dry and coarse, Sora appreciated the company.

She couldn't say how long it'd been before the cabin door swung open and sunlight poured in. Aquira bolted upright, growling until she realized who it was. A stout dwarf appeared in the entry, with a nose like a pear and a beard that seemed not to have seen a blade in years.

"All right, lass," Tum Tum's gruff voice said. "The time for sleepin and depressin be over."

"Please, leave me alone," Sora said, and rolled over.

"Not happenin. I know ye ain't a bit happy bout our situation and neither be I, but we be lost and nearly out of food."

Sora sat up. "We're lost?"

"As a giant in Hornsheim," he said with a chuckle. "What did ye expect? All I know about sailin I learned watchin the wharf from me bar and ye've been pissin the days away in here. Not that I be complainin, if ye'd been of the right mind we'd be out of food long ago."

Sora swore.

"Just give me a few minutes to get properly dressed," she said.

"As I said, not happenin. I know if I leave here, yer just gonna flop back down on that soft, comfy bed and drift off again."

She knew he was probably right. She grunted and got out of bed. She wasn't naked, but she wasn't dressed either. It was dark, and the dwarf turned around to give her privacy, especially after Aquira screeched at him.

After wiggling into a pair of pants and pulling on a sack-like tunic—both she'd found in the quarters—she said, "Okay," and they went out onto the deck. Aquira flapped up and landed on her shoulder.

The sunlight hit her full in the face, causing her to squint. Water sprayed her cheeks, reminding her she was still alive. Climbing the five stairs from the cabin doorway, she breathed in the salty air. She had to admit; it felt good to get out of that room.

"Where are we?" she asked.

"In the middle of the ocean," Tum Tum said.

He wasn't lying. There was blue everywhere—blue ocean, blue sky—except to what she thought was east where the skies were beginning to darken. Sora had to grab a railing to keep grounded and avoid feeling dizzy. All around them, there was no land or steady horizon. It vacillated with the crests of waves, up and down, side to side, an interminable wall of water.

She swallowed hard. "That doesn't look good," she said.

"That's why I be waking ye," Tum Tum said, "Easy to sail alone when ye let the boat do the drivin, but now there be a storm comin and I ain't barely good on a bright day."

Sora's head hung a little, and her shoulders followed.

"What's left for food?" she asked.

"Still got some fish I caught, but since the previous owner didn't eat nothin dead, there wasn't much in the way of stores."

"Please don't remind me about him." Any thought of Kazimir, the upyr who'd hunted her and Whitney through Winde Port, would make her remember how he'd wanted to feed on her blood until she was dried out. Which would remind her of her unbridled rage as he threatened Whitney's life, and then what had happened to both of them.

"Apparently, he had a love of apples cus there was a bunch of em," Tum Tum said. "Most be dried up and rotten by now though. If ye be wantin some sweet fish stew of me own invention, there's some on that pot over there."

He pointed toward the galley, which was really just a covered, flattened portion of the ship with three walls and a cauldron.

The thought of food had her stomach rumbling. She'd only eaten every few days and only when she couldn't manage any longer. She imagined if she had a looking glass, she'd barely recognize the woman in the reflection.

"I must be gaunt," she said to no one in particular.

"Fair as the day I met ye," Tum Tum responded.

What he hadn't said was that they'd only met about two weeks ago, and even then, just a day or so before they'd ended up on this ship together.

She quietly made her way toward the food, all the while eyeing the steadily approaching storm.

Tum Tum trailed a bit behind her.

"I'm sorry, Tum Tum," she said softly.

"Sorries be for the past," he said. "Let's just get off this damned boat."

Sora laughed and nodded as she ladled some of the food onto a tin plate. She raised another spoonful for Aquira, who devoured it in a single gulp, nearly breaking the spoon too.

"Looks great," Sora said. "Aquira seems to like it."

"Trust me; it's not." Tum Tum laughed this time. "I serve drinks. Leave the food for me cooks. Or well… left."

Sora pursed her lips and raised her bowl to him in solidarity. If there was one thing she understood, it was losing one's home. Then they took a sip of the stew together, and she stifled a gag. Tum Tum wasn't lying. The fish was dry and filled with bones, and the broth was tart.

"Where do you think Whitney is?" Sora asked after a long silence and forcing herself to get half the bowl down.

"Not here." he answered. "Not here, lass, and that's all we be knowing. Best not dwell on what we can't change."

Tum Tum returned to the helm while she ate, eyes closed, ready to nod off. She'd have cried if she still had tears left, but instead, she stood and walked back out onto the deck. By now, a dense fog had rolled in. The storm still loomed a bit off in the distance, but it was approaching at an uncomfortable rate, and the wind was picking up. The ships sail flapped loudly.

Sora regarded Tum Tum, seated at the helm. It was he who slept now, and she hated him for it, imagined he was dreaming of snow-covered mountains and far-away lands, pretty dwarven women and gold-filled mines. She knew it was unfair. Tum Tum knew Whitney too. He might have even known him better than she had. It was easy to forget that between him leaving Troborough without saying goodbye, and her finding him escaping Redstar's prison, was nearly a decade of adventures. She'd give anything to hear him exaggerate about another.

Piss in the wind, as Whitney would have said.

What mattered now was how to get to where they wanted to go so she might be able to figure out where they were. It was her magic that disappeared them. She knew it wasn't Kazimir's because he had no interest in Whitney. No. Whatever had happened sprung from her fingertips, and the strange power growing within her. Her abilities had always come with the cost of blood. It allowed her to keep them in check, but occasionally, like in the Webbed Woods, or when she lit Winde Port on fire, she lost control. She'd promised Whitney she wouldn't let that happen again, and she'd lied.

"You're out there somewhere," she whispered into the wind. "I know it."

She couldn't, however, answer the question of where without first finding land before she and Tum Tum starved. That was step one. Don't starve. Then she could figure out a way to get to Yaolin City, where she and Whitney were headed before everything went south. Based on everything she'd learned from Wetzel, only her Panpingese ancestors, and their great mystics, fully attuned to drawing on the powers of Elsewhere, could help—if any who still knew anything even remained now that the Glass Kingdom ruled their lands.

As she stared quietly upon the continually shifting horizon, white crests rising and falling, a mass of what seemed like land peeked through the rolling fog.

Maybe we're in Panping already?

She'd never sailed before so had no idea how fast it should go. This was by far the furthest from home she'd ever been, and thanks to Afhem Muskigo and the Shesaitju rebellion she had no home to go back to for the second time.

"Tum Tum!" she called.

"Aye?" he said, sleepily.

She thought about the stories she'd heard over the years when sailors would occasionally pass through Troborough and hunker down in the Twilight Manor on their way to Yarrington. Sora would usually sit and listen to the bards play their songs and over-hear some of the tales. What was it they would shout when they spotted land?

"Land, whore!" she cried.

Tum Tum muttered a curse as his head sprung up from resting on a spoke of the wheel. Then he laughed. "It's land ho, lass." He waddled over to Sora by the bow. He squinted and said, "I dun't see nothin."

"Right there," she pointed. "Just beyond the veil of…"

Her voice trailed off at the same time she'd realized her mistake.

"It's not land, it's another ship!" she yelled. "That might be even better than land."

"Unless they be pirates," Tum Tum remarked.

"Those are just tall tales told by sailors looking for attention," she said. "The Glass Kingdom drove them all out… right?"

They both stood and watched the approaching ship which was more than twice the size of theirs and had three times the sails. As its silhouette grew, it pierced the veil of fog and Sora's heart sank into her stomach. The sails were dark as night, and the flag flapping in the now buffeting winds bore the image of a chipped skull with blood leaking from its eye-sockets and mouth.

"Are those…" Sora couldn't finish.

"Not just tales, lass," Tum Tum said quietly.

They both swore.

"Mayhaps they won't be seein us," he added.

"I think it's too late for that," Sora replied.

The ship lurched, the boom and sail swinging over their heads. The sound as the wind caught the fabric was loud as thunder, and Sora and Tum Tum realized they were both crouched in fear. Aquira's claws dug into Sora's shoulder, only one leg still on as she flapped with all her might to combat the gust.

"We've got to get you inside." She grabbed Aquira and tucked her under her elbow before running to the captain's quarters.

Cold, wet rain slashed against Sora's skin like needles as she ran. They were far enough south to escape the bitter cold of winter, but the rain still came down like ice. She locked Aquira inside before it got even worse, the wyvern screeching in protest.

In a matter of minutes, it went from a light sprinkle to a deluge. Their ship rocked uncontrollably in the growing waves, even as Tum Tum took the helm to try and keep them steady. The dark, pirate vessel maintained a straight on approach.

"Best be preparin for what's to come," he said.

"Which is?" Sora said.

"The end."

The seconds ticked by like hours, and the sky turned a sickly shade of green. The ocean lost its blue, as if somehow it could become even less inviting. Now it was gray like death and decay, the waves rising high all around them, blotting out even the clouds.

"We can't just sit here and wait for them to board us," Sora said. She turned and raced back to her cabin. She returned a moment later with Wetzel's knife in hand.

"Are ye plannin on us hackin down twenty pirates all by ourselves?" Tum Tum asked. "Face it, lass, whatever they be wantin, they'll be gettin. We may as well play coy and ask to join the crew."

"Don't underestimate me, dwarf."

"Long as you don't underestimate them," he retorted, pointing a stubby thumb toward the ship that was now only fifty meters away.

Sora walked out to the center of the deck and drew a thin line of blood across her hand. Sacrifice, to draw on the powers of Elsewhere. She raised her hand toward the boarding vessel. Flame sizzled at her fingertips as she pulled on that haunting, indescribable power within; but it never formed further.

Driving rain stung at her wound and washed the blood away, and after whatever she'd done to Whitney, her body was still weak. She could usually feel the energy of Elsewhere percolating in her gut, but now it was distant, fleeting.

"C'mon," Sora willed her body. "Don't do this again!" She cut her bicep, deeper this time. Her hand and forearm were numb to the abuse, but as the soft skin split apart, it came with a forgotten pain. She fell to a knee, wincing, but she didn't give up. A pathetic stream of fire swirled around her hand, then arced off into the pirate ship.

The rain quickly extinguished even the magical flame, and all that was left was a singe on the ship's hull.

Several dirty men peered over the side of the rail. The frigate or galleon—Sora knew nothing about the names of ships—drifted close and it occurred to her that their vessel could literally fit inside of it.

"Prepare to be boarded!" a gruff voice shouted, barely audible over the whipping winds. Grappling hooks soared over the watery expanse and found purchase in the wood of the corsair. Several pirates swung across, landing and rolling to a standing stop before drawing short, curved swords.

Rough hands seized her from all directions. Sora swung at them with her knife, but it was pointless. The men were stronger, and no matter how she tried, she couldn't get the fire to come. She told herself it was the driving rain keeping her spark at bay before it formed, but she knew that was a lie. Every time she looked inward for the call of Elsewhere, Whitney's face flashed through her mind.

Tum Tum protested even louder as they ripped him from the helm, lashing out with curses she didn't even know existed. A plank lowered with a loud *thunk* when the two ships were close enough to one another.

The pirates jeered at her, and she found herself wondering why evil men were always so gross. Rotting teeth, messy beards, scars going every which way. Last time she'd been faced with a situation like this, Whitney had shown up just in the nick of time, stealing a caravan from a bunch of vile mercenaries, and together, they rode off into the proverbial sunset. Not this time. She would have to handle this on her own.

"There's nothing worth taking here," she said, throwing one of them off her arm. The end of the sleeve tore.

"I beg to differ, little lady," one said, looking her up and down like a piece of steak. He went to wrap her arms around her waist.

"Get your hands off me!" She squirmed, but it was no use against so many of them. And even as her fresh blood mixed with the rain, she couldn't will Elsewhere to respond beyond the tips of her fingers.

That would have to be enough.

She grabbed her assailant's arm and he squealed like a stuck pig in response to the heat of her palm. "Iam's light, what was that!"

Sora slipped under the grasp of another and ran toward the captain's quarters. Tum Tum was by the helm, still fighting to break free. She could hear Aquira inside making a racket over the storm. The wyvern might be enough to change the tide.

Sora looked back at the ruffians in pursuit, and when she turned to the door, her path was blocked. The man before her cut an imposing figure. He stood more than a head above Sora and three above Tum Tum. A long, thick beard fell from his chin, black with strips of white running vertically at nearly perfect intervals. His heavy, silver clasped boots landed on the deck of the small ship with a horrifying thud.

"All hail Grisham 'Gold Grin' Gale!" one fat lump cried from behind. "Scourge of the Seas, Ward of the Waters, and King of the Pirates!"

"All hail!" the rest echoed.

Sora didn't know how to react.

Of all the pirates in the world...

Whitney boasted about his time spent with Gold Grin a few times. She didn't usually believe him about these kinds of things, but she had to admit, a bit of hope coursed through her body.

"Aye, let go of me ye shog bucket!" Tum Tum screamed as they tried hauling him toward her.

"Just relax," Sora said, but it was too late. One of the pirates clubbed Tum Tum hard over the head, and the dwarf collapsed to the ground, unconscious.

"Tum Tum!" Sora lunged for him, and a mess of grimy hands pulled her back.

The hulking man who could be none other than Gold Grin looked down at her. He grinned, and Sora learned how apt his name was. Lots of men had yellow teeth, but his were gold as autlas and sparkled just the same.

"Where's yer cap'n?" Gold Grin asked, scanning the ship over Sora's head.

"We don't have a captain," she answered.

The men laughed. All but Gold Grin.

"Where's the rest of the crew?" he asked.

"We don't have anyone else."

A few men laughed again, but most took the cue from their leader who remained stone-faced.

"Ye thinking this a joke?" he asked.

"No joke, my Lord," Sora said. "It's just the two of us. We were three—someone I believe you may know."

If the pirate were listening, he didn't show any sign of it. He strolled off toward the captain's quarters and threw the door wide open.

"Fortist, Hestor," Gold Grin shouted to two of his men. "Tear it apart!" He leaned into Sora and grinned even wider. His breath smelled of ale and fish. "And I ain't no lord, pretty lass."

Two of the pirates began giving orders to the rest, and in

seconds they had fanned out like ants from a mound. Gold Grin joined them and headed down the stairs into holding.

"Please!" Sora yelled. "Just listen!" She went to step, but the deck was slick and rocking side to side with the tremendous waves. She slipped, and was immediately hoisted back up by a couple of men. As could be expected, their hands wandered wherever they desired.

"You don't understand!" she started.

"Naw, ye don't understand, wench," one of her captors said. "This be our ship now, and ye might stay alive to keep us company."

Everyone within earshot laughed, but Sora finally had enough. The familiar surge of Elsewhere returned, and this time she forced herself to think of Kazimir, Muskigo, and Redstar; all those who'd ever tried to hurt her. Anyone but Whitney. The gash on her arm itched, begging her to draw on blood offered. Flames erupted from her and scorched the men on either side. They cried out, and even those holding Tum Tum backed away.

The pirates shouted about witches and demons, but one voice broke through the din of insanity.

"Aren't ye a special one?" Gold Grin clomped back toward Sora and stood, eyes fixated on her. In his hand he twirled half of King Liam's crown, fingering the glass. "This be a mighty good fake."

"That's no fake," Sora said, panting. Gold Grin approached her as if her hands weren't currently wreathed in embers. "That belonged to King Liam himself."

"Only one king around here," one of the pirates said, voice shaking.

Sora looked at Gold Grin and smiled. "You're the king of the pirates, huh?"

"The ones that matter," he chortled.

"Aye! Boss, look what I found!"

Sora turned toward the captain's quarters where a skinny little runt of a man came running out holding Aquira by the neck. She flapped and squirmed but couldn't get free. He had a singed sleeve for what it was worth, and the one next to him was full of bite marks.

"Leave her be!" Sora shouted, her fire growing brighter and stronger.

"A Panping mystic with a wyvern?" Gold Grin said. "Now there be a story I'd like to hear."

"Put her down," Sora demanded. "I won't ask again."

Gold Grin motioned for the pirate to release Aquira. The wyvern turned and snapped at the man. He drew his hand back, fearful. Two long flaps brought Aquira to Sora, and she tucked under her arm where the wind wouldn't send her flailing. She coughed, sparks dribbling down her chin to join Sora's flame.

Last time their powers combined, half of Winde Port went alight. She knew what would happen if she released energy like that on a ship, but a part of her didn't care. A part of her wanted to send all these grimy souls who thought they could do whatever they wanted to anyone with no consequences to the bottom of the ocean, even if she went with them. But then she'd never find out where Whitney was.

"What's a pretty, powerful woman like ye doing out at sea with naught but a dwarf for company?" Gold Grin asked, moving closer. She raised her flaming hand, but it didn't stop him. The man showed no fear as if her magic was just the beginning of the wonders he'd seen.

Despite her having the perceived upper hand, Sora was fearful of any man who didn't flinch in the presence of magic.

"Whitney Fierstown," she blurted as Gold Grin drew close enough for her to smell the fish on his breath.

He leaned back. She could tell from the change in his features that the name meant something to him, just what was yet to be determined.

True to his name, a wide grin began to stretch across his sun-beaten face. It looked like leather stretched across Mr. Gregor's tanning frames.

"What did you say?" he asked, slowly examining the faces of his men.

Sora still couldn't judge which direction her choice to invoke the name of Whitney Fierstown would take her.

"You know him?" she asked.

Every last one of the men nearly doubled over with laughter. Gold Grin merely stood there, same grin plastered across his face.

"Do we know him, boys?" Gold Grin shouted.

None stopped laughing long enough to provide an answer.

"Aye," he said, leaning in again, "I know him weller than any man be wanting to know any lying, thieving, picaroon. Had a date with Stumpmaker Jack, he did." The man motioned to his neck and drew his finger across his throat. "Escaped with more than his life that day."

They all laughed again, and Sora swore to herself.

"Left this crew as the only man to ever steal from Grisham 'Gold Grin' Gale, he did!"

Gold Grin took one last step forward. Aquira growled, but Sora's flame began to weaken from drawing too long on the power. She knew she'd made a mistake. *I should have known better than to think Whitney left a good impression on anybody.*

"Left here with the respect of each and every one of us too!" Gold Grin exclaimed after a brief silence. "Where be that carousing rapscallion?" He grabbed her by the shoulders and shook her.

"What?" she asked, stunned.

"He be on this crew? This ship? He be a bucko of yers?"

"I—he—I," she couldn't manage more than a stammer until Gold Grin stumbled backward, chuckling.

"He was. I—I don't know where he went. He just… disappeared."

Still laughing, the pirate king said, "Sounds like Whitney Fierstown, the scalawag! Bet he stole this crown as well, didn't he?"

"Yes." She hoped her face didn't betray her sadness. "At least, that's what he claimed."

"Then we've all been flimflammed by the same rotten scoundrel. What be yer name, love?"

"Sora," she said, then added, "and this is Aquira."

The wyvern growled.

"And that," she pointed to the still-unconscious dwarf, "is Tum Tum."

"Aye, he'll be fine," Gold Grin said. "Throw a bucket on him, Nevin!"

A hunched over, well-fed pirate Sora assumed was Nevin grabbed one of the buckets Tum Tum had been using to swab the deck and tossed it on the dwarf.

Tum Tum awoke in a startle, scrambling to his feet, and readying his fists.

"Where they be? I'll kill em all," he muttered as he stumbled around the deck.

"It's okay, Tum Tum," Sora said over the laughter of the pirate crew. "They know Whitney."

Tum Tum grumbled something, but Sora couldn't make it out. He plopped down on the deck, clearly exhausted.

"What are ye doing on here all on yer own?" Gold Grin asked. "Gods. Whitney didn't drive ye to kill him and toss him overboard did he?"

"It'd be about time!" one of his men hollered.

"We were sailing for Yaolin City before getting lost," Sora said. "I'm… I'm a trader."

"I'm all for liars girl, but usually traders be… well… having something to trade!"

More laughter came.

Sora didn't overthink. Whitney taught her not to when spinning a lie. She reached into the folds of her clothing and removed the sealed writ she and Whitney had taken from Tayvada Bokeo in Winde Port after he died. The one that indicated him a member of the Winde Trader's Guild. Sora had used it on Afhem Muskigo to trick him into helping her, and now the poor, murdered man would ensure her life again.

Gold Grin took the sopping wet papers and shook them off. "Winde Trader's Guild, eh?"

"Yes, with my… uh. My husband. He died in the Shesaitju attack on Winde Port. Gave his life so that I could escape alive. I need to reach Panping as soon as I can to settle his affairs." A tear rolled from her eyes even though she wasn't trying to cry. *Pieces of truth*. That was how Whitney had taught her to lie, and now she realized that she'd partly been talking about him.

"You hear that, Gold Grin?" the grungy, wiry pirate beside him said, missing an eye and more than a few teeth. "She's available."

Gold Grin's slapped him in the back of the head.

"Ye can see all the wonders in the world, but you can't teach a scoundrel manners," Gold Grin said, "My condolences, me lady."

Sora sauntered toward him. She knew she couldn't hide the grief and fear wracking her face, but she let her figure do the talking. Out to sea for Iam knows how long, with only disgusting men for company, Gold Grin was easy prey. She lay her hand gently upon his forearm.

"Please," she said meekly. "All me and my friend want is to sail to Yaolin City unharmed, and bring some closure to Tayvada's family." As the words left her lips, she vowed that if she made it, she'd do just that. Let them know he died a hero to his people, and that he'd saved her life twice now.

"You plan on heading through them waters?" Gold Grin asked, pointing to the east. "Not likely this little ship will take ye through unscathed with only two of ye. Plus, there be pirates about!"

The man he'd just hit chuckled.

"I'll tell ye what," he said. "Give me this here crown, and we'll take ye where ye be going, right boys?"

"Aye!" they all shouted.

Sora bit her lip. She knew Whitney would freak out if he knew she'd bartered the crown, but what choice did she have? Neither she nor Tum Tum had a clue what they were doing out on the open seas. And as much as she didn't want to admit it, Whitney was gone, maybe not dead, but somewhere else. The only people who might know where were through the torrent.

A tear welled at the corner of Sora's eye. The crown was all she had left to remember him by. But it wouldn't do her any good at the bottom of the ocean. She lowered her head, closing her eyes against the thought. *He wouldn't want me to die out here all alone, or give up on finding him.*

She stuck out her hand. "Deal."

Gold Grin grabbed hers and shook. She tried to avoid staring at his stained fingernails. "I don't suppose them papers can get me and me boys into Yaolin without the guards taken shots at us. I haven't been to a proper city since I sunk my first Glass galleon."

"I... I'm not sure."

He leaned in and flashed his golden teeth once more. "Well, it won't hurt to try... us at least." He laughed, then snapped his fingers to his men. "Prepare a bed for our new guests and strip this vessel for all she's worth."

"Aye!" his men echoed.

He placed his hand on Sora's back and led her to the plank so she could look upon his galleon. "Welcome to the *Reba*!" he said, spreading his arms wide. "There be one rule and one rule only; None of that fire magic on me ship and we'll get along just fine. Wood and flame don't exactly make the best of friends."

Sora swallowed the lump forming in her throat. Riding with pirates wasn't the way she expected to reach Yaolin City, but it was too late to turn back now. She couldn't help but think that Whitney would approve.

"No fire?" she said. "I think I can manage that."

III

THE THIEF

"There's a very simple explanation for all of this," Whitney said. "It's a dream. It's a yigging dream. Tomorrow, I'll wake up, and I'll be in some inn on the shog side of Yarrington. Or better yet, a brothel in Latiapur."

Whitney looked over at the pale, terrifying man beside him. They were in the boat that beached ashore when they arrived in what he'd been told was Elsewhere, courtesy of one of Sora's unpredictable spells.

Well, he looked over at the apparition of a pale man because he still believed he had to be asleep.

Kazimir, the white-haired upyr, hadn't said more than two words together since they boarded the rickety boat. Whitney kept an eye on him the entire time, waiting for when the man would try to throw him overboard and finally succeed in killing him.

"No, really," Whitney continued to himself, "you don't understand how much sense this makes. I think I must be in some sort of extensive sleep. Maybe I've been poisoned—I've never been poisoned. Huh, I'd always thought it would hurt more."

The boat creaked as the dark, robed figure who stood upon the bow paddled through the endless sea with a long, knotted oar. He answered only to the name the Ferryman, but he too hadn't spoken since they set off. The silence drove Whitney mad.

"There's no way I was rescued from a jail cell by the Wearer of White after stealing the King's crown, just coincidentally ran into my childhood friend Sora, slew a yigging goddess in a gods-forsaken forest, and then ended up in Elsewhere next to a gods-damned upyr," Whitney decided. "I'm asleep. It's the only reasonable answer."

A foot connected hard against Whitney's arm. He yelped.

"Can't feel pain when you're asleep," Kazimir said.

"I doubt that's true," Whitney said.

"Just be silent," Kazimir growled. "Your tongue is the only thing that could make Elsewhere worse."

"You're not too great a companion either, Kazimir," Whitney grumbled under his breath as he laid back. "*Kaz*imir. What kind of name is that anyway?"

The upyr ignored him, as he had for the last how many hours. So, Whitney stared up at the night sky. It wasn't any sky he'd ever seen. No stars twinkled. If Celeste and Loutis were present, they were hiding well.

"It's kind of a reddish-purple," Whitney said. He looked at Kazimir again, who was pointedly looking away, off toward the horizon. "The sky," Whitney continued. "Makes sense. The water is dark and bloody, why wouldn't the sky be the same?"

Whitney laughed nervously to himself as waves gently lapped against the side of the boat. He'd long since learned to ignore the cold, spectral hands reaching over the side of the boat. They grasped but could never grab hold of anything. The deep wailing echoing off the surface of the Sea of Souls was nearly a lullaby now that they'd proven to be harmless.

"I remember someone telling me the ocean wasn't really

blue," Whitney said after a brief silence. "The real ocean that is. Can you believe that? They said it's just a reflection of the sky."

Whitney didn't care if anyone listened. He loved to hear his own voice.

"But this, I can't believe its real. Do you know how long I've been ignoring priests' words about the punishments of Elsewhere? My whole life—yet, here it is. The Sea of Souls. That is, of course, assuming I'm not asleep."

"Where are we going, old man?" Kazimir finally questioned the wizened old Ferryman.

When he didn't respond, Kazimir launched himself to his feet and stepped over Whitney. The little boat rocked furiously, and Whitney had to grab the sides to steady himself.

"Hey, watch it!" Whitney complained.

"Will you answer me, Ferryman?" Kazimir barked. "I've already been through this gauntlet. I refuse to play these games again. Do you hear me!"

He reached out to grab the Ferryman by his robe. As if he were one of the lost souls beneath the surface, Kazimir's hand went right through him. He let out a cry of frustration that barely sounded human. It occurred to Whitney it was likely because the man wasn't human.

"Just settle down," Whitney said. "It'll all be over soon when I wake up."

"You think this a game, thief?" Kazimir spat. "You have no idea what kind of torment awaits you on the other side of this sea."

"And you do?" Whitney asked with a smile.

"Explicitly."

A sudden movement beneath the waters stole Whitney's breath and sent the boat into a spin. Kazimir stumbled, nearly flailing over the edge and into the deep, his otherworldly grace and agility gone. Whitney scrambled again to grab hold of the vessel. The Ferryman didn't respond in the least.

"What was that?" Whitney asked.

"You're about to get a taste of Elsewhere, boy," Kazimir replied.

Water, red as wine, rose up on both sides of the boat and showered over them. If the blue Torrential Sea was a mere reflection of the sky, this was nothing like it. The thick liquid stuck to Whitney like blood, making him hope it wasn't. Something whipped across the waters and slapped down, causing another spray and a swelling wave that threatened to overturn their vessel.

Whitney swore.

Again, the thing rose up and slapped the surface of the deep. One end of the boat sailed into the air and slammed back down. When the onslaught of sea spray ended, Whitney shuddered and stumbled backward. The creature had pulled up alongside them and leveled the gaze of one giant, black eye upon Kazimir. Whitney couldn't see any more of it through the thick water, but that was enough to know how enormous it was.

A shadow cast over them and Whitney looked up to see another tentacle the size of a church steeple rising. Right before it crushed them, a bright light burned from the top of the ferryman's oar. Whitney shielded his eyes—then, just as quickly as it all started, it stopped. The creature was gone.

Heart pounding, Whitney said, "Shogging exile, what was that?"

He turned to Kazimir, who looked paler than before, now a sickly white, like the haggard moon Loutis. Whitney imagined he looked similar, but if a ruthless upyr was frightened, then he couldn't even imagine what else would come. Whitney turned to the Ferryman.

He was gone, only his oar left where he once stood. Whitney

swore again as he crawled toward the edge of the boat to peer down into the dark water.

"Hello!" he shouted. The only reply was his echo and a pair of spectral hands reaching up toward him which sent him stumbling back into the boat.

"Gone," Whitney whispered. "He's yigging gone. Just like that? He yigging left me alone with you?"

"Yes," Kazimir sighed, still refusing to look at Whitney. "He tends to do that and, in this case, we're lucky."

"All right, that's it." Whitney stomped his foot. The boat swayed, and he thought better of doing it again. "Who in Elsewhere are you really and how do you know about… Elsewhere?"

"Just row the boat," Kazimir said.

"What, so you can shove me off and fulfill your blood pact?"

Whitney promptly found his throat closed off by a powerful hand. Kazimir was close enough for him to have smelled his breath if the overwhelming stench of the Sea of Souls wasn't vying for the award for worst smell ever.

"If I wanted you dead, you never would have stepped foot on this boat," Kazimir said. "Best not to be alone in Elsewhere."

Whitney spent the whole trip so far trying to get under Kazimir's skin—hours, maybe an entire day, it was impossible to tell—now, he'd welcome the neglect. The upyr's dark eyes bore into him as if piercing his very soul. Only when he turned his head away did Kazimir release him.

Whitney crumpled in a heap. Kazimir kicked the oar into his gut.

"Why do I have to row?" Whitney murmured, more to himself than his dreadful companion.

"Because someone has to." He returned to his seat and went back to staring at the vast nothingness.

Whitney absentmindedly started rowing. Nagging the upyr was all fun, but seeing that rage again reminded him how near he'd come to having his body drained of blood while he was still alive. Or Sora's. He shuddered.

Wherever they were, dream or not, at least here, in the middle of nowhere, he couldn't hurt her. But if all of this was a figment of his imagination, he had to think that their reunion was as well. Which would mean that the only woman in the world he cared about still harbored years-old hatred toward him for leaving Troborough without so much as a goodbye.

He focused on rowing to take his mind off all of it, but it just brought new concerns. The feeling of the oar against the water was unsettling. He could sense the wood smacking against the bodies of all the lost spirits teeming beneath the surface, which was odd since they couldn't touch him.

"Are we even going the right way?" Whitney asked. "You know we got all turned around when that thing hit us?"

"The right way for what?" Kazimir asked. "Who knows where that wretch was bringing us this time. Any direction is as good as another."

"Okay, Mr. Deadman with all of the answers, what was that thing that attacked us then?"

Kazimir exhaled sharply and said, "It is a wianu. We call him Dakel un Ghastrin."

"And that is?"

"Roughly translated. 'Guardian of the Dead.'"

"A friend of yours?" Whitney asked.

"Hardly," Kazimir said. "He's hunted, trying to kill me for a thousand years."

"Why didn't it?"

"Apparently, the Ferryman wants you to see the other side."

"Iam's light you are cryptic." Whitney sighed. "So, is the old man dead?"

"Has been for longer than Pantego has existed."

Whitney gave up expecting answers from the upyr, rolled his eyes and turned back to the sea.

He wasn't sure when he'd resolved himself to the idea of talking to an upyr in the middle of Elsewhere, but here he was. Somehow, in the grand scheme of things—Kazimir trying to murder him, kidnapping Sora, working for Darkings—things on Pantego seemed unimportant.

It wasn't that Whitney wanted to make friends—the man was a monster unlike any he'd known before—it was just that, surrounded by the bloody ocean, any company seemed preferable to being alone.

"What about food?" Whitney said. "What if we get stranded at sea?"

"Hunger is an illusion here for mortals like you. You will ache and crave because that is what you were used to, but here, you will never eat your fill, and you will never starve."

"Dreaming," Whitney muttered to himself as he paddled. "I'm dreaming."

"You're not dreaming, thief. I promise you this, we are here, and we aren't leaving anytime soon."

"If you can't feel anything in Elsewhere, then we aren't in Elsewhere," Whitney said after a long spell of silence."Kazimir let his head fall back as he exhaled. "I didn't say you feel nothing. Trust me; you will long for the days where you felt less."

"Well, that makes sense because I feel terrified. I'm pretty sure I just urinated in my pa—where the yig are my pants?" Whitney glanced down and realized he wasn't wearing any clothing. "There's no way. We've been naked this whole time?"

How in shogging exile did I not realize?

He shifted his frame, suddenly acutely aware of his shame. His cheeks went red. He covered his nethers with one hand, and then his eyes went wide. "We can't be in Elsewhere."

"And why is that?"

"Now I feel shame."

"That's all up here." Kazimir pointed to his head. "It is the affairs of the body that have no bearing here. The need to shog or piss. To eat or drink. Even the air you breath is your mind working out of reflex. There is no air here, only the void."

"What about you and your…" Whitney swallowed. "Hunger."

"Gone."

"I was wondering how you've been resisting this handsome, bare neck."

"Just because the need is gone doesn't mean I wouldn't take pleasure in draining you, thief. You're just lucky Elsewhere seems to have a purpose for you."

"If I can't feel, why did I feel you kick me?"

"Oh, the pain of violence remains very, very real."

Whitney felt his heart racing but figured that was a trick of his mind as well. He tried to let the repetitive motion of rowing soothe him. It wasn't working, but it kept him occupied if not distracted.

"You've been here before?" he asked.

"Every time I close my eyes," Kazimir responded.

"A bit dramatic, don't you think?"

"I am not being dramatic," he said. "It is why we do not sleep. We upyr are already dead. When we allow ourselves to drift, we find ourselves in this very place. It is how I know our guide. It is how I know the beast."

"So, we're in your dream?"

"No. Dead men don't dream."

Kazimir lay back and closed his eyes regardless. Whitney tried to get him to keep talking a few times, but if the upyr couldn't sleep, he was an excellent actor. With his arms folded over his chest, Whitney wished he'd place them lower.

An indeterminable amount of time passed as he rowed, no end in sight. There was no sun or moons to track the day or night. The sky remained dark red, same as the water only still. There were no gulls or spouting whales, just the gentle song of the spirits. Whitney's eyelids grew heavy. His head fell off to the side a few times as he struggled to stay awake. He leaned on the oar and finally gave in.

"You can't sleep in a dream," he told himself. "Sora's going to wake me up with a bucket of water back on the sea." He blinked a few times, minutes passing each time as he dozed off. Then, suddenly, they reopened, and he noticed a few bumps sticking out from the endless seascape through a layer of fog.

"Hey," Whitney said.

No answer.

He extended his leg and kicked Kazimir in the foot without looking over at his disgustingly pale, naked body. The upyr didn't argue or respond, just sat up.

"What's that?" Whitney asked. "Is that land?"

Kazimir peeked over. "Looks like mountains."

"Yes! They are, aren't they! Oh, gods, get me off this boat, and I'll worship all of you for the rest of my life." Whitney started rowing harder, the resistance of the spirits growing stronger.

He kept at it. His arms burned with soreness even though he'd hoped Kazimir had been wrong and he wouldn't feel pain here. Nobody gets hurt in dreams after all.

"Uh, why are those mountains moving?" Whitney asked.

The more he rowed, the more land appeared on either side of the mountains, extending to the horizon in either direction. The land drew closer, gaining shape through the fog, but the hills never seemed to grow no matter how close they got. Then, they vanished beneath the sea. Whitney's brow furrowed. A break in the land, the mouth of a narrow river, appeared. Whitney felt the current pulling on the oar and stopped rowing, but it was like no river entry he'd ever seen. The water drained in front of them as it towed the boat forward.

"Those were no mountains," Kazimir said, eyes snapping all the way open. "He's returned." He hopped to his feet just as a massive tentacle, missing its tip, shot up into the air and slammed down in front of their boat. Whitney soared back as the water swelled, but Kazimir caught him and tossed him down. He pried the oar out of Whitney's grasp which had tightened out of reflex.

Kazimir stabbed it out over the bow and struck the beast in an eye, eliciting a roar that would have stopped Whitney's heart if adrenaline didn't have it thumping against its rib cage.

"I thought you said it didn't want to hurt me!" Whitney said.

"The ferryman is gone. Now you're just in the way." A tentacle lashed at him, and he sprawled out to duck under it. Whitney stayed on the floor of the boat and dared not rise. He considered kicking the upyr overboard to save his own skin—it was the least the upyr deserved for all he'd done—but Whitney's muscles had seized.

A tentacle burst through the bottom of the boat, rising like a disgusting column of lumpy skin and suction cups. They soared into the air, Kazimir nearly flipping over the side of the boat and doing Whitney's work for him. The vessel tilted forward, and they both slid toward the bow.

Whitney found himself staring down into the face of a creature larger than a dozen zhulongs. Its many tentacular appendages waved around beneath and above the surface like so many snakes preparing to strike. Its two large eyes stared back at him, wider than any wagon wheel in Yarrington, and both of them as dark and soulless as Kazimir's, like they were related somehow.

It let out a primal scream—something Whitney would have never considered possible from any sea creature. With its giant maw open, rows upon rows of razor sharp teeth could be seen, hunks of flesh lodged between them, and they were being lowered into it.

"I'm dreaming," Whitney told himself. "I'm dreaming, I'm dreaming."

"It is not time yet, beast!" Kazimir shouted. He snapped the oar in half with his foot. The wianu shook the boat, and Kazimir flipped over the side, falling straight toward its mouth. He grabbed onto a tentacle before being carved to pieces. Swinging, broken end of the oar in hand, he stabbed it into one of the beast's eyes.

The wianu cried out, the sound so primordial it snapped Whitney back to attention. Its tentacles thrashed, and the boat went with them, snapping in half at the stern. Whitney held onto the front half as it flew through the air over the beast, then slammed into the mouth of the river.

Kazimir leaped from tentacle to tentacle as it tried to grab him. He didn't move lightning fast as he had back in Winde Port, but Whitney had never seen such precision.

The beast's head exploded from the surface behind him, blood black as pitch leaking from its eye. Its teeth gnashed, and it caught Kazimir on the back with one last desperate swipe of a tentacle, knocking him into the river ahead of the half-a-boat Whitney clung to.

Whitney stuck a leg out as the boat went by, now caught in the river's current. Kazimir grabbed hold of it, and Whitney reeled him in.

The wianu crawled up onto the land, a mess of tentacles allowing it to stand. Its screeches filled the air, but it didn't follow. Whitney didn't know if it was because the river grew too narrow, or Kazimir's blow had hurt it too badly, but he wouldn't complain.

"What the hell did you do to piss that thing off!" Whitney yelled.

"Only what I had to," Kazimir said through a series of coughs.

The swift current whipped them around a bend in the river

which got thinner and thinner. They hit a rock, and the front of the boat broke open before it started spinning. Now Whitney and Kazimir held onto what was essentially a piece of debris.

The rapids whipped them until Whitney could feel his fingers beginning to give way. He cursed himself for rowing so hard toward mountains that turned out to be a giant octopus monster. Brackish water filled his mouth, beat against his eyes.

Then he let go.

He tumbled through the water, blind, terrified. His shoulder hit a rock, lucky it wasn't his head, and he flipped around. He screamed, though only bubbles came out. He found himself so dizzy he wasn't sure which way was up. Then something squeezed the back of his neck and heaved him out of the water. Whitney looked from side to side, in shock. Gone was the raging river carrying them in from the sea. Gone were the echoes of the crying wianu. He wasn't sure how he'd been drowning, because now they were within a gentle stream. Kazimir stood in the chest-high water, holding Whitney up, allowing him to cough up water. The remnants of the boat floated on ahead.

Kazimir gazed back, eyes still bright with adrenaline. Then he drew a long, tired breath. "We're safe from it here, I think."

"You mean you're safe." Whitney shook himself free and fell back into the water again. His head dipped, but his feet found purchase in the soft river-bed.

"Do not think the beast innocent. It hungers for souls and would not hesitate to devour yours."

"Maybe I should have left you back there so we could test that."

Kazimir didn't reply, but he didn't have to. Now that things had calmed Whitney couldn't help but wonder more about what he was thinking saving the upyr who'd only just threatened to kill him back with Sora. He imagined Kazimir wondered the same.

He cursed his talent for acting first and thinking later.

"So where is here?" Whitney asked once he waded through the water enough for it to be at his waist, where he finally felt like he could breathe. Whether the air around him was real or imagined, he was desperate for it.

"The boat's destination is different for all who arrive in this realm."

"Are your answers to everything so vague?"

"It is the nature of this place."

Whitney stifled a groan. Hills rose and fell, there was a forest downriver, and smokestacks billowing from beyond the river's crest. He put a hand through his hair, grimacing from his sore shoulder. "Shog in a barrel," he said as he took another look from side to side.

"What is it now?" Kazimir questioned.

"Shog. In. A. Barrel."

"What is wrong?" Kazimir asked more directly.

Before Whitney could answer, a young boy came jogging down a path toward them through the brush.

"Greetings travelers!" he exclaimed. "Welcome to Troborough!"

IV

THE KNIGHT

Torsten's dirty, bloodstained hands wrapped the rusty bars of his own personal cell in the deepest dungeon beneath the Glass Castle. From there, he imagined how many wrongdoers and miscreants had stood in that very spot—how many of them he'd put there. Cultists, murderers, and thieves, like Whitney.

Now, he was stuck on the same side as all of them. Damned to hear the eternal grousing of those in the dark, dank cells around him who proclaimed their innocence as if they'd forgotten how to say anything else.

If Elsewhere was as legends described—a place where one was cursed to endure their greatest fear over and over for the rest of eternity—Torsten couldn't imagine worse. His only solace was knowing he wouldn't be one of the prisoners left to decay, forgotten. Redstar wouldn't have that. One morning, Torsten would be dragged outside and hanged before his people as a traitor.

And that was what broke his heart the most, even though he knew it was wrong. He knew his only concern should be the Glass Kingdom, left in the hands of those with unclear motives, but if Redstar had proven anything, it was how weak Torsten truly was.

His fingers slipped from the cold metal, and he fell back against the stone floor. Cobwebs in the corner were his only company, gathered around a stick-shaped object which he dared not get closer to observe. Some cells had port-holes, but not his. His had chain-links hanging from the ceiling and more on the floor. Attached to one was a solid, iron mask with only a few holes poked in for air.

Redstar was a cruel and spiteful bastard, putting Torsten in the very cell he himself had occupied after Torsten brought him back from the Webbed Woods. The very cell he'd been chained in, accused of cursing the then-Prince and purporting himself as Uriah Davies, before suddenly, nobody seemed to care anymore.

Torsten fought the urge to pound his fists into the stone. Instead, he used them to prop himself up onto his knees. He regarded the moldy ceiling and closed his eyes.

"Iam," he said.

"Ain't no gods down here!" an old coot in the adjacent cell cackled.

Torsten ignored him, sliding further into the cell and lowered his voice to a whisper. "Iam, I cannot say if You have abandoned me, though I would not question it if You have. I have failed You, mind and body. I have sinned beyond forgiveness in the murder of a brother of the Shield, Sir Havel Tralen. And I have failed to bring to justice a rebel responsible for so much death."

He paused to gather his breath. For so long, when he spoke with Iam, he could feel his God around him, as if wrapped in His loving embrace. Now, Torsten felt hollow.

"Forget me if You must," he said. "Let me rot down here, but do not forget about them. A devil wearing human flesh walks amongst Your most devout, plying them with a silver tongue.

Perhaps we have allowed Your light to wane in this past years, but You mustn't abandon them. They need You now more than ever."

"You think your god can hear you all the way down here?" Redstar said, his voice like needles stabbing Torsten's brain. He leaned against the bars of the cell, the light of a torch illuminating him so that the mark covering half his face was like pooling blood.

Torsten didn't answer.

Redstar picked something from his teeth, probably leftovers from some great feast had in honor of the 'Hero of Winde Port.'

"The realm of the buried belongs to a different deity," he said. "Perhaps you appeal to her?"

"Did you come here to gloat, Redstar?"

"Gloat? Why ever would I do that?"

"Because you've stolen everything you've ever wanted."

"Oh, Torsten. You have me all wrong. It pains me so to see you like this. Pains me to have been forced to do what I did for the good of the kingdom."

"Then walk upstairs and tell the King of your lies. Tell him exactly how you cursed him, and not all the fiction of you helping him see the truth. But how you wanted revenge for being shunned by your sister and left behind in the tundra by Liam. Tell him how you stole the face of Sir Uriah Davies."

Redstar sighed. "I can do all of that, and you'll still be the only one of us whose hands claimed the life of a fellow King's Shieldsman."

"Just leave me to exile!" Torsten barked, his fist pounding the wall. His knuckles split open against the immovable stone.

"Oh, but I have come to like you so much. After everything that's happened between us, it's almost as if... as if I created this version of you. As if I'm writing your story."

"You're no god, Redstar."

"Now that we agree on, but I do know one thing. This, in

here, is not where or how your story ends. The Buried Goddess promises so much more."

"Do you truly believe all the lies you spout? You foretold her glorious return back in the Webbed Woods, but where is she?"

"Sitting on the throne you so cherish, in the ears of your king."

Torsten scoffed. "Face it, Redstar. She remains buried as she ever was. I looked into Pi's eyes; I saw no all-powerful goddess in them. I saw his father."

Redstar allowed a grimace to show just for a second before he regained his infamous, shog-eating grin. "Nesilia's time is coming. She lies just beyond the veil, waiting to step back into the world she helped create at Iam's side."

"But she isn't here." Torsten leaned forward, realizing that he finally had the upper hand in one of their spats. "You didn't expect that, did you? All this scheming is just you biding time."

"Preparing her domain for her true arrival."

"Just admit it. You're as lost as the rest of us."

"Do you remember the hymn I recited in the Woods? 'Eye always wary and never known fear—'"

"Not this drivel again." Torsten rolled his eyes.

"'Abruptly disrupted by a single shed tear,'" Redstar continued. "'Beneath soil and stone, the Lady awaits. The heart of her lover shall ne'er abate.'"

"Enough. I remember the damn song."

"Then perhaps you can help me." Redstar sat and folded his legs. "I've studied those ancient etchings of the God Feud endlessly alongside the hymn inscribed around its border. It was supposed to bring her back from Elsewhere, you see. The blood of Bliss spilled by a servant of both Iam and Nesilia. We killed the Spider Queen together. You buried her blood with Pi's orepul beneath Mount Lister. Yet all that rose was the boy and her whispers. My Lady's true essence remains trapped in the prison made by Iam."

Torsten's throat went dry. *The orepul?* He'd been so busy with the kingdom; he never examined the night Pi was reborn in detail. He'd believed it was Iam's hand, or Redstar's curse finally wearing off. But now he knew why the boy king was so unpredictable and disconnected. If it wasn't a miracle of Iam that brought him back, it was unnatural, dark magic that should never have been trifled with.

He's a liar, Torsten reminded himself. Every word from his mouth is poison.

"You didn't put all that together yet?" Redstar remarked, clearly noticing the shock written all over Torsten face. "Yes, my thick-headed friend. Pi lives again thanks to blood magic."

"He died from it too," Torsten snapped.

"That was never my intention, but I can't say it's been bad for me." He raised his arms, gesturing to the fact that he was free.

"Yet your goddess remains buried."

"Not for long." He scooted closer like he was listening to a lecture from Holy Wren. "There's something in all the signs that I'm missing or ignoring. Something forgotten."

Then she will arise, in glorious day
    Through will and through fire, her enemies slain
    Forgotten, abandoned, but no longer bound
    From Elsewhere and exile, she'll receive her crown

"She will arise," Redstar said. "But when? How? Something is missing."

"Well, I hope you search forever."

"If that is what it takes. But I hear her, even now, telling me the answers I seek are somehow connected to you."

"I'll die before I help you."

"Oh, please. A few days down here, you'll be looking forward to my visits. Don't worry, dear Torsten. Together we'll find out what was missing, and by the time this year's Dawning comes, our Lord and Lady will be reunited in this realm again."

"Leave him be, brother."

Torsten was ready to drive his fists even harder into the stone from frustration when he heard Oleander's familiar voice, somehow both soothing and authoritative at the same time.

"Sister!" Redstar exclaimed. He pulled himself to his feet. "What a delightful surprise. Come to visit your favorite knight?"

"What I've come for is none of your business," she replied.

"Of course. The former Wearer and I were merely discussing his responsibilities in this transition of power. It will be so difficult deciding on a new Wearer who can finally live up to the reputation of Sir Uriah Davies. I'd take on the mantle myself but, Arch Warlock, dradinengor, Prime Minister; my responsibilities are endless these days."

"I'm sure you'll find a way. Now leave us."

Redstar turned to Torsten. The way the flame caught his brown eyes and marked face made him appear like a demon. "I look forward to seeing your story unfold, Torsten Unger."

"I suggest you hang me now then," Torsten said, seething. "Because the only way this ends is with my sword in your spine."

"I'd best be sure not to wear armor then to make things easier for you."

Redstar bowed with a grin and a flourish, then left. He bumped into Oleander on his way out, offering a halfhearted apology. A moment later, the Queen Mother appeared at the bars. She wore a pleased expression, her nose turned up at Torsten as if he were any other prisoner. But he could see the pain behind her bright, blue eyes. The dungeons weren't a fitting place for a woman of her majesty. Dust caked across the bottom of the same exquisite dress she'd worn in the Throne Room.

He rushed across the cell, wrapped his bloodied hands around the bars again and stuck his face through as far as he could.

"Oleander, I—"

"You were supposed to kill him," she cut him off.

"I was supposed to do many things, but we… I… underestimated Muskigo."

"I spent every second you were gone enduring my son's chastising until he finally began to speak to me somewhat like his mother again. I saw my precious boy in him. And now Redstar arrives to continue whispering in his ear and warping his mind. Already Pi ignores me."

"Then you kill Redstar!"

Her hand struck with the quickness of a desert snake, slapping Torsten across the face. Her long, manicured nails scratched his cheek. When he looked back up, he could see the pangs of regret painting her features before she forced her lips into a straight line.

He took her hand. "My Queen," Torsten said.

She pulled away. "You are not Wearer anymore. Dare touch me again, and you'll lose your hand on top of your dignity."

Torsten drew a deep breath. "I failed him, Oleander. For that, I am sorrier than you could possibly imagine."

"Do you know what it's like, seeing Redstar walk these halls with that damn grin on his face, barking commands? He was a rotten boy, and I was happy to leave him behind in the north when my Liam came. I never thought he could get worse."

"Then stand up to him. Help Pi see what a snake he really is."

"You think I haven't tried? Magic, parlor tricks, and heroics… I can't compete with that. All I can offer is my love and whatever happened to him when he passed on for those short days; I don't think he can feel love again."

"So, you allowed Redstar to throw me in here and take control of the King's Shield? Why, because you're scared Pi would be upset with you?"

"Because I don't want to lose him again!" she screamed. The way her voice echoed in the dungeon sent a shiver up Torsten's spine. A few other prisoners hollered lewd remarks, and they were lucky she was so focused on him otherwise they might've found their necks in a noose.

It was then that Torsten noticed the handmaiden lurking in Oleander's shadow and he remembered Tessa, the handmaiden she had so ruthlessly executed in a fit of rage. He'd spent so long trusting that Oleander and her soft spot for him was the key to fixing everything, but had somehow ignored how things got so bad in the first place. He forgot who ran things after Liam grew too sick to talk, or when Pi was unconscious and dead.

It all made him feel incredibly foolish ever thinking Oleander might've supported him back in the Throne Room. He knew everything she did was only for her son. And he knew what lengths she was willing to go to for him.

"The kingdom of Iam is in peril, Your Grace," Torsten said, unwilling to back down. "I know how much you care for Pi, but we've both been played for fools. If we don't try something drastic, we—"

"Fools?" The laugh that followed dripped with sarcasm. She was back to her old tricks. "How dare you. You had one simple task Torsten, and you didn't just fail to kill him, you let him become the greatest hero the kingdom has known since my husband."

"You think I don't know that? For Iam's sake, I'm in a dungeon!" He squeezed the bars so tight his hands lost their color. "I know all you want to do is earn Pi's affection, but someone has to stand up to him. Someone has to show him the light of Iam."

"Of all people, you should see," she bristled. "Iam has abandoned us. We're all we have."

Torsten lost his grip and staggered backward. To hear her say that... She had been born in the same land as Redstar but spent most of her life in Yarrington at Liam's side. She became as much a woman of the Glass as anyone. It wasn't acting. From the moment a younger Wren bathed her in Iam's light and cleansed her soul, Iam became a part of her.

"You can't believe that," Torsten stammered.

"You're blind not to. He teaches us not to kill, but do you know what I felt when I had all those people hanged?" Torsten's heart nearly stopped. In the months since that happened, never once had Oleander brought up what she'd done. "Nothing. Iam didn't stop me. He didn't punish me. All I wanted was to embrace my child again, and now that's possible."

"Then protect him from the monster upstairs, at least."

"Redstar now claims it was him and his goddess who brought Pi back."

"Redstar claims a lot of things."

"I don't care how it happened, only that it did. I will earn my son's love in the manner of my choosing, but you were meant to kill Redstar so that he never blamed me for stealing an uncle he admires for whatever gods-forsaken reason."

"Then let me out of here, and I'll do it. Even if it means I suffer an eternity in Elsewhere, I'll do it for this kingdom. For you."

"So you can find a way to make him more powerful?"

"What then? What would you ask of me?"

"Nothing. It's too late now, Torsten. If Redstar isn't lying and all his nonsense about the Buried Goddess is true... I won't let my rotten brother cause any more harm to my child if I insult her by having her voice on this plane killed."

"Oleander, please listen to me. These past months I have seen miracles with my own eyes, and they did not belong to him. There is no her."

"There is in the land I come from. And if I simply appeased my brother when he visited muttering his madness about fallen gods a year ago, none of this would have ever happened."

"So, you'd turn your back on Iam? After all His light has blessed you with?"

"I turn my back on all but my son." As if to demonstrate her words, she whipped around and snapped her fingers for her hand-maiden. The young girl hurried forward and placed a bowl of steaming, fresh stew on the floor. She went to slide it under the bars, but Oleander clicked her tongue in disapproval, and she left it outside the cell. It was within reach, but the message was clear enough.

"That is for all you have done in service to my family," she said, her back still turned. "Enjoy it. It's the last thing you'll ever get from me."

She started walking away. Torsten mustered the courage to press his face back against the cold metal.

"Answer me this, my Queen," he said. She stopped. "Why did you come to my room that night if you don't trust me? In your heart, you must know that all I want is what's best for this kingdom."

Finally, she turned back and approached the bars. There was rage in her eyes, but also a playfulness that reminded Torsten all too much of her brother. He'd never seen a resemblance between them until that moment.

"I did trust you, more than anyone in this damned castle," she said. "But like I said then, my husband got to have all the fun in the world with every whore in every corner of Pantego, from here to Panping. Why shouldn't I get to?"

Torsten sunk back, wondering how he could have been such a fool. Blinded by the touch of her lips. He'd lived so long, hoping that he was a better man than the vagabonds in taverns groping at barmaids, but now he knew he had all the same weaknesses. Perhaps he'd had them all along.

"Oleander," he said softly, "can you do one last thing for me at least?"

She didn't answer, but she didn't leave. She simply kept glowering. He knew her well enough to know that meant she was listening.

"Send for Wren to visit me," Torsten said. "If I am to die in the cell, I'd like to talk to Iam one last time, and it's clear He's listening to me no longer."

"Goodbye, Torsten."

"Please, Your Grace."

She left without a response, her handmaiden scurrying after her like a trained wolf. Torsten knew well enough that a non-answer from her wasn't a no. She could be incredibly impish when she was agitated, much like her brother.

Now she and Redstar were the only two speaking into Pi's ear, and Nesilia if Redstar was to be believed. The only two influencing the fate of the kingdom Liam had brought to such heights. Torsten wondered if maybe deep inside, Oleander wanted to see the kingdom crumble. For the man she claimed to love so deeply, she often cursed with equal vim.

Liam wasn't perfect.

It was a hard truth to admit, but it was true nonetheless. He'd had his vices, a short temper with his wife who took so long to produce a male heir or a lust for any woman who flashed a smile and a bit of flesh. In the end, that was likely what got him sick. Yet, Iam had chosen him to spread the word of his chosen kingdom. For all the death and suffering he brought to Pantego in that crusade—death which inspired men like Muskigo to rebel—he also brought a decade of peace not known in all of history.

As Torsten leaned back and stared into the surrounding darkness, he vowed not to sulk and let everything he loved fade. If Liam was flawed, Torsten was a monster, but so long as he drew breath, he would come up with a way to unseat Redstar. Whatever it took.

The Glass Kingdom had nobody else left...

V

THE DESERTER

Rand Langley woke the same way he had nearly every time he'd allowed himself to drift asleep over the last few months. Drenched in sweat. It didn't matter that it was the heart of winter in the dead of night and so cold that frost hadn't abandoned the tiny window of his tiny apartment since before he could remember. He'd become exhausted from fighting sleep, hoping to ward off the terrors.

Exhaustion won.

"It's okay, Rand," his sister Sigrid whispered. She rolled over in her bed. Their narrow mattresses rested side by side against the wall, a dusting of snow at their feet, blowing in from an ever-growing crack in their window.

Rand continued to breathe heavy, squeezing his eyes shut to drive out the noise that had plagued him for so long. The threads of rope stretching as it swung, creaking, over and over. It was like the sounds of docked ships rocking in the waves, only in his head, the rope wasn't moored to a quay.

"Just breathe, brother." Sigrid crawled to his bed and stroked his sweat-wet hair.

She hummed the same tune their mother used to when they were kids in Dockside. A Ship to Nowhere, about the poor dreamers sitting on the edge of the docks, wondering where the great vessels came from and where they were heading. Rand and Sigrid used to sit by the water, and he'd sing to her, but now he didn't know the words. It was before the King's Shield. Before...

"I need a drink," Rand said. He threw off his ratty sheets and edged his way passed Sigrid's bed.

"Rand, it's the middle of the night," she said. "What ye be needing is sleep." She spoke with a Dockside affection; one Rand managed to break as he rose through the King's Shield and spent more time amongst nobles.

He ignored her while pawing around the room in the darkness, only a bit of moonlight coming through the clouds lighting his world. Their last candle was a melted clump of wax in the center of their only table, which Rand banged his knee into and cursed. Then he found an empty bottle of wine and cursed louder, throwing it down in disgust.

"Rand, please," his sister said, taking his hand. "We can't afford anymore."

He shook her off. "You're a barmaiden," he replied. "Take some."

He rifled through their cupboard and found a jug of ale. Not even bothering with a mug, he lifted it to his lips. Only a few, stale drops remained. "Gods-damned, empty yigging..."

Rand's voice trailed off as he slammed the clay jug on the table just as Sigrid went to stop him. Shards flew out in every direction, and a chunk of table snapped off.

"Dammit, Rand!" she squealed.

Rand stood, fuming. The taste of ale was just enough to make the terrors of his mind worse. *Creak, creak, creak*, the taut rope swung like his own mind was taunting him. He raised his hands to his temples and screamed. It was the only way to stop the thoughts.

A neighbor banged on the thin wall to quiet him, dust billowing through the thin ray of moonlight.

Rand fell to his knees, panting. The creaking rope was now accompanied by the sound of thick blood trickling to the floor. More waking nightmares. He could see the bulging eyes of the handmaiden Tessa as if she were right in front of him, tongue swollen, purple, and hanging limply from her lips. Only there has been no blood dripping from those he hanged.

Rand opened his eyes and saw his sister, seated on her bed. The tear on her cheek glistened with Clora's light, but she fought back any more as she clutched her hand. A piece of the jar had left a deep gash on her palm.

"Sigrid, I'm so..." he stammered. He crawled over and took her arm. Blood streamed down her forearm onto the floor, seeping through the cracks in the faded wooden planks. She pulled away, unable to look at him. He tore a strip off his bedsheets and gently wrapped her hand. She was the injured one, yet his fingers shook as his body yearned for another drink.

"Yer getting worse, Rand," she said softly. "Yer going to kill yerself drinking so much. I... I don't know if I can keep helping ye."

"I know. It's just," he paused, looking up at her. "It's the only thing that helps me stop seeing her face. All the others, they're blank. The same. But hers, I can still see the tears streaming from her eyes as the white went red and her neck tensed. She was the most beautiful girl I'd ever known and I—"

Sigrid finally gave in and clutched his face. Rand could smell the iron in the blood on her hand, but he didn't care. "It wasn't yer fault," she said. "The Queen made ye."

"I could have run."

She put on a smirk. Rand knew it was all a façade to try and cheer him up. "And never see me again?"

"I just wished I'd told her how I felt. That from the moment I entered the castle, she made even the Queen seem hideous. That I'd offer anything to see her smile in the hall as I passed. One last time."

"And I'd offer anything to see ye smiling again, li'l brother."

Rand swallowed the lump forming in his throat. "Then help me."

"I'm scared I can't." She stood and crossed the room. She picked up a single, bronze autla from a bowl. It scraped as she slid it over the rough wood. "This be the last of the pay for yer prior cycle in the Shield. Everything I earn downstairs goes to keeping this dump. It's all we've got, Rand."

"We'll find a way."

"We keep saying that, but we don't. I can't be the only fighter. I know ye can't return to yer post, especially after ignoring the call to Winde Port, but there's got to be something ye can do. Someone in this city is always looking for muscle."

"I don't want to hurt anyone ever again."

"Then haul cargo down by the docks. More Longboats from the Drav Cra're arriving every day now they're allies. Do something, Rand. I… I feel like I'm falling apart supporting us both these past months. I can't even imagine what ye've been through, but I can't be doing this alone no more."

"You're right. You should be off getting married to some great man. Having children on a farm outside of Westvale. You deserve the world."

"Listen to ye, speaking all proper-like. I don't care about deserving; I just want to survive winter." She returned and kneeled in front of Rand, staring straight into his eyes. "Please, find a way to forgive yerself. We can go to church and kneel in the light of Iam if ye want. He can show ye that none of this is yer fault."

Rand didn't respond. For months, his sister had been begging him to attend service, but how could he bring himself to stand before Iam after what he'd done?

"Fine," Sigrid said. "I guess we'll both freeze in this awful place together." She stood and grabbed a cloak from a hook on the wall.

"Where are you going?"

"On a walk. If ye won't go and seek out Iam, then I will."

"Sigrid, wa—"

The door slammed before he could get the words out. Her footsteps echoed down the hall, then nothing. All he was left with was the soft whistle of wind coming through their window.

For those few seconds alone, he stared at his sister's blood and considered never taking to the drink again. Then a gust of snow powder blasted his cheek and stirred his thoughts. Salty, fishy air mixed with the faint smell of blood. He wondered how those hanging bodies faired against the elements when winter took, if the cold frosted their eyes like glass.

Rand looked up at the rotting, wood ceiling which warped down to one corner. "You really have abandoned us, haven't you?"

He pulled himself to his feet and peered out the window. Sigrid walked through the alley out to Port Street, drawing her cloak tight for warmth. The clarity in which he could see her, even through the dirty glass, meant dawn was approaching. He didn't have much time.

He rushed to the door and grabbed the bronzer—blood money —then headed out without bothering to lock the door behind him. There was freedom in knowing they had nothing worth stealing. The dark hall on the second floor of the Maiden's Mugs Tavern had a few more rundown apartments, but Rand was interested in the tavern itself.

His eyes closed as he descended the stairs. The floor of the tavern wasn't much better, but he'd manage. Relief was so close. Not a soul was around, and the bar was cleaned up nice. Gideon Trapp ran a clean establishment, which was a lot to say for Dockside. He didn't, however, take good care of his lodgers.

The storage room was locked, but the tapped barrels of ale stacked along the wall were merely plugged. Rand unsealed one, grabbed a mug, and let it pour. *Stealing...* It went against everything a member of the King's Shieldsman should stand for.

He didn't care. *Trapp shouldn't make it so easy.*

He let the mug fill halfway, then raised it to his lips and guzzled it down. The Dockside stuff had a sour tinge—nothing like Old Yarrington mead—but he was so used to it now, it went down like water. And every ounce down his throat was like one turn of a gear loosening the vice squeezing his head. He hated himself for breaking his vow so quickly, but after Tessa's horrid, decaying face began to blur in his mind, the guilt vanished. He wiped his lips, then went to fill the mug again. He was just about topped off when a hand slapped the bar counter behind him.

"Ye gonna pay for that?" a man asked.

Rand turned slowly, mug in hand, and saw Gideon Trapp standing behind him. The man had a gut the size of one of the kegs and shaggy mutton chops running down the sides of his head to draw attention away from his balding pate. His teeth were a rotten shade of yellow, like any man born in Dockside who never left.

"Are you going to fix our window before my sister freezes to death?" Rand asked, taking a step closer, looking down on the man. Months of wallowing had eaten away much of the muscle he'd earned in King's Shield training, but he still towered over most Docksiders.

"I told you, I can't do nothing till we thaw out a bit."

"By then you'll be scraping our bodies off the cold floor."

"Better than the streets. Now, I'll ask again, are ye gonna pay for that?"

The portly man didn't back down, just puffed out his soft chest then grabbed Rand's wrist. Rand's forearm shot forward and barred Trapp's throat, slamming him against the stack of barrels. He pushed harder and harder until spit bubbled in the corner of the Trapp's mouth as he struggled to speak. It was only when Rand heard that familiar gurgling of a clenched airway that he realized what he was doing and backed off.

Trapp fell to the floor, gasping and pawing at his throat. The sight made Rand envision another of his victims besides Tessa's. With full clarity, the bearded visage of the royal physician, Deturo, flailing as the noose tightened and the color fled his cheeks passed before his eyes. He blinked a dozen times, trying to force the vision away.

Rand reached into his pocket, removed the last bronzer he had left to his name, and slapped it down on the counter. In the same motion, he grabbed the mug and headed upstairs.

"Yer lucky yer sister has such great… mugs… or ye'd both be out in the cold!" Trapp rasped.

Rand stopped and regarded the man. In a district so poor, only the dishonest were so obese. Rand could have killed the fat slob in a second if it wouldn't have left his sister without a proper way to make a living. There were worse taverns, which would ask more of her than to show skin.

"Speak about her like that again, and I'll drown you in your ale," Rand said.

"I don't care what you used to be; you won't get the jump on me again. Now get out of here. One more screw-up, and I'll tell yer sister she's through! Don't care how pretty she be. Ye can take it up with Valin, or go crawling back to your friends at the Glass Castle, deserter."

It was no secret to anyone in Dockside who Rand was, or what he'd done. There weren't many from the place who rose so high. The only reason the crown didn't barge through his door to drag him away and punish him as a deserter was because Docksiders kept their mouths shut.

"Just leave her out of this," he growled.

Rand's hands quaked as he turned to leave. He used both hands to grip the mug, ale sloshing over the rim. It wasn't rage, though he was desperate to unleash some on the man. Just the thought of being so near the sweet release had his entire body aching.

He waited until he was back in his room. Downing a second full mug of Dockside ale was enough to make him feel light as a feather. It tasted like swill, but that just meant it kicked like an angry zhulong. Plus, he'd been drunk so long, it was like his body forgot how to act any other way.

"I'll show ye a screw-up," he hiccuped to himself, his accent breaking through training. He made it two steps across his room before he tripped over the chair leg and came crashing down on the floor face-first. His lip split open, and splinters drove into his hand as he failed to break the fall.

Rand couldn't bring himself to get back up, laid flat across the floor, and that was when he noticed the glimmer of the armor tucked under his bed, the metal forged with glaruium from the heart of Mount Lister.

Despite the dust and snow powder covering the room, somehow the King's Shield armor remained clean, so polished he could see his reflection in the chestplate. There wasn't even the faintest dent or scratch, for even though he'd claimed the lives of dozens whilst wearing it in the name of the Queen, it had never seen battle.

He barely recognized the man who stared back in its reflection. Bleeding, eyes puffy and red, cheeks gaunt from malnourishment. He reached out to crawl toward it, and his fingers brushed through his sister's still-wet blood on the floor. Now, Gideon Trapp would be riding her even harder thanks to Rand causing more issues downstairs. Drunkenly stumbling through the tavern, knocking over tables every other day was bad enough, but striking the owner?

"Some knight," he whispered as he dragged the armor out and lay it across his hay bed. He could remember proudly standing in it, still donning the helm of the Wearer of White before Torsten returned to reclaim it. He could remember being in the castle bailey, ordering his men to string up the innocent at the command of the mad Queen Regent. He could recall Tessa's face, heartbroken, knowing the feelings he'd held inside for so long and feeling them just the same.

And even then, Rand had said nothing. Even then, he was a loyal knight serving his monarch. All he had to do was speak out, and maybe Oleander's wrath would have turned to him instead of her handmaiden. It could have been him hung from the walls like meat in a butcher shop, putting an end to his miserable life.

It was then he knew what needed to doing. For the first time in a long time, Rand's mind was clear.

"I'm so sorry, Sigrid," he whispered as he tore his sheet out from under the armor, then took his sister's. He tied the ends together while muttering, "Ye'll be better off, ye will."

He stood on the bed, tying one side securely around a ceiling beam, and with the other, he tied a tight noose around his neck.

Staring down at his armor, he began reciting the words of the King's Shield. "We are the Armor of Yer Holy Kingdom. Our lives are given freely under the sight of Yer Vigilant Eye so Yer children may thrive in this world Ye have blessed us with." He sniveled, closed his eyes and drew a deep breath.

"I shielded nobody but meself," he sputtered through tears before mustering the courage to continue.

"We are the right hand of Iam. The sword of His justice, and the Shield that guards the light of this world." He hung his head. A tear rolled down his cheek and splattered on his armor. He wasn't sure how long he stood there, a minute or an hour. To take one's own life was a sin by the teachings of Iam, but he was bound for Elsewhere anyway. Eternal torment in the bowels of the underworld was all he deserved.

There was a knock at the door. The sound startled him, and his feet slid hard to the side, knocking the mangy bed out from under him. His feet dropped, stopping a good half-meter from the floor. His neck wrenched upward, the cloth tightening around his throat so fast the corners of his vision went blotchy.

Sigrid! he thought, imagining his sister finding him like this. He grasped at the cloth and flailed his legs to try and pull the bed back. His toe caught its edge, but the wood frame cracked, and the bed tipped. His body swung the other way, his vision growing blurrier as he struggled.

At a certain point, he gave in and allowed his eyes to close. There was no fighting anymore. He could almost see the other side and the end to his torment. All he could hear was the creaking of the cloth pulling on wood.

Suddenly, something wrapped his legs and lifted him. Air rushed down his throat, filling his lungs with new life. He gasped awake from the precipice of unconsciousness. He rolled his eyes to look down with his peripherals and saw two arms around them. Then, taking another breath, they became more manifest, covered in the loose sleeves of a white robe. Just as suddenly, they vanished, and Rand's weight once again pulled him toward doom.

Just before he could wonder what cruel trick this was, the bed reappeared beneath his feet. He tapped with his bare feet until he found footing. The relief was immediate, unlike anything he'd ever experienced. Even laying down after a hard day at training under Sir Unger or Sir Jolly couldn't compare.

He felt a body against his and fingers against his neck. The handmade noose lifted over his ears, and without the support of it, his wobbly legs gave out. He collapsed onto a man's chest.

Chest stinging from exertion, throat burning, he steadied his breathing, every one like a tendril of ice as the cold air went down.

"It's okay, my child," the man said, laying Rand down on the bed, his voice still indistinct. "Breathe."

The world came slowly into focus, and with it, the man hovering above him. Rand thought he'd died and gone to Elsewhere when he saw him, that this was some demon's trick. For cradling him and rubbing his back as if to beckon the air in, was the unmistakable face of Wren the Holy, High Priest of the Church of Iam.

VI

THE MYSTIC

As a lover of music, Sora could say with certainty what she was listening to was no such thing. Three of her new pirate companions picked and plucked at strange, home-made-looking instruments of a variety Sora had never seen before and hoped she'd never hear again.

To see such hardened and grizzled men drinking and being merry, laughing and joking; it was unsettling.

She'd only been on Gold Grin's pirate ship for a few hours, but already she wanted to go back to her little captain's quarters and sleep. If she weren't afraid of offending Gold Grin, she'd have already retired into the small quarters they'd provided for her far below the deck. It being separate from the rest of the crews' bunks by only a curtain didn't have her any more eager.

Aquira was alrcady there although she'd protested at letting Sora wander off unprotected. Sora knew it wouldn't help anyone to have a wyvern flittering about, least of all, Aquira. The pirates were all spooked by her, something about ancient Panpingese curses. In Sora's experience, Aquira had been anything but a curse. The llttle, winged reptile had saved her life more than once.

She let her head fall into her arms folded on the table in front of her. She tried to imagine the music being better than it was; tried to imagine it was Fabian "Feel Good" Saravia, her favorite bard who'd frequently come through Troborough.

It was no use. It was trash. Brigands without an ear for music gallivanting around because there was nothing else to do on the high seas—besides stare at her now. She noticed one of their gazes fixed upon her while the grubby man tapped his foot along to the sorry excuse for a tune.

She turned sidewise and self-consciously raised the neckline of her dress. Then she allowed her mind to drift toward Yaolin City and her plans once she arrived. The problem was, Whitney was supposed to be her guide. She knew nothing of the city— even being Panpingese. Their customs were as foreign to her as she was to these pirates.

It reminded her of her first day of church in Troborough. Father Hullquist stood at the altar beneath the glittering Eye of Iam and read from ancient scripture. The villagers sang hymns with him, then one by one were invited up the aisle to bask in the pinhole shaft of light piercing the center of the Eye.

Those first days, fresh off the caravan of war refugees, she felt so out of place. Wetzel had barely spoken to her above an incomprehensible grumble and had her towing supplies all over town. It wasn't until a tawny-haired boy slapped her on the rump as she trembled before the priest and said, "You're up," that she was able to breathe properly. From that day, she and Whitney had been inseparable.

Until he left…

"Left," Sora spat to herself. At first, the pirates were a distraction, but now that she'd settled in, her mind returned to those dark places which had her confined to her quarters on the corsair for so long.

This wasn't like the time he'd abandoned her in Troborough

and set off to find adventure she could barely dream of. She'd been responsible this time. Wherever he was, Sora had sent him there.

"Girly," came Tum Tum's voice, pulling Sora from her ruminating. "Yer gonna hafta move on someday. Why not start?"

Tum Tum was a nice enough man, even for a dwarf. Sora hadn't known many dwarves. Even those who'd plowed through Troborough on the occasional caravan usually kept to the Twilight Manor, filling Hamm's coffers with coin and their gullets with ale. But if there was anything to be learned from how she'd been treated in places like Bridleton and Winde Port, it was people are people no matter what race.

Tum Tum sat beside her and threw his feet up onto the table. He was clean. Really clean. The pirates treated them well, allowing them to bathe in heated salt water which was great for their wounds. Tum Tum's now-untangled hair and beard were combed and braided. She didn't know what the standard of beauty was for dwarves, but she'd imagined he was on the handsome end of the scale.

They were in what she assumed to be the pirate ship's galley. It was a massive galleon, so many times larger than their little corsair ship it was impossible for her to guess just how many rooms there were. All she knew was it was comforting to know that someone besides her and Tum Tum—someone who was skilled in naval fairing—was piloting the ship.

The galley, like the rest of the ship, wasn't ornate, but it was homey. It was clear the pirates took care of their vessel. Trinkets and paintings lined the walls, all appearing to come from different places—loot displayed like trophies to their greatest conquest, not unlike Liam's Throne Room

She'd have never thought such dangerous men would be so meticulous about their ship decor or the quality of their food, but they showed great care even to the smallest details. Looking down at the chopped mutton before her, drenched in thick, rich gravy, topped with kernels of corn, she wished she had an appetite.

"Haven't touched yer food," Tum Tum said.

"Where did they get sheep?" Sora asked.

Tum Tum shrugged and snatched a piece from her plate. He made a deep, satisfied moaning sound as he bit into it.

Sora once again regarded the musicians—if they could be called that. Big, toothless grins plastered their faces. One with a patch over an eye drummed on the top of a clay mug with the tips of two dirks.

"Whitney would have made some cheesy joke," she said to Tum Tum without looking at him, "about how they were a merry band of pirates. Then he'd have thought himself a genius for the play on words."

Tum Tum laughed. Sora smiled.

"Aye," he said. "Whitney could tell tales with the best of em. Never could tell where his jokes ended and his adventures began though." He took a deep breath, then lifted his pint. "To Whitney. It's a quieter life without him."

"Yeah," Sora said, not having a mug of her own to lift. "To Whitney..."

As tears welled in the corner of her eyes, she realized she hadn't cried since they left their ship. It felt like a personal record after what happened.

"What if I killed him, Tum Tum?" she asked. In the days since, she'd never been able to ask that question out loud. She couldn't bear the thought.

"Ye did what ye had to," Tum Tum said. "If ye hadn't, that gods-damned vampire'd have done it and we'd all been dead. Ye saved our lives, lass. Ye should be celebrated. I know Whitney wouldn't have had it any other way. Ye should have seen his face when I assumed the two of ye were married back in Winde Port.

Cheeks red as an apple." He chuckled. "Matter of fact, make believe this party be for ye, for savin our skins and riddin the world of that monster. Ye deserve it."

"I deserve nothing!" Sora snapped. "You know what I did? I burned down a whole city, and I killed my best friend or worse."

"Now stop it!" Tum Tum stood, shoulders barely clearing the height of the table. "Ye did no such thing. That place was overrun by them gray men, and ye saved us all. In yer own way, ye even saved Whitney from a much worse fate."

The music stopped as their host, Gold Grin, appeared within the threshold of the galley. Even across the way, she could see his teeth glistening in the light of the candles.

"Carry on, boys!" he exclaimed.

The men cheered, and the music struck up again, a little more lively and a lot less in tune. The feet clomping on the floor sounded like they were keeping the beat to at least a dozen different songs.

Sora watched as Gold Grin picked up a silver goblet and made his way toward the table where she and Tum Tum sat with a skip to his step.

Sora raised her head and furiously wiped her eyes. She didn't know why, but she didn't want the man to see her in such a state. Probably something Whitney had told her. Showing weakness to pirates was the quickest way to wind up one of their wenches.

"That's more like it," Tum Tum said, his back to the pirate, not knowing the reason for her sudden change in demeanor.

"Guests!" Gold Grin addressed them. "Hoping yer comfortable?"

"Damn," Tum Tum said. "Comfortable that is. We be damn comfortable. Anything beats sailing toward nowhere."

Gold Grin looked to Sora, and she managed a nod.

"Good to hear," Gold Grin said. He pulled up a chair and sat with its back facing the wrong direction. He crossed his arms and leaned in before continuing. "Now tell me, what makes ye want to go to Yaolin… really?"

He examined Sora from head to toe. Usually, it made her shudder when men looked her over like she was meat at a butcher, but there wasn't a hint of malice in Gold Grin's eyes. For the terror of the seas he claimed to be, he seemed quite the gentleman.

"As I said, my husband died, and I want to inform his family in person," Sora said. "Whitney was an old friend, and helped us get this ship and start sailing before leaving us for the gulls."

"Codswallop," Gold Grin said. "Try again."

Sora blinked. "That's the truth."

"Aye, so let me get this straight. I save ye from certain doom, we welcome ye onto our ship, into our home, and ye lie to my face?"

Sora glanced at Tum Tum. The dwarf shrugged. "Can't say I ain't curious meself."

Sora swallowed the lump in her throat. She wasn't sure why she cared so much about guarding her true purpose. Sure, Gold Grin might not take kindly to being lied to and change his mind about taking them to Yaolin, but that wasn't the real reason. He seemed decent enough despite his title. But the last person she'd opened up to vanished, and the thought of doing it again made her stomach churn.

"Honestly, I need to know more about where I come from," she said, battling back the sick feeling. "Who I am, why I can do what I do, how to control it better." She pictured her outstretched hand back on the corsair ship and the blinding light; Whitney and Kazimir there one second, then gone another. Then she recalled the Webbed Woods when she released a blast of energy that subdued a powerful warlock, or in Winde Port when Muskigo was on the cusp of victory before her fire spread as if fueled by her rage. She even remembered Redstar's face when she healed Torsten's wounds in the forest.

It was nothing any normal blood mage without decades of experimenting like Redstar had should be capable of, she knew that now. Nothing her teacher Wetzel even knew enough to teach her.

"That's more like it!" Gold Grin slapped the table hard, and so deep in thought, Sora jumped. "Ye got yerself a special gift there, lassy. I'd been trying to learn some magic myself in my travels, but some of us just ain't got the gift."

"It's not as great as it seems," Sora said.

"Trust me, girl. I've seen more horrors at the hands of men playing with magic than any other, but I've seen some good too."

Gold Grin gently took Sora's hand. She tried to pull away out of instinct, but Grisham politely asked, "May I?" and she gave in. He slowly unwound the cloth bandage around her palm and studied the many scars.

"Blood magic, aye?" he asked.

"Yes," Sora replied softly.

"I've seen the Drav Cra use it. Very powerful, very unpredictable in weak hands. Never seen a Panpingese lass doing it, but I suppose there aren't many mystics left after the war."

Sora leaned forward. "But there are some left?"

"Ah, so it's a mystic ye want to meet?" he asked, grinning. "Rumors say they're out there. They ain't on the seas though, and impossible to find. Trust me; I've looked. It's said the ancient mystics found a way to live forever. Hogwash probably, but I'll be damned if me and my mates don't keep an ear open for the secrets. Sail the seas for all of time!"

"Live forever, ye say?" Tum Tum asked.

"What about making someone disappear?" Sora asked.

Gold Grin scratched his chin. "Not sure. What, were ye

wishing ye'd make that scallywag Whitney vanish? Cus then I'd understand!"

Sora choked on her next breath. Gold Grin's brow furrowed like he knew he was on to something.

"Well, I don't know nothing about disappearing," he said, "but I heard some say the mystics learned a way to travel to Elsewhere itself. That they hid there after the war. Seeing as how nobody talks about them now, probably got stuck there, where nothing living should be."

Sora turned to Tum Tum. "You don't think Whitney—"

"I just be a dwarf good at pourin ale," Tum Tum said. "All this mumbo-jumbo talk makes me head spin."

"Look, if Whitney wronged ye, ye wouldn't be alone in wanting revenge, lass," Gold Grin said.

"He didn't wrong me," Sora said.

"Ah, so he broke your heart."

"No," she protested, but her expression must have betrayed her words because Gold Grin's smile gave credence to his name.

"The boy always did fancy himself a ladies' man. Stealing a woman like ye from her husband though, I'm impressed."

"He didn't steal me—"

Gold grin waved his hand to quiet her. "I ain't here to judge, lass. Whether yer husband truly be dead or yer going back to him after a dalliance with that lying thief, I can promise ye I've done far worse."

"I'm not sure about that." She closed her eyes and could see the flames devouring Winde Port, feeding off her anger.

"Bah," Gold Grin spat. "That rat bastard is fickle as the wind, so I say move on."

"Now, now, he wun't too bad," Tum Tum butted in. He'd had a few ales by then, and the words flowed right out of him. Sora stayed quiet and tried her best to listen, but something Gold Grin said had her distracted.

Mystics hiding in Elsewhere.

"I met him in the Dragon's Tail when I was just a mere miner," Tum Tum explained even though nobody asked. "He convinced me to follow me dream and travel south. 'Open a pub,' he said after we spent a week deep underground searching for the mythical Brike Stone."

"Did ye find it?" Gold grin interrupted.

"We found a stone all right, but it wasn't magical, much as he claimed it was. I think he just wanted to get to the fresh air. 'Why do anything we don't want to?' he always used to say and lived it too. Minute we got out, he gave me some staff he took so I could buy a lot on Winder's Wharf, much good it's doing for me now."

"You had it easy," Grisham said. "Old Whitney joined up with my crew a few years back. We were riding on my first; hand built it myself. The *Sea Hawk* was a fine vessel, but Whitney spotted a Glass Kingdom galleon alone on the Torrential. Convinced me to try and take her and start an armada. Ye know how convincing he can be."

"Like a silver-tongued devil," Tum Tum snickered.

"So, we did it, and we took it. And next thing I know, Whitney's sailing off the other way in the *Sea Hawk* with a few deserters."

Tum Tum smacked his head with his palm. "And ye didn't kill him?"

"We set off on him full tilt when I realized: somehow he'd shoved all our plundered riches into barrels and set them into the water for us to grab. All I was short was a small, mangy ship and a few unloyal crewmen. Now I've got the *Reba* and the best crew in Pantego!" His men took a momentary break from their raucousness to cheer in approval.

"Never's there been a man so equally able to frustrate and show ye everything ye really want," Tum Tum said.

"Yeah..." Sora whispered.

"So where in Elsewhere did he disappear off to then?" Grisham asked. "Always a thrill to hear about one of his great escapes, even if it came at your expense lass." He nodded Sora's way, but she stayed quiet.

"He pulled off the greatest trick of all," Tum Tum said. "There we were on that ship, beset by a vile killer. An upyr, believe ye me. He had Whitney by the neck and Sora here was going to use some of that magic to save em. A flash, then bam, they're both gone. Never seen a thing like it in me life."

Gold Grin shot Sora a knowing look. A man like him had likely seen so much of the mysterious in their world; she wasn't sure why she was surprised he'd pieced some of what happened together, at least as much as she had herself. She did her best to mask her grief, but that apparently wasn't good enough.

"I see," Gold Grin said. "Boy always was so quick with his fingers it was like magic."

"Just like magic," Sora said. Just as she went to lean on her palm, a thought popped into her head. Her eyes lit up.

Where in Elsewhere is he… For the first time in many days, a weight lifted off her heart. If the mystics could access Elsewhere, not just feel it working through them, but genuinely obtain that plane as Gold Grin said, could that be where she sent Whitney and Kazimir? It wouldn't be the first time she'd pulled off a magic feat seemingly only a powerful mystic should've been capable of. And if that's where he was, maybe they could help her get there. It made more sense than anything else.

Either he was alive and trapped there, or dead, and damned to spend eternity there. He sure as Iam wasn't destined for the Gate of Light, if it even existed. The only other option was that Kazimir had powers the books on upyrs never spoke of and somehow teleported them somewhere else.

"Look, lass," Grisham said. "If ye want to meet a mystic and figure out whatever in the gods' name happened, I can't help ye, but Yaolin is the best place to start looking."

"So, you don't care that I lied about why I wanted to go?" Sora said.

"Care?" he chuckled. "Like I said, whether it be dead husbands, fake husbands, or mysteries of magic; they don't matter to me. Ye be a friend of Whitney Fierstown, and that be enough. Plus, I've already got this!" He pulled out the half of the Glass Crown and placed it on the table. "If Whitney weren't lying, this'll be worth a fortune, broken or not. Where better to sell it then Yaolin?"

"Even *if* he's lyin again, it's got enough gems," Tum Tum said, ogling it.

"Eyes to yerself, dwarf." Gold Grin laughed and hid the crown again.

"You didn't meet the Shieldsman who caught him," Sora said. "If you had, you'd know this is one time he's being truthful."

"Shieldsman and the Glass Crown? Now, this I've got to hear." He banged his empty tankard to get one of his men's attention. "Fortist, fill me up. I've got a tale to hear."

So, Sora told him. With the glimmer of hope instilled by the information about mystics she'd learned from him, talking about Whitney didn't completely fill her with dread.

She explained all about how he'd stolen the crown from a royal masquerade celebrating the late king's last birthday, though she could only tell it how Whitney had and he tended to exaggerate. She found it strangely healing to be speaking of him, especially considering her company. Never in her life did she imagine she'd feel welcomed by a pirate with gold-clad teeth.

She finished the story of the crown, and they shared long laughs, which felt good compared to weeping in solitude. By the end, Sora was eating and drinking, and felt her spirits begin to rise a bit. Her toe even tapped along to the off-time beat and dreadful singing.

They shared more stories of adventures, not just featuring Whitney. Gold Grin of battles on the high seas she could barely fathom, or of how his ship got its odd name, the *Reba*. He'd been lured, nearly to his doom, by the song of a mermaid by that name. When he'd shown the fortitude and strength to deny her seductions unlike any man before, she called off the many storms and waves meant to bring death to the crew and invited him to her waters.

"She was the only woman I ever loved," he said. "And she didn't even have the parts I'd once thought necessary for loving!"

Tum Tum told of crazy nights in his tavern which only he found hilarious. Sora tried to match them, but every story she told went back to Whitney. Because without him, she'd never done anything more than hide out in Wetzel's shack and learn how to make a fire in her hand.

So, she spoke of Whitneys rescue from the Yarrington dungeons by Torsten's hands, and about his rescue by her hands in the Webbed Woods, and then about how Muskigo and the Shesaitju attack rescued him just as he was about to be hung by Bartholomew Darkings. She began to see a pattern.

"Right good fellow he was," Tum Tum said, rubbing tears of laughter from his eyes at the vision of Whitney fleeing with a noose flapping in the wind at his back.

"Aye, despite him being a no good jollywanker!" Gold Grin exclaimed. They laughed again, drunker now.

Sora just smiled and closed her eyes. Whitney had a knack for being rescued, and if there was a chance, even in the slightest, that he and Kazimir were banished to Elsewhere in her blind rage —she was going to find a way to bring him back.

VII

THE THIEF

"Shog in a barrel," Whitney said for what must have been the tenth time in as many days.

"I don't know what that means, Mister, but I'm sure if we've got it, we'll be happy to share it," the boy replied. His clothes were dirty but well-kept. His hair, tawny brown and messy, his face red and blotchy like he'd just spent the afternoon rolling around by the river.

"We haven't had anyone new come through here in as long as I can remember," he went on. "Lots of folks are gonna be happy to see you both."

Whitney looked at Kazimir and suspected very few people had been happy to see him in centuries.

"Uh, yeah." Whitney started. "So, this is Troborough, you say?"

"You've never heard of it?" the boy asked. "I guess that makes sense. It's pretty small compared to Yarrington. I hope I get to go there one day." He stared off toward the barely visible mountain in the distance, peak sliced clean across. "Father says we'll go for a Dawning when I'm older."

It was then Whitney realized the deep purple sky had lightened. Little, white, puffy clouds now painted themselves against an amber sky, the color of Sora's eyes. Whitney wasn't sure when that happened. Green grass swayed along rolling hills, and the smell of horse shog in the distance met his nostrils.

"Gonna be here long?" the boy asked.

Whitney regarded Kazimir, who remained silent as a corpse. When the upyr didn't respond, he said, "Just passing through, I think."

"Travelers, huh?" The boy's eyes lit up. "Are you hungry then?" he asked.

Whitney glanced down at his stomach. After running through Winde Port without a bite to eat or a wink of sleep, then rowing across Elsewhere, he felt like he should have been starving, but Kazimir was right, his stomach neither grumbled nor cramped as it should have. The thought of food, however, had him salivating.

"Starved," he said. He both meant it and didn't, which made no sense, just like the rest of this strange place.

"Great!" the boy said. "Let me show you the farm! We've got plenty of food, and I bet Pa will let you stay in the barn. We don't get many noble visitors here."

"Noble," Whitney repeated to nobody in particular, instinctually puffing out his chest.

"It's gonna be dark soon if you want to get going. Don't wanna make Pa mad."

Again, Whitney looked to Kazimir in disbelief that he was in a position where he had to rely on the murderer. Kazimir nodded him along.

"If this is where the Ferryman wanted you, you'd be wise to follow. But remember this, thief, there's no, 'just passing through,' in Elsewhere."

"What if it isn't where he wanted me?" Whitney asked.

"Pray to whatever god you believe in it is."

Whitney found himself standing firmly in place. Everything with the upyr was grim, but that didn't stop his mind from churning with possibilities, all of them awful. The stories fathers told about Elsewhere, and how demons would pluck out your organs while you watched; all the mystical hogwash he'd ever heard was starting to feel all too real.

"C'mon, we better hurry." The boy took Whitney's hand and pulled him along in the direction of the town. The act made Whitney look down, and then he remembered what he looked like.

"Hey kid," Whitney said. "Think we could stop by the tailor and pick up some clothes first?"

The boy stopped.

"Clothes?" he asked, looking Whitney up and down like he was insane. "Those are nicer than anything you can buy here."

Whitney peered down again and noticed he was now wearing clothes—dark pants, white silk tunic, and a cloak worthy of a Darkings. Kazimir the same. They looked like proper noblemen.

"How did?" Whitney said, incredulous.

"I bought mine from the tailor, Gilly." The boy snapped his cloth collar. "Well..." He leaned in close. "I didn't buy them." He continued on his way.

Whitney touched his clothes, pulling at fabric, fingering his cloak until Kazimir nudged him in the side. He grunted for them to keep following.

As they traveled, Whitney's jaw increasingly dropped. He was dumbfounded. Troborough looked just as he'd remembered it growing up.

What mess did you get me into this time, Sora?

In the distance, he could see the Julset twins' place. The corners of his mouth peaked at the thought of afternoons spent snogging in their backyard, wondering but not caring which one it was, Becca or Kayla. Then, next door was old Charles Whelfork's place and Farmer Branson's farm. It all looked like it had when he was a kid, not like the last time he'd visited, and certainly not like it had after the Shesaitju attacked and burned it to dust and ash.

Then he saw something that made the air catch in his throat and the contents of his stomach swirl. He may not have been able to feel hunger, but he felt the sickness gurgle within at the sight of Wetzel's little shack down back at the riverside. It was the place Sora had grown up and apparently learned magic, unbeknownst to him. Wetzel was the town healer and herbalist; the place you went when prayer at the church wouldn't cut it.

Whitney started veering off the path toward it.

"Hey, Mister." The boy pulled him away. "You don't want to go there."

Whitney didn't listen. He released the boy's hand and continued on his path.

"I said, Mister! You don't want to go there."

Every muscle in Whitney's body froze a few meters away from the shack. He tried to push forward to Wetzel's door but felt compelled back to the road until he was, once again, striding alongside the boy. He wasn't even sure he could remember how he got back there.

"What are you doing, thief?" Kazimir asked.

"I don't know," he said. "I wanted to go see the shack but... I… I couldn't."

"You don't carve your own path here."

"I always do."

Kazimir ground his teeth. "The Sanguine Lords must truly be angry to strand me here with such a fool."

"The farm is just over there, beyond the town center," the boy said, pointing.

He started running again, waving Whitney and Kazimir along.

They passed the Twilight Manor and a small oak whose leaves were turning that wasn't so small the last time he'd seen it. Whitney's was so distracted by the tree that he nearly plowed over the boy when he stopped in the middle of the courtyard.

"That's the Twilight Manor," he said. "Dad says it's the porthole to Elsewhere and exile, and only rotten sinners go there."

"Sounds like something my old man would have said too," Whitney said to Kazimir. The upyr walked at a brisk pace behind them, refusing to run. He wore the jaded glare one does when being dragged to church on the turning of the moons. Like it was all too routine.

Whitney stole a glance to the sky. It returned to blood red, only now one of the moons peeked out from soft clouds. Whitney never paid much attention to the moons if he wasn't forced to during Dawnings, but now, Celeste the bright moon was nowhere to be found. Loutis hung alone in the sky, haggard and skull-like, no light shining from it and barely able to be seen.

He didn't even have a chance to ask about the moons before his gaze turned down and he noticed that the old Troborough Church of Iam stood in ruins across the plaza. The bit of stone around the altar remained standing along with half a statue of Iam's Eye, but the rest of the place was burned down, charred. Whitney couldn't remember a time when the church was in such disrepair except after the Shesaitju's razing. A blind priest sat, legs folded, before the ravaged altar. Only he too was different, with dark skin like a man from Glinthaven and not the old, white-haired priest Whitney remembered growing up.

"What happened to the church?" Whitney asked.

The boy slowed. "Not sure," he said. "Burned down before I was born and the Crown hasn't sent anyone to fix it."

"Then where do you all... you know... pray?" Whitney recalled how many hours of his life he must have spent in sermons within that unimpressive building. He'd never cared for all the pomp and circumstance, but it was undoubtedly a big part of his childhood.

The boy stopped to observe him quizzically, tilting his head, but never answered the question. After a brief moment of silence passed between them, he said, "C'mon, my house is this way," and continued down one of the roads.

"Even the creators of this place cannot abide prayer to the one who damned them here," Kazimir said, catching up to him. "This is where you grew up, isn't it?"

"How can you tell?"

"I hated where I grew up too."

Kazimir passed by as well, leaving Whitney staring at the devastated church. He swallowed the lump forming in his throat, and followed, unable to take his eyes off the out-of-place priest. A cloth wrapped his blinded eyes, but he seemed to be looking straight at Whitney, through him.

Whitney turned away quickly and jogged to catch up to the boy. Something about the imposter was familiar, and it sent a very inhuman chill up Whitney's spine.

Loutis still hung alone in the sky when their young guide led Whitney and Kazimir to a wooden fence surrounding farmland.

"Welcome to my home!" the boy announced. "I hope Ma made candied plums. Farmer Branson grows the best plums."

Whitney's legs stopped working. His mouth fell so wide he thought it might've soon touched the ground and filled with dirt.

"This is…" He couldn't get the words out.

"You are dull as a wizard's blade," Kazimir said.

"You knew?"

"I told you this isn't my first foray through this realm."

"You, mighty assassin of the Dom Nohzi, have been to this town? My house? I—I mean, my parent's house?"

"Elsewhere is different for every traveler, but nearly all the problems of men seem to stem from their homes, no matter how it looks, or who occupies it."

Whitney's home was exactly as he had remembered it—or

how he'd chosen to forget it. He never even went to take a look when he'd returned to the Twilight Manor what seemed like ages ago and was challenged to steal the Glass Crown.

It was a simple farmhouse, wattle, and daub with a broad, thatched roof. Over the years, Whitney's father had begun reinforcing the frame with long pieces of timber, and it looked like he was in the midst of repairing the roof. It might have been one of the nicer houses in Troborough, but that wasn't saying much.

The boy ducked under the fence and waved to them. "Come along."

"You—you live here?" Whitney asked.

The boy turned and grinned. Whitney felt the air flee his lungs.

"My name is Whitney," the boy said without prompting. "Whitney Fierstown. I know, it's a girl's name. Ha, ha, very funny." The boy stood staring, waiting eagerly for Whitney and Kazimir to respond to a joke Whitney knew too well. He'd spent his entire childhood getting ahead of the game before other children teased him first.

"My name is Kazimir," Kazimir said. Whitney had no idea he could sound so polite. The boy offered a broader smile and nod of approval. Whitney couldn't believe a child—himself—could look upon the pale upyr with his snow-white hair and dark, soulless eyes and not be gripped by terror.

The boy then turned to Whitney.

"I'm Whi—" Whitney began before Kazimir interrupted.

"Willis."

"Yeah, Willis Blisslayer." Whitney took a step, then had to grab hold of a fencepost to keep himself upright.

"Want to meet my parents?" Young Whitney asked. "I'm sure they'll love company."

"Doubtful..." Whitney said under his breath.

"Huh?" the boy said.

"Would love to," he said, forcing a smile. He didn't. In fact, he wanted to turn tail and run the other direction as fast as he could, but just as he had been led away from Wetzel's shack, he was compelled toward his childhood home. His legs moved, seemingly disconnected from his thoughts.

They walked down the dirt path Whitney had walked a million times before. He hadn't been there since the day he left at sixteen, but it all felt familiar—eerie even. A candle burned in what Whitney knew was the kitchen window. Several of them, in fact. He could remember how comforting that sight was every time he'd return after playing by the river with Sora or getting into trouble alone. His mother would be in there with a white smock covering her plump figure, probably pulling some kind of fruit pie from the oven, so it had time to cool before dinner was through.

He could smell the roast duck wafting through the window. Then, he heard something that reminded him of why he'd left in the first place.

"Iam's light, Lauryn, that's gotta be a whole week's worth of butter you used!" His father shouted, somewhere inside. "No wonder you keep growing."

Again, Whitney stopped and swallowed hard. "Maybe we should find someplace else for the night? I always preferred the Twilight Manor." He fought the urge to keep walking and finally spun around to leave, but the next time he blinked he found himself facing his childhood home again.

"Nonsense!" Young Whitney shouted. "Didn't you hear that? Pie!" He licked his lips before running toward the house. When neither Whitney nor Kazimir moved to follow, the boy called back, "Lazy as you are ugly?" He laughed.

Kazimir grinned, and not the wicked sneer that made grown men shiver that Whitney was used to, but a mortal one, like he was delighted. "This will be fun," Kazimir remarked.

"How do you figure that?" Whitney asked.

"You're about to be as annoyed by you as the rest of us are."

Whitney rolled his eyes and continued ahead, but then a thought crossed his mind that he wished would go away. "If this is Elsewhere... and you're... how do you know you didn't?"

"Because I'm here, in your Elsewhere." Kazimir shoved by him; only Whitney didn't go flying onto his rump. All that supernatural strength the upyr had displayed in Winde Port, he was now no stronger than all the countless drunks who'd nudged by Whitney over the years.

Up ahead, Young Whitney threw the front door open and cried out, "I'm home, and I've brought guests!"

"I hope it's not that little knife-ear orphan!" his father shouted.

"Hush," said the voice of a woman. Her finger was still over her lips as she rushed into the mudroom. She was large for a woman, and her messy apron couldn't cover it. But her red cheeks and warm smile were sweet as spring after winter. She'd left work at a bakery in Yarrington to live with her husband and never looked back. Just like Whitney hadn't when he left the farm behind, not even when he'd heard that a plague passed through Troborough's water supply and claimed his parents' lives.

"Hi, sweetheart," she said. "Did you have fun?"

"Did you get into more trouble this time?" his father questioned.

"No!" Young Whitney shouted defiantly.

Big Whitney knew precisely what that tone meant. He had gotten into trouble, and by the look on his face and the redness of his cheeks, it was pretty serious.

The boy's father—Whitney's father—stood in the doorway leading into the sitting room, two hundred pounds of muscle and a beard down to his heart. He looked the way he'd always looked, like he'd just worked the whole day. That's all Rocco ever did, after all. From the moment the sun rose to well after it set, taking only the yearly Dawning off to relax. For all his work, they still lived in this shog house, in a shog town, just west of nothing but more shog.

Kazimir elbowed Whitney, and he realized he'd been making a face like he smelled the shog.

"Who're these vagabonds?" Rocco asked.

"They're not vagabonds, Pa," Young Whitney said, then turned to Big Whitney and said, "Are you?" He smirked before Big Whitney could answer. "This is Willis and Kazimir," he said. "I told them they could stay for dinner and then sleep in the barn."

Rocco took a few lumbering steps toward the two. He got so close to their faces, Whitney could feel the whiskers tickling his skin.

"We look like an inn?" he asked.

"Nope, you're right," Whitney said. "We'll head right down the road to the Twilight. It'll only cost a few autlas."

"Nonsense," his mother said. "Rocco, you said it yourself, this is too much food for the three of us. Why don't we let them stay? By now, the Twilight will be full of ruffians. Nobody these two fine gentlemen would want to deal with."

Whitney thought his mother was about to receive a wallop, but instead, Rocco nodded and with a snort said, "Fine, Lauryn. They can work off their share on the farm first thing in the morning before they head off. Big harvest tomorrow."

"Yippee!" shouted Young Whitney.

"Yippee, farm work," Whitney whispered sarcastically to himself. He'd dedicated his entire life to escaping the tedium of farm work, and now, somehow, he was at risk of it again. He decided he'd play along with Elsewhere's games, enjoy his mother's cooking—which was one of very few good parts about Troborough—then slip out in the night to find a way out of… whatever this was.

"Better than spending autlas on room and board," Rocco said.

Lauryn invited them to a too-small table in a cluttered kitchen where she had the feast laid out. Roast duck with fingerling potatoes and cabbage. It looked delicious.

Whitney stared at his mother, just as he'd remembered her. When she and his father passed from illness, he'd probably been across the world on some adventure. He wouldn't have come back even if he'd known. He preferred never to see his dad again and wanted to remember his mother with some fondness. Truth was, he resented the woman for sitting by while his father did whatever he wanted, treated them both however he pleased, and slandered Sora and any other foreigner relentlessly. He was a nobody yet she let him act like he ruled Yarrington.

"Where you from, sirs?" Rocco said, shoveling a large, juicy bite of duck into his mouth.

Kazimir shot Whitney a look that said, "Think this through." He was glad for it too. He might have blurted Troborough out of reflex, and then who knows what mess would follow.

"Yarrington," he said instead.

"Figured as much," Rocco replied, mouth still full. "You don't look like the type who've done a day's work in a long time." Lauryn kicked him under the table, but he ignored her and grinned. "We'll fix that tomorrow, huh?"

Whitney held his tongue. "Yes. I suppose we will."

"Pa, if they're helping you, does that mean I don't have to?" Young Whitney asked. His mouth was full of food as he talked as well, though when he did it, it wasn't nearly as repulsive.

"What, so you can go play around with the knife-ear and the old codger who'dun took her in?" Rocco questioned.

"Not at the table Rocco," Lauryn muttered under her breath.

"The war with her kind got your aunt and uncle killed, boy!" Young Whitney's gaze snapped toward Rocco upon being

scolded. For a moment, staring at the sad expression of his minia-
ture doppelgänger, Whitney forgot which body he was in.

"If King Liam didn't decree that we take in refugees," Rocco
went on, "she'd be on the streets wit—"

"You sure look awfully familiar, Willis," Lauryn said, cutting
her husband off. "Have you been here before?"

After a pregnant pause, Whitney said, "No."

"Hm, guess you just have one of those faces. And where are
you from?" Lauryn asked, turning to Kazimir. "I haven't seen hair
that white on a man your age in all my life."

"The far north," Kazimir said.

"You don't look like a Drav Cra heathen," Rocco remarked.

"Brekliodad."

"Oh, how fun!" Lauryn said. "I've never met anyone from
there. What brings you so far south?"

"Yeah, Kazimir old pal, what does bring you so far?" Whitney
said.

"Work," he answered.

"Then you've come to the right place," Rocco said. "It's about
time someone your age learned the meaning of hard work. Too
many soft hands around these parts."

Whitney wished his old man could experience Kazimir's
"work" firsthand. If he'd known what the upyr was, he'd be
calling for the King's Shield. Only they'd never bother coming to
such a worthless town in the first place.

"Pfft," Whitney said before he could stop himself.

"Excuse me?" Rocco's glare could have shot icepicks.

"Sorry, had a stray hair on my lip."

Young Whitney sniggered into his napkin.

"I see," Rocco said, placing another bite of duck in his mouth,
eyes fixated on Big Whitney.

"My dear, you haven't touched your meal," Lauryn said to
Kazimir after a brief silence.

"I'm not hungry." Kazimir regarded the food, his lip twitching with disgust. He pushed the plate away.

"I see." Lauryn frowned. Her head tilted to the side, and she stared at him so intensely it looked like she was going to cry. Whitney didn't remember her ever acting that way. "You should eat. I can make you something else." Her head tilted the other way. "I can make you something else. I can make you something else." She stood to go to the kitchen.

"This is fine." Whitney grabbed a piece of duck and held it up to Kazimir's face. "More than fine, right old friend? Nice, bloody duck meat for you."

Kazimir snagged it. Just the smell had him looking like he was going to gag. He closed his eyes, tilted his head back, and dropped it into his mouth like he was eating a worm, then he swallowed in a single gulp.

Whitney would have taken pleasure in how miserable Kazimir, the man who tried to kill him and drink Sora, appeared if his mother's strange behavior wasn't so unsettling. As soon as Kazimir had his bite, her head straightened, her smile returned, and she continued eating like nothing had happened. Neither Young Whitney nor Rocco even seemed to notice her repeating herself like Gold Grin Grisham's parrot before Whitney accidentally set it free.

"Is it pie time?" Young Whitney asked after another long moment of silence.

"Not until you're done," Rocco said. "And even then, you'd better slow down before you end up a tub of lard like your mother." He laughed a mirthless laugh and his mother chuckled awkwardly.

Big Whitney closed his eyes and clenched his jaw. He felt a hand rest upon his thigh under the table and squeeze. When he opened his eyes, he saw Kazimir giving him another warning look.

His mother said nothing and Young Whitney stuffed his mouth with all his food. Then he opened his mouth and said, "Ah" for his father to see.

"Oh, yes," Lauryn said. "Blueberry and lemongrass with flakes of ginger." She looked at Young Whitney. "Some Panpingese merchants came through today with buckets of fresh ginger. Did Sora go see them?"

Big Whitney rolled his eyes. *Typical.* His parents figured every place on earth was as small and insignificant as Troborough. As if every Panpingese person in the world knew each other, even the ones who hadn't been since birth.

"Oh, yes," Young Whitney said. "I believe that was Sora's mother you bought that ginger from. Oh, wait. No. She's dead. Maybe Uncle killed her?"

A fist landed hard on the wooden table, sending silverware and goblets soaring, their liquid contents covering the table and dripping onto the floor. The same fist reached out and grabbed Young Whitney's ear.

"You want to get funny with your mother, I'll make your ears look like that little wench's," Rocco said. "That what you want?"

He pulled so hard Big Whitney thought he might succeed in his threat. Without conscious thought, he grasped at his own ear.

A ruckus outside suddenly drew everyone's attention. The sound of the front gate opening and footsteps dragging on gravel. Whitney—Big Whitney—sat up tall and craned his neck to see out the window. Through the bare branches crisscrossing over the opening, he saw the shadows of a band of men crossing the yard.

His head spun on Young Whitney so fast he heard his neck crack.

This is that night?

"Oh, you foolish boy," Whitney said under his breath.

"What's that noise out there, dear?" Lauryn asked Rocco as if Whitney weren't already looking. "It's a little late for visits, no?"

"I don't know, but I'll see to it." Rocco got up and made his way to the front door.

"Go to your room," Big Whitney whispered to Young Whitney, quiet and intense. "Trust me."

A moment later, just as Rocco reached for the handle, the door kicked inward, splintering at the frame and slamming hard into his forehead. The blow sent him reeling backward so hard his head rebounded against the wall. Lauryn yipped.

"What is this?" Kazimir stood and asked Whitney.

"What do you think?" Whitney said. "The kid is me."

Young Whitney was midway up the stairs when the first of the men entered the room. Big Whitney's jaw dropped. He remembered the night fairly well, though he'd blocked much of his past from his conscious memory. He'd stolen jewels from the wrong travelers and was caught. Only this wasn't the thug he'd recalled breaking into their home. This was Bartholomew Darkings.

VIII

THE DESERTER

Rand blinked at the sight of the blind man whose responsibility it was to carry the voice of Iam on Pantego. It must have been a heavy burden to bear, especially when so much about Iam's caring nature now felt like a lie to Rand. Strangely still, the old man's presence brought him a sense of peace during a time that peace had been so elusive. All the pain wracking Rand's body seemed to wash away beneath Wren's gaze until Rand tried to speak.

"Father..." he rasped, his throat like the streaming magma from Kal Driscus in the far east.

Wren shushed him. "No need to speak." His wrinkled arms were frail, but somehow, he was able to prop Rand up against the wall to rest. Then Wren looked to the ceiling, traced his eyes with his fingers, and muttered something under his breath.

"I..." Rand coughed. He could barely formulate words. "Why?"

"Iam guided me here to save you from eternal damnation, Sir Langley. I'm glad I listened."

"I'm no knight."

Wren the Holy smiled, his face creasing all over, chasms digging deep into his flesh. If Rand ever pictured what Iam might look like, it was the man standing before him; a fatherly presence, with a long, white beard that spoke of many years on Pantego. The only difference was that he always imagined Iam with old eyes teeming with untold wisdom, and Wren had only gaping holes where his used to be.

"No matter what you are, life is precious," Wren said. "To take it, in anger or grief—there is no higher sin."

"Not even taking the lives of so many innocents?" Rand barely managed the question, but once he did, he saw his error.

Wren's face contorted into sadness. No, not sadness. Pain.

"Those were not your fault, my son. I know how difficult living with such things can be. How impossible it can be." He pressed the palm of his hand against the side of Rand's face. Rand could hear the coarseness of Wren's skin against his beard. "Knight or beggar, all must endure. I know it may not seem it, but the light of Iam is with you, child."

The man's touch sent Rand's skin to goosebumps. Either that, or it was a cold gust of air and snow slipping in through the crack in his window. "Trust me, Father. Nobody is with me."

"Yet, here I am."

Rand sat up. The burning in his throat had diminished slightly. It was still incredibly sore, but the act of speaking no longer felt like a trick of magic. "How?"

"Let us just say that an old friend needs your help."

Rand laughed, then coughed again. "Look at me. Who could I possibly help?"

Wren rose to pace the room, bones creaking. Somehow, even sightless and in tight confines, he didn't bump anything. He stopped by Rand's set of Shieldsman armor, leaning against the wall. Apparently, when Rand sent his bed flying his armor went with it.

"You took a vow to shield this kingdom and the faithful," Wren said. "I know what you did, Rand. I was there. And I saw what your Queen ordered you to do. You thought you were serving your kingdom."

"I was a coward."

"Then so too am I," Wren said, his vacant eye-sockets aiming toward Rand. For a moment, Rand swore the man could see him. "There were men of the cloth hung in her wrath as well. Priests I hand-picked to serve in the castle's chapel. I looked the other way because, for all the Queen's wrongdoing, Iam saw fit to raise her child from the grave, I don't care what the heathens say. He showed me that the Nothhelm family's time is not yet through."

"Maybe it should be." Rand wished he could take the words back the moment they escaped his lips. He expected the Holy Father to be shocked, but the old man nodded and wore a relieved smile as if happy to see he wasn't alone in that thought.

"Perhaps." His face turned toward the floor. "Rand, did you know that it was I who crowned our greatest king atop Mount Lister?"

Rand shook his head.

"I placed the Glass Crown upon his head, and it was one of my proudest moments as High Priest. I knew without question the man he was and who he'd become."

"He was perfection in Iam's sight."

Wren laughed this time. "He was a whoremonger with a lust for bloodshed when it suited him."

Rand nearly toppled over.

"But Iam, in His grace, found the greatness of the man to outweigh his flaws. For we are all imperfect. It is what makes us human, and it takes a long life to find the inward light of Iam in it's purest form."

Wren returned to Rand's side and lay a gentle hand upon his shoulder. "That day, crowning Liam, I felt something strong course through my veins. Hope. It is a feeling I have not felt in a long while, yet today I feel it once more. There is hope yet for the Glass Kingdom. It all starts with you."

"With all due respect, Your Holiness. I think you've come to the wrong place."

"Perhaps Sir Unger meant a different Rand Langley, former Wearer of White, who lived in a 'shoghole of a flat above a shoghole of a tavern' when he sent me here to beseech you."

Wren smiled, and Rand sat up further. The only thing more shocking than the priest's language was the name that spilled off his lips.

"Sir Unger sent you?" Rand asked.

"Directly, yes."

"I guess he tired of begging me to return himself."

"He wished he could come, but that is no longer possible. You're not the only disgraced Wearer in Yarrington any longer."

"What did she do to him?"

"She is the least of our concerns. Yarrington has been invaded. Quietly, peacefully, the enemies of Iam flood these walls from the cold, bitter North. The worst among them, Redstar, whispers in the ear of our king."

"The Queen's brother? I thought him dead."

"Dead?"

"Last I saw, Torsten returned from the Webbed Woods with him as prisoner, set to be hanged for his crimes."

"Is Dockside so forgotten by the castle you haven't heard? The Drav Cra are here, and it was by invitation of the King himself."

"Not Dockside." Rand stood and crossed the room toward a row of empty jugs of ale. He sat at the table. The urge for a drink hit him like a crashing wave now that the pain had subsided. He realized his hands were shaking. Luckily, there was nothing left to drink.

"I see," Wren said, disappointed.

"All I know is the young Prince—"

"King," Wren corrected.

"Yes, my apologies. The young King Pi came back to life, and we're at war with the Black Sands." Rand stared at the old man. That fatherly warmth was gone, replaced now with fear. "I know. Not exactly the hero Torsten painted."

"Then perhaps it is not a hero we need. Torsten said you are the only Shieldsman he can trust."

"Now I know this is a dream. I'm still hanging on that rope, aren't I? Ready to die."

"You are here, and now. The Queen's treasonous brother has stripped Torsten of his rank, claimed the ear of the King as his newly instated prime minister, and stolen victory in the battle of Winde Port. His heathens fill the capital, their warlocks spreading their lies to the faithful. If we do not act fast, there will be nothing left to save."

Rand swallowed the lump in his throat. He'd noticed an unusual number of fur-clad, Drav Cra traders passing through the Maiden's Mugs, but little else. Every day since the moment he handed Torsten back the white helm and left the castle behind was a blur. Just the ropes creaking over and over and over...

"Rand, it's time you put your armor back on," Wren said.

Rand squeezed his eyelids tight, then tried to focus on the High Priest. "I don't know what you possibly think I could do."

"'Cut the head off the true snake,' as Torsten so mildly put it. Traitors and deceivers abound, but there is only one who can be traced to all of it—one whose actions led the Queen down that horrid path you suffered."

"I didn't suffer!" Rand snapped. "They all suffered. Priests, doctors, council members... Tessa!" He couldn't believe himself, yelling at the High Priest of Iam.

"And we can never change that," Wren interjected calmly.

"We can, however, ensure that Iam's light shines brightly on the future. Redstar would cover this world in darkness in the name of his Buried Goddess. He must..." Wren paused. His lips parted, but the word he was searching for didn't come. And that was likely because it was a word no man of peace like him had likely ever uttered before in such context.

"Die," Rand finished for him. "Is that what this is all about?"

"It is a sin even to think, but like your friend Torsten, I would rather suffer eternity in Elsewhere than watch Pantego succumb to madness."

"So, you come to an expert on killing?" The words stung as they came out and in the back of his mind, he could hear Tessa and the others begging for mercy.

"I come to a sworn knight of the King's Shield. A man who vowed to safeguard this realm, and who hasn't been manipulated by an imposter like the rest. Perhaps there are other Shieldsmen to be trusted, but the only one I trust is locked in a cell, and he told me to find you."

Rand shook his head. "I don't... I'm done killing."

"That is why it must be you. Our king is young and impressionable. If we wait any longer, our great cathedral will be a ruin for warlocks to dance and spill blood on. Who knows what they will do when the light goes out upon the Dawning next week. If I could do this for the kingdom of Iam, I would. But I am too old and too frail."

"And I'm a drunk."

"No one is perfect. Not me, not the great Liam. All his countless mistakes litter Elsewhere—bastards all—but we are the best he could do. We are small, jealous humans, yet he put faith in us as his creation. It's time we do something for him and protect his chosen realm from the fallen."

Rand drew a deep breath; then a chuckle slipped through his lips. Before today, he couldn't remember the last time he'd laughed at anything, no matter how slight. "The sermons in Dockside are nowhere near as poetic as yours, Your Holiness."

"That is something I will have to remedy."

"Rand, are you—" The door swung open, and Sigrid froze in the entry. The loaves of bread under her arm fell. "Your Holiness." She fell to her knees and circled her eyes with her fingers.

"Stand, dear," Wren said. "You are Rand's..."

"Sister," she finished for him. "Why are you... I mean..." Her words trailed off as her gaze stopped on the noose of tied blankets still hanging from the ceiling. Then on the upturned furniture and armor.

"We're doing Iam's work, my child." Wren stood, groaning softly as his old legs stretched out. "Now, I do think it's time to return to the cathedral. There are a few honest folks left in this city if you look hard enough, and the Dawning approaches. Must be prepared." He shuffled past Sigrid to grab his cane from against the wall. Sigrid hurried over to help him to the door.

"Your Holiness, what do you expect me to do?" Rand asked.

The High Priest stopped at the door, then glanced back, again wearing his warmest smile like it was second nature. Perhaps it was. After all, he was the father to all the faithful in Yarrington. Had Rand's own father lived long enough, his might have grown equally reassuring.

"To receive that armor is a rare thing, an honor," Wren said. "There are few in this city who have it, even fewer living beyond the castle walls. If you remain loyal to Torsten, the one you seek now sits, an imposter in the chambers you and he once occupied." Wren traced his eyes in prayer, then hobbled out of the room.

Sigrid watched the door close all the way, then turned, brow furrowed. "Am I losing my mind?" she asked.

Rand didn't respond. All he could think to do was rush across the room and wrap his arms around her.

A heavy gust of sea wind tore in through the window. The

already loose knot of the tied sheets Rand had used to try and kill himself came undone, the cloth fluttering harmlessly to the floor. He squeezed Sigrid tight and kissed the top of her head.

They were all each other had since their parents died when they were still young. He stepped back and took in the sight of her. He'd almost stolen even that from her—made the shogpile she called a life even worse. He caught a whiff of her tangled hair, the familiar scent of salt and spilled ale heavy in it.

A second later and Wren might have been too late to save him. As he pulled Sigrid closer, he couldn't help but wonder if perhaps he was wrong. If Iam hadn't yet turned His eye away from him.

IX

THE MYSTIC

Sora awoke to the sound of gulls. She sat up, stretched, and yawned. Aquira flopped over and snorted, ash spraying like powder from her nostrils. The warmth of her scales felt nice in contrast to the cool air beneath the deck of the *Reba*.

It took a minute or three for Sora to realize what the sound of gulls meant.

"Land!" she shouted. She sprang up from her bed and bounded toward the door, grabbing her dress on her way out. She pulled it down over her body even as she climbed the stairs. The hatch opened. Bright light poured in and blinded her. The sounds of hurried commotion assaulted her ears, and with her vision temporarily impaired, it was all overwhelming.

Gold Grin's men barked commands, ropes thrummed, and sails battled with the wind for dominance, their flapping loud as Muskigo's army marching down the streets of Winde Port. Somewhere in the distance, bells rang out.

Her eyesight returning, Sora could see the visual representation of all the sounds. Excitement stole over her, something she thought she'd never feel again, but there it was. After weeks spent on the sea, anything other than the vast bluish-gray landscape of ocean and sky was a thrill to see.

To add to all the racket, she heard the clattering of little claws against wood and looked down to see Aquira standing next to her, blearily blinking her four sets of eyelids.

Sora scooped her up and held her tight against her chest.

"We're here, girl," she said, taking a few steps out onto the deck. She turned and looked up at the helm where Gold Grin stood. It was then that she realized the ship's black sails with a bleeding skull had been switched out for unmarked white ones.

"Aye, lassie!" he shouted. "Come on up and see your homeland for the first time!"

By now, Sora had come to like the pirate. She hadn't seen much of the world, and in her limited experience adventuring with Whitney, most men were cruel brutes. Torsten thought her a monster, Bartholomew Darkings a pest, Kazimir a meal, and Whitney…

She'd been nervous to step upon the *Reba* at first, but even though Gold Grin was some dastardly pirate feared across the seas, he treated her as she would think any decent man would a woman. He reminded her of Muskigo, and that scared her, but she smiled back up at him and climbed the short flight of stairs leading to the stern-side deck.

Grisham held the wheel steady and peered off into the distance.

"Yaolin City," he said, a sense of awe in his voice. "No more beautiful nor magical place in all Pantego, except maybe Glinthaven."

Sora couldn't muster a response. She followed Grisham's gaze and saw the capital city of her people. As far as she could see, tiers upon tiers of buildings with sweeping, red-tile roofs plastered a cliff face. It seemed nearly impossible. When she squinted, she could see dark little dots scurrying like ants along the rocky terrain. Wooden staircases connected the tiers, and more little dots covered those, with waterfalls cascading amongst all of it.

"It's huge," she said.

"No place like it," Grisham repeated. He reached out to scratch Aquira beneath her chin as she flapped hard to fly along with the ship. Even Aquira had come to like the man over the weeks they'd been on the *Reba*. "No place at all."

Sora's features darkened.

"What's wrong, lass?" Grisham asked, noticing.

"How am I ever going to find what I'm looking for in a place so big? It was hard enough for Wetzel to teach me to light a candle and I'd lived in his home."

Sora had shared enough details of her life with the self proclaimed pirate king for him to know about Wetzel and how he taught her. Grisham had been particularly interested in the many tomes explaining how to perform magic spells until he'd found out they'd been burned along with the rest of Troborough.

"Aye, difficult indeed," he said. "But I'm sure someone of your particular talents'll have no trouble."

"You're too kind," Sora said. She lifted her arm for Aquira to land, but it was more to hide her reddening cheeks. "Come on Aquira, let's go find Tum Tum. You'll excuse us?"

Gold Grin nodded. "I don't own ye, lass."

Sora hurried down a small flight of stairs to the galley where she found Tum Tum, as always, by the food.

"Aye, girly!" he exclaimed. "Pull up a crate." His beard had grown unruly during the journey. Sora couldn't believe how fast dwarf hair grew.

"But Yaolin is so close," she said. "We need to get ready."

"Sometimes I forget ye've never been on the sea, so worldly ye seem. It'll take another half-day to close that distance over water. No point goin hungry, I always say."

"Half a day?" Sora asked.

The first mate himself, a pirate named Fortist, dragged a crate toward the pot for Sora. Aquira growled. She still hadn't forgiven the man for how he handled her on the day Grisham's men boarded their old ship.

"Thank you, Fortist," Sora said, then tapped Aquira on the snout. "I'm sorry about her."

"I deserve it, miss." Fortist bowed and backed away. "Cap'n always says that a pirate who can make friends always has an army."

"Yer cap'n is as wise as his teeth be… well… gold!" Tum Tum burst out laughing, and a few others joined him. It was clear now that his belly wasn't just full of food, but that once again they'd dug into the ale despite it being just past sunrise.

Sora rolled her eyes. *They can't be perfect. They are pirates after all.*

After a hearty meal, Sora retired to her quarters to pack what meager belongings she had. The pirate crew had been kind enough to supply Sora out of their massive cache of loot with the things men had no need of. She tried not to notice the gold or jewels in the crates as well and dared not ask where they were taken from—for her own sake and peace of mind.

Her first day on board, she'd been given several changes of clothing, all in the style common to wayfaring Pantegans. She finished lacing up her leather bodice, adjusted the waistline of her pants, then put on a pair of leather gloves she'd specifically asked Gold Grin's men for. They ran high up her forearms, covering the blood magic scars. She clicked her tongue, inviting Aquira to crawl up her sleeve to perch on her shoulder.

"I wish I were a little more prepared," she whispered to Aquira. "I was really counting on Whit, you know? He knows the place. I'm not sure how I'm going to find the Bokeos to let them know about Tayvada let alone hidden mystics. Iam's light, Aquira, I'm even assuming the man still has living family and that they didn't live and die in Winde Port along with so many others."

Sora had taken to talking to the wyvern, speaking her thoughts instead of keeping them bottled up inside. It was how she passed the quiet moments without dwelling on Whitney and how she could undo what had been done.

There were times when Sora thought her little reptilian companion understood every word—like when she'd used her fire breath to rescue Sora from the hands of Kazimir in the old, battered church steeple. In the present, if Aquira understood a word, she hid it well. She scratched her head with her rear claws then rolled over on the bed, belly facing the ceiling, and stretched.

"Yeah, girl, your kind aren't used to being cooped up on boats either, are they?" Sora said.

"Lass?" Gold Grin's voice boomed from above.

"Coming!" Sora emerged to find Gold Grin waiting at the top of the hatch.

He extended his hand. "Gonna need them papers of yers."

"My papers, already?" she said, hand moving instinctively to cover the pocket of her leather pants. "For what?"

He laughed. "Ye think the govn'r of Panping tells his men to just let pirates into his capital city?"

Sora didn't argue further. She produced the papers Whitney had taken from Tayvada Bokeo's corpse back in Winde Port. Grisham snatched them, inspected them, then handed them back, grinned, and said, "On second thought, best ye handle this. I be fairly famous for the grin."

Sora reluctantly returned a smile. Making believe she was a helpless traveler on the road in need of help from a passing caravan, or Father Gorenheimer's altar server was entirely different from trying to fool the city guard in a land unfamiliar to her.

She took the papers back and glanced toward the city. They were close now, close enough that the people were no longer dots lining the cliff faces but she could even make out faces. And ears. Sure, the steel armor of Glass soldiers patrolling glimmered here and there, but thousands upon thousands of people worked, walked, and generally lived life with ears just like hers. She felt something she didn't even know she wanted because she didn't know it existed.

Belonging.

"Where are the docks?" she asked.

"Follow me," Gold Grin said, already on his way back to the helm.

He gave the wheel the slightest turn, and the course shifted toward a giant, dark hole in the face of the cliff, piercing the city and with a waterfall pouring over it. As they approached, Sora grew concerned that the tall mast wouldn't clear the opening. The closer they got, the bigger the hole appeared to be until she realized the sheer immensity of it. The *Reba* could have fit twice stacked within the cavern.

"Hold on, lads!" Grisham shouted. "'Bout to get mighty wet in here!"

The ship passed beneath the pounding waterfall. The force of it knocked Aquira from Sora's shoulder, and as she sprawled to grab the wyvern, she saw that Grisham already had. He lifted Sora by the back of her shirt. One foot into Yaolin and her new clothes were already drenched.

"That's how we swab the deck round these parts." He removed his hat and flicked it to get the water off.

Light bloomed on the far end of the cavern. Every sound of the ship echoed. Waves slapped against the side of the hull, causing the wood to creak, and then bounced back to collide with the hard stone. After a moment, Sora fell into the gentle tempo of it all. It was like nature's song, peaceful, serene.

She closed her eyes and let the rhythmic sounds wash over her until a hot, white light painted her vision through her eyelids. She opened them and was immediately forced to squint.

They emerged into a great lake. The city and all its colorful, tiled roofs stretched all around it, rising up three rocky hills like the fingers of giants grasping for the clouds. Between them, walls rose high to keep out invaders, with the sea and cliffs guarding the side they'd arrived from. Hundreds of large ships were docked along the coasts, and hundreds more little fishing boats with square, ruffled sails floated within the vast waters.

"A beaut, ain't she?" Tum Tum said, sidling up to her.

He was right in every sense of the word. The sheer mass of the place made Sora wonder how Liam managed to conquer it. As she took it all in, she only saw the one entrance by sea through the waterfall, walls, and hills everywhere else.

How did he ever bring a fleet and an army through? Wetzel didn't have any books that told that story. It was a testament to the man's prowess as a military leader.

Then she thought of all the people who'd lived peaceably here before the Glass brought their heavy fist down.

"I've never…" She couldn't find the words.

"No one has until they has," Gold Grin said.

"What's that?" Sora asked, pointing at a tall tower on a small island in the middle of the lake. A series of stacked, terraced layers comprised it, made from smooth red stone carved with bands of bas-reliefs depicting men and women in robes. At each landing, tapering up to a top which vanished into the clouds, bare plants and twisting vines grew, void of all color. It was the dead of winter, but the air in Panping remained temperate, so Sora wasn't sure why they didn't grow.

More trees surrounded the base, budding from the centers of still pools of water. A bronze gate sat on four sides of the round tower, each with a large gem set in the center. One red, one blue, one yellow, and one green. Before each gate stood a row of clay statues depicting armored soldiers holding spears.

"That be the old mystic tower," Gold Grin answered.

"Was before Liam took over," Tum Tum added.

"They were a strange folk, them mystics who ruled this place. I heard tale they stored their books and secrets in that tower, but it's been sealed ever since Liam left this place."

"They say water used to fall down each layer from the top, and that plants of the wildest colors ye could imagine grew up the sides."

"Aye, it's true. I saw it once as a boy. O'course, I was peeking through the tiny slit of a prison cell, so maybe I was dreaming." Gold Grin laughed.

Sora didn't have time to think about a response before Gold Grin started throwing orders around to his crew, directing the ship toward the city's least crowded of many docks. His crew scurried around the deck and up the masts like spiders, reeling in sails, swinging booms. If the city weren't so spectacular, Sora would have been enthralled with the performance. It was better than anything the troupes passing through Troborough ever put on in the town square.

Before she knew it, they pulled up alongside the dock and secured the ship between a Glass warship and a small fishing boat. She'd expected a few bumps after how rocky the escape from Winde Port proved to be, but Grisham's crew were artists on the water.

With the ship successfully moored, Grisham "Gold Grin" Gale, one of the strangest and most powerful men Sora had ever known, placed his arms around Sora and said, "Anyone official be seeing me here without an understanding, and we might find trouble, even with this old girl wearing the white of Parlay. Get us clear to stay, and find us a way to debark without trouble, aye lass? The boys want to see what kind of trouble they can get into here and it ain't often we get hold of some legal trading papers."

"I'll stay here and wait until we're clear," Tum Tum said. " A dwarf will only complicate things down there. But you'll find me at The Ruby House at sundown. I never been here, but Whitney always said it's the best place on Xiahou Boulevard."

"The Ruby House. Xiahou Boulevard. Peaceful passage." Sora nodded then looked up at Grisham. "I can't thank you enough for this. You have no idea what it's been like since me and Whitney started adventuring together."

"Aye, trust me, I know how things be with him." He squeezed her a bit, then took her by the shoulders and looked straight into her eyes. "Always a pleasure to have a proper lass on board. Ye tell the world that old Gold Grin ain't just a monster of the seas."

Sora chuckled. "I will."

His lip twisted. "On second thought, tell them we ravaged yer bones and made ye wish for death. Fear be a great motivator!" He laughed heartily, then opened her hand and placed a bag stuffed with gold autlas in it. It was more than she and Whitney had earned in Winde Port, and he gave it over like one would an apple.

"Give this to the guards, and they won't look twice at this ship," he said. "Now go on. There was a bargain struck between us, and I believe my end be upheld."

He gave her a gentle shove toward the lowered gangway. She stepped lightly, unsure. But as she neared the docks, she felt invigorated. Somewhere in this vast city were the answers to all her questions: who she was, why she could do the things she sometimes did, and where Whitney was.

Aquira nuzzled against her neck and closed her eyes. Sora took comfort in the wyvern's soft purrs. She stowed the coin purse, then drew in a deep breath and noted how different the air smelled compared to anywhere she'd been before. No salt from water, and no shog from men up to no good. It was fresh, crisp, and a bit like the first budding flowers of spring.

Her foot crunched onto gravel as she made landfall.

"Jinszi," said a Panpingese man waiting on the dock almost immediately. He gave Aquira little more than a cursory glance. Apparently, wyvern's weren't such a curiosity in the east.

"I… uh. I don't speak Panpingese," she said.

The man rolled his eyes, apparently a gesture that transcended culture, and said, "Papers."

"Oh, yes. Right here." Sora handed the man the trading documents.

He looked at the papers, then at her, then Aquira, then back at the papers again. He waved back to a pavilion, where Sora now noticed the host of Glass soldiers sitting around playing gems. One of them groaned, then stood to approach.

The Panpingese dockworker held up the papers for him to see. He shielded his eyes from the sun as he gave them a look-over, then snatched them out of the man's hands to scrutinize.

"You don't look like a Tayvada," he muttered.

"No," Sora said simply, then forced herself to look as sad as she could manage. "My husband. He's dead, and I've come to deliver news to his family and return with the last of his goods." She pointed to the galleon behind her.

The man followed her finger, then his bleary eyes finally opened wide enough to show concern, but it was not for her loss. His hand fell to the grip of his sword. "You do know whose ship that is, don't you?"

"I do." One look was all it took him. Perhaps she underestimated how infamous and feared Grisham truly was. Though other than switching out their black sails on approach, he didn't try to hide anything. Now that Sora wasn't on the ship or in a storm, she could see the distinctive shape of a golden mermaid statue perched on the *Reba*'s prow. There couldn't be another like it in all Pantego.

"Come on, Higgin, your turn!" shouted one of the Glass guards beneath the covering.

The guard named Higgin glanced back at them, and his expression caused them all to stir from their game. Two rose and started toward him.

"They helped me escape the fighting in Winde Port," Sora said. "I assure you, they're flying white because all they wish for is a few days on land and to trade away their wares."

"Trade *their* wares?" Higgin replied. "You do realize what pirates do, don't you, Miss Bokeo?"

The reference to her as Miss Bokeo nearly shook her, but she found her resolve and mustered the same air of nobility she's used back in Winde Port on the rebel Muskigo. All of Whitney's lessons on lying and thieving were paying off.

"I'm not a fool," she said, "but these men helped me and the Winde Trader's Guild." She acted wounded, vulnerable, even getting her eyes to water. Then she pulled out the purse and stuck it in the man's gut. "I owe them."

The guard glanced down. All his worries seemed to melt away. He raised a hand for his men to stop approaching. "Go help them," he ordered the Panpingese dockhand, pointing to another ship down the docks.

"Fine." The guard stowed the purse. "They cover that damn prow, they can stay, but you didn't deal with me." He handed the papers back. "You have one day tree of charge, as is customary due to your husband   late husband's position in the guild. After that, they'll be charged the regular rate of... two hundred autlas per day. Understood?"

"Two hun—" Sora caught herself. It wasn't her money, and with the loot Grisham's boys would be selling off, that was probably pocket change. "Thank you." She forced a snivel. "I'll never forget how you've helped me."

"No, thank you, miss. And please, forget." He turned, then glared at Aquira. "And get your pet in a damn cage if you don't want to be stopped again. All those things manage is trouble."

He returned to his game of gems with his mates, and with a lot more to bet now.

"Don't listen to him," Sora said, scratching Aquira's chin. "You're no trouble."

Sora turned back to the *Reba* and waved for one of the crew to get Grisham. She couldn't believe how happy the site of him peering down over the side made her. She explained to him the terms of them staying, and the great pirate tossed her a smaller pouch of autlas of her own to help her in this strange new city.

"Good luck lass!" he shouted down as his crew hooted in celebration at being welcomed to Yaolin. "And when you see that whelp Whitney again, tell him he owes me a ship!" He burst out laughing, and his men joined in. Sora wouldn't miss the stench of their breath or how raucous they could be, but she'd never forget him.

Thanking him one last time, she headed back toward the city. She had no idea where to start, but the Winde Trader's Guild papers, a sack of autlas, and a sad story were a good place to start. It was much more than she and Whitney had when they got to Winde Port seeking passage.

She spotted the dockworker who'd greeted her and hurried to him.

"Sir?" she said as he tied a knot around a cleat to hold another ship in place. He didn't answer. It wasn't until she addressed him again that he regarded her, but didn't stop working. "Do you know where I can find the Trader's Guild?"

"That a joke?" he asked.

"I'm sorry?"

He pointed toward a giant edifice just behind them. "Big building, round dome, bronze ship statue."

"Thank you so much." Sora reached into her pocket to find an autla for him, then reconsidered. "One more thing?"

The man released a loud sigh and pursed his lips.

"Can you tell me the way to The Ruby House?" she asked.

His eyes went wide, and his face turned bright red. "Madam…" He laughed awkwardly. "I don't—why would you… such an establishment is no place for…"

Sora blushed. "Never mind. I'm sorry I asked. Thank you for your help." She handed him a coin, and he bowed three times before scuttling away.

Sora swore to herself she'd give Tum Tum a good smack for embarrassing her when the time came. Reaching up with her right hand, she scratched Aquira on the top of the head and whispered, "You ready, girl?"

The wyvern purred and readjusted herself as Sora set off down the quay. A short staircase led up to the city streets. When she reached the top, she stopped and turned back toward the lake. The view was breathtaking. She'd seen Trader's Bay near Winde Port, but that was little more than swamp and sharp rocks in comparison. This looked like the place Iam would choose for his throne.

Clear across the water she could see small pagoda style houses surrounded by bamboo forests. Personal-sized vessels lined the bay near the homes like ferryboats intended to give the illusion of being a part of the vast city. The water itself was so still, it was almost crystalline, even around the coast of the mystic's tower. Here and there, bulbous formations of rock topped with moss jutted out.

When she turned around, she was staring at the Winde Trader's Guild. The entrance was shaped like a giant ship made of bronze. She looked down and frowned, realizing how underdressed she was likely to be. There was no time to worry about that.

The interior changed her opinion. The guild hall in Winde Port had all the trappings of a noble mansion, but this one was far more reserved. Unadorned walls, with those leading deeper inside made of what seemed like paper and grids of wood. The only decoration were tapestries along the walls portraying cities from around Pantego in a symbolic nature. She recognized Yarrington by the Glass Castle and Mount Lister; Winde Port by the pier filled with ships that no longer existed.

A short and stout Panpingese gentleman awaited her in the lobby. He sat on a cushion directly on the floor behind a low desk and wore a style of clothing she was not at all familiar with. It was a bit like layered robes, but more tightly fitted, and the shoulders were broad with tassels nearly tickling the ground. He barely glanced up from a pile of papers upon which he scrawled in black ink with a thin brush.

"Shi shi," he said.

"Shi shi," Sora responded. It was all she knew in Panpingese. She'd learned how to greet travelers who made their way through Troborough long ago.

The man said something else in Panpingese and Sora raised her hands and smiled. "I'm sorry, that's all I know of your beautiful language."

"I see," the man said in perfect common, seeming disappointed. "What brings you to the guild?"

"I am looking for the Bokeo family."

The man's eyes narrowed. "What business have you with the Bokeos?"

She considered sticking with the story of her and Tayvada's ill-fated marriage, but anyone who knew the man would know that was a lie. "I know—knew their son, Tayvada," she went with instead.

"Yes, sad news."

"Oh, you've heard?" Sora asked a little too eagerly. She caught herself and toned it down. "He was a good man."

"Yes, we've all heard. The family has been in mourning since word arrived of his unfortunate murder in Winde Port. A shame what happened there. It's miraculous any of our people made it out alive, and with the rebels holing up in Nehejab, things will only be getting worse down south."

Sora nodded her agreement, the horrors of what happened in Winde Port flashing through her mind.

"Will that be all?" the man asked.

"Do you know where I can find them?" Sora asked. "I was there wh… when he… passed on. I'd like to offer my condolences."

"I'm not sure that is wise."

Aquira perked up and shuffled on Sora's shoulder, then released a shrill sound that caused the man to jump.

"I'm sorry about her," Sora said. "Aquira, stop that."

"Aquira?" the man asked, for the first time peering up enough from his work to see her. "Is that…. That's Tayvada's wyvern?"

"It is. As I said, I was there when he passed."

"Aquira didn't like anyone but Tayvada. If that is her—"

"Like I said, it is her."

"In that case, Lord Bokeo would be most interested to hear your tale, and I'm sure they'd all like to have Aquira back."

Aquira backed down but still growled softly.

"Back?" Sora asked, a wave of sadness passing over her. She'd gotten used to having the wyvern's needlelike claws digging into her shoulder, and it had been nice having someone to talk to now that Whitney was gone, even if Aquira never answered with more than a growl.

"I'd suspect so. A wyvern of that rare stock is worth its weight in gold. Is this your first time in Yaolin?"

"Unfortunately."

Again, his disappointment showed. "Okay. Just follow this road with the statues. That's Xiahou boulevard. Take a left when you reach the end and look for Bones and Tomes—Lord Bokeo owns a small bookstore, and the family lives in the home adjacent to it. If he isn't there, please, do not disturb them at home—they deserve time to grieve the loss of their son."

Sora nodded, and Aquira screeched.

"Thank you, Mr…"

"Kyoto," he finished for her.

"Thank you, Mr. Kyoto," Sora said, and turned to walk away.

"Oh, and Miss?'

Sora looked back.

"Take care of Aquira until you speak with them," he said. "You have no idea how valuable she is."

X

THE THIEF

"Is that—" Whitney didn't dare speak the name of the man who'd entered his parent's house out loud. Bartholomew Darkings was unmistakable. His fat belly was clad in a colorful silken shirt, unbuttoned halfway and more expensive than anything in the Fierstown household. His gold chains jingled, bouncing against his hairy chest.

"Elsewhere has a way of doing that," Kazimir said, also apparently recognizing the man who'd hired him to kill Whitney. "It's time to hide. This isn't our battle."

"Shouldn't we do something? You can kill all of them in the blink of an eye."

"In Elsewhere, always take the path of least resistance."

Kazimir opened the coat closet, and he and Whitney hid before the men could see them. They watched through a crack as Rocco yelled from the ground, blood dripping from his forehead.

"This is an outrage!"

"Where's that little rat?" Darkings spat, his mustaches bobbing atop his upper lip.

"How dare you!" Rocco scrambled to his feet.

Five more men shoved their way into the house and pushed him aside.

"Tear the place apart until you find it," Darkings ordered. Two men clambered upstairs and the sound of things breaking traveled down the flight.

"Rocco," Lauryn cried. "What's going on?"

"Sirs, you must leave this instant!" Rocco demanded.

Darkings ignored him and sauntered into the kitchen.

"Oh, roast duck," he said, eyes unfolding over the dinner table. "How quaint. And is that blueberry?"

"Blueberry and lemongrass… w-with a t-touch of ginger," Whitney's mother stammered, though there was no mistaking the hint of pride in her tone even as her voice quivered.

"Get out of my home!" Rocco shouted.

"Boys, shut him up." Darkings snapped his fingers before pulling out his father's chair and picking up a fork and knife. He stabbed a piece of duck and shoved it into his mouth, then moaned in ecstasy.

The remaining three thugs accosted Rocco, two grabbing his arms and a third punching him in the gut.

"Please, don't!" Lauryn cried, starting to stand.

Darkings pointed his knife at her and said, "Sit."

She returned to her seat and smoothed her apron.

Whitney took a step, but Kazimir held him back.

"Did this happen?" he asked.

Whitney nodded. It did. His younger self even managed to squirm upstairs and hide during the brunt of the action. He drew on the deepest chasms of his memory to try and piece the rest together.

"Then don't make things worse," Kazimir said.

"I can't just watch this."

"They aren't really your parents. Just wait."

Rocco's lips pursed in anger just before he took a balled fist to the face. He clattered to the floor, taking a table and flower vase with him.

Darkings took another bite of the duck then looked at Lauryn. "You made this? Quite good, quite good."

"W-what are you d-doing in my home?" she asked.

"Is there anyone else here?"

Lauryn looked to Rocco, and his father shook his bloody head. "No," she said.

"It turns out there's a young boy who lives here, your son perhaps?" Darkings waited, but Lauryn said nothing. "Well, he stole from the wrong man today. We're just here to recover what was lost and teach the boy a lesson."

"Boss!" one of the thugs called down. His footsteps grew louder as he clomped down the stairs. He held Young Whitney by the scruff of the neck. "This him?"

Darkings stood, wiped the corners of his lips with a napkin, and threw it down over the plate. He made his way to the bottom of the stairs.

"Get off me!" Young Whitney shouted, kicking his feet frantically. "It wasn't me."

Darkings grabbed him by the jaw and forced him to look into his eyes. "You stole from me. Me! Do you know who I am, boy?"

"By the look of it," Young Whitney said, teeth clenched, "the King's jester."

Darkings slapped the boy hard with a ring-covered hand. Big Whitney seethed.

"No!" Lauryn yelled, finally getting up the courage to leave the kitchen table.

Darkings pointed a finger at her and said, "Stop, before you join your husband and make things worse for your boy."

"Please, just leave them alone," Rocco grated. "You got what you came for now get out of my house. He's just a boy."

Big Whitney's gaze turned to Rocco, bloody-nosed and eyes

that would surely be black and blue in the morning. He remembered all this happening, though not the parts where his father tried to protect him.

Just then, another thug came barreling downstairs waving King Liam's Glass Crown in his hand. "Got it, Mr. Darkings."

"I don't know how it got in there!" Young Whitney shouted. I swear it wasn't me. "What the yig-and-shog?" Big Whitney whispered. His younger self had only stolen jewelry that day, not the Glass Crown.

"You don't get away with anything in Elsewhere, thief," Kazimir said.

"Wonderful."

Darkings removed a dagger with a red jewel buried into the hilt from his belt and raised it to Young Whitney's nose.

Lauryn whimpered.

"Get out, now," Rocco warned. "I had two guests here, sent them after the bailiff the moment we saw you coming."

"You heard him, boys, it's about that time to head off." He lowered his dagger, and his man dropped Young Whitney, who ran to his mother. Then they began ransacking the cupboards and all their unfinished dinner. That's what the real thugs did before punching Rocco one last time and burning the barn down on their way out.

Whitney finally recollected how he'd been punished for months after. He had to help his father rebuild the barn, harvest the fall crops, help the Father Hullquist—who wasn't the father in this version of Troborough—prepare for post-Dawning festivities and wasn't allowed outside their fence. Work had him too exhausted even to sneak out. It was the longest he'd gone without being able to spend time with Sora until he left Troborough for good.

"Your boy's got talent," Darkings said. "But he's got to learn that there are consequences to getting caught." Darkings plucked a candle off a window-sill and headed for the back door. He grabbed Young Whitney again on his way, tearing him from Lauryn's arms. The boy kicked and thrashed, but was too small and weak.

"Let him go!" Rocco started to rise, but one of the thugs kicked him hard, ensuring he stays put.

This was the moment. That first time Whitney got caught nipping more than a bronzer. The thug hadn't hurt him, only tossed him in the dirt and made him watch as the barn burned. Besides being punished, his father never let it go, and his mother never looked at him the same. Smiling when he returned for supper grew more and more difficult for her, until it stopped altogether.

Before Kazimir could stop him, Big Whitney threw the door to the closet open.

"Stop!" he shouted. "I did it!"

"I don't know who you are," Darkings said, stopping by the door. "but we saw the boy do it."

"You think that little punk-kid is capable of devising a plan like that? I did it. Paid him to help because I figured even a boy could rob fools like you."

Darkings looked back at Young Whitney. "Is that true boy?"

Young Whitney looked at his ma and pa, then nodded. "Yes, sir," he said, just as Whitney imagined his younger self would, eager never to take the blame. "He told me I was doing the right thing."

"That's right, It was me," Big Whitney said. "Whit... I mean Willis Blisslayer, bester of brigands, the filcher fantastic himself. So, let him go."

The thugs dropped Young Whitney to the floor and moved toward Big Whitney, seizing him and dragging him to Darkings. Whitney had hoped, by that point, Kazimir would've burst out and made quick work of them, but the upyr remained hidden.

So much for saving him from that sea beast…

"Do you know who I am?" Darkings asked.

"Pretty sure the boy just told us all," Whitney said. "Court jester?"

"Everyone here is a comedian. What an entertaining little town. What's this little shoghole called?" Darkings turned back to his thugs.

"Troborough, boss."

"Well, why don't you teach this Troborough trash a lesson? It's a shame; we'd have let the kid go. He's just a kid, after all. But if you did it…" He frowned at Whitney. "Well, that's a different story."

One of the thugs approached Whitney wielding a heavy club.

"You don't have to do this, Barty," Whitney pleaded. "You got the Crown back, right? No harm done."

"What did you call me?" He seemed confused, then looked at his thug. "Make it hurt, would you?"

The club-wielding thug reared back. At the same time, two things happened: Rocco rose and propelled himself at the man, and Whitney heard the sound of a door opening behind him. The club came down hard. Whitney winced, clenching his eyes shut.

A white blur passed him on his right, and Kazimir unleashed a flurry of attacks on the men, though in Elsewhere he was too slow to stop everything and the club found purchase with a loud crack, and a groan. Only, the groan wasn't Whitney's.

Whitney cracked open one eye to see Rocco, his father, on the ground, face scrunched up in pain and holding his knee. The thugs who'd been holding Whitney faced Kazimir's wrath and were face-down on the floor, dead.

"Get him!" Darkings shouted.

Kazimir used his momentum to spear another thug, driving him to the floor. The upyr rolled to his feet.

Whitney, now free, elbowed Darkings in the nose and blood flowed freely.

The remaining thugs dropped into what passed as fighting stances, although they were little more than brutes using their size and raw strength instead of any real skill.

Kazimir reached back, and in one fluid motion, grabbed two knives from the table and threw one. It lodged itself in one of the thug's throats. He then wrapped his arm around Bartholomew Darkings, who was holding his probably-broken nose, and pulled him in, the other knife at his throat.

"Tell your men to get out of here and never return unless every one of you wants to look like that." Kazimir wrenched Darkings' neck, pointing his eyes down at the gurgling thug.

"You will not get away with this," Darkings said.

Kazimir flicked his wrist, and the tip of the blade caught Bartholomew Darkings' ear.

"Okay, okay!" he blubbered. "Let's go boys."

Kazimir waited until the surviving thugs were out of the house before walking Darkings to the front door and shoving him down the front steps.

"Do not return," Kazimir said.

Whitney sidled up to him in the doorway and threw the Crown. "Don't forget this!" It hit Darkings in the back of the head, and the fat man stumbled before turning to snatch it up.

Whitney turned to see Young Whitney staring, stunned and speechless. Lauryn knelt by Rocco's side, cradling his head. Whitney gave his younger counterpart a sidelong glance and the boy wiped his nose with his sleeve.

"Rocco," Lauryn whispered.

His father groaned and sucked in air through his teeth.

"Are you okay?" she asked.

"Where's the vagabond?" he asked.

"Right here, Whitney said.

"Thank you for what you did, taking the fall for my boy," he groaned. Whitney could tell the man was in incredible pain. "It was stupid, but thank you."

"He was aiming for me," Whitney said, unable to believe what he was seeing. This was not how the night he remembered had unfolded.

"You were trying to keep my boy safe, and for that, you have my eternal gratitude."

Whitney never heard his father say a single kind thing about him growing up. He glanced over at Young Whitney, who hid his face. Big Whitney grabbed Rocco's wrist and tried to lift him, but the man squealed and crumpled back to the floor.

"Are you okay?" Whitney asked. He couldn't believe he was asking that question of his father.

"I can't feel my legs, he said. He gritted his teeth and squeezed his eyes shut.

"Oh, Rocco," his mother said, crying. After a moment hugging Rocco, she pulled back and yelled, "Whitney! Go get Father Drimmond and Wetzel, now!"

Big Whitney nearly started running, then remembered who she was talking to.

"C'mon," Kazimir said, grabbing Whitney. "Let them handle their own affairs. Let's get rid of this body."

Whitney got stuck carrying the thug by the heavy end. Weight didn't seem to be any different in Elsewhere, the thug may as well have weighed a ton. Whitney had to stop a few times to catch his breath on what Kazimir had assured him wasn't air before they reached the creek at the back of his family's property.

"Right here," Whitney said, groaning. He and Kazimir tossed the body of the dead thug into the brush by the creek. He remembered burying stolen treasures nearby as a kid and even saw the glint of something shiny under a pile of rocks.

He gave the body an extra hard kick into the current so it

wouldn't ever come back on the Fierstowns. Someone might find it down a ways in some other worthless town, bloated and unrecognizable—if there even were other towns in Elsewhere.

Whitney exhaled and fell against a tree stump. He couldn't die from hunger in Elsewhere, but he was exhausted all the same. Kazimir too seemed winded without his supernatural, upyr abilities.

"You were *supposed* to jump out with me," Whitney said.

"I warned you to take the path of least resistance," Kazimir replied.

"What's the point of having an upyr companion if I can't beat up some thugs who have it coming?"

"Do you still not realize where you are, you ignorant, son of a—"

"Hard to insult her now that you've met her, isn't it?"

Kazimir exhaled through his teeth. "You said this is all your memory, didn't you?"

"Sort of, only I didn't rob Darkings, and it wasn't the Glass Crown." Whitney stuck out his chest. "It took a more refined thief to pull those off."

Kazimir appeared to hold back another insult. "Was your father hurt then?"

"No, just a few bruises from being punched. They burned down the barn and made me watch as punishment, and I—well, younger me—got stuck helping rebuild it for months."

"All these years and you still haven't learned there are consequences."

"What, I was just supposed to watch it happen again? What is the point of the place if I'm just supposed to relive every yigging memory?"

"That is precisely the point, thief." Kazimir stood and brushed his pants. "This isn't your game. It's theirs." He looked around, and Whitney followed his gaze but saw nothing but trees. "Give an opening, and you'll lose your mind faster. So, stop acting like an impetuous child and let's hope your father is all right. There's no telling what *they'll* do if he's not."

They set off back toward the house. Whitney took a second or three to let the words sink in. He knew Elsewhere tortured fallen souls, at least that's what the Church of Iam preached. Good, honest people went to live out eternity in paradise through the Gate of Light, but what happened to those who were magically exiled to Elsewhere by their best friend alongside an upyr?

He hurried and caught up to Kazimir. "You should have taken down that fellow with a club before he ever started his swing," Whitney said. "I've seen you move ten times faster."

Kazimir bit his lip. Whitney noticed it wasn't only anger twisting his features, but frustration. "I didn't this time."

A few clever quips popped into Whitney's head. He settled on silence. Maybe the upyr had even fewer of his abilities than Whitney thought, as slow now as an average man. Even if that were true, Whitney was smart enough to know he still couldn't take him in a one on one fight without a chance to cheat.

As they approached the farmhouse, the town father—who was now of Glintish decent for whatever reason—caned his way out of the house toward the exit gate at the edge of the Fierstown property. Whitney held it open for him.

"Thank you, my son," he said. "Praise the Fallen."

Whitney froze in the gateway, and it wasn't because of the priest's refusal to praise Iam, but because of the man's face. The cloth wrapped around his eyes made it difficult to tell, but it was clearly not Father Hullquist. Not only in skin color, but the man looked exactly like Torsten Unger.

"Torsten?" Whitney said, but the man ignored him as if he'd said nothing at all.

Whitney blinked hard. Still Torsten. It was just like how Dark-ings had appeared as another figure from his childhood.

It's just Elsewhere messing with you, Whitney told himself. *Just play along, like the blood-sucking upyr said. You always wanted to try your hand in an acting troupe.*

Wetzel suddenly plowed by Whitney. The old codger wore his usual rags, hollowed out shells and dried fruits dangling from his neck, each holding odd potions and powders. He was the strangest man Whitney had ever met, and Sora, as a child, used to say the same. She said they rarely spoke, meanwhile he'd secretly been training her in blood magic.

Seeing him made Whitney wonder if she had any other secrets, such as having exiled someone else to Elsewhere with her power before. Then he worried that she might be with him—he wasn't ready to see her.

Luckily, only Lauryn and Young Whitney followed behind, the latter looking anxious and cowering behind her. Whitney couldn't tell if his nervousness was for his father, or for the repercussions of what he'd done. He had no experience in worrying over Rocco after all.

"How is he?" Whitney asked.

Kazimir stood off to the side, watching, but not speaking.

Wetzel stopped and scrutinized Big Whitney. "Who is this?" he asked, leaning in uncomfortably close. His skin stunk of muck from trolling the riverbank, searching for herbs. He pulled something from one of his many pockets, a feather, and waved it in the shape of an eight front of Whitney's face. His eyes widened, he opened his mouth, then closed it again.

"Wetzel, this is Willis," Lauryn said. Her eyes were puffy and red.

Wetzel craned his neck to look into Whitney's ear, then grumbled, "Your color is wrong."

"What?" Whitney asked.

"Your color. It is wrong."

"Uh, thanks?" Whitney said.

Wetzel grumbled again, then continued back into town, all the strange containers hanging all over his rags clattering.

"You'll have to excuse him," Lauryn said. "He means the best, and he is the only healer we have."

"What did he say?" Whitney asked.

"Father Drimmond prayed for him. Blessed him. He's asleep now." Her voice shook. "Wetzel said… he said…"

"It's okay, take your time."

"He's... he's...." Lauryn's face fell into her hands as she tried to mask her sobbing.

"His back is broken," Young Whitney said for her. "They said he's never gonna walk again without a miracle from the fallen gods."

"I thought I told you to stay inside!" Lauryn snapped.

"I—I didn't mean for this." Tears welled in the corner of his eyes, then his head sunk and he sulked back toward the house. Big Whitney found it strange seeing himself so somber. He hated being sad; in fact, he couldn't remember the last time he let that feeling overtake him. He rolled with life, improvised—and now he wondered if it was that nature Elsewhere planned to prey on.

"I'm sure he never imagined this could happen," Whitney said.

"He's always getting into trouble," Lauryn said, voice clogged from crying. "It was bound to catch up to him eventually."

Whitney frowned. Burned barn or crippled father, the result was the same. His mother's love would wane every time she looked at him.

"I don't know what we're gonna do," Lauryn sobbed. "The farm. The house. Who's going to finish the roof? Tend the land? We can barely afford help right now, and the King's taxes keep going up with the wars in the South. Oh, gods…"

Whitney thought about the sacrifice Rocco made, then the things Kazimir had said to him. He didn't like the upyr, but he'd had experience with Elsewhere. It was Whitney's fault the man—this version of him at least—was crippled. Had he just stayed in that stupid closet, everything would have been fine.

"Don't you worry about a thing," Whitney said. He turned to Kazimir and said, "We'll help."

"You will?" Lauryn's eyes lit up. "We don't have much to pay, but…"

Whitney shook his head. "Forget about that. We have nowhere else in this whole world to be. We've been looking to settle down."

"Oh, bless you, kind sirs." She threw her arms around Whitney. He nearly hugged her in return before remembering that as far as she knew they'd just met. He didn't realize, however, how much he'd missed the warmth of her hugs.

"I won't let you do it for free," she said, barely able to contain her excitement. "How's ten bronzers a day sound, and you can sleep in the barn, and have supper for as long as you're here? "

"That's fine, right Kazimir?" Whitney nudged the upyr and earned a glare that made his heart feel like it'd jumped into his throat.

"Bless you ten times over!" She went to hug Kazimir, but the man's demeanor was enough to scare off a starving Westvale whore. She settled for a bow.

"You have no idea how much this means to us," she said. "And it'll do good for Whitney to have such fine gentleman as you. Especially with his father…" She paused, and her enthusiasm faded. "Well, anyway… I'll talk to Rocco about the details. For now, there's more than enough room in the barn, and I'll set down blankets. Sorry we don't have more."

"We've slept on worse." Whitney grinned, and she did the same though hers brimmed with sadness.

"Path of least resistance, right?" Whitney said, pleased with himself as she waddled away back to the house. "What can be more simple and boring than farming? It's why I left to find some excitement."

Kazimir grimaced, said nothing, and headed off toward the barn. Whitney all but patted himself on the back. If Elsewhere wanted to try and throw him, he was up for the challenge. He could play the good guy in their game until he found a way out of this gods-forsaken place.

XI

THE DESERTER

"What will ye do?" Sigrid asked.

She and Rand sat side by side in the mouth of an alley at the end of the docks, a blanket wrapped around their shoulders. They were at their favorite spot in Autla's Inlet, named after the first King of Glass. Once home to the wealthy and influential of the city, the area was destroyed by a storm off the Torrential Sea the likes of which none had seen since. Those who survived moved to higher ground, taking up residence in the district just beyond the castle walls in what is known as Old Yarrington. Now surrounded by the slums of Dockside, the homage to the Father of Glass was one small step away from insulting.

In the warmer months, Gunter, a merchant old as the docks themselves, worked a stand behind them. He peddled the best mussels this side of the gorge and likely beyond. Rand wouldn't know. He'd never traveled so far. He used to toss them one every day when they were children. Now Gunter wanted coin like everyone else.

He'd been Wearer of White, but he'd never been anywhere. Given the highest honor the Kingdom offered someone without a noble name, yet he'd only seen their little corner.

He sneezed. On top of it all, he felt as if he was coming down with sickness.

A stiff breeze blew in from the ocean, carrying flurries of snow with it. Tall waves from the Torrential Sea broke against jetties at the mouth of the inlet, tossing ships in the ice-cold water within. Most belonged to the Glass Kingdom, but there was an unusual number of longboats moored along the curved docks. Glassmen from Crowfall and further north would see those square, patterned sails and pointed prows bearing the imagery of the Buried Goddess carved into the wood and fear for their lives. They were the ships of Drav Cra raiders and having never been farther north than Westvale, Rand had never seen them before.

Presently, one sailed in from the darkness of the sea before them. A fur-clad warrior at the bow barked orders to more than a dozen rowers. Their shields hung along the sides of the hull, painted in all manner of heathen imagery.

It had always been custom for Liam's training Shieldsmen to be sent north to protect towns against Drav Cra raiders, but as peace painted the land and the Glass grew stronger, there'd been fewer raiding parties to defend against. When Uriah Davies wore the helm, he'd been known to still send his men into the cold to test their mettle—but Torsten had been too preoccupied with a dying king to focus much on his men.

Rand didn't blame the man—after all, look at what he himself had accomplished during his tenure as Wearer serving under the foreign Queen Oleander. Nothing but murder. She was one of the northerners in another life after all.

After Liam's illness became visible and he was kept within the castle to maintain appearances, and Sir Uriah disappeared, Rand started to hear tales of the Drav Cra returning to their old ways. The heathens had once again begun looting, raping, and pillaging as much as they could manage before vanishing to return to their tundra in ships just like the one before him. Rand knew it was true because half the uprooted refugees wound up in Dockside after their homes were torched.

If Wren could be believed, these Drav Cra killers were now taking up residence in the very castle Rand swore to protect.

"Rand," Sigrid said, tearing Rand from his reverie.

"Sorry." Rand shook out his head. "It's just those ships; I'm not used to seeing them here."

"Yer just noticing, are ye?"

"Apparently."

"Been getting worse for a month now, brother. They come into the Maiden's Mugs, trying to trade trinkets for ale or just slamming down an axe. We're all too scared to ask for autlas."

Rand shivered as the wind picked up.

"Here," Sigrid said. She went to share more of the blanket with him, but he pushed it back.

"I'm fine," he said, sneezing again.

His hands would tremble regardless, his body desperate for a drink. His head throbbed as well. It'd been so long since he allowed himself to feel anything, he almost welcomed the pain to accompany his sore throat.

"Ye ain't fine," she said. "If Wren didn't show when he did ye'd have—"

"But he did," Rand interrupted before she could remind him.

"Was a miracle, it was."

"It was an old man come calling at a lucky hour." He didn't even know why he was being so stubborn. He too had wondered whether Iam's hand had intervened.

"Is that all ye'd call it?"

"No," he said, then pulled a bit of the blanket over him and scooted closer to his sister. "A reminder, maybe. That the vow to take the Shield is one made for life, and I turned my back on it. I should have been killed the moment that happened, but Sir Unger never lost faith, even though I had."

"Ye aren't considering going back for true, are ye?"

Rand hung his head. He couldn't help but picture Torsten chained up in a dungeon like an animal. "I don't know."

"After the things ye did? All they made ye do? I spent months keeping Sir Unger away from ye, brother. Look at what they done to ye." She clasped one of his hands in both of hers. "I know it was Wren the Holy they sent this time, but they don't deserve ye."

Although Rand knew the love with which they were offered, the words stung him harder than a slap in the face. "Torsten Unger was the most honorable man I ever met in that gods-forsaken castle. Perhaps he is the most honorable man I've ever known."

"Where was he when the Queen Mother started hanging everyone in her way?"

"Doing whatever it took to serve the kingdom the right way."

She squeezed his hands tighter. "Iam gave ye a second chance. Don't throw it away acting as their murdering thug. Let's leave all of it behind. Leave this place, go somewhere south where it's warmer."

"With all my heart, I wish I could."

"So, yer going back?"

"It's my duty; I'm just… I'm not sure I can do what they need me to."

"Of course, ye can't. Ye ain't a killer, Rand, I don't care who they're needing to die. Ye never have been. Ye joined them to protect people, just like ye've always looked out for me."

"Not recently." He turned and looked straight into her eyes. She looked so much like their mother. "I'm so sorry for everything I've put you through."

A tear rolled down her cheek as she stared back. She released his hands so she could wipe it away, then turned to snivel.

"For the first time in months, I don't feel like yer a stranger. I don't want them to destroy the good man ye are again."

"I can never bring back those who died so senselessly, but if I have a chance to help bring them justice? The chance to stop the person behind all of this?"

"Rand, I won't stop ye, but—"

The blanket snapped from off their shoulders. Rand whipped around to see a group of three Drav Cra men. Their skin was white as the snow falling around them. Thick, braided beards dropped from their chins, getting lost in the gray pelt of their furs.

The biggest of them scrutinized the ratty blanket. "No wonder why so many of you Glassmen freeze in the deep winter." He laughed. The others joined him.

"Such a pretty thing under there though," another said, gawking at Sigrid. He was gaunt with a sharp, hawkish nose permanently broken in two places.

"Give it back," Sigrid demanded.

"And such fire too."

"I think you fellows are lost." Rand stood and positioned himself in front of his sister. His heart began to race, reminding him how sore his ribs were from nearly hanging to death.

"Damn right we are," the big one said. "We just sailed in at Drad Skaardi's request expecting to see the grand city of Yarrington, and all I see is yig and shog."

"Except you, little lady," the hawkish one said. "I hear southern ladies'll do anything."

"If you're looking for women, I suggest you head down the other end of Dockside," Rand said. "Valin Tehr runs a brothel called the Vineyard where you could get whatever you can imagine."

"Oh, but I never had much of an imagination," he said, taking a step closer. "I want her. She looks so… ripe."

The man grabbed Sigrid's arm. Rand shoved him away.

"Don't touch her!" he snapped. A few locals strolled by, glancing over, but otherwise minding their own business. That was how things were in Dockside. Nobody got involved in another's business unless they were left with no other choice. As for guards, they were rarely seen. It was why Rand joined the King's Shield in the first place. To try and make the forgotten corner of Yarrington he grew up in a better place.

The big one drew a hatchet and raised it to Rand's throat. The sharp edge scraped across the short hairs on his neck.

"Or what?" the man asked. "Look at you, shaking like a true southern flower."

Rand caught a glimpse of his hands, still involuntarily shaking. "I'm warning you," he said.

"Haven't you heard, Glassman? We share this city now. It's only right for you to share her with my friend here. It's… what do they call it? The law."

The hawkish one grabbed Sigrid and yanked her forward, wrapping his arms around her. She squirmed and tried to push him away, calling for Rand to help, but his whole body seized. All he could see was Tessa and the others, necks forced into nooses on the command of the Crown.

Sigrid elbowed the man in the groin and broke free. He grabbed the back of her shirt as she tried to escape. It tore in half before she slipped on the icy dock and hit the wood hard. The savage grabbed her leg and dragged her back screaming.

"Rand!"

The leader chortled. "That this puny little man's name? More like runt."

The screams of all the voices of those who'd suffered filled Rand's mind, mixing until, through the chaos, he heard his sister scream his name. His vision focused. His eyelids peeled open. Suddenly, he was back with Sigrid, the freezing air biting at his nose. His years of training for the King's Shield kicked in, and he didn't think—he just acted.

He punched upward, catching the big one in the elbow. It didn't break the bone but extended his tendons so he couldn't get any strength behind his swipe at Rand's neck. The blade sliced off a few hairs from Rand's unshaved chin as he twisted out of the way. The big man lost his balance, and a kick to the jaw finished the job. He tumbled off the docks and into freezing water.

Rand heard the unmistakable hum of steel through the air. He ducked beneath the swinging hatchet of one of the others, then barreled into him shoulder first. They hit the floor and rolled over. Rand held the man's weapon-arm back with both hands and earned blow after blow to the ribs. Rand head-butted the Drav Cra heathen just above the ridge of his nose. They both came away dazed, but Rand had existed in a fog for months now. He recovered quicker and pried the hatchet out of the man's loosened grip.

He drew it across the man's throat, shoved him aside, and faced the belligerent savage who'd first grabbed his sister. The man had a knife to Sigrid's throat. Tears filled her eyes, already starting to freeze upon her cheeks as she cried Rand's name.

"You're gonna regret that, Glassman," the savage said.

Rand squeezed the grip of the hatchet so tight the wood creaked. *Creak, creak, creak.*

"Let her go!" he roared, focusing his anger.

"Or what?" The savage slid the blade closer to her jugular, drawing a bit of blood. "I swear, I'll gut the pretty whore like a fish and make you watch as I take her—"

Without so much as a warning, Rand threw the hatchet as hard as he could. The blade sunk into man's forehead, the front of his skull crunching. He collapsed, and Sigrid twisted her body with him so that his knife only drew a shallow scrape along her neck. She gasped for air as she crawled out from under his arm.

Rand ran to help Sigrid to her feet. Only once she was upright did he take a moment to breathe. One of their assailants gurgled, blood pouring out of his split throat. The big one splashed around in the water, his movements slowing as the cold set it. He was dead already but didn't know it, and the one who started it all was still, eyes stuck wide open in shock. A flake of snow fell upon one, landing like a speck of dust on glass.

Rand scanned his surroundings. A homeless woman cowered in an alley, burying the face of her child against her bosom to shield him from the horrors. A dockhand gripped his broom, unable to move. A few more down the way helped the incoming Drav Cra longboat into a slip.

"Rand… they… they were going to…" Sigrid was shivering uncontrollably, both from terror and from all the snow filling her torn and tattered dress. Rand could feel the goosebumps all along her exposed skin.

"I know," he said. "They can't hurt you now."

"Are you sure they're…"

"They're dead."

He yanked the hatchet free of the man's cranium with a satisfying *thunk,* hung it from his belt, then swept up Sigrid and helped her toward the Maiden's Mugs. Not a soul approached them or the bodies. No one said a word. In the deep winter, if you died in an alley, your rotting corpse might not be found until Spring. That was the way of things in Dockside, the strip of Yarrington by the water's edge in South Corner.

Halfway home, Rand locked eyes with one of the Drav Cra standing on the prow of the arriving ship. There was a wild look in them. Rand quickly turned Sigrid down an alley and away from the man's gaze. A few beggars who'd taken up residence beneath strung up tents rattled pewter mugs for money, not realizing that

Rand and Sigrid were equally poor now thanks to Rand's weakness.

They reached the Maiden's Mugs and quietly made their way for the hearth. A few drunkards looked Sigrid over on her way by, unable to help themselves with her dress so torn. All those men in for an early round before her shift had likely dreamed of seeing more of her. Her smooth, milky skin showed now even more than in her barmaid uniform. It didn't matter that her lip was split and her teeth chattered from the cold.

Rand stopped to pull the neckline of her ripped dress up as high as he could, then noticed a pair of Drav Cra seated in the corner, speaking in their heathen language and laughing over pints. He led her as far away from them as possible on his route to the hearth. A fire crackled, and he carefully set his sister down on one of the tavern's few cushioned chairs.

"There ye are, Sigrid!" Gideon Trapp called over. He approached from the side, cleaning out a mug. "Almost sundown. Ye'd better get dressed."

"Get her a blanket," Rand asked.

"What'd ye say to me, thief?"

"I said to get her a gods damned blanket!" Rand slammed on the nearest table. Every pair of eyes in the room fell upon him, except those of the Drav Cra.

Trapp's face twisted with rage. Rand could tell he was preparing to curse in response until he got closer and noticed Sigrid'a condition.

"Who did that?" he said. Not in a way that showed concern for her, but as if a precious possession of his had been damaged.

"I'm not going to ask again, Trapp."

Finally, the portly man hopped to and went to storage, returning a moment later with frayed sackcloth probably used to cover barrels. Rand tore it from his hands and wrapped it around Sigrid's shoulders.

"There you go, Sig," he whispered. Now it was she who shook uncontrollably, and it was Rand's turn to care for her. He tucked the cloth tightly over her chest. She stared up at him, eyes agape in horror, but no other part of her moved. Seeing her in such a state of complete shock made Rand feel ill. He may have been the Shieldsman, but she'd always been the tough one—always wanting to go hunting with Rand and their father when they were younger, never shying away from elbowing a handsy customer in the gut as a barmaiden.

"Either of ye gonna tell me what happened?" Trapp questioned, his hairy arms crossed over his belly.

"What happened is you're going to keep her right here by the fire for the rest of the night," Rand said.

"No way. She can clean up, but I need her on the floor tonight. She's all I got."

Rand's fist and jaw clenched. He rose to his full height and glowered down at the man. "If I hear you have her working, I swear to Iam, you'll pay."

Gideon Trapp didn't back down. He rose up on his toes and shoved his face toward Rand's. "Who the yig do ye think you are? She don't work, yer both out on the streets."

"I am a..." His voice trailed off. He wanted to say what he was, to claim he was a knight of the King's Shield out loud, but his brain wouldn't let him. Instead, he said, "I swear to you, Trapp, one word she's working, and someone will hear about what's in the crates shipping through your basement for Valin Tehr. I may not have any friends left at the castle, but I know how to get word to them." Rand kept his voice low so nobody, especially the Drav Cra in the corner would hear.

The color fled Trapp's chubby, red cheeks.

"Drinking doesn't make me blind," Rand said. "Now fetch her some warm tea."

Trapp grumbled something under his breath as he turned.

Rand made sure he headed straight for the bar. All the barkeep did was help smuggle in manaroot from the Eastern Panping Region for one of Yarrington's more vocal leaders of the underworld. That was tame for Dockside, but the root was outlawed after the Panping Wars. Panpingese Soothsayers were said to use it to help magnify their connection with Elsewhere. For everyone else, it was a powerful sensory amplifying drug popular in brothels.

What Rand didn't mention was that it was his sister who'd told him about Trapp's dealings soon after he moved in with her. Somehow, in his alcohol filled stupor, Rand held on to that bit of knowledge. All those long months she'd managed to take care of him alone after he abdicated his duty and came stumbling home to hide in forgotten Dockside, he couldn't even do the same for her without needing a bit of her help.

"Everything is going to be all right, Sig," he said as he kneeled by her side and took her hand. He could tell she wanted to thank him for dealing with Trapp, but her lips merely parted. "Just stay right here and keep warm."

"Wh—what are ye gonna—gonna do?" she replied, teeth still chattering.

"Keep you safe this time." He kissed her on the top of the head, realizing it was the same thing their mother used to do when one of them got hurt, then he headed for the stairs. He paused at the bottom, eying a full mug of ale in the grip of some grimy, off-duty dockhand. He watched the liquid foaming, sloshing against the side. His whole body tingled merely from the sight, but he shook his head out and scaled the stairs.

It was clear now what he had to do, and he couldn't do it with his head in a fog and his vision blurred. He threw open his door and strode to the opposite side of the tiny room. Then he stopped and stared down into the reflection of his armor.

It was time to wear it again. Time to serve Iam and those closest to Him.

Redstar, the wicked man who'd cursed the Queen Mother's son and driven her into a spiteful rampage, needed to die. And he wasn't going to do it for Wren or Torsten or the King's Shield. He was going to do it for his sister and Dockside who'd suffer under the Drav Cra occupation more than any other part of Yarrington and to find justice for those murdered at his own hand like Tessa.

No matter what it took.

XII

THE MYSTIC

Sora walked slowly, cautiously. Yaolin City was larger than any place she'd ever been and unfamiliar in all regards.

Statues of all shapes and sizes rose on both sides of the street, every ten paces. Upon closer examination, Sora noticed they'd all had their faces rearranged. None of them were exactly alike, but she knew without a doubt, they were intended to be the visage of King Liam the Conqueror.

Her heart sank for her people. These statues must have been idols of Panpingese emperors or gods, but now they were all desecrated—history abolished for the sake of a far-off king who was now dead.

And now, from this vantage, she was even more in awe of Liam managing to conquer such a massive city. It was twice the size of Yarrington at least, not to mention it had been ruled by mystics capable of bending the world to their wills.

It was immediately clear, however, that the Glass presence in Yaolin City remained strong. Blue and white flags hung from many buildings, totally out of place against the earthy tones and terra-cotta roofs, guards posted at every corner. It was more security than Winde Port had by a long shot, despite being twice as far from the Glass Castle. Muskigo's active rebellion probably didn't help with that.

Still, through shop windows and on the streets, Sora saw smiling faces and generally happy-looking people, both Panpingese and Glassmen. It was a jarring juxtaposition to the Panping Ghetto in Winde Port where she'd seen children begging for coin or scraps of food.

"Come off the adventure, miss?" a lady said, appearing in front of her. Dresses and fine clothing hung along the porch beside them. "A pretty girl like you could use some proper clothing. Take your measurements?"

"I… no, thank you." Sora ducked away.

"Finest dumplings at port!" shouted another. The aroma coming from his stand was intoxicating, but she didn't have time to waste on trying food just yet.

As she traveled down the statue-lined boulevard, she read all the store signs—or she tried to. Half or more were in Panpingese, others had both languages but used strange words she didn't understand. She stopped when she spotted one that said: Clairvoyant of the Mystic Arts.

"It can't be that easy," Sora said to Aquira who wasn't listening. She was huddled against Sora's neck, probably terrified by the busy streets.

Sora stepped up to the threshold, and a Panpingese woman wearing a dress covered in jangling jewelry emerged from behind a shimmering curtain. She wore a ridiculous amount of makeup that made her look like a street performer.

"Welcome to—" she stopped, her eyes widening. "I am sorry, madam. I am sorry." She dropped to her knees and kowtowed. "Here. Here."

She gathered a pouch from beneath the folds of her dress with one hand and raised it without looking up. Sora didn't take it, and the bag fell to the floor, spilling open to reveal dozens of gold autlas, enough to live comfortably for a year.

"I've not been able to pay in some time," she said. "Business has been scarce since the seas became unstable from the war to the west."

Sora knelt quickly and shoved the bag back toward the woman. "What are you talking about?" she asked. A few minutes in Yaolin and people were trying to give her more autlas than she'd ever need. No wonder Whitney loved this place.

"Lady, please forgive me," the woman said. "There's far more there than I owe. Spare me, I beg."

"Stand up," Sora said.

The woman was reluctant, but she stood.

"Who are you?" Sora asked.

"I'm no one, my Lady," she said, still purposefully avoiding eye-contact.

"I'm no lady. Why do you call me that?"

The woman laughed, but then her expression quickly grew dour. "This is a test? You are one of the..." she lowered her voice, "...Secret Council, are you not? Your aura, your power... It is—"

"Me?" Sora said. "What in Iam's name is the Secret Council? Wait." Sora leaned in close, a glimmer in her eyes. "Are you talking about the Mystic Council?"

"You charlatan! Thief!" the woman shouted, wiping her tears. "You have wasted my time and brought fear upon me without reason. Please, leave this place." In an instant, she swept back into her shop, the curtain fluttering behind her.

"Mistress!" Sora shouted. She pulled the veil back and called again, but there was no answer. The room was empty but for a circular table with a small, glass orb set upon it.

"Iam's light," Sora exhaled. "What was that?" Aquira flew off her shoulder and landed on the table, circling the orb and sniffing it. Sora approached slowly. The walls were all white and unadorned, the ceiling black as night. But there were no other trinkets on shelves like there would be in a shop of curiosities.

She reached for the orb and gently lifted it from a jade stand with prongs like dragon claws on three sides. She felt nothing. It was heavier than it looked, but nothing more than a globe. She returned it and extended an arm for Aquira.

"Come on, girl," she said. "We need to find your family."

She headed back outside onto Xiahou Boulevard, bustling with traders, guards, performers, and all manner of other things that go on in capital cities. Most people shared her features, but most men wore the same strange silk robes as Mr. Kyoto and most women, flowered dresses with flowing fabric belts tied into bows. It was then that she realized how far from home she truly was, and how little she understood about this new world, even if she had been born there.

Sora shuffled along until she saw a large sign with words written in Panpingese. She recognized the letters but couldn't read the words. The image of two bones and a book spread open was burned into the wood, which indicated she'd found the place she was searching for.

Sora felt Aquira peep over her shoulder and the wyvern began to purr.

"You recognize this place, huh?" Sora asked.

The wyvern made a series of chirping noises.

As Sora approached, two Glass soldiers stomped toward her from the opposite direction.

"Clear the streets!" they shouted absentmindedly as they talked to one another, laughing. "Clear the streets!" People listened, flooding away from the road without protest or delay. However, those with shop stands took longer. One earned a shove, knocking over the beautiful calligraphy pieces he was selling.

"Speed it up!" the guards ordered.

Sora continued ahead, the distance between them closing and the bookstore resting in between.

"Aye! You!" one shouted. She stopped, and they filled the gap. "If you don't speak the common tongue, you are in violation of the law."

"I do!" she said.

"Then you're just insolent?"

"Me? No! What?" Sora stammered.

"We said, 'off the streets!' yet, here you are."

"I'm just trying to get home," she lied. "I'm sorry. I live right there." She pointed to the rooms above the bookstore, and the men let their eyes follow.

They regarded her suspiciously for a moment, then one said, "Get going. Now! We have a parade to set up for."

"Sorry," she said and rushed by.

She felt a yanking behind her, then heard a squeal.

"What's this?" one of the guards asked.

She turned around and saw the men prodding Aquira who was being held by the frills and throat, wings batting against the man's armor. The way he held her kept her from being able to open her mouth and spray fire or claw at the man. This wasn't the first time they'd dealt with a wyvern.

"Put her down!" Sora demanded.

"Oh, found your voice, huh, wench?" The other guards pulled their swords halfway from their sheaths.

Wench?

Sora couldn't believe what she was seeing. She thought Panping would be different, that somehow being in her own land, she wouldn't suffer the same prejudices. Apparently, she was wrong.

She felt the gentle tugging of Elsewhere from deep within, begging her to make the sacrifice necessary to burn the men to a crisp but she stifled it before it managed to take hold.

"She is my friend, and you are hurting her," Sora said calmly. "Please, put her down."

"Aye, that's a bit better. But what if we want to keep her?" He turned to the other man. "Never ate dragon before, have you?"

They laughed.

Aquira squirmed, her muffled squeals somehow even more distressing than if she were permitted to howl.

"Maybe we bring them both to the Overlord?" the guard said.

"Supposed to call him Governor Nantby in public," whispered the other. He had an incongruously small head and a pugnacious goiter on his neck.

"Whatever," said the first, running his fingers along Aquira's tail.

"She's a wyvern," Sora said, "and I think you're making her angry."

"I know what she is, *girl*. And they aren't supposed to be on the streets without a muzzle, by word of the Governor." The guard, still laughing, leaned in and scratched Aquira under the chin. "Aw, is the little pest getting angry?"

Aquira thrashed hard enough to shift the man's grip so she could snap at him, taking a chunk off the man's finger. He dropped her and swore.

"Kill that little shogger!" he commanded.

The other guard hesitated as Aquira reared back, spreading her wings wide. Her wingspan couldn't have been more than a meter, but she still cut an intimidating figure.

They gathered their nerve and began inching forward, Aquira let out a shrill cry, and a blast of flames burst forth from her maw toward the sky. Sora could tell it was restrained. Had she wanted to, Sora was sure the little wyvern could have burned them all in their armor and watched as their ashes filled the wind.

Aquira flapped her wings and rose, hovering at about head-height, then screamed again.

This time, the guards didn't stick around. "Get that thing under control or else!" one yelled as they turned and ran down the street, nearly knocking each other over with the effort. Once they were a safe distance, Sora reached out and coaxed Aquira back to her shoulder.

"Let's go before they bring more," she said. "And thank you for holding back on those creeps."

She squeaked what Sora liked to imagine as 'you're welcome,' and then they continued into the bookstore. The door jingled on her way through, which startled Sora. She looked up to see a bell tied to a string in front of the door.

Clever, she thought.

"Hello?" she said softly. When no one answered, she called a little louder.

Books were everywhere—on shelves, tables, stacked on the floor. More books than Sora had ever seen. The closest she'd ever been to such a library was in Wetzel's shack, but those sprawled around the floor could have fit on one of the hundred shelves throughout the store.

She strolled through, taking it all in, reading the spines of the books. There were stories as well as learning books. Another shelf had nothing but scrolls piled nearly to the ceiling. Most were in Panpingese, but some were in common, or... she wondered what they called her language here. *Glassenese*? Others still were in languages she'd never seen before.

She stopped at a shelf with leather-bound tomes and fingered a few of them.

"Hello?" she called again as she walked toward the rear of the room.

She rounded a corner, putting the shelves behind her, and found another section of the store. More shelves lined the walls, but these had various artifacts resting on them. There were skulls and bones, jars, both large and small, filled with liquid, strange creatures floating within.

Aquira hissed. Sora turned around and saw bottles similar to Wetzel's potion bottles at an alchemy table. Within were concoctions, none of which Sora recognized, made with powders and herbs ground up using the mortar and pestle beside them.

"Ah, I thought I heard someone," said a voice from behind her.

Sora's hand instinctually fell to her knife as she spun around, bumping a shelf and causing a jar to topple. Aquira swooped down and caught it before any real damage could occur.

The man laughed as he slid closed the translucent door leading to an adjoining room. He wore a robe similar to the doorman at the Winde Traders Guild, but this one looked expensive—judging by the patterned, gold threading.

"I'm sorry," Sora said. She glanced down, realized she still had her fingers wrapped around the grip of her knife, and quickly let go. "I called out, but no one answered."

"You've done nothing wrong, dear," the man said. "Welcome to my humble shop. Are you finding things as you desire them to be?"

His back was impossibly straight, hands folded behind his back. After the initial shock wore off, Sora noticed the resemblance.

"Lord Bokeo?" she said.

"At your service." He bowed, which she found odd for anyone called Lord to do to anyone not a king.

"I am—"

"I know who you are Sora." He took a couple of steps, smiled wide and said, "Aquira."

The wyvern flapped her wings and soared to the man. She purred and nuzzled up against his face.

"Warm as ever, aren't you?" he said. "Have you been well?"

Aquira nodded.

Sora's mouth opened slightly.

"Are you still sure about this one?" he asked Aquira who nodded again. "Excellent."

Aquira rose up again and returned to Sora.

"Did you just…" Sora started. "Did you understand him?"

Aquira squeaked and bobbed her head.

"She understands?" Sora asked Lord Bokeo.

"She does a lot more than understand," he replied. "You are an extraordinary young woman, Sora."

"What do you mean?"

"Oh, dear, there's so much to discuss." Lord Bokeo took a few steps and reached out, offering her his arm. "We've been waiting for you."

"That's impossible," Sora said, backing up. "No one knew I was coming here. No one. I came to tell you of your son's unfortunate death, but apparently, you already knew about it."

"Knew about it? I've been expecting it."

The breath fled Sora's lungs. "What?"

"The Ancients have been waiting for you for some time, my dear. I knew—Tayvada knew that someday the gods would come calling."

"His death is the work of no god!" Sora bristled, thinking about Kazimir. "It was the work of a monster."

"All things are works of the gods."

Aquira purred, and Sora jumped. She had been so distracted by the man's words she almost forgot the wyvern on her shoulder.

"Relax, my dear, and I'll show you the world," Lord Bokeo said.

It sounded like something Whitney would have said. She stood, mouth agape that a man across Pantego somehow knew her name, just as the demons in the Webbed Woods had.

"I know this is a lot to take in, Sora," Lord Bokeo said, stepping closer. "There is much you do not know, and much you will discover, but as it turns out, time is short."

"Short for what?" she said. "Do you not even care about your son's passing?"

"My son made the sacrifice expected of him. We all have our purpose, dear. That was his."

Sora grew frustrated. She'd wasted valuable time away from her quest to find out what happened to Whitney. All to give her best to Tayvada's family and tell them how beloved he was in Winde Port. Apparently for no reason.

"Tell me, what is on your arm?" Lord Bokeo asked.

"My arm?" she said, surprised by the sudden shift in conversation.

"I mean upon your skin." He inched toward her, cautiously.

Sora pulled back.

"Please, Sora, I mean you no harm," he said. "Trust an old man. If you cannot trust me, trust your friend." He pointed to Aquira.

"I'm starting to feel deceived by everyone, including her."

"You cannot tell me you never suspected she understood your words?"

Sora couldn't deny it. The wyvern was either incredibly perceptive, or she took instruction through spoken language. The answer was probably both.

Aquira whined and lowered herself to the floor.

"Do not blame her," Lord Bokeo protested. "She was merely following commands."

The wyvern nuzzled against Sora's leg. Her warmth and the roughness of her skin oddly comforting.

"Now, may I?" Lord Bokeo asked.

Sora bit her lip and conceded. "Fine."

He moved close enough to roll her sleeve back. When the marks on the top of her forearm revealed themselves, she reeled back, but he tugged a bit on her wrist, straightening her elbow. Then he started to pull down her gloves.

"Just as I imagined. What are these?" he asked, pointing to the scars.

"None of your business," she said. Ever since Wetzel allowed her to practice blood magic, she'd been self-conscious of the scars on her hands and arms. Not only because the Glass Kingdom outlawed blood magic, but because nobody else had them. It was hard enough to fit in as a Panpingese refugee in a small town raised by the town kook.

"They are precisely my business." Lord Bokeo walked toward the shelf housing jars of fine powders. He pulled one, seemingly at random, and returned to Sora. While he perused the shelf, she considered running away, but still, curiosity had her pinned to the floor.

"What is that?" she asked.

"Will you trust me? I believe I possess the answers to all of your questions."

Sora nodded.

Lord Bokeo unscrewed the jar's cover and swirled the contents. "Stay still, even if it burns a little."

Sora flinched ever so slightly as he shook the contents of the jar onto her arm, careful to coat each scar. He was right, it burned, but she'd experienced worse pain every time she sliced herself to access the powers of Elsewhere.

After the burning subsided, Lord Bokeo bent over and blew away the powder.

Sora sneezed. When she opened her eyes, every scar on her arm and hand was gone.

"What the yig and shog?" She covered her mouth. "Excuse me, I'm sorry, Lord Bokeo."

He chuckled. "It is fine."

Her eyes went wide, and she said, "Wait, you do magic?"

"It was not magic, my dear. It is what learned men call alchemy."

"I know what that is." She'd watched Wetzel brew potions and toxins enough. She'd rarely seen him perform any blood magic himself, but he preferred to think of alchemy in the same light.

"Then you know that in many ways, it works like magic," he said, echoing Wetzel's sentiments. "But Alchemy calls upon the laws of Pantego and its elements. Magic breaks those laws through Elsewhere, and always it comes with a cost." He took her other hand and revealed those scars.

"So then, you know?" Sora said.

"That you do magic? Yes, but those days are over. Soon, you'll never need to mutilate your body again."

"You don't understand," she said. "I must do magic. I have to…" She was going to tell him of her need to see Whitney returned to this world, but remembered she had only just met the man, even if he'd somehow known her by name.

"I did not say you wouldn't do magic. But this barbaric way, this blood magic. That is the way of animals who would defile this world. You are above it. If you allow, I can make preparations for your training."

"Training for what?"

"Your bond to Elsewhere is strong, Sora. The gift courses through your veins. It always has. We wish to teach it which veins to travel. Wetzel could only instruct so far."

Sora swallowed.

Lord Bokeo smiled. "Yes, I know of the old badger as well." He put his arm on her shoulder and led her to a wall with a painting the size of a man. "You've not been forgotten, Sora. The Secret Council has watched you for some time."

Sora was too stunned to fight his guidance. The painting depicted three Panpingese warriors dressed in blue robes. She wasn't sure how she knew they were warriors, they held no weapons, but even in the painting, they bore a particular strength.

Rolling his fingers along the edge of the frame, Lord Bokeo stopped toward the bottom. Sora heard an audible click. Rising, he gave the frame a hard yank. The painting swung away from the wall, revealing a stone staircase.

"Come," Lord Bokeo said. Aquira screeched and flapped forward, following him as he descended.

"You expect me to follow you down there?"

When no response came, Sora looked from side to side. All the room held were dusty old books, and there was hardly anything fearful about a librarian. She hoped. Regardless, Tayvada's strange father clearly had a more intimate knowledge of Elsewhere, and that was precisely what she needed.

She took a deep breath, then hurried to catch up. She did, however, have the good sense to keep her hand on her weapon as she did. She was about halfway down the dark stairwell when she heard a creak as the painting closed behind her. All the light disappeared except for a faint, bluish glow emanating from the bottom of the staircase.

"Almost there," Lord Bokeo said.

"What is this place?" she asked.

"It is the Dixia Shanyow, or roughly translated, The Underground."

"Dixia Shanyow," Sora repeated softly.

"Many years ago, even before King Liam the Conqueror arrived and sowed discourse amongst our people, the Mystic Council became keenly aware of a time to come where they would not be welcome with arms wide open as they had been for so many centuries."

They reached the landing which opened into a chamber of engraved stone. Great statues of beasts Sora didn't recognize lined the walls on both sides. Water spewed from their mouths into pools, the ceaselessly rippling water, mesmerizing. In the middle, a platform bridged one side to the other.

"Those are wianu," he said, yanking her from her reverie. "The great sea beasts. Legend says they retreated when the Drav Cra expanded their tent stakes into lower Pantego. They have not been seen since the establishment of Westvale, their first city."

"They are…"

"Beautiful," Lord Bokeo finished for her.

"I was going to say terrifying, but I suppose beauty can be scary."

"Yes," he said, giving her a sidelong glare, "I believe that to be true as well."

"You were saying something about the Secret Council?"

"Ah, yes," he said, slowly proceeding across the bridge. He raised his voice over the gurgling of the fountains. "The Mystic Council decided it would be best to find quiet solace for a time, to bide time and wait for the age of Glass to fall."

"That could take centuries."

"For the remaining Ancients of the Mystic Order, centuries would be like days. They do not fear time and death the way the rest of us do. They can afford to wait."

"You mean to say they are immortal?"

"Not exactly," he said as they reached the other side. "They can be killed, but there are none outside of Elsewhere who we believe possess the power to do it. They went to great pains to survive after the culling of King Liam, sacrificing much of their power in this mortal realm to endure. All to ensure your future."

Sora assumed he meant the future of all Panpingese, but still, the words caught in the back of her mind somewhere as if they were intended only for her.

Massive, stone doors stood in their path, intricate markings covering both sides. Sora recognized some of the letters as the Panpingese alphabet, although she couldn't say what any of the words meant. Other lines and circles created patterns and shapes, but if they represented anything, she couldn't tell.

"How are you involved in all of this?" she asked.

"There will be much time to answer questions, although I believe you'll find all your questions will be answered in short time," he said. "To sate your curiosity regarding me, I am but a gatekeeper. My family was not blessed with the gift, my son especially, but our loyalty to the Council has never waned."

That explained why Kazimir didn't take to Tayvada's blood like a drug after he drained him. Before Sora could inquire further, Lord Bokeo raised his hand to the door and fit his finger within one of the engraved circles. Tracing it around, then to another, and then a straight line down to another series of loops. A deep growl sounded and shook the very stone upon which they stood. Dust billowed, and the door cracked open.

"Speak only when spoken to, Sora," he said. "This is very important."

Sora nodded. She wasn't sure what else to do.

Inside, she expected to see a giant, soaring cavern, but instead, it was a reasonably sized, circular room—twenty or thirty paces across. She followed Lord Bokeo to a raised dais the same shape as the room itself. The chamber was cold. Unnaturally cold. The chill pierced through Sora's layers as if she were naked and even then, her skin did nothing to keep it away from her bones.

She shivered.

Lord Bokeo stepped up onto the dais and beckoned Sora to follow. He climbed. She climbed. When he sat in the center with legs crossed over one another, Sora watched.

Placing his hands together, palms flat, Lord Bokeo inhaled, and in one breath said, "*Lu hwan, oolanxio!*"

Suddenly, as if reality itself changed, Sora saw seven thrones materialize around her in a circle. She looked to Lord Bokeo, who held a finger against pursed lips.

Turning back to the thrones, Sora now saw figures seated upon them. The one straight ahead of her wore a robe of blue, and the others wore yellow flecked with darker shades of yellow. All seven raised their hands and grabbed hold of their hoods, drawing them up, casting deep shadows over their faces.

"Sora, the one with no place to call home." A voice spoke, but Sora wasn't sure from which of the figures it had come.

Sora remembered what Lord Bokeo said about staying quiet and looked to him. He gestured for her to respond, though she wasn't sure how to.

"It is... I," she stammered and immediately felt ridiculous. It's what Whitney would've said, never the one to feel out of place no matter how bizarre the situation. She regarded Lord Bokeo again, and he nodded in approval.

"Aran Bokeo, we thank you for your service," the voice spoke again. "You may leave."

"Wait," Sora said, then cringed.

Lord Bokeo flinched but still rose and walked toward the door. He shot Sora a look that seemed to convey his condolences for the wrath she was about to suffer. Aquira shifted nervously as well, reminding Sora she was there.

The blue robed figure stood and stepped down from the throne. "Bokeo, wait." The voice sounded feminine as it hovered in the air.

Sora heard the shuffling of Bokeo's boots as he stopped.

"Our guest wishes for you to stay," the figure said. "Is that right?"

"I... uh.... Yes, my Lady," Sora said, hoping she addressed her correctly. She wasn't sure why she cared if Lord Bokeo, a relative stranger, remained, but even a face familiar for but minutes was preferable to these robed figures who reminded her of Redstar's followers in the Webbed Woods.

"Then please, stay."

"Yes, Ancient One," Lord Bokeo responded, bowing. Sora took note of the title.

"Do you know why you are here, Sora?" the woman asked.

"No, Ancient One," Sora replied.

"Aquira tells us you are special."

"May I ask you something about that?" Sora asked.

The Ancient urged her to continue with an elegant wave of her hand.

"I do not understand how Aquira told you anything when she's been with me since nearly the day we met," Sora said.

"Aquira is not average, just as you are not average." The woman turned her shrouded face toward Aran Bokeo as if waiting for approval, and they exchanged a nod. "Many years ago, when the gods spoke of Tayvada's sacrifice, we sent Aquira to wait for you."

"For me? I'm sorry, I still do not understand. I… I grew up in a small village far from all of this. An orphan of war, that's all."

"The Well of Wisdom showed us that in Tayvada's passing, you would finally be ready to return to us. To fulfill your destiny."

"My what?" Sora fought back the sick feeling within her belly. To think, Tayvada might have died because of her, just as Whitney possibly had. She couldn't believe it. "Tayvada didn't pass, he was murdered by an upyr who was hunting another… my friend."

"The cause of his death matters not. Only that his lifeblood was spilt. Aquira knew the moment she met you at the guild that you were the one for which we have waited so long. When she told Tayvada, he accepted his fate, as you must."

Sora looked to Aquira. The wyvern blinked her two sets of eyelids, then bobbed her head, frills wriggling.

"She speaks now?" Sora asked.

"Not with words. In time, you will learn to communicate with her, and she will be your aid as we embark upon this great journey. It is time to fulfill your destiny."

"And if I refuse?"

Behind her, Aran Bokeo winced. She was uncomfortably aware of the eyes of the other six hooded figures on her even though their faces were shrouded.

"You will not," the Ancient One said. "Allow me to show you the glory that awaits you in the new Mystic Order. This may be jarring at first…"

"Wait—" Sora said, but it was too late.

The Ancient One stalked toward her, and no sooner had Sora reached for her knife then the mysterious woman waved a hand in front of her eyes. Sora felt a sensation she'd become all too familiar with. Elsewhere tugged, just as it had when the guards held Aquira, as it had when she knew Kazimir was around, as it had so many times before. Only, usually the haunting sensation came from within, but this time it seemed to envelop her.

Heat washed over her body and sweat poured down her brow. Her head swam like it had when Whitney bought her a second drink at The Lofty Mare back in Yarrington.

Without thinking, she took a step and felt faint, then the familiar sting of Aquira's claws digging into her shoulder vanished. She spun, searching for her wyvern companion who was nowhere to be found. The quick movement almost made her fall over. Something about the room was wrong now. The lines didn't match up. The place where the wall would normally meet the floor now connected with another wall. Come to think of it, she wasn't even sure the floor was the floor anymore.

The thrones were gone, and so were the figures seated upon them.

"Lord Bokeo?" Sora called, but he was gone too.

Another shift, and Sora found herself falling to the side. She tumbled from the dais and expected to feel pain as her shoulder collided with the floor, but she felt nothing.

She hadn't even realized she was clenching her eyes shut. When she opened them, she was floating.

"Sora," spoke a matronly voice from somewhere. At first, Sora thought it was the Ancient One, but the voice was different. It sounded far off and distant, like someone talking under water.

Sora tried to turn, but with her feet no longer touching the ground, even the smallest movement came at an incredible cost. She finally managed to rotate and face the doorway leading into the room with the bridge and water. Breathing was difficult. Everything around her, she noticed, was the wrong color. No, not color, just shade. Everything was darker, redder.

Something raced toward her, wings flapping. A bird maybe. No. The wings were too big, flapping hard, fast. She recoiled as it got nearer, but it went right through her.

Then fire came. Hot fire. Bright, blinding. She shielded her face from the sudden onslaught of heat.

When it passed, she heard another sound. Her name. The voice was familiar and screaming. Over and over she heard the voice calling her name. There was panic within the word, desperation even. She knew immediately, the voice belonged to Whitney.

"Whitney!" Sora shouted and heard her name come back in reply. She fought against everything to find him, wading through darkness just to get a glimpse. She peeled away another layer of darkness and could just make out his face in the distance, but as she went to call out again, another presence stepped before him. Pale of face, eyes like daggers; a nightmare. Kazimir.

The mere sight of him caused her to jump, and then she fell. She screamed Whitney's name and could hear him shouting hers, the sound growing more and more faint as she plummeted. Then she stopped, and his presence was gone.

"Whitney?" she said. A series of torches surrounded her and suddenly ignited. Sensation returned to the flats of her feet, dirt between her toes. Everything was still wrong, red, purple, different—plus, now, she was no longer inside Dixia Shanyow. Those words came easily to her, like she'd known them all her life.

"*Dixia Shanyow*," she said aloud, and then, "*Tsu shensughu ywen zhun tahuet feng yaris tsu weyong ywen hou.*"

She not only spoke the words in Panpingese, but she understood them. Earlier that day, she could do little more than say hello in the foreign tongue, now she was speaking sentences.

"*The spirit of the gods is found in the one with the will of fire,*" the Ancient One's voice echoed, translating what she'd said back into common.

A sudden rumble tore her from her reverie, and the ground began to shake. Her feet stayed rooted, even as winds blew fiercely, whipping dirt and sand. Slowly, like a worm wriggling from beneath the soil, a rock poked through the surface of the ground. It continued to rise, eternally, yet in an instant. Time meant nothing to Sora as she watched.

When it stopped, she stood staring at something she'd only seen from a great distance. Mount Lister, in all her glory, cast a long shadow over her. She recalled the only other time she'd seen it close up, when she stole off from Wetzel's shack in search of Whitney and wasn't there to protect him from raiders. She'd only made it to the hills in the western fields before she became overwhelmed by the size of Yarrington.

Even then, she'd never seen it like this.

It was then she realized she'd only thought the mountain stopped rising. It continued into the clouds, ever growing.

The earth shook once more, but this time Sora found it difficult to stand. Small stones pelted her feet and ankles, and she backed away from the spot where dirt and grass collapsed into the earth. A pale hand broke through the surface, grabbing hold of anything it could. Its muscles flexed, and an elbow appeared, then a shoulder.

She expected rent flesh and yellowing bone like that of a dead man, but the hand was smooth as a newborn babe.

A second arm broke through, and with it, a face.

Before she could register the terror in her heart, she stood face to face with the most beautiful woman she'd ever seen. Her long, black hair, flowed like a flock of ravens behind her, catching the wind. Her eyes were entirely white; her irises only a shade off-color. She wore the most beautiful dress Sora had ever seen—a burial gown fit for a queen.

Her pale skin wriggled all over, and Sora feared maggots covered her until she realized what caused the movement. Small, budding roots and they sprouted leaves.

This strange, buried woman should have been a vile thing of the grave. Instead, she was perfect. Her arm extended. A long finger traced the outline of Sora's face.

"Yes," the woman said. "Yes."

Sora tried to step back but couldn't.

"Do you know me?" the woman asked.

Sora took a deep breath and said, "I know of you." She wasn't sure how, but she knew exactly who she was looking at. Nesilia, the Buried Goddess. She who Redstar and his wicked warlocks worshipped above all else. Nesilia was magnificent, stunning. A power pulsed from her like all the waters of the oceans coalescing into one massive tidal wave.

Nesilia's brow furrowed, drawing attention to the fact that they were little more than lines of moss across her forehead. "Then tell me what you know of me," she said. The words came as a gentle request, not a command.

"Awful things, yet now I fear they are mostly lies and myths, my Lady," Sora said. She hadn't even meant to call her that, but in the goddess' presence, she struggled to find any other title.

Nesilia smiled, then gestured for her to continue.

"I've heard from the men who worship Iam that you were… are the false goddess. Evil and without a heart—but I met evil. Bliss was pure evil. You… you're something else."

Nesilia still smiled but said nothing.

"I've heard from your followers in the North that you and Iam were lovers, that he saved you by cursing Bliss—the One Who Remained—but I think both tales are too different for either to be trusted in their entirety and both people too flawed." As the answers flowed through her lips, Sora wasn't even sure if she was in control of what she was saying, like her deepest, unconscious thoughts were slipping out.

"Smart girl." As Nesilia spoke, vines spread from her feet and ankles, slinking ever closer to Sora who didn't dare move. "But what do you believe?"

"Truly?"

"Truly."

"In my heart, I chose to believe the story of love. That Iam created Elsewhere for the gods and goddesses who rebelled, but you, he loved. After cursing Bliss, he let you stay buried beneath his throne so he'd never be far from you."

Something new washed over the goddess' face like a shifting shadow.

"I'm sorry, my Lady, if I offended," Sora said.

"He wanted to punish that witch… that vile and heinous crea-ture," Nesilia said, her voice growing louder. "She thought herself so beautiful, so perfect. So, he stole her looks. Cursed her to become the creature you met. He thought it would be the ultimate punishment. Send all the rebels to Elsewhere except the one who struck out against me, his love, his Queen!"

As she said the last word, the ground shook, and sharp, jagged rocks rose up around them like the talons of a carrion bird.

"He cursed her, but he blessed her as well! She may have become a beast, but he let her retain that which gods love most: the fear of our creation. All of the world feared her—even those who didn't know she existed. Each time they saw an eight-legged pest scurry across their floors, their fear fueled her."

"But for me..." Nesilia pressed a hand against her heart. "He said he loved me! Said he wanted me close. He could have saved me, built me a throne upon His Mountain. Instead, the very earth healed me."

Nesilia stroked the vines which now covered her arms.

"Even the lesser gods were free to rule Elsewhere," she went on, "but I was the one who was cursed! What's worse than being a dreadful beast?"

When she hesitated, Sora wasn't sure if she expected a response. Sora stuttered until Nesilia's chin fell to her chest, and a black tear, like sap, ran down her cheek.

"Being forgotten," Nesilia said softly.

"My Lady... I..." Sora stopped. All her life, she'd heard the Church of Iam preach against Nesilia and her role in starting the God Feud, even more so than the other fallen gods. Then, she heard Redstar speak of her glory and giving her life out of love. At the time she thought little of it, but now, as Sora looked upon the Buried Goddess, she could only feel pity.

"I am so sorry," Sora finished.

"For what?" Nesilia questioned. "It was not you who abandoned me."

"I—no... it was not."

"Why have you come to this plane?" Nesilia asked, jolted from her sadness in an instant.

"I was sent by an ancient mystic, I think. She said I would see the glory that awaits me."

"So, look upon me, girl. Feast upon my glory and do not forget it!"

The world began to swirl again. The mountain rumbled as Nesilia's scream rang out, then it broke into countless pieces, scattering and showering down around Sora. She cried out even though none of the stones touched her.

Suddenly, Nesilia's face was all she could see, filled with fury. Yet there was something else there. That sorrow and loneliness remained within her colorless eyes even as her features twisted with rage. In that moment, Sora wanted nothing more than to be close to the goddess, to embrace her and soothe her pain.

And with that, Sora's entire world collapsed around her.

XIII

THE THIEF

Following a hearty breakfast made by Lauryn, accompanied by the kind of awkward silence one would expect at the table after a thieving son gets his father crippled, Whitney and Kazimir set out to harvest.

It had been a long time since Whitney gripped a sickle, but it didn't take long to find his rhythm. It also didn't take long before he remembered all the reasons he'd left the farm to begin with. Between the fragments of vegetation pelting his skin, the hot sun, and the bugs buzzing around, he was itchy and irritable.

Young Whitney was outside as well, supposed to be helping, but instead kicking around rocks by the barn with his head down. Whitney didn't bother him. He couldn't believe his younger self would feel such guilt, but then again, the real version of himself had never got his father's back broken. Barns are easier to mend than bones.

"You know what I hate?" Whitney asked.

Kazimir ignored him, as he'd been doing all morning. He simply worked, quiet and drone-like, hacking away. After all this time together, Whitney still couldn't get a read on the man. The ruthless, rule-bending killer, happy to fall in line and listen to all the ingrates in this phantom Troborough. It was hard to fear him now.

"The color brown," Whitney answered himself. "I miss anything that isn't brown. Look around you. Brown fields, brown houses, brown roofs. Even the horses and goats are brown. Shog, even their shog is brown. That's why I left this place—well, that and a million other reasons."

"Yet, here we are, harvesting barley in Elsewhere," Kazimir said.

"You know what I realized?" Whitney threw his sickle to the ground. The tedium of work gnawed at him like a swarm of angry locusts.

"What?" Kazimir didn't even bother looking up from his work.

"We wouldn't be here at all if not for you."

"Is that so?"

"Let's see," Whitney started as he approached the upyr. "First, you appear like a creep from the shadows of some murdered guy's bedroom. Then, you kidnap my… friend. Then, you try to kill us both."

"And I'd have succeeded if your mystic *friend* had the slightest clue how to wield her magic," Kazimir growled. He stabbed his sickle down and looked to the sky. "Trapped here, thanks to an accident."

"Oh, poor you," Whitney shoved him.

"You're going to regret that."

"You aren't as tough without your spiky teeth, dung breath." He wasn't sure what came over him. Kazimir was right; he was the one who'd committed to helping run the farm. Kazimir just played along for reasons Whitney still couldn't understand. But Whitney pushed him again, harder this time.

As Kazimir stumbled back, a sound drew Whitney's focus to

the creek. Young Whitney was behind the barn out of view of his house, throwing stones at fence posts with a young, Panpingese girl with long, jet-black hair. Whitney hadn't even noticed that the boy had somehow slipped away.

"Sora…"

It was the only word Whitney got out before he felt Kazimir's balled fist connect with the side of his head, and then the cold earth came up to meet him.

Whitney came to, sprung to his feet, and dropped into a fighting stance, but Kazimir was nowhere around. It was no longer morning. The sky was dark again, and to Whitney's chagrin, a deep purplish maroon, as unnatural as could be. Whitney realized he must have been knocked out cold. His ears rang, and he saw starry blotches before his eyes.

A high-pitched laugh came from behind him, and he spun. It echoed, and he turned again. Soon, the sound surrounded him, feeling vaguely familiar. Suddenly, a horned head popped up from beneath the barley field. Its golden yellow eyes gleamed as it cackled. It was dark, so Whitney couldn't make out its features as it climbed free of the ground, but he immediately recognized the satyr.

When he, Torsten, and Sora were in the Webbed Woods, they'd encountered the beasts and only survived through the interference of Redstar disguised as Uriah and his dire wolf, Gryff.

Gryff wasn't around to help this time.

Another satyr arose, snickering. Then another. And another still. They soon surrounded Whitney and were closing in. One spoke, its voice sounding feminine, but distant and difficult to understand.

As they grew ever closer, their features began to form, and Whitney blanched.

"Sora?" he whispered.

Each of them looked the same, and each of them looked like

her. They were arm's length away, and he felt the heat of their breath. One opened its maw, and its Sora-like features began melting away and their faces morphed into thousands of little bugs. Some flitted around, snapping their tiny mouths at him. Instead of the expected buzzing sound, their collective wings mimicked Sora's voice, and it sounded pained.

Whitney felt something crawling on his leg and looked down. Spiders covered his feet and ankles. He tried to shake them off, but he couldn't move. His heart pounded, his clothing, soaked with sweat. He wanted to throw up but couldn't.

The flying insects swarmed, swirling around him. His vision was now completely obscured, shrouded in total darkness. From within the darkness, a giant spider emerged. As his eyes followed from the ground up, the legs and thorax faded into the body of a woman. She was completely naked.

Bliss, the spider queen and the One Who Remained.

He tried again to run, tried to do anything. He opened his mouth to scream, and it was immediately filled with hundreds of bugs. He felt them teeming on his tongue.

Bliss spoke, and his gaze met hers, but once again, instead of the face of Bliss Whitney had encountered in the Webbed Woods, Sora's stared back at him.

She charged him, and when he fell backward, his world went black again.

Someone screamed Sora's name, hysterical.

After a few shouts, Whitney realized it was him. His eyes protested but finally shot open, and he was staring into the glaring sun, surrounded by blue skies. He heard himself, his younger self, talking to him, but couldn't make out the words. Then he heard another voice. When he shifted his eyes, all he saw was a giant white blotch. He blinked, trying to focus.

"Why is he screaming my name?" the voice asked.

"I don't know. Say, Mr. Willis, why are you calling my friend's name?" Young Whitney asked. "How do you know her? Are you okay? Where's your friend?"

Big Whitney sat up. Finally, he could see clearly, and he was face to face with Sora, exactly how he'd remembered her looking as a kid. From her hair and her scrawny frame to her stunningly amber eyes.

"Why are you calling me?" Sora asked.

"I was dreaming," Big Whitney said.

"Ick." She looked repulsed. "About me?"

"I—I don't. No, I have a friend named Sora, too."

"You do?" Sora asked. There was something in her voice Young Whitney wouldn't have noticed, but Big Whitney did. Hope.

Whitney cleared his throat and stood. He stared at the little girl, the spitting image of Sora—because it was her. It was every bit her as the woman he'd left on a ship in the middle of Trader's Bay. Every bit her as the one who'd saved him from Redstar... twice.

"Mister? You know another Sora?" Young Whitney asked.

"Yes," Whitney said, clearing his throat again, and tussling her hair. "She's beautiful, just like you."

Little Sora blushed.

Young Whitney scowled. "Gross," he said.

"Be nice, Whitney," Sora said. "Didn't he take credit for that dumb stunt you pulled yesterday?"

"Yeah," Big Whitney said. "I've been waiting for a thank you."

"A lot of good it did..." he grumbled. "Come on." He grabbed Sora by the arm. "Let's go."

"It's almost supper time, won't your mother—"

"I need a break from their sad faces, and besides, that guy's too old for you."

"Stop it!" Sora punched Young Whitney in the arm before they ran off toward the creek, though not before he shot Big Whitney another dirty look. The sight of them together made Whitney's eyes well up.

"She used to punch me like that," Whitney whispered as they skipped away.

Whitney wiped sweat from his brow, still shaken up from the vision. Then he swatted a bug on his neck. He stuck his tongue out as he wiped its guts off on his pants.

He decided that his younger self was right; a break was in order. He made his way to the house, drawn by the scent of a fresh cherry pie. The back door was always open, and he let himself in.

"Mrs. Fierstown?" he called. It was weird calling her that, and he'd, more than a few times, almost called her 'ma' already.

"Where's your friend?" Rocco asked. The day after his injury, Whitney and Kazimir carried a bed down from upstairs and set it up in a downstairs room with a window that looked out over the farm. He'd barked all morning for Young Whitney to get to work before passing out in his bed, subdued by herbs brought over by Wetzel.

"Not sure. Probably off skulking in shadows," Whitney said.

"What's that supposed to mean?"

"I don't know," Whitney snapped.

The words hadn't any sooner left his lips than he'd regretted them. Memories of being badgered by his father returned, and he couldn't help himself. He braced, waiting for his father's wrath.

"Fine." Was all Rocco said, which pissed Whitney off more. If he'd lashed out like that when he was a child, he'd have a painful date with a belt.

"Fine?" he questioned. "That's it? Fine? If I'd have said that to you twenty years ago, you'd have threatened to tear my ass from my hind or some crazy thing that made no sense. Fine?"

"Twenty years ago? What is wrong with you, boy? The sun… the heat's getting to you. You'd better rest." Then he muttered under his breath, "Nobles."

"Are you yigging kidding me? Rest? Since when is anyone allowed to rest around this gods-damned farm?"

Whitney was now directly in front of Rocco and shouting in his face, spittle speckling his lips. The fact that the man was laying down and couldn't even get up completely escaped him.

"Enough."

Kazimir appeared out of what might as well have been thin air and stood between Whitney and Rocco.

Rocco's fists were clenched along with his jaw. "I thank you for this kindness, but get your friend some water and shade or you'll both be without a bed tonight, that understood?"

"Maybe we'll just—" Kazimir gripped Whitney by the arm and shoved him outside before he could finish.

"Yes, sir," Kazimir said. "It's just the sun, I'm sure."

Rocco gave Whitney one last glance, then closed his eyes, moaning. "I knew they couldn't be trusted with this," he grumbled.

Kazimir gave Whitney another push on his way out the door.

"Get off me," Whitney bristled.

"If you insist on acting like a child, I will treat you like one," Kazimir said.

"If you haven't noticed," Whitney said, voice still raised, "the child version of me is down there by the river. He'd leave now if he knew what's good for him. Take Sora with him."

"A roof. Fresh food any time. I would have killed to grow up in a place like this. I did kill."

Whitney stared for a moment, then huffed. "You don't get it. The bastard is impossible."

"Excuse me?"

"My father," he spat the word from his mouth like it was a bit of maggot-filled meat.

"You get him crippled, now complain about an attitude you instigated?"

"This isn't really..." Whitney drew a long breath. "He and I just shouldn't be in the same place for long."

"Well, this was your idea. 'Simple and easy,' you said."

"You don't understand," Whitney whispered, shaking his head.

"What, a Glassman who hates his father? You're as predictable as the day I caught you."

"Do you have any idea how predictable everything about you is? Just cos you're a bloodsucking demon doesn't mean you have to look like... like this." He flattened his palm and lifted and lowered it, gesturing like he was showing off a cow at market. "You're the spitting image of my childhood nightmares."

"A nap in the dirt wasn't enough? I should kill you where your stand."

"It wouldn't count," Whitney retorted.

"What?"

"That's right. This ***fool*** is starting to figure things out. You can't toss me away and leave me here, can you?" Whitney scoffed. "Your Sang-whatever Lords won't count it as dead and clear your blood pact. That's why you're following me around like a hen. Hoping we come out of this crazy place side-by-side."

"My desire was the orphan mystic. And neither you nor this foul place will keep me from her."

"Well, there she is!" Whitney smirked, gesturing back toward the river. "I may be many things, but I know how to sniff out a liar. I've learned from the best." He nodded in the direction of his younger doppelgänger. "You're scared to fail. No, wait… you think the sandwind Lor—"

"Sanguine ," Kazimir growled.

"Whatever. You think they're keeping you here as punishment because you went too far and still couldn't get the job done. Killing Tayvada, bloodletting Sora. They know you've been naughty."

Kazimir's features twisted with rage. Whitney placed his hands behind his back so a part of him could twitch with fear while the rest of him stood strong. He'd taken his gamble, and now he had to stick with it. He laughed.

"Ruthless Kazimir is superstitious!"

Kazimir's whole body tensed and Whitney prepared for another blow to the head. Instead, the upyr stalked away. "When I do get out of here and find your friend, thief, know that I'm going to drain her in the most painful ways imaginable."

"*If* you find her. Far as I can tell, we aren't leaving this place, and the Sora here doesn't know mystics from cow dung."

Kazimir didn't stop walking.

"Hey! Where the yig are you going?"

"I'm done arguing with a child," Kazimir answered without turning around or stopping. "I'm going to rest for the first time in longer than I can remember. You can handle this problem yourself."

"What is wrong with you?" Whitney asked, following him into the dark barn. "You're a gods-damned upyr, and you're acting like a trained house cat."

"When you've been here as many times as I have, you learn a thing or two. No one is saving you. Nothing you do will make anything better. Play by their rules, and you might get along easy. I'm not a cat, and I'm sure as this is Elsewhere not an upyr anymore. Not here, at least."

"Well, you might give up, but I won't. I'm going to get out of here. I've escaped the Glass Castle more times than I can count—and that was just in the past few months."

"One day and you nearly got yourself kicked out of here. Tell me, what do you think you'll be doing in Elsewhere if you can't handle farming. Hanging from the Eye of Iam to be picked out by ravens for all eternity. I see no other possibility for you. This isn't the Glass Castle. You're playing in the territory of angry gods now." Kazimir laid down on the hay and closed his eyes.

"Yeah well, these gods haven't met me. I killed a goddess, and I'll kill every one of them if I have to. I'm done playing. I won't waste any more of my life here." Whitney picked up a sickle, slammed the barn doors open, then started off toward the edge of the property.

"You're wasting your time," Kazimir said, having abandoned his hay to follow.

Whitney ignored him. He thought he could handle playing the helpful stranger, but it was clear that was a bad idea. He had them —bad ideas—from time to time, albeit very rarely. He crossed back through Troborough. As usual, nothing was going on. Whitney heard some of the townsfolk discussing the latest gossip, and almost all of them seemed to be talking about what happened to Rocco and the strange travelers kind enough to help him like that was the biggest thing that had happened in all of their lifetimes.

"I'll give you a game," Whitney grumbled. "Damn, lazy upyr tricking me into sitting around doing nothing." He swung the sickle in anger, and the townsfolk gathered outside the Twilight Manor stared at him.

"Just a mysterious traveler passing through!" he shouted.

Their heads turned with him. It made his skin crawl. Even the priest version of Torsten watched him though he had no eyes.

Whitney held his breath and picked up his pace.

"Ferryman!" he shouted as he walked down to where they'd

been dropped off in the river. Wetzel's shack sat far to the left of him, roof covered in moss and a broken water-wheel off to the side. The old codger fumbled with something out back, cursing to himself.

"Ferryman!" Whitney yelled again. He sloshed into the water and looked from side to side, as if the boat would appear, completely repaired.

"Yigging exile," he cursed. He looked back toward town and saw that a few of the townsfolk had gathered atop the hill, still watching him, whispering to one another. He snapped the sickle shaft over his knee and stormed up passed them, pants soaking wet.

He found the town stables to be empty, wondering why he'd ever thought there'd be a convenience like horses in Elsewhere. So, he marched down the main, western road on his own, doing his best to ignore all the prying eyes of anyone he passed.

"Not going to wait around in this dump," he grumbled. "I'll go where things happen."

He stopped at the edge of town, rolling hills before him. Eventually, the dirt road would intersect with the grand, stone-paved Glass Road which led straight to Yarrington. He turned back. Dozens of townsfolk were now congregated, Wetzel among them, and out-of-place Torsten, even Lauryn, staring at him like she had no idea who he was.

"Have a good eternity," he said, performing an exaggerated bow, then set off down the road. Just as a smile crossed his face, he slammed into something he couldn't see, and collapsed to the ground, his tailbone landing on a rock. Pain shot all the way up his spine and further. His nose hurt... his whole face hurt.

"What the..." He popped back up and crept forward with his hand flat. It pressed against an invisible boundary. He whipped back around, brow furrowed, and all the townsfolk began to break away.

"Drunken fool," one said.

"Poor, lost soul," said another.

Whitney patted the unseen surface separating him from the Glass Road, taunting him. He sensed a shadow creeping up on him.

"Wonderful," he said. "We're stuck here, aren't we?"

He turned, and Kazimir stood in the road. They'd spent the entire day bickering, but now Whitney saw an unfamiliar expression on the upyr's face. It seemed like pity.

"You're starting to get it," Kazimir said.

"There has to be a way out."

"Not for you." Kazimir walked by him and stretched his hand through the invisible wall. The world rippled around his fingers like water as it passed through.

"What the!" Whitney nudged him aside and slapped his palms against the same part, only for them to be blocked. "No, there has to be a way out."

"There isn't."

"You're a yigging liar!" Whitney kept going, skirted along the barrier and running his hand along it as if it were a wall. "There's a way out; there's always a way out." He kept going, running now, until he found himself back around on the other side of Wetzel's shack, shin-deep in the river.

"What kind of place is this!" Whitney shouted. He kicked at the water, then fell to his knees.

"I've been trying to tell you," Kazimir said. "I have all of Elsewhere I could be, but I'm staying here because this is your Elsewhere, and just as you are unable to leave, the wianu are forbidden to enter."

"So, you're scared?"

"The beast exists beyond life and death. Only it can destroy me, and I have too much left to do before I die."

"If it can kill you, doesn't that mean it can do the opposite. You know, send you back?"

"I do not know. We do not face them here by choice, where they're at their most powerful."

"But you can leave? You can go find one of the fallen gods or whatever and tell them we don't belong here."

"And they would care not. For you do belong here, and I belong nowhere."

"I don't. You were there, on that ship. We didn't die."

"But you're here, and only the dead inhabit this place. Mistake or not, your soul is in exile. Never to return."

"You said it yourself. You've been here before many times. Not just when you closed your eyes."

"It is the nature of becoming upyr. To become of both realms as the wianu is. Untethered. The newest of us always pass through this place, and encounter all its challenges as their minds come to grips with what they are. Knowing I was going to wake from this nightmare as the Sanguine Lords saw fit, I never cared."

Whitney looked up at him, tears in his eyes. "So now you've come to gloat?"

"No. Seeing a man grasp for purpose when there is none, even if it is you, brings me no pleasure. You're dead Whitney Fierstown. There is no going back. The Sanguine Lords punish me, but not because you failed to die, but because I wasn't the one who killed you."

Whitney's throat went dry. "So, you expect me to just… stay here?"

"It is all you can do. I hoped you would see on your own, but the people I've sent here aren't expecting miracles. They're dead, and they know it."

"Well, I'm not. There's a way out of everything, and if this really is all Sora's fault, she's up there figuring out how to reverse it."

Kazimir exhaled, then laid a hand on Whitney's shoulder. Whitney winced out of reflex.

"I've seen many strange things, but for men, Elsewhere is permanent," Kazimir said. "There is nothing your friend can do. Fight the truth if you must, but do yourself a favor and make things easier on yourself. Be the man you think it's impossible for you to be, because there is no worse torture, and that is all this foul place feeds on. One day, the Sanguine Lords will pardon my failure. I will wake up on the other side, and I won't be here to keep you from turning this nightmare into true exile. Until then, don't ruin my rest."

The upyr walked away, leaving Whitney to stare down into the water at his reflection. Dead him still looked like the him he knew, at least until the broken shaft of the sickle floated into his knee and disturbed the water. He grabbed it and considered ramming the pointy end through his own chest. His hands shook but eventually dropped it.

If Elsewhere was like this, he couldn't imagine where he'd wind up should he die a second time. He looked up and saw Wetzel hurrying Young Sora indoors. Apparently, she had returned from the Fierstown's, probably kicked out once Whitney's parents saw her. She looked at him before the door slammed behind her. Straight at him.

Ever since he'd gotten to Elsewhere, he'd had this eerie feeling like people were looking through him, but not her.

"He's wrong," Whitney told himself. He stood, clenching the shaft so hard his knuckles turned white. "Maybe I am dead, but I don't belong here."

An invisible wall may have trapped him in Troborough, but he'd been trapped in worse places. He'd find a way out, and if he couldn't, he still had Sora out there in Pantego, seeking out true magic from the mystics. She'd sent him here, the girl who'd grown up in that shack, and he had to hope she wouldn't stop until she found a way to undo it.

Even if it took years, he'd wait. He'd keep his mind. If Elsewhere wanted him to live out the nightmare of being a worthless farmer in a worthless town, he'd be the best damn farmer there ever was.

XIV

THE DESERTER

Rand's armor felt heavy as he made his way to the heart of Yarrington. Every suit of Shieldsman armor was reinforced with glaruium mined from within Mount Lister, the sturdiest and rarest ore Pantego offered. They were passed down from generations, re-fitted for each man by the castle's eldest blacksmith, Hovom Nitebrittle, who'd trained beneath dwarven artisans to become the only Glassman possessed of the skills to work the metal.

Now, Rand's had a loose fit. He hadn't realized how much muscle he'd lost since he fled his post. The vast, open fields he'd spent days and nights training and exercising in had been replaced by a room the size of a horse's pen and enough alcohol to drown the horse.

The training of a Shieldsman, however, was eternal. He'd learned that lesson well at the docks. He may have never wanted to kill again, but defending Sigrid was different. As Wren said, he would agonize in the bowels of Elsewhere if it meant creating a better world in which for her to live. He was already destined for that rotten place anyway. Until the Drav Cra were driven from the city, a Docksider like her would never be safe.

Yarrington Square was different from Rand's memory. Usually, when a harsh winter came, the merchants kept to the southern portions of the kingdom. But with the Drav Cra in town —they were an entirely new customer base. Maybe they didn't have autlas, but they were out in droves buying things that were of no use to nomads living in the far north. Formal clothing, pottery, furniture; items they'd never seen before, but they seemed eager to get a taste of Yarrington.

They traded their weapons and furs for all the southern trinkets and fineries, hauling it all back to leather tents just beyond the city walls, where their women, children, and elders lived while their army helped secure the kingdom.

There are so many. Have they all abandoned Drav Cra? Rand wondered.

It all seemed so incredibly innocent until Rand looked a little closer. For all the Drav Cra marveling at useless items, they were also sharing their clothing with Yarrington. Furs from bear and wolves—oversized coats, boots and gloves—all crafted by masters of keeping warm through the coldest winters, and in that way, they were winning over the locals. Even in the square, painted warlocks by the walls invited Glassmen into their circles for prayer, drawing bloody symbols on and around a slain goat, and surrounding it with candles and burning incense.

Idols to the Buried Goddess were worshiped without fear of reprisal.

"Yarrington is being invaded. Quietly, peacefully, the enemies of Iam flood these walls from the Drav Cra." Wren's words echoed in Rand's mind.

He could see why even young King Pi might see the beauty in this blending of cultures. But it all seemed incredibly calculated.

The Drav Cra never stayed put for long. They were raiders

and nomads, playing the part of wholesome guests until they decided to be raiders and nomads again. They were used to striking at small villages around Crowfall and even as far east as Hornsheim, yet here they were, welcomed into the walls of Yarrington. Perhaps the number of warriors present was few with others out fighting rebellion, but he'd already seen first-hand how little they thought of southern men and women. All the realm believed that the rebels were south in the Black Sands, but they were forgetting to look right underneath their noses.

"Repent!" shouted an old man on a podium where the Square met the Royal Avenue. He wore tattered, brown robes and had his head shaved with the eye of Iam painted large and sloppily across his forehead, indicating him a monk of a more fanatic sect of the Church of Iam known as the Order of the Holy Eye. They rejected the Kings of Glass as chosen and heeded only the direct word of their God.

"Brothers and sisters, you must repent!" he continued. "You welcome these heathens and destroyers with open arms. Those who would deny our holy Lord His glory!"

A crowd of Glassmen started to gather around him. Guards took notice and inched closer. As Rand instinctually did the same, he remembered that, as far as the world could see, he was one of them—higher ranking, in fact, than any of them.

"The boy seated upon the throne does not speak for us!" the man continued. Spittle flew from his mouth as he spoke with such vim it looked like he might burst a blood vessel. "Only Iam can. How many of these monsters slaughtered our kin in the North? They are children of the great deceiver. She who tricked the heathen gods in the feud over Pantego. She who lies buried beneath that very mountain!" He stuck a finger out toward the flattened summit of Mount Lister presiding over the city.

"Bah! You'd all be roasting on Shesaitju spits if not for us," said a Drav Cra warrior who'd remained behind with his people as he passed.

"Even now, they mock us!" the monk said. A few grumbles of agreement broke out. "These corrupt men. These depraved men. Heathens!" The monk turned his wrinkled finger in the direction of the warrior who'd spoken. In that moment, the surface of peace melted away as a dozen angry eyes fell upon the warrior.

"We must not stand idly by while they ravage the realm of Iam. Brothers, we must take up the sword and drench His holy realm with their heathen blood. We must bury them with their goddess, or they will do the same to us!"

More cheers rang out, this time with more vigor. The crowd, stirred like a nest of angry hornets, turned upon the nearest Drav Cra warrior. The guards battled against the masses to reach the rabble-rousing monk.

"How many of your kin have died in their raids!" the monk shouted.

"My brother died in Crowfall thanks to them," a man in the crowd called out.

"How many of your children have been sacrificed to the wicked cults who worship the false goddess with them? They are the very spawn of Elsewhere! It is time we tear the imposter, Redstar, from his seat in the castle and burn him in the fires. We will ensure he'll never see the Gate of Light nor his blasphemous Skorravik."

"Aye, why don't you savages go back to your tundra!" another voice cried out to the Drav Cra warrior who'd spoken up.

The warrior didn't leave. In true Drav Cra fashion, he turned to face his accusers and drew his battle-axe. "Which one of you wants to die first, then?"

Rand took a few steps closer. In the faces of the incensed crowd, he could see the truth of the situation. The tension boiling over would eventually lead to Yarrington's ruin. If the entire Drav

Cra horde was near the city, even a small squabble like this could ignite the flames of open war. Perhaps that was what Redstar wanted. He'd already done enough horrible things to weasel his way into power, and Rand likely didn't know the half of it.

"That's what I thought," the warrior spat. "A bunch of southern flowers."

"Heathen scum!"

A man burst through the crowd and charged the Drav Cra warrior. The swing of his battle-axe sent the Glassman back onto his rump. But the Glassman wasn't alone. All it took was one to show bravery, and now a good portion of the crowd stalked toward the warrior.

"Kill the savage!" a local screamed, waving his hand to coax the mob forward, but his body froze mid-stride. His eyes darted side to side, the only part of him able to move.

"Nesilia is the one true!" Three men, garbed in crimson robes, wearing emotionless white masks appeared behind the warrior. Each had one hand raised, fresh blood trickling from their palms, and gripping a knife in the other. They weren't Drav Cra warlocks, but members of the Cult of the Buried Goddess. They were a group Rand had dealt with even in his short time as a Shieldsman. Usually relegated to abandoned basements or caverns beyond the city, now, they found themselves emboldened by unexpected allies.

"Donning masks doesn't make you one of us!" The warrior whipped around and slashed even at his saviors. They retreated just as more guards arrived to hold back the swelling mob.

The Glassman attacker let out a breath as he collapsed to the dirt only to be trampled by his own people with sights on both the cultists and warrior.

"See how they turn us all against each other!" the monk yelled. "Tricksters and demons in human form!"

The chaos allowed Rand to shove his way through the edges

of the crowd and seize the monk. There was truth to what the man was saying, but men like him had a knack for starting fires.

"You want to get everybody killed?" Rand questioned as he dragged the monk west along Royal Avenue toward the Glass Castle. The glass spire presided proudly over the city, shining even with the sun veiled by snow and clouds.

"I speak only the truth," he answered.

"Well, you can enlighten everyone in the dungeons."

"Don't you see?" he cried, manic. "You have been deceived!"

"Would you shut it? I'm on your side."

With his armor on, no one questioned Rand as he entered the Old Yarrington. He kept his head down so he wouldn't be recognized, but he had no idea where his post should be. He wasn't even sure he was supposed to be in Yarrington and not out in the field subduing the rebel Black Sandsmen. At least with a rabble-rousing fanatic from the Order of the Holy Eye in tow, he'd be subject to fewer inquiries unless he ran into the Shieldsmen's Taskmaster, Lars Kesselman.

They reached the bend in the road where it ran parallel to the castle's outer walls. The sight of them stopped Rand in his tracks. The walls were bare now, the wind howling along their flat faces, but he could still picture the bodies, ropes tied around their necks, creaking together as if part of a symphony.

Rand squeezed his eyes shut. "Focus," he whispered to himself, hands trembling and head aching.

"You are troubled, brother," the monk said. "We of the Holy Eye can help you."

"Quiet," he grumbled. He opened his eyes, and the bodies were gone.

Soon I'll be free of them, he told himself. Soon all will be made right.

They reached the gates, where a few Glass soldiers stood guard. He expected them to question him, but instead, they parted for him to pass. Redstar may have set up camp in the castle, but Rand's order still held sway among the commoners.

"Sir, allow me?" one of the guards said, motioning to the monk.

"Excuse me?" Rand said, surprised.

"Is he a prisoner? I'll take him to the dungeons."

Rand swore under his breath. He'd hoped to use the monk as a means to traverse the castle with a ready excuse. "I've got him," he said.

"Sir, I insist. You shouldn't have to sully your armor in that pit. Please, let me do my job?"

It was a sincere request from a good soldier. Rand sensed a future Shieldsman in that armor. "What's your name?" he asked.

"Garihad, sir. Garihad Yulniz."

"Yulniz, eh?" Rand said.

"Yes, sir. I believe you must know my father."

"I've heard of him." Phillip Yulniz was a revered and retired member of the Shield and had served as Taskmaster under King Liam and Uriah Davies years back.

Rand sighed and handed the monk over. "He's a rabble-rouser from down in the Square," he said. "Do what you do, soldier."

The soldier pounded on his chestplate in salute, pride on his face, then grabbed the monk and headed around the back of the castle. Rand considered giving the monk a message for Torsten before he was gone but decided against it. After Redstar was removed from the equation, Torsten would be free. Plus, according to Wren, Torsten occupied the lowest, most secure sanctum of the castle dungeons. It was nowhere a mere fanatical preacher would be held.

Rand slowly crossed the bailey. A legion of young Shieldsmen trained on one side. Sir Nikserof Pasic sat overlooking them, chatting with Hovom, the castle blacksmith, and another Shieldsman Rand recognized as Sir Austun Mulliner. Nikserof behaved like a commander, but Rand had only known of two King's Shieldsmen able to act in such a way in Yarrington. There were captains in every city throughout the kingdom, but here, Torsten was the commander, and if he wasn't around, Sir Wardric Jolly had always been his second, just as he was for Torsten's predecessor.

Neither was present now.

Sir Nikserof wasn't green at least. Rand remembered a few lessons he'd received from him in swordsmanship. He was an expert at that subject, but still, he was no Torsten Unger.

Rand drew a deep breath when he realized he was standing still again. Being back at the castle brought all the horrid memories to the forefront of his mind. He turned his head away from the Shieldsman and continued toward the castle gates. Even with his now-shaggy hair and beard, he might be recognized. His days as Wearer, although few, were memorable.

He turned, facing the other end of the bailey where a group of Drav Cra warriors practiced throwing their axes at dummies. Their chief strode through their ranks, barking at them in their harsh language. He had a beard that looked like it'd never been cut, with a bald portion along the right side of his jaw where a series of deep scars lay. The white paint covering the right half his face only seemed to accentuate them, like he was proud of how near he'd come to death.

It was as strange a sight as Rand had ever seen. Painted, fur-clad Drav Cra warriors before the backdrop of the Glass Castle. And while tension remained between the commoners in the Square, these groups of soldiers paid no attention to each other, whether good or bad. Whatever had happened in Winde Port left them fused by battle.

Savages, literally at the gates, trusted enough that nobody was keeping so much as a wary eye on them. So much had changed it made Rand's head throb. He tried to gather himself, leaning against the statue of King Fentomir flanking the Great Hall entry.

He looked up and saw the visage of the Fentomir, then let his eye wander down the line until it rested on King Liam's statue. After a moment, his gaze drifted to the slab of rock that would eventually be carved into the likeness of King Pi. Rand couldn't help but wonder what kind of legacy the young boy would leave.

In his mind, the image shifted into the birthmarked face of the chieftain Redstar. He shuddered at the thought of the Glass Kingdom falling into Drav Cra hands.

He was pulled from his reverie when, out of the corner of his eye, he noticed the outer wall's gate crank where he and his soldiers had forced Tessa to her death. He could remember that look on her face like he was there. Betrayal, sorrow; a mixture of all the awful things a person could feel.

"I shouldn't have come here," he whispered.

He knew he was drawing attention to himself, muttering under his breath and shaking his head like a madman, but he couldn't help it. Her shrieks hammered around in his skull. Calling out his name, just like how Sigrid had when the savages got their hands on her.

Am I really any better?

"You," someone addressed him.

He turned and saw the source of all his pain. Oleander Nothhelm, wife of Liam the Conqueror and the mother of the Miracle King, approached him. Her dress was long and lovely, the same deep blue color of her lips and nails. The last Rand saw her, she was frazzled and broken, yet now she was the picture of royalty. Even after everything she'd done.

"Are you dull?" she asked, snapping her fingers in front of his face. "Shieldsman, I'm talking to you."

"Y-y-your Grace," Rand managed to squeeze through lips, paralyzed by an onslaught of emotion. His hand fell to the pommel of his longsword before he could think about it.

She leaned down and stared into his eyes. She was going to

recognize him, blow the whole thing. She was going to recognize him, and he'd have no choice but to kill her, no matter how much he fought the desire.

"Will you just stare at me?" she asked. "I swear, ever since Torsten went away, the quality of your order is..." She grabbed Rand's jaw. "Would you look at your Queen." She emphasized each word like she was scolding a child.

The front of Rand's head pulsed with pain as he forced his blank stare to meet Oleander's. He didn't want to look at her. He never wanted to look at her again. His fingers slowly wrapped the handle of his sword. All he had to do was draw it, and the source of all his pain would be wiped from the face of Pantego.

"That's better," she said, then released him. "Since the kingdom is left without a Wearer, I need you to go fetch my impetuous brother."

Rand swallowed. She was literally inviting him to the room of his target. All so easy. All he had to do was hold steady, and he could fix everything. "What..." His voice cracked, and he cleared his throat. He felt like he was holding his breath deep underwater. "What shall I tell him?"

"Tell him his king needs him. And Shieldsman, your duty is to do what I ask and nothing more." She groaned and stormed away, her heels clacking along the courtyard's marble perimeter. "These Shieldsmen are going to be the death of me," she muttered before disappearing into the castle.

Looking down, Rand released a mouthful of air and realized his sword was halfway out of its sheath.

Shieldsman.

Everything she'd put him through, and she had no idea who he even was. He could see it written all over her face like she was talking to any inferior whose name she'd never bothered to learn. She'd rarely gotten his name correct even when he stood guard as Wearer directly outside her chambers.

"By Iam I need a drink." He shook out his hands, then headed across the courtyard toward the West Tower, keeping his head low. If she didn't recognize him, he doubted anyone else would, but he still had to be safe.

Three guards walked by chatting. "I hear Sir Unger let the rebel afhem escape down at Winde Port," one said. "Probably helped Yuri Darkings free the Caleef too."

"No, Sir Nikserof was there," said another. "Said he fought like a madman to get them out alive, then just snapped and lost it, blood-crazed."

"I heard he drove his blade straight through Xander's heart back in Winde Port, he did," said the third.

"Yeah? I heard worse, that it was he who slew Sir Wardric Jolly outside Winde Port, not that Darkings traitor."

A wave of sadness passed over Rand. He'd served under the old Shieldsman Wardric who'd been around in the order forever and refused to wear the White after Uriah Davies died. There was no finer Shieldsman, and now, while Rand drank himself to oblivion, Wardric had been killed at the hands of traitors. Rand understood very few rumors in his drunken spell, but the news of Yuri Darkings, the former Master of Coin, conspiring to free Caleef Rakun of the Shesaitju from King Pi's grasp was information he retained.

"Don't be ridiculous," the first guard said.

"Fine... was a Black Sand's wench at the Vineyard who told me, I'll admit."

The other two laughed.

"All that time sharing the mad Queen's bed, I'd lose it too—" his comrade nudged him as they noticed Rand passing. They nodded in acknowledgment.

Sharing her bed? Freeing Rebels? Killing Sir Wardric? Rand couldn't believe how busy Redstar had been sullying Torsten's good name. One would think the vile heathen would honor a debt of gratitude to Torsten for allowing him to return alive from the Webbed Woods. Now, instead of answering for his crimes against the Prince, Redstar now served directly under young Pi as prime minister, a position which had gone unoccupied for many kings passed.

Rand glanced back one last time at the slab of stone that would be King Pi's statue. He circled his eyes and ducked into the East Tower. As he turned back, he collided with something and heard a clattering on the floor. A younger gentleman stumbled, and Rand reached out to keep him from falling too.

"My apologies," Rand said.

"Yes, yes, yes," said the young man.

Rand recognized him, thought him an assistant to the Master of Rolls before realizing he had a young page following behind him. Then he remembered that he'd been there when the former holder of the title, Frederick Holgrass, was hanged at the request of the Queen—that he'd fulfilled her request.

Focus, Rand, he told himself as his hands balled into fists.

Liars, monsters, and strangers abounded in the castle where he once happily served. It could all be traced back to Redstar. From Uriah Davies vanishing, to the cursed Prince nearly dying and driving Oleander to do unspeakable things.

He had to trust Wren the Holy. He had to trust Torsten.

He rushed by the new Master of Rolls without bothering to help with the mess. It earned him a glare, but there was no time to dawdle. If he were discovered, everything would be for naught. He'd be hanged for abandoning his post, or worse, thrown into a dungeon to live forever with what he'd done.

He scaled the stairs of the West Tower two at a time. Wren said Redstar was in the Wearer's chambers—Torsten's chambers —and Rand knew well where they were. Another noble or council member Rand didn't recognize passed by as if Oleander had driven away every familiar face in the castle.

He reached the long hall at the second highest level of the castle, where councilmen and other dignitaries kept their quarters. The Wearer of White's room was first down the line as if he were meant to protect all the rest. The shield of the kingdom's noblest nobles.

A Drav Cra warlock stood outside, wearing a ratty cloak and discolored furs. A necklace of bones and totems fell to her narrow waist. Her expressionless face aimed forward, with eyes staring off into nothingness as if her soul was already in Elsewhere. She may have been pretty once, before she let her hair go wild and covered her face with paint like a demon, white beneath her nose and solid black above.

Rand grew up like any other proper Glassmen, attending services at the changing of the moons in the name of Iam, receiving His light at the weekly congregation his end of Dockside, honoring the Dawning. Other than being forced to shirk the lazy accent of his upbringing, he'd never been good at learning; otherwise, he might have gone on to study the holy scripture. But he was always good at fighting, at defending his sister even though she rarely needed it. The King's Shield—sworn protectors of the Iam's chosen kingdom—seemed the only possible choice.

To see a faithful servant of the Buried Goddess guarding the very chambers reserved for Rand's leader... suddenly it put everything into perspective. He knew what he had to do. He knew why he had to do it. But only now was he entirely sure he was going to.

The corridor was empty except for the warlock.

"I must speak with Redstar, by request of the Queen Mother," Rand said.

The woman didn't bother to face him. "Arch Warlock, Drad Redstar is busy and must not be disturbed. Tell her she can wait."

"She said it's in regards to King Pi. It seemed urgent."

"There is only one being who requires urgency."

"Please…" Rand begged, letting his shoulders sag. "Do you know what the Queen Mother will do to me if I return to her alone?"

"His convention with the goddess will conclude in due time. You are free to wait, but hers is the only scorn you should fear, knight."

"Okay, I'll, uh… I'll wait right here."

He went to step by the warlock, keeping his defeated tone and posture. The warlock's eyes stayed unfocused. Rand took two steps, then whipped around and swung. His glaruium-hard gauntlet crashed into the warlock's jaw, and she went down in an instant. He'd never been one to hit a woman, but chivalry died for her when she chose to be a warlock.

Rand waited for her to spring up, but she remained still.

"So much for your goddess' powers," he whispered. He approached the door cautiously. It was unlocked. The knob turned with a barely audible click, and he slowly pushed it in. First, he saw the familiar relics of Shieldsmen past lining the walls. Then, sitting with his legs folded in the center of the room, was Redstar.

He was completely naked, palms raised to the ceiling, and covered in thick blood. His infamous birthmark stretched down the side of his neck and over his shoulder. Rand never realized it was so extensive. Every inch of his back was scarred—sword marks, frost burn, and even animal bites. All the windows were covered in sackcloth, the wavering light of dozens of candles surrounding, illuminating him.

Redstar muttered under his breath in a strange language, his fingers twitching. Arrayed on the floor before him was a series of stone shards fitted together like a puzzle to create a mural of imagery reminiscent of the stained glass designs of the God Feud found in Yarrington Cathedral. He recognized Mount Lister in the center and the Eye of Iam above it, but much of the rest was unclear including strange, florid inscriptions which wrapped its border in a foreign language.

Rand slowly unsheathed his longsword and approached him. He drew steady breaths, kept his footsteps light, and forced his mind clear. It took all his King's Shield training to do the latter, but he managed. At the same time, he battled his training—battled his instincts of knowing that stabbing an unarmed, unarmored man in the back wasn't the way of a Shieldsman. But he was a Shieldsman only in appearance, and even then, barely. He'd failed a long time ago. At least this failure might right all his wrongs. He knew such an act would likely keep him from entering the Gate of Light and earn him a place in Elsewhere, but he didn't care. As he prepared to strike, he hoped that maybe, perhaps, he was performing the work of Iam.

Remember me well, Sig, he thought to himself.

One last step and he thrust his sword toward the base of Redstar's skull. The tip stopped just short as if a shield had blocked it, but there was only air.

Rand glanced up from the blade and saw one of Redstar's bloody hands closed into a fist, blood squeezing out from the creases.

"I wondered how long it would take you to get out, Torsten," Redstar said, flippantly.

He stood and strolled to his bed. The muscles in Rand's arms tensed as he struggled, but his arm was frozen along with the rest of him.

He tried to speak, but even his mouth was forced shut by the magic.

"Ah, not Torsten. You two share the same aura." He chuckled as he put on his robe. He released his fist and said, "Speak."

"What devilry is this!" Rand questioned.

Redstar turned. He had a grin smeared across his face. "The same aura, indeed. He sent you, didn't he?"

Rand said nothing; he merely grimaced as he continued his futile attempts to move.

"Your eyes betray you, knight," Redstar said. He picked up a dagger from atop the stone mural. The handle was carved from bone and the blade curved. The same foreign language found on the mural was etched into the hilt. The edge was still wet with the blood from his sliced hands.

"And your heart betrays you, heathen," Rand snapped. "You will not make it out of this room alive."

"Another insufferable zealot? I swear, I thought only your former master was cut from so rigid a cloth."

Sweat glistened on Redstar's forehead, and streaks, commingled with blood, drew lines on his crimson birthmark. Redstar kept his voice firm, but Rand could see the dark rings hanging beneath his eyes like bloated coin purses. Whatever dark ceremony he had just been involved in clearly had him drained.

"Wait," Redstar said. "I recognize you." He squinted as he scrutinized Rand's face, then began to cackle. "You're the Wearer who replaced Torsten, aren't you? The coward who tucked tailed and ran from my lovely sister? Just like everyone else."

"Release me from whatever this is, and I'll show you cowardice," Rand growled.

Redstar leaned in close. His grin vanished and his features darkened. "You? A deserter and a drunk? I can smell the ale in your sweat. It reeks of weakness. Are you the best Torsten could find to come for me? I suppose after his little performance at Winde Port, the Shield is even less loyal to him than I expected. I thought perhaps that Pasic fellow, Nikserof, but you? I'm insulted."

"You—"

"Don't speak!" Redstar raised his other hand and pressed his fingers together. Rand's lips sealed again, and this time he couldn't even groan. Redstar then glanced back at the stone mural and the circle of candles around it. "Is this another test, my goddess? I have done everything you ask. Why do you not return to your realm in full?"

Rand remained frozen but noticed that Redstar had to take a breath before the last sentence. He was straining, winded. All the signs were showing of a man in a sparring duel ready to be overtaken, down to the way he held his slumped shoulders.

So Rand pushed with all his might to move his sword. It stung with unimaginable ferocity, but he didn't back down. He wanted to scream at the top of his voice, but his lips were sealed. He pictured Sigrid with a knife to her throat from one of Redstar's savage followers. He pictured Tessa's rotting corpse swinging in the wind at the command of the sister Redstar drove to madness. And then, he remembered himself, vision going black as the sheet tightened around his throat. Ready to give up until Iam's highest servant arrived to give him one final task, to give him purpose.

His lips suddenly parted, and he released a scream that shook the heavens. His sword hand twitched, and while he wasn't in complete control, he was able to swipe upward. The blade, forged by Hovom, the castle smith, cleaved Redstar's hand from his wrist. The Arch Warlock stumbled backward, gawking down at the stump on the end of his arm as blood gushed.

"The madness ends today!" Rand declared. Suddenly, he was free of the dark magic. He charged forward and swung at Redstar, who ducked and spun around. Redstar's gaze fell to his dagger, still gripped by the cloven hand.

Rand came at him again. The tip of his blade sliced Redstar's robe as he evaded another blow. He was quick as the dire wolves of his homeland, but Rand didn't stop. He measured his attacks, desperate to finish him.

"Enough!" Redstar finally roared.

Rand's blade stopped inches from the warlock's heart, then flew from his grip as he soared backward. He slammed into the stone wall so hard it cracked, arms and legs spread. Redstar remained on the other end of the room, panting like a wild beast. Two streams of blood trickled down from his nostrils, and his pupils filled the entire iris of his eyes.

He used his stump of a wrist to hold up his other arm and thrust them both forward. Rand felt as if the magic intensified by a hundred times as it crushed him against the wall.

"You think you have weakened me?" he growled. "The more of my blood that falls to the earth, the stronger my connection to her power!" His fingertips remained inward, and Rand's glaruium armor started to tighten around his body, constricting his throat, bending his ribs. Rand could do nothing but gurgle.

"Do you feel that?" Redstar said. "You fools have spent centuries mining the stone imbued with Nesilia's power after Bliss struck her down and Iam was too weak to save her. Coating yourselves in a shell of her protection. None of you were bright enough to even question why the stuff was so strong." He clenched his fingers more, and the armor squeezed so tight Rand couldn't breathe. "Others are difficult to control but you, Shields-man, it's like you're wearing strings."

Darkness nipped at Rand's vision. He felt like he was back in his shoddy room above The Maiden's Mugs, swinging from the rafters with a noose around his neck. *Failing Sigrid. Failing himself. Failing everybody.*

"You thought that you could destroy me, her Hand?" Redstar said. "You pathetic, little fool. I will wear your bones."

"You will not lay a finger on another of Iam's children," someone said from the doorway.

The pressure exerted by Redstar's magic let up. Rand was still pressed against the wall, but as his armor expanded back to its proper form, he found himself able to breathe again. He and Redstar both looked to the entrance, and Rand was greeted by a familiar sight to eyes blurred by strangulation. Wren the Holy shuffled in with his cane. His scarred face where his eyes had once been scrunched up, leaving crow's feet as if he were in pain.

"I suggest you leave, old man," Redstar said. "We wouldn't want you breaking anything."

"Wren… go," Rand rasped.

"I will leave when you let the boy go." He walked in further and positioned himself between Rand and Redstar. "Not before."

"You would protect a murderer willing to stab an unarmed man in the back?" Redstar asked. "Though I suppose that was the way of your God's champion, Liam. Win, no matter how many orphans are left behind."

"Enough posturing!" Wren said, projecting his voice with a timbre no man his age should bear. "Your pettiness and lust for revenge are going to bring this kingdom to ruin."

"Then I will sleep in its ashes." Redstar raised his hand high again, and Rand was compressed from every direction.

"This man came at my request. If you must have blood, take mine, but you will let him go."

"No, Your Holiness," Rand grated. "You still have a part to play."

"Release him!" Wren slammed his cane down in front of him with both hands. The floor cracked like he had the strength of a giant and the crystalline Eye of Iam carved upon the handle began to glow. The blinding light folded in front of them as if it were a shield. Redstar's hold completely vanished, and Rand collapsed to the floor, gasping for air.

"Yours isn't the only deity with tricks up her sleeve," Wren said. Redstar's bloody limbs remained outstretched, the air between them rippling from magical energy. Wren's shield blocked it all and seemed even to push Redstar back. The sheets whipped off the bed and the many relics around the room clattered to the stone floor, several shattering. The rest of the warlock's face went red to match his birthmark as he drew on Elsewhere to break through.

Even once air filled his lungs, Rand remained frozen on the floor, shocked. People often spoke of Wren and other priests performing feats of healing that could be described as no less than magic, but he'd never seen any of them do anything like this. Wren turned back to face him. Heavy beads of sweat ran down the High Priest's forehead, and Rand wondered if the man could somehow see even without his eyes.

"You must run, Rand Langley of Yarrington," Wren said.

Rand stared at the spot where the man's eyes should have been.

"I won't leave you." Rand reached down, grasping his fallen longsword, and went to charge, but Wren stuck one of his arms out to impede him. The cane shook in his other hand, the preternatural light beginning to flicker.

"I cannot retain him much longer." Now he sounded every bit as old and brittle as he appeared. "He's stronger now than either of us ever imagined."

"He'll kill you."

"He'll kill us all," Wren said. "Torsten put his faith in you and so did Iam. Prove it was not misplaced."

"I… I don't know what to do," Rand said, voice quavering.

Wren's lips creased into a smile. "I never have. Now go. Perhaps Torsten was wrong in thinking this great act could be completed alone."

Rand's gaze darted between them. Redstar slowly battled the energy expelled from Wren's light shield and approached the cane. He wore the expression of a wolf crouched above its prey, ravenous and ready to pounce—barely even human.

"You've gone too far now, holy man!" Redstar shouted, crowing like a madman. "My Lady and I will break you!"

Darkness now filled even the whites of the Arch Warlock's eyes. Wren's legs and arms quaked.

"I won't fail you," Rand said. "I'll find another way." He bolted for the door. He stepped over the unconscious body of the female warlock, then heard shouting. He glanced the other way and saw a host of Glass soldiers bearing down on him. That was when he realized he was leaving the private chambers of the royal uncle with a bloodstained sword and armor, standing over a body.

They were coming from further down the corridor, so he took off toward the stairs that would lead back to the bailey. As he skidded around the corner, a Shieldsman was ascending. The knight went for his sword, but Rand leaped over him, slamming into the wall at the next landing. A blade hummed toward his head, but he ducked under it before continuing down the stairs.

Horns sounded throughout the castle, vibrating in the stone. Some were familiar, belonging to the Shieldsmen. Others had a wild sound to them, and he recalled the terror of Drav Cra longboats lining the docks in South Corner.

Rand knocked a candelabra down behind him to slow the Shieldsman at his back, then hurried for the Great Hall. He slowed his pace when he reached it, remembering what he was wearing. He sheathed his sword where the blood was most apparent and kept his head down as chaos broke out all around him.

He had no idea what to do. Wren placed his faith in him again, even after his latest failure, and he'd gotten himself surrounded. He considered making a run for the dungeons to free Torsten, but he'd never make it down now that the castle was swarming—the whole city likely too. An assassination attempt on a member of the royal family, no matter how awful he was, couldn't go unanswered.

Dockside was the only place in Yarrington he knew he could hide out and regroup. The poor folk there never talked, proven by how he'd remained there even after deserting the shield. Torsten had found him, but he imagined that more a result of the man's prowess than anyone ratting.

Rand veered toward the front gates and picked up his pace. Shieldsmen and Drav Cra flowed in from the bailey in a steady stream, none seeming to notice them. Rand was nearly through the gates when the Shieldsman from the stairs hollered, "Seize him!"

Rand glanced back and dozens of eyes fell upon him. He didn't wait around. He sprinted through the great doors into the bailey. Horses were tied up along the wall, and he sliced the rope on one before mounting it. A soldier was already at the castle gates, cranking them closed.

Rand spurred the horse onward, kicking at its side, driving it to pound its hooves into the dirt. Once the gate sealed, he'd be doomed. Barking sounded as dire wolves raced out from the bailey's stables and gave chase. Rand's horse squeezed through the closing gates just in time, barreling through a few guards. The wolves scratched at the wood and howled. Arrows clacked against the snow-covered street behind him from archers on the wall.

He yanked on the reins and sent the horse toward the busy marketplace. A quick glance over his shoulder revealed a few glass soldiers on horseback. He kicked his horse's haunches again, but they were going downhill, and the streets were slick with frost. The horse's front hooves slid apart, and it dipped, launching Rand forward.

He slammed into the street, and he skidded into a mob, knocking the legs out of many before rolling to his feet. Things had heated up since he left the Square, and guards were busy keeping the tensions between the populace at bay. The din of cursing citizens drowned out the horns from the castle.

Rand took one quick look up at the men chasing him, then shoved his way through the mob. By the time he was through, he'd lost them and was safely into the back alleys leading down to South Corner and Dockside.

Wren the Holy had called upon Iam to give Rand a second chance at making things right in Yarrington. The next time he'd be ready, he just had to figure out his next move. One thing was clear after witnessing Redstar's power firsthand—he couldn't do it alone.

XV

THE MYSTIC

The moment the darkness around Sora faded, she found herself standing within the circular chamber where Lord Bokeo brought her to meet the Ancient One and who Sora surmised were what remained of the mystics Liam conquered. She slapped her hands against something soft and supple out of reflex. Lord Bokeo took the hits like he deserved them.

"It is fine, my dear," he said, grabbing her arms to stop her. "Tell me, what did you see?"

Sora spun a quick circle, desperate to find Nesilia. At that very moment, she needed more than anything to see her again.

"Nesilia!" she cried out, but no answer came.

Lord Bokeo pulled her close, eyes wide like saucers. "You saw the Goddess of Earth? Where?"

"I was there," Sora said, eyes still darting around the room as if she'd suddenly appear again. "I was in Elsewhere."

"Elsewhere.... You were in Elsewhere?" he said, urgency saturating his words. "What did you see?"

"I told you." She pulled herself free. "I must go back. I have to go back. Send me back!"

"Sora, please. Stop," he said. "The Ancient One, Aihara Na, would not have sent you to Elsewhere."

"There's no mistaking that feeling, Lord Bokeo. I was there. I heard my friend who is stuck there. I saw Nesilia. It was all so real. I... I know what communing with Elsewhere feels like and I was there."

The emptiness she'd been feeling in Whitney's absence was now magnified by her being with him, even fleetingly in the ethereal realm, and the hole left in the wake of Nesilia. Her presence was intoxicating. Sora had never wanted to be closer to anyone ever, and that brought a sense of guilt. Whitney was trapped in a nightmare with the monster Kazimir, and she let herself be distracted from that awful fact in the presence of Nesilia.

Sora surveyed the room and the now-empty thrones. "Where are... they?"

"You were unconscious for some time. They gave me the honor of waiting for your return."

"Aquira," Sora said, suddenly and turned quickly, looking for any signs of the wyvern.

Lord Bokeo squeezed her shoulder and tried to get her to focus on him. "Breathe, Sora. Do not worry. Aquira is well known to the Council. They are... catching up."

Sora shook him off. "Would you just tell me what's going on? Why did she send me there? Why?"

"The Ancient One sent you nowhere. She merely shows you the truest parts of your soul."

Whitney, Sora thought.

"She gives you insight into what was and what is to come," he continued. "If you saw the goddess... please, try to have peace. I know this is all very confusing and hard to grasp, but the Ancients

—they've been expecting you for many years, well before Aquira told them your time had come."

"But I came here. I chose to be here. I..." Sora finally drew a few deep breaths to calm herself. Enough to look the man in the eyes. "How did they know? I don't understand anything she told me."

"It has been heard on the wind and in the waters. The call of nature beckons forth the heart of the gods."

More riddles. If this is what was left of the once mighty Mystic Order Sora had read about, able to move earth and summon storms, they now reminded her more of Redstar. Always talking in circles. But what Lord Bokeo said reminded Sora of something that happened in her vision of Elsewhere.

"While I was in Elsewhere—"

"You were not there," Lord Bokeo interrupted. "You must trust me on this."

"Wherever it was then. I heard something—or rather, I said something. It doesn't make sense to me but, maybe you could?"

"Tell me," Lord Bokeo said.

"Tsu shensughu ywen zhun tahuet feng yaris tsu weyong ywen hou."

"How do you—"

"When I was in Else—there, it was like... I don't know how to explain it, but I can understand your language. *Yi zhu naji mei tong.* I guess... I can speak it now too."

A smile spread wide across Lord Bokeo's face. "They were right."

"Who was right?" Sora asked.

"The spirit of the gods," Lord Bokeo, whispered to himself as he took her by the arm and pulled her down the stone steps, "is found in the one with the will of fire."

"I know how it translates but what does it mean?"

In response, he took her by the arm and said, "Come. It means time is shorter than I'd thought."

Lord Bokeo led her back out to the bookstore. It was still light outside, but the sun was well along its descent. Sora pulled back on him at the door to stop them. He'd been in such a rush it caused him to stumble and knock over a few worn books.

"Lord Bokeo, I'm not going a step further until you give me some answers!" she demanded.

He promptly released her and tended to the fallen books. She thought she could hear him whispering to them under his breath. When he finished, he glanced up.

"Please, indulge me just a moment longer," he said. "I promise the answers will become clear to you. We aren't going far."

She bit her lip, looked back at the dark staircase they'd emerged from, then conceded. *I've come this far already…*

Lord Bokeo led her outside and rushed through the streets, forcing her to keep up. They dodged Glass soldiers along the way who were finishing clearing Xiahou Boulevard.

"What is all this?" Sora asked, referring to the barricades stanchioning off the road, fearing it truly was Winde Port all over again.

"Tonight begins a weeklong celebration called, *Gyuan Jie—*"

"Festival of Ghosts," Sora translated without a second thought.

"Yes, indeed. It is an ancient celebration of our people—those who have passed on to be with the gods."

"And the Glassmen allow this?" she asked, thinking about the defaced statues which now all resembled King Liam.

"King Liam didn't, but when he left Panping in the hands of Lord Phillipi Nantby, the Governor welcomed it. They enjoy it as much as we, and it leads into the Dawning, providing extra time for leisure. With as much drinking and carousing as goes on—they care not what reason we give them for partaking."

As they continued, Sora saw a building that stood out, wrapped by a porch on all four sides. Upon its gates sat two stone monkeys. Their hands were broken off at the wrists and patched in between them, as if an afterthought, was an Eye of Iam.

"What is that place?" Sora asked.

"In the days of the Council, it was a temple to Heragi, God of Misfortune. Now, it is like all of our temples, a Church of Iam."

"That is awful," Sora said.

"It makes them comfortable, which keeps everyone happy."

"It still seems wrong."

"The people have taken to the Glassmen's faith in the name of peace, but we know the other gods are stirring. These are sacred sites of communing with gods. Just because the effigies and the names change, does not mean the power does. It is something the Glassmen could never understand."

They walked the rest of the way in silence, climbing marble flights of stairs until they came to a stop at a long, public balcony overlooking the lake where Gold Grin's ship docked.

"Beautiful, isn't it?" Lord Bokeo said.

From so high, the lake looked like a mirror, the setting sun casting a pinkish hue over it. The shadow of the abandoned tower of the defeated Mystic Council stretched long toward an outcrop of rock at the edge of the lake. Sora followed the shadow to the shore where it fell upon another tall structure. She followed the coast, noting several such spires. That was when Sora realized that the mystic tower also served as a massive sundial.

"Breathtaking," she marveled.

"Sora," Lord Bokeo said, turning to her, "what do you know of the gods?"

"Which gods?"

"Our people once worshiped the Many and the Few—*Pinyun*

tsu chahn ji duo. Or simply *Pinyun.* Now they embrace Iam. Iam is not our enemy, but his followers have created him to be such."

"I know little of your gods, only of Iam and a bit about Nesilia. I—my friends and I, ended the life of another whom we were told was a goddess. But I am not so sure. I didn't think gods could die."

"Bliss—the One Who Remained."

"Yes!" Sora said, then her eyes narrowed. "How did you know?"

"Your fame precedes you in many ways. The destruction of the deformed goddess brought confirmation to the now-Secret Council of your preparedness. It was no accident you found Aquira soon after."

"That is what the Ancient said, but I still don't understand."

"May I tell you a story of the gods?" Lord Bokeo asked.

"Will it explain everything?"

He smiled. "Perhaps everything. Perhaps nothing." He motioned to a stone bench facing the lake, and they took a seat.

"Many centuries ago, before the molding of man, before even the forging of the dwarves by Meungor the Sharp Axe, the gods made tabernacle upon this earth," he began. "Pantego was vast, far vaster than any world in which they'd dwelt before.

"Upon this very spot, rising above these cliffs stood a majestic mountain, and the gods all called it home. It was rare to find any of them upon it, they were far too busy playing and shaping the world, but it was home nonetheless.

"One spring morning, when the dew was just so, and the flowers bloomed, bringing with them the fragrance of the eternal planes, the gods were spread widely throughout the land. Our legend tells of the Emperor God—the most powerful of all gods —call him Iam if you'd like, but our people did not. He decided the mountain should reflect the beauty of its inhabitants. So, with his great hand, he scooped up the rock, grass, and all that was within, and carried it far across the western horizon, searching for the place of greatest beauty. When he found a vast ocean and green, fertile land, he left it. Weary from his travels, he rested before making the trek back to the others to share with them the news of his findings."

"Mount Lister..." Sora whispered.

Lord Bokeo nodded "When the gods and goddesses returned," he continued, "and saw their beloved home was gone, they wept until they were dry and their tears filled the chasm left by the mountain. They created something new and possibly more beautiful even than the mountain. This very lake. But the gods would not be content; they missed their mountain. They cried out to one another, demanding justice be served to their Emperor God. One rose up, higher than the rest. The Goddess of Death and Darkness. You knew her as Bliss."

"She, more than any, would not stand the barb at the hand of the Emperor, for she still did not know that what he did was for all their benefits. So, she called together the thousands—gods and lesser gods. Even those who'd long since abandoned the mountain in hopes of forging their own peoples and lands—Meungor the Sharp Axe, god of dwarves, Bilnor god of the giants, Vilnor, his brother, god of the frost giants, and many more.

"When they found the Emperor God, he slept peacefully upon his new home. Only he wasn't alone. For it was only with the help of the Goddess of Earth that he moved the mountain, and she saw his wisdom. Bliss led the charge, even though the Goddess was her sister, carrying with her the full weight of the scorned gods. But none could match the Emperor's strength, and none would hear his words."

"Before long, the gods had forgotten why they battled or who they were angry against. They turned on one another, fury driving them to destroy each other. The violence of gods tore a rift in the fabric of reality, creating Elsewhere and damning them all within.

Now they all, the *Pinyun*, crave to once again return to this land. But we cannot allow it. This is why I know the wise Aihara Na would not have opened up a gateway to Elsewhere. It is too dangerous."

It was quiet for some time after he finished and they stared upon the lake. The shadow of the tower stretched so far now in the fading daylight it scraped along the western coast of the city.

"The tower," Sora said, breaking the silence. "What is it really?"

"It was once a place full of life and magic. The Red Tower—the home of the Mystic Order for millennia. Liam, when he outlawed magic, first made the Mystic Council seal it—with magic of all things! Could you imagine? As if that could stop those few mystics who remain. Within lies the knowledge of every mystic ever to walk Pantego, where the Well of Wisdom still bubbles."

"Then we should go," Sora said.

Aran Bokeo laughed. "Your eagerness may be the end of you, Sora. Tonight is an important night for our people. I would encourage you to clear your mind of all this until the time has come for your training."

"Why not start now?"

Lord Bokeo's legend of the gods sounded just like all the others she'd heard, a story, nothing more. The mystics might have feared opening Elsewhere because of them, but that meant they knew how. Which meant she could learn.

"The time will come quickly, and it will not be easy," Lord Bokeo said. "Do not rush it, for it will not be pleasant. Tonight will be a night you will not soon forget, as will the nights thereafter. There is much to appreciate about the Festival of Ghosts. Just try to take it all in. Do you have any autlas?"

"Plenty," she said.

"Good, good, good. Then I recommend you head to the

Emperor's Quilt and ask for a room overlooking the lake. The views tonight will be spectacular. If they are booked, tell them I sent you."

"And they'll believe me, just like that?" She wasn't sure if the Panpingese were just an overly trusting people, but in the Glass, people required proof.

Lord Bokeo chuckled. "I own the place."

"Of course you do…"

"Now, I suggest you try to enjoy the night. Forget about all this and see your homeland for the jewel it truly is." Lord Bokeo stood and brushed off his robe.

"Wait. You said my questions would be answered. You've only given me more."

"Sometimes, the quickest route to enlightenment is the longest path around the desert." He bowed, then left her.

Sora watched as he descended the marble stairs and disappeared. She considered following him, but couldn't take any more riddles. Then she considered seeking out Tum Tum, but the thought of finding him in a brothel brought a sour taste to her lips.

Instead, she decided to heed Lord Bokeo's suggestion. She was exhausted, mentally and physically, and a plush bed at an inn owned by a wealthy member the Winde Traders Guild—and evidently the Secret Council—sounded about right.

Finding the Emperor's Quilt was no trouble at all, especially now that she could understand Panpingese. She could even read it now. She rented a room using Lord Bokeo's name and plopped down on a luxurious bed. The cool lake air blew in through an open balcony. At least, it felt cold to her. She'd gotten used to sharing a bed with Aquira out on the sea, who was like an oven when she slumbered.

Sleep was impossible to come by anyway. Sora's mind replayed the meeting with the mystics, and then Nesilia, the sound of Whitney's voice calling to her. Her mind swam in the many mysteries.

She'd heard Whitney there in Elsewhere, just like Gold Grin said. She was sure of it. All she needed to do was enter again, find him, and figure a way to bring him out. If she'd put him there alongside Kazimir in the first place, certainly she could remove him. And if anyone could teach her how, it was the strange, hidden mystics she'd just encountered.

But it wasn't only that. For so long she'd sought to belong. The mystics were her people, both in race and in their ability to answer why she had this strange power that seemed to extend beyond any normal blood mages. She'd set off with Whitney to find them, and now, she had.

A chance to understand.

So, as she lay, staring at the wooden ceiling, she decided she would see it through. Whatever it was the mystics wanted. It was the only way. She would learn about her power, bring Whitney back alive before it was too late, and leave Kazimir behind where he could never harm another innocent soul like Tayvada Bokeo again.

Having a clear path calmed her enough to finally start to doze off, until a loud bang caused her to shoot upright. Shouting followed, coming from downstairs in the streets.

She swung her feet off the bed, but two more deafening blasts had her covering her head and ears. Terrified.

XVI

THE DESERTER

Watchtower bells echoed from every direction. Guards flocked down streets, sending Rand through back alleys. By the time he passed through South Corner and into Dockside, their footsteps were distant, lost to the chimes of moored ships and the rasp of beggars.

Nobody would question him here, and the guards were so scarce it'd take some time for the search to reach the grimy place. Rand threw his back against the nearest wall and finally took a moment to breathe. He couldn't get air down fast enough. His chest felt like it was going to implode, and the armor still felt tight from Redstar's dark magic even though it was normal again.

He considered tearing it off, then noticed the dirt-covered boy kneeling next to him, a tin outstretched and rattling.

"Spare a bronzer, Sir Shieldsman?" he asked, then coughed.

Rand regarded the child, skin and bones, a product of Dockside. *Saving the realm is enough.* He could worry about saving Dockside later, plus, the child likely had more autlas to his name than Rand did.

Rand started off at a brisk walk without a backward glance.

Keeping his shoulders straight, he bore the proper poise of a true Shieldsman. He took steady, slow breaths through his teeth, so he wouldn't appear anxious. The cold air made his teeth sting, but the pain made it easier to focus. Docksiders didn't talk to guards, but during the winter months, when there was little to do but survive and gossip, rumors spread like wildfire. A Shieldsman decked out in armor having a panic attack wouldn't remain a mystery for long.

It was dusk by the time he reached the Maiden's Mugs. Before anything, he had to grab Sigrid and get her out. Trapp knew his name, and so did Redstar. It wouldn't be long before word reached these parts and while Docksiders didn't talk, money did. The reward for turning him in would be too much for a sleazy tavern owner like Gideon Trapp to deny.

Grab Sigrid, find shelter, free Torsten. That was the best plan he could come up with. It was clear he couldn't take down Redstar alone, but with him maimed, the two of them might be able to. Torsten's renown as a warrior was unparalleled. Wren had provided Rand a chance to strike again and he…

Wren, Rand thought solemnly. All his church-going life, he'd received Iam's light, but he'd never seen such a display of power in His name. He could only imagine what Redstar would do to the High Priest once he broke through the shield of light the old man had summoned. Rand vowed not to let the distraction go to waste.

He stopped outside the doors of the Maiden's Mugs, drew a few deep breaths. The regulars would be arriving soon, finished with their shifts down at the docks. One had already arrived.

"Shieldsman blessin our li'l corner today?" a drunkard arriving at the same time said. Rand recognized him from other nights imbibing.

"Impossible to get a proper pint in the castle," Rand replied. Stay calm. Act superior. Don't draw attention.

"Impossible to find a proper lass too, eh?" he chuckled.

"There be a bar wench here who's pretty as spring. A li'l flower blossom for winter."

Rand knew who he was referring to, but let it slide. "I'm not here for chitchat, just a drink."

The man shrugged. "Suit yerself."

He pushed the door open and stepped inside. Rand followed close behind and bumped into his back when he suddenly stopped. Rand was about to curse him as any Shieldsman would a drunkard, then realized what caused it.

The tavern was abandoned, tables overturned, ale spilled all over the floors. All of Trapp's storage barrels, broken apart, the bar cleaved in two. There were no bodies, but a few splatters of blood were counted on the floor, mixing with ale.

Rand heard a whimper and pushed the drunkard aside to rush toward the sound. Gideon Trapp slumped against the wall behind the bar, ale trickling onto the top of his head from a broken tap. One of his legs bent like a galler's, the wrong way at the knee. His nose was broken and bleeding profusely.

"Trapp, what happened?" Rand questioned, kneeling at his side.

The man's bleary eyes blinked open. His gaze went from Rand's face to his armor, then widened. "So... it is true?" he wheezed.

Rand took him by the shoulders and shook. "Trapp!"

"The savage... he... every guard in Dockside went running toward bells; then he stormed the place."

"Where's my sis—" Footsteps creaked upstairs. Trapp raised one trembling arm and pointed to the ceiling.

Rand shoved him aside and ran for the stairs, unsheathing his sword as he went. A thud followed heavy footsteps and low voices speaking in Drav Crava. Besides his, there were a few apartments upstairs—every door was open revealing ransacked rooms. Beds were flipped, cabinets raided, and in the first room, a man lay sprawled out, groaning on the floor. His face was a flat, bloody mess.

"Where's the one who did this, girl?" a deep voice questioned.

It was coming from the direction of Sigrid's room. Rand couldn't hear the response, but it was muffled and frantic.

"You dragged me here for a girl?" another Drav Cra man answered. "Nesilia's grave… don't you know you can pay for them here?"

"Quiet. I'll never hold an axe again thanks to this little wench."

"Is it just your axe your worried about holding?" The second man cackled.

Rand stopped just outside his door and peered in. A Drav Cra warrior he didn't recognize sat on the table—his table—biting on a piece of the stale bread Sigrid had only recently brought home. A wooden shortbow was slung over one shoulder and a full quiver over the other. A hatchet-axe still dangled from his hip. Apparently, ransacking the place was too easy for him to bother using it.

Behind him, the savage Rand had pushed into the bay had Sigrid pinned against the cabinetry by the throat with his left forearm. His weapon hand hung slack at his side, empty, the skin of his half-clenched fingers discolored from frostbite.

"Now, you whore," he said, "I'm not going to ask again. Where is your man?"

One eating, one crippled. Rand was out of practice, but he liked his odds. He was just about to speak up and answer the devil when Sigrid grabbed a kitchen knife and stabbed her assailant in the shoulder just below the neck. He dropped her and staggered, but didn't go down, the stab missing anything vital.

Sigrid scrambled to the far corner of the room with nowhere to go.

"Bitch!" he barked, tearing the knife out. He stalked toward her, blood staining his furs red. His compatriot burst out laughing, at least until Rand stormed in and cleaved his head from his shoulders in a single, mighty swipe.

"Step away from her," he ordered, his sword directing the remaining savage with a twist of the wrist.

The Drav Cra warrior turned, a steady stream of blood now pouring down his shoulder and chest. As soon as his eyes laid upon Rand, the corner of lips, still purple from the swim in ice-cold water, curled into a smile.

"And here I thought I'd have to go looking for you," he said. He playfully flipped the knife and dropped into a fighting stance, but the man's feet were set wrong, telling Rand it wasn't his dominant hand.

"I'm right here," Rand said. "Sig, get behind me."

She went to move, but the warrior slowly rotated so that he'd be directly between her and Rand. "She's going to watch you die, soldier-boy. No water to push me in this time."

"They're all right about you people. Infesting this city like a sickness with your vile ways."

"I've seen very well what Glassman are capable of. You were probably a pup when the coward Liam invaded my clan to take his Queen. Oleander isn't the only one of us who got forced to bed that night."

"The Queen came of her own free will because she saw what it was like to live in the light."

"'The light,'" he chortled. "All I see outside are clouds."

"You'll see black soon."

Rand charged him and swung. After striking air twice, it was clear to him that he'd gotten lucky down on the docks accidentally knocking this one into the water so fast. The man was nimble as a hare. Rand went high, and the Drav Cra spun around low, slicing Rand where his armor bent at the knee.

"Rand!" Sigrid yelped. She was at his back now, both of them with nowhere to go.

"Stay back," he told her.

The Drav Cra warrior rolled his shoulders and cracked his neck. "Been a long time since I had a fair fight, but I only need one hand to kill you."

Rand charged him again and brought his sword crashing down. The man evaded, rolling to the side. Grabbing Rand by the neck, he flung him into the cabinets headfirst. Rand's ears and forehead were stung by splinters.

"Now where were we, girl?" the man asked, turning to Sigrid who now fully cowered in the corner.

Rand pulled himself free and leaped back into the fight. The warrior dodged without looking, then whipped his frostbitten forearm around and smashed Rand in the face. Rand stumbled back, but not before thrusting his weapon. The man purposefully caught the end of the blade with the palm of his crippled hand. Skin sliced as the metal sunk through, but if he could feel it at all, it didn't show. Once the sword pierced through the other side, he wrenched it out of Rand's grip.

The warrior placed his foot against the wall to spring toward Rand. It went through the thin wall like a sheet of parchment. Rand tried to take advantage, but before he knew what hit him, the warrior lashed out. The now bloody, frozen wrist forced Rand's head down and kept it there as the savage's knee rose to meet Rand's jaw.

Rand flew back, the table cracking in half beneath the full weight of his body and armor. He saw stars but felt the savage on top of him. Blood still poured from the man's neck, now drenching Rand.

"Because of you, I'll never be a dradinengor!" His good fist slammed into Rand's face. "I'm going to drag you into the water. And you'll freeze as I show your girl what a true man is like." He flipped the knife over again and held the blade to Rand's eye.

"Get off him!" Sigrid screamed as she came at him.

His frozen hand snapped up, smacked her across the face, sending her to her knees.

"Don't touch her!" Rand shouted. He went to push the savage off, but the knife returned to his eye, blade glinting so close he could see how red they were in the reflection. He hadn't had a good night's sleep in days, and now after all he'd been through since he decided to string himself up by the neck, he was going to die by the hands of a coward picking on a woman half his size.

Rand, in a last-ditch effort, forced his hand up and dug his gauntleted finger into the man's neck wound. The savage screamed, but easily swatted Rand's hand away.

"Stop fighting, flower picker," the Drav Cra warrior said. "You'll be with the Goddess underground soon. You just—"

Blood sprayed across Rand's face, and the full weight of the warrior fell onto his chest. Rand dragged himself backward, wiped his eyes, and saw the arrow sticking through the savage's neck.

Sigrid stood holding the savage's shortbow, the string still thrumming. Her cheek was split open. His gaze went there first, then to her usually calm eyes. He'd never seen such rage in them.

"Monster!" she yelled. She tore another arrow from the quiver, took two long strides, then straddled over the savage. He still clutched at his neck as he gurgled on a mouthful of blood. She screamed again and brought the arrow down into his chest. Once, twice, again and again, until his eyelids froze open and his limbs wilted, his chest looking like a pincushion.

Tears streamed down her cheeks as she screamed and threw the bow aside, then kicked the fallen assailant repeatedly in the face. Rand regretted how long it took for him to get up and comfort her, but eventually, he caught her arms and pulled her into a tight embrace.

"It's okay now, Sig," he whispered. "I'm back now."

She squeezed him, then shoved away and punched him in the chest. "I heard the bells, I thought…"

"I failed, but I got out. I had to get back here to you, but it seems you didn't need me. How in Iam's name did you learn to shoot like that?"

She sniveled, then released a low chuckle. "Ye weren't the only one paying attention when father took us hunting."

"Father's still saving us from beyond the grave."

"It was a lucky shot," she confessed.

"I'm starting not to believe in luck. Come on." His knees were still shaky, and his legs burned with soreness now that the adrenaline stopped pumping. After months of sitting around drinking, he'd been through more real fights in the last day than his entire service in the King's Shield.

It was clear someone wanted him alive.

"Where are we going?" Sigrid asked.

"Anywhere but here. Redstar's turned the whole Shield against Torsten as he performs some dark ritual in the Wearer's own chambers. We have to stop him, but it's clear I can't do it alone."

He took a step away, but Sigrid's hand fell upon his cheek, and she turned him back. "It's not your fight anymore."

Rand nuzzled her hand, then removed it. "It is. I don't know why, but it's like this is what I was born for. If I don't, Redstar will make this city a playground for his heathen horde, and more good women will be…"

"I understand," she replied solemnly. "But if ye can't do it alone, who can help?"

"Redstar has Wren the Holy in his grips now too, and the King's trust. So, I'm going to free Torsten so the King's Shield may do what it's meant to and shield this kingdom. He defeated Redstar once before, and he made a mistake putting his faith in me alone. But right now, we need to get out of here before the guards arrive."

Sigrid nodded, hurried to the table beside her bed, and grabbed a few items including a necklace. Rand recognized it. The thing belonged to their mother; a bit of bone from a Panpingese sea creature whose name Rand couldn't remember carved into the shape of a water droplet on a rusty, metal band. Then, she hefted the shortbow and slung it over her shoulder. "Just in case," she said, shrugging.

"Smart," Rand replied. He retrieved his sword and a loaf of bread. He had no keepsake from their parents to take with him. No belongings but for the Shieldsman armor on his back. The very armor he'd earned in the name of his parents to try and make Dockside—their home—a little brighter.

"Okay, let's go," Rand said. He took Sigrid's arm and caught her staring at the body of the man she'd killed. The first one was always the toughest, even if it was a monster. "He deserved it," Rand assured her.

"I know." She swallowed hard. "Iam forgive me anyway."

"He will. Now we just have to make sure He has a kingdom left to watch over."

Rand towed her along back down the hall. Groans sounded from within the other rooms as the victims of the Drav Cra recovered from the raid. Downstairs, Gideon Trapp lethargically swept up broken bottles, his wounds slowing him down. The drunkard Rand had arrived with sat at the bar with a pint in hand, utterly oblivious to the chaos. A few others had trickled in as well.

Rand understood well. Most people from Dockside needed to drown out the thoughts of their shoggy lives, and no mess would keep them from their favorite watering hole.

"There ye are," Trapp snapped. He tossed aside his broom and met them at the base of the stairs. "This were yer fault, weren't it? First, ye get my best server hurt, now this?"

"We're leaving, Trapp," Rand said. He went to shove by, but Trapp stood his ground.

"Oh no, ye don't. Ye'll both be working to pay off all of this, ye hear me?"

"She's done here. We both are."

"I don't care what ye think ye know," Trapp said, "ye ain't getting out of this. Valin will hear about this."

"He cares so much he didn't even have a guard looking over the place. Sigrid is done. Step aside."

Gideon Trapp turned to her and softened his tone. "Siggy, don't listen to this drunken brute. There ain't no better work than this in Dockside for a lady like you. Haven't I been good to ye?"

Sigrid shoved a ball of fabric into his gut.

"What's this?" Trapp said. He held it up. It was the skippy outfit he made her wear while serving.

"He ain't a drunken brute," she said. "He's my brother, and yer a right piece of shog ."

Rand flashed Trapp a grin, and then he and Sigrid pushed by.

"Don't ye dare walk away!" Trapp shouted. "I own ye, ye filthy whore's daughter. When Valin finds out what ye cost him—"

"And what did they cost me, Trapp old chum?"

The front door swung open and in strode the last person in Dockside Rand ever wanted to see. Out of instinct, he stopped to place one arm in front of Sigrid while the other hand fell to the grip of his longsword. Dockside had no mayor or constable, only a guard captain who kept as close to Yarrington proper as he could. Even the Master of Ships stayed at the castle and rarely visited.

Valin Tehr was the power. He had been for all of Rand's life. If you stepped into a shop or tavern, it was likely he received taxes from the owners on top of what they paid the Crown. His right leg, scrawny and deformed from birth, made the man walk with a permanent limp and use a cane plated in gold. Even his face, with its oversized chin and wide-set eyes, was nothing to look at, but his mind more than made up for it.

Valin had been a thorn in the side of the King's Shield for many years, though some felt him a necessary scourge. With fear and gold, he kept Dockside in line and its people working hard enough that the Crown turned a blind eye to his more nefarious dealings.

"Mr. Tehr, sir... I...I," Trapp stammered like he was talking to a king. With the way the gangster dressed, however, he may as well have been. And while the man had no King's Shield, a dozen or so thugs entered alongside him.

"Who did you insult this time to bring such destruction?" Valin asked.

"It wasn't me, sir. This, this, drunkard angered the Drav Cra. They came bursting in before we opened, right through the lock."

"Drav Cra and a Shieldsman? I pay you good money to stay inconspicuous."

"Sir, if you don't mind, me and my sister were leaving," Rand said. He took a step, the thugs shadowed his movement, grinning like wild men.

"Not so fast." Valin dragged his misshapen leg forward to get a closer look at Rand. "I know you, don't I, kid?"

"Please, Mr. Tehr," Sigrid said. "We really need to be gone."

"I say who is 'gone' anywhere here!" Valin barked, emphasizing Sigrid's Dockside accent. He spoke with the refinement of a true noble.

Rand pulled his sister back, his fingers wrapping the hilt of his sword now. "In the name of the King's Shield, move aside."

"Yes, no one has more respect for the Shield than I, isn't that right boys?" His crew laughed. One went behind the bar, filled a mug and passed it to another who'd shoved aside the drunk and stole his seat. "Thing is, you're Rand Langley. Wearer for a day, disgraced for a lifetime. And the word is you tried to murder the King's uncle in his own chambers earlier today."

Rand's throat went dry. His palms started to sweat. Inch by inch, he slid his sword out of its sheath.

Valin clicked his tongue in disapproval. "I know everyone in Dockside, kid. You can hide from the Crown. You can hide from Iam. But you can't hide from me." He began to pace, every thud of his cane unnerving Rand further. "I've been keeping an eye on you. Not every day a Docksider earns the Shield," he went on, "but every time I reached out so you might use your post to help this place we call home, you ignored my call."

"I have no quarrel with you, Valin," Rand said. "My father worked at your dock when he was alive, and you paid him well, kept food on our table. I meant no offense in rejecting your advances; I merely wanted to focus on my training."

"Who am I to scorn good old-fashioned hard work? Still, it hurts me that you went off and forgot this place. You had so much potential."

"I never forgot I... Look, I know what you bring in through this place. Let us go, and the secret goes with us.

Valin edged closer, and Rand's heart raced. The man could hardly walk, and he didn't bother carrying a weapon when his thugs could handle things for him, but growing up in Dockside, there wasn't a soul who didn't know that crossing Valin Tehr meant taking a nice swim out into the Torrential Sea.

"Are you threatening me, Rand Langley?" he asked. "You gonna get your Queen to hang me over the walls like the others?"

Rand pictured Tessa and the others swinging in the wind but squeezed his eyes to drive out the image. People in Dockside didn't pay attention to Glass Castle affairs. It was what made it such a good place for him to shirk his duties. Clearly, Valin knew enough for the whole district.

"No threat... I just... we need to leave," Rand said.

"Going to take another swipe at Redstar? Castle halls not bloody enough for you?"

Rand didn't say a word. Instead, he drew his sword a little further, wary of the thugs surrounding him. Sigrid clutched his arm.

"Why didn't you cut out his black heart the first time, you fool!" Valin laughed and banged him in the pauldron with his cane. His men joined in, and after a short while, Rand forced a nervous chuckle as well.

"If you let us go, I will," Rand said.

Valin eyed one of his men. Unlike the others, this one was older, more refined. His shirt was neatly tucked, and his graying hair combed. All Rand could focus on, however, was his glass eye painted entirely white. He had the sharp nose and noble brow of a man from Brekliodad, as well as a curled, white mustache no westerner could possibly grow.

"Confident, chap, isn't he, Codar?" Valin asked the man.

"Indeed, sir," Codar answered, Breklian accent thick as syrup.

"Too bad. You've got the whole guard in a mad scramble looking for you, kid. Like you're more important than the missing Caleef." Tehr smiled. "You don't have the Caleef, do you?" He leaned in, pretending to look behind Rand. "You aren't getting close enough to that filthy warlock to smell him now, let alone kill him."

"I don't have a choice," Rand said. "Iam needs me."

"The boy is needed by Iam Himself?" More chuckles from the thugs sounded, now nearer.

"They would do well to watch their manners," Sigrid bristled. "Wren the Holy himself asked this of him."

"Ha! The Holy Father asked a sinner to sin?" Valin looked toward the ceiling, closed his eyes, and traced one of them with his finger. "Guess its better to use a sinner than a saint, if there are any left. What is this city coming to?" He looked to Codar as if expecting an answer.

"It is impossible to tell," Codar said.

"Barbarians surrounding us, sharing our mead and nobody in the castle can do a damn thing. Hell, I don't even know a soul in that place anymore, and I used to have the whole council on retainer. You hung a few who owed me a favor."

"Redstar started it all," Rand said. "Now he'll see us fall to ruin."

"And you're going to stop him? You, the hangman who let the mad Queen run wild? If you ask me, it's about time we got a whole new family up in that keep, but I'm happy here in my little fiefdom so long as whoever's on the throne keeps out of it."

"As long as Redstar has the King's ear, the Dockside you know will become a hunting ground for barbarians. I can help stop it."

"Not alone you can't." Valin smirked, then turned to his men. "Get this place cleaned up and grab my shipment. A Shieldsman needs our help rooting out the savages, and I live to serve the Crown."

XVII

THE KNIGHT

Torsten tossed a tiny rock against the wall and let it roll back to him. Then again, and again. It was the best way he'd found of staying sane in the dungeon. Even then, he wasn't sure it was working.

Sitting, waiting for news from Wren the Holy about Rand Langley's mission made it even worse. He'd staked the fate on the kingdom first on Oleander showing a shred of mercy and sending for Wren. When she did, he'd put even more trust in a deserter of the King's Shield to take down an Arch Warlock.

He was running out of faith.

"Yer gonna to need something bigger than that to break out," the old kook in the adjacent cell said. When he wasn't snoring, he couldn't go more than five minutes without having something to say.

"I'm not trying to break out," Torsten replied.

"Ye'll be the first then."

Torsten remained silent, rolling the stone over in his fingers.

"I gave up too." The old man coughed loudly. "Been so many years down here, I dun't know what I'd do outside no how. I be a charm of good luck though. Ye go, try and break out. I bet ye do it."

Torsten clenched his jaw and held his tongue. He had no interest in making friends, but there was nothing else to do. And in the stifling darkness, the silence was an easy place to lose oneself.

"Please, by Iam, tell me how an old man trapped down here could possibly be a good luck charm?" Torsten said.

"Each bastard what gets shut in near me, gets out. Not long ago, upstairs, some handsome devil tricked me into tryin and got out himself instead." He hacked out a laugh and a cough simultaneously. "Called himself the greatest thief in Pantego. Stole my freedom, he did."

Torsten allowed his head to sink back against the wall. He couldn't help but smirk. There was no question in his mind who the man was referring to.

"Then, they shoved me down here and some Drav Cra warlock, all metal, and masks, get's put right where you are," the old man continued. "Ye think I talk too much; guy wouldn't shut it for a second even after they muzzled him."

Torsten sat up. He crawled over to the bars and stuck his head through as far as it would go. "Redstar?" he said.

"Yeah that… that sounds familiar."

"He escaped?"

The old coot peeked through as well, made visible by the flickering torch outside his cell. His face was so loose with age it looked like it was melting off his skull. Only a handful of rotting teeth remained in his mouth, and when he grinned Torsten caught a whiff of the foulest smell imaginable, and he'd endured the sewers of Winde Port.

"Ye shoulda seen it," he said, ignoring the question. "The gods damned new King hisself came down here every night and talked to him. Sat right outside the cell yer in now. I swear on me bastard son, there ain't never even been a Royal Councilman willing to stay down here, and I been locked up since Liam could walk. I'm innocent of course, but ain't no one with them decision-making ears be willin to listen."

"You didn't answer my question. Did Redstar escape?"

"I wouldn't say that."

Torsten slammed on the bars. "Old man! I need to know."

"Iam's light, ye really are a nutter ain't ye? The King let him out hisself. I know it was him because of the crown, ye see, and the stature. I didn't even know Liam had a son." He cackled. "But I'm guessin he didn't when I was locked in."

Torsten backed away and hung his head. "Did you hear anything they had to say, or were you too busy yammering?"

"If I did, I wun't tell you." Torsten heard the man's knees drag across the floor as he slinked back into the corner.

"I don't have time for this. What did they say?"

"Ye have all the time in Pantego, ye biff. Gods… even the warlock'd be better company than ye—least he sang some songs."

Torsten squeezed his fist and slowly drew air through his teeth. "Please, tell me."

"Now that's better!" The man guffawed. "It wasn't too much really. Just some apologizin for doing what had to be done to open eyes, talk about Iam and the Buried Goddess. All borin stuff. The warlock was much more entertainin when he was mutterin to hisself alone. But, of course, he got invited right out by the King hisself. See? Charm of good luck."

"If only it were thanks to you. That man is a foul, no good—"

"Monster," someone addressed him from the opposite direction. Soft footsteps approached from around the corner, then a familiar face outside his cell was painted orange by the dim torch-light, the birthmark covering half of it as dark as red wine.

"Redstar," Torsten growled.

"That's the man!" the old coot said excitedly. "Walked right on outta here like he—"

"Quiet." Redstar raised his left hand and squeezed his fingers, a bloody bandage wound around his palm. The old man went silent in an instant. "I told you I would be visiting, old friend," he addressed Torsten. "How are you faring down here?"

"I preferred when it was quiet," Torsten said.

"Must you always be such a grouser? Come, Torsten, I'd like to show you something."

"If you open that door, I will kill you."

"And them?" Redstar snapped his fingers, and two King's Shieldsmen approached, their heavy boots shaking dust from the walls. The first was Sir Nikserof Pasic, the most veteran of his order remaining within the Glass Castle. His arm wound had healed. The other, Sir Austun Mulliner, whom Torsten had wounded so deeply outside Winde Port. "Will you murder them too, just like last time?"

Torsten hurried to the bars and looked Nikserof in the eye. The Shieldsman refused to look back. "Nikserof, you must not listen to a word he says," Torsten pled. "Can't you see how he's deceived you all?"

"They are under strict orders to keep me safe, by the King himself," Redstar said. "After a man of your order—former order —tried to kill me in my quarters, they're lucky they aren't all hanged. But that man wasn't really one of them, was he, Torsten?"

Torsten's heart sank. He hadn't yet heard from anyone, but that meant Wren the Holy was able to reach out to Sir Rand Langley to redeem himself through the death of Redstar. Clearly, he'd failed.

"What did you do to him?" Torsten questioned.

"Far less than I should have. He escaped like the spineless rat he is."

"Turning to a Deserter?" Sir Mulliner said. "By Iam, what happened to you in Winde Port?"

Sir Nikserof didn't say a word.

"I thought you were better than turning to deserters and ale-soaked cowards to do your dirty work," Redstar said. "You have abandoned honor in your mad quest to prove me something I'm not. Your men see it too."

Torsten again tried to get Nikserof to acknowledge him, but now understood why he wouldn't. Taking the vows of the King's Shield meant serving for life, and Rand Langley had abandoned the castle after Torsten returned, leaving nobody to answer for why so many had died. By their code, he should have been hanged.

Torsten realized then that he could have attempted asking Nikserof to do what was necessary and take down Redstar. They had fought together in Winde Port, bled together. Instead, Torsten went to a deserter for help—failed—and again played right into Redstar's hands.

Torsten shifted his gaze to Mulliner, who stared back, eyes full of frustration and judgment. Torsten closed his eyes and let his chin fall to his chest.

Sir Nikserof removed a ring of keys from his belt and began unlocking the cell door.

"Nikserof, whatever this is, there's still time," Torsten said without looking up. "I know I don't deserve to wear the White, but he will destroy you. Hang me if you must, but set him beside me."

"Sir Pasic," was Nikserof's only reply as the keys fumbled within the lock. *He's nervous. Perhaps he might still welcome the opportunity to tear the warlock down.*

"Some of the King's Shield know how to obey the command of their king," Redstar said. "It shouldn't be so difficult as it's in the name, but you seem intent on undermining him at every turn."

The lock clicked, and the door swung open. Nikserof and Mulliner entered and seized Torsten's arms to cuff them. Austun then gave him a hard tug.

"Would you listen to me!" Torsten implored. "He doesn't serve the King; he only serves himself!"

"Relax, Torsten," Redstar groaned. "This isn't your execution. I simply want to show you something."

"Nothing you show me will change a thing."

"We shall see." Redstar grinned. "Come."

The Shieldsmen dragged Torsten along. Behind their group, he noticed Freydis following, soundless and reserved, yet Torsten knew madness stirred just below her surface. Nikserof still refused to look at him, and Torsten wondered if he were being controlled by black magic at their hands. The old coot in the adjacent cell sat against the wall, pawing at his mouth, seemingly unable to open it.

Torsten paused to look in, and Redstar took notice.

"Ah, my apologies," the Arch Warlock said. "The Lady has been so kind to me with her power of late, sometimes I forget." He spread his fingers, and the old man gasped for air. He remained cowering in the corner, quiet for once.

They led Torsten to the castle's entry hall. He'd made himself busy the entire way trying to talk sense into Nikserof, and not getting an answer. He even tried talking to Mulliner, although he knew it would do no good.

When they reached the vast space, drowned in the colorful light of all the stained glass in the clerestory, he was silenced. Glass soldiers, Shieldsmen and Drav Cra warriors patrolled and guarded the castle's every corner. The Northern savages were no longer merely at the gates, but inside them making themselves comfortable.

Torsten stole a glance into the Throne Room. Pi stood in the center of the room, engaged in a heated conversation with Oleander. Or, rather, it was heated on one end. Oleander towered over the boy. She was tall by any standards, but next to her son, she appeared a giant. Her cheeks were flushed, and her hands whipped around dramatically as she spoke, but Pi remained the same stoic boy he'd been since emerging from the Royal Crypt.

Oleander threw her arms up in frustration. Pi shook his head solemnly, then turned and headed toward his throne. Oleander made a move toward the Great Hall and locked gazes with Torsten through the open doors. He expected a glower, but she seemed relieved to see him.

"Torsten, I must have a word with you immediate—"

The doors slammed shut in her face without anyone pushing them. Torsten heard Freydis snicker and looked back. She had a bloody hand raised. Oleander pounded from the other side, her muffled shouting indiscernible.

Torsten's pulse raced. He was about to have a chance to beseech the King again.

"Take him to my quarters," Redstar said, smiling. "He won't want to miss this."

Torsten veered toward the doors and was about to call out to Oleander when his escorts jerked him back.

"Please, I must speak with her and the King," Torsten protested. "I must speak with them!" He thrashed with the full weight of his towering body. The Shieldsmen had to anchor their feet to keep him in place.

"Sir Unger, this isn't the time," Nikserof whispered into his ear.

Hearing his title whispered caused Torsten to stop fighting, and he was promptly towed to the stairs of the West Tower. It meant that at least a smidgeon of respect still remained. That didn't change how foolish he felt. All his life in the Shield, he'd hauled hundreds of criminals to the dungeons. He always wondered where they found the gumption to fight the inevitable.

Nearly all of them struggled as if they had a chance against soldiers or Shieldsmen with their hands cuffed.

Now Torsten understood. They fought it because in their hearts they believed they were innocent. Not every criminal was as self-aware as Whitney had been. Torsten couldn't help but doubt himself—to wonder if maybe he was wrong. If somehow, he'd imagined Redstar's many slights. After all, the only others there that night, a year ago, when Redstar cursed Pi and fled, were Uriah, who died shortly after, and Queen Oleander. When it came to Pi, the Queen never saw things clearly.

No, Torsten told himself, shaking the thoughts out of his head as Nikserof and Mulliner dragged him onto the stairs. The wolves were circling no longer. They now made their home within the camp, and their pack leader would devour everything in his path.

"Nikserof, Mulliner, you have to see the madness in this," Torsten said as they ascended the stairs. "Drav Cra in our very halls." He nodded back toward Freydis who followed them at a safe distance.

"Now isn't the time for this," Nikserof said. Mulliner remained silent.

"Soon there will be no time."

They pulled him to a halt at the landing of the second highest floor of the castle, just around the corner from Torsten's old chambers. Nikserof leaned in to whisper in his ear. "Many of our men defend against the Black Sands. We're outnumbered."

"And we don't need a traitor's help," Mulliner snapped.

He shoved Torsten into the passageway. Torsten staggered forward but couldn't mask his smirk as he found his balance. Mulliner may have been unreachable, but Sir Nikserof wasn't lost to lies.

I'm not alone.

They stopped outside of Torsten's former Wearer's chambers. Two Drav Cra warlocks stood outside, rags and trinkets draped all over them. Both turned simultaneously toward them as if they were connected.

They extended their arms and silently beckoned Torsten into the room. Freydis rattled off to them in Drav Crava. One left, and she took his place guarding the door.

"You may enter," she said.

The Shieldsmen released Torsten, and he took a few cautious steps toward the doorway. These were his chambers, but he couldn't help but feel that something was different. He stopped.

"Are we still the Shield that guards this kingdom?" he asked Nikserof.

"Always." The knight replied.

"We are," Mulliner said at the same time, indicating that Torsten wasn't one of them. Then they set off back toward the stairwell.

Spirits lifted by one of their answers, Torsten entered the chambers that had served him and so many Wearers of White before him. He barely recognized it anymore. All the arms of former Wearers which once festooned the walls like relics were askew or fallen. An entire wall was cracked as if a boulder had slammed into its center. Droplets of blood covered the floor, the largest splatter on a mural, its stone canvas pieced together like a puzzle.

That uplifted feeling vanished almost as soon as it'd arrived. Torsten could never forget that painting Redstar once showed him which depicted the God Feud in a way that painted Nesilia, the Buried Goddess, as Iam's ally and lover. The notion itself was ridiculous, contradicting the Holy Scripture and every glass shard of artwork decorating churches of Iam—both ancient and new. In true history, Nesilia and the One Who Remained, whom Redstar called Bliss, were the two instigators of the feud that nearly reduced Pantego to rubble. Hundreds of gods and goddesses died or fled, never to be heard from again. The One Who Remained defeated Nesilia after they turned on each other.

Iam watched in horror as all his kin ravaged the land that, together, they created. With all others weakened, he created Elsewhere and banished what remained of the gods there for all eternity. All the horrid creations of unspeakable power they conceived to help in their feud joined them. Iam was left with both the feeblest and fairest of their creations; dwarves and men, beings of flesh, blood, and bone. He shed his light upon them from the heavens above, hoping for a day when all the fighting initiated by his fallen ilk might end.

It was the sad story of Pantego's birth, once intended to be the crowning achievement of the gods. But even they fell prey to jealousy and contempt. Only Iam stayed true, and Torsten had long ago dedicated his life to that truth by following King Liam. His conquest to bring all Pantego under a single banner was everything Iam loathed, but Liam understood the cost. To do whatever it took, even sacrifice the sanctity his very soul to create a peaceful world of tomorrow. A world where man would stop squabbling over false idols and dedicate themselves to the light of the One True.

Now, Redstar sought to undo all of Liam's painstaking work.

Torsten squeezed his fists tight. There were ancient weapons all around him. If he could find a way to break the chains on his wrists, he could get out and finish what Rand couldn't. He wasn't sure why he trusted the broken-down deserter to take down an Arch Warlock alone.

The axe of Sir Quenton Carlsbad lay on the floor, its shaft cracked in half a century ago in a war with the dwarven kingdom of Elnor. If Torsten could get the right angle, he might be able to snap the chain. He'd have to deal with the two warlocks outside, who may be listening to his very thoughts for all he knew. All he'd have to—

"Fair Yarrington!" someone announced. Torsten was immediately drawn to the window which looked down over the castle's entry gate. Redstar stood atop it with Pi on one side and Wren the Holy on the other. In the bailey, at their backs, were all the members of the now-worthless Royal Council. Arrayed behind them, King's Shieldsmen and Drav Cra warlocks and warriors, Nikserof at the head of the former, and Drad Mak, the latter.

A crowd had formed down on Royal Avenue, staring up at their lords. It was common-folk, mostly; the only people stirred by affairs of the kingdom. The nobles down the way were happy to stay in their Old Yarrington estates, letting the world pass them by so long as their coffers remained full.

"I stand before you, humbled by the acceptance of my people, and the trust of your king," Redstar continued. It was only then that Torsten realized it was he who'd been speaking. He'd never heard the Arch Warlock project his voice so loudly. "It has not been easy coming to this strange, vast city. I've been working hard to learn how things work so that I might earn the title given me by your King as Prime Minister, his right hand."

"Ain't no Drav Cra ever be one of us!" a member of the crowd shouted, encouraged by a smattering of cheers.

"You don't belong here!" cried another.

"I have heard all the rumors and lies about how I came to be your Prime Minister!" Redstar said, ignoring them. "But today I stand before you, begging you to put aside our differences. Do you not remember we all hail from Drav Cra long ago? Oh, what the years have done to our minds, our memory fails us. Has this alliance not brought us back to simpler times? Times when we were one? Has it not proven the brilliance of your late King in taking my lovely sister, Oleander, as his wife?"

Torsten scanned the platform. Oleander wasn't present. As Queen Mother, she should've been standing by the side of her son, but Redstar stood there in her stead.

"Lovely as gold-plated shog!" someone else in the crowd hollered, drawing laughs.

"Where is the murderous shrew?" asked another.

Pi glared in their direction. Without anyone needing to ask, two hulking Drav Cra warriors delved into the crowd, grabbed the men who'd spoken out, and hauled them, screaming, back through the bailey.

"There are still those who ignore fact," Redstar continued. "Since the moment King Pi was brave enough to call on his family for help we have claimed resounding victory at Winde Port, as only Liam could have done. All of Pantego now fears our great army again, but there are still some among us who deny this success." Redstar lifted his arm and drew back his sleeve. The crowd gasped, Torsten did as well. There was only a stump where his hand used to be.

"A member of your King's Shield accosted me as I slept. A man, still loyal to the former Wearer Torsten Unger, whose mind was so ravaged by battle he took the life of one of his own. I have been left scarred but not disheartened. For as my life seemed to be coming to an end, a sign—a light from the heavens shown. Wren the Holy arrived at my room at the exact moment of betrayal and disarmed my would-be assassin." Redstar extended his remaining hand and placed it on Wren's shoulder, and smiled warmly. "The voice of Iam saved my life."

Murmurs broke out. Wren limped forward, leaning on his cane, his hands shaking so much Torsten could see it even where he stood. Wren moved like a decrepit old man, and even nodding in agreement with Redstar seemed a struggle. Torsten had seen him only days earlier when he sent him to find Rand, and he appeared healthy. He'd been an old man since Torsten first met him, but never had he been feeble.

"Some of you are loathed even to speak the name of the Buried Goddess!" Redstar announced, stepping forward, arm around Wren's hunched back. "Some of you believe she is wicked. The bringer of the God Feud. Deceiver. Just as we, for so long, thought Iam our enemy. But it is all of us who have been deceived. History, twisted over eons by liars and cheats who have forgotten the love shared by our holy Father and Mother."

"Blasphemer!" someone in the crowd called out.

"Hang him!"

"Crucify him!"

"Silence!" Pi bellowed. His voice, like that of a giant, filled the air, sending a chill up Torsten's spine. In an instant, the crowd grew so quiet he could hear the clattering of glaruium armor far down below. "You speak ill of my uncle and your Prime Minister. The next who does shall speak no more."

With that, the silence lasted. There was no question that the common-folk of Yarrington remembered the sight of Oleander's slaughter, dozens swinging from the walls by their necks. Torsten wasn't sure if Pi would do the same. He'd seen such a glimmer of hope in the boy outside of Redstar's influence—but that was the problem. There they stood, side by side.

"Thank you, Your Grace." Redstar bowed to him, then turned back to the crowd. "For too long we have fought in mind and body! We have imagined our gods to be enemies until we believed it ourselves, down to our very cores. But I have seen the truth. I have seen it written in texts older than the Glass Kingdom itself, and I have seen it here." Redstar faced Pi. "Our Miracle King, brought back from the earth."

He returned to Wren's side, knelt, and took the holy man's hand. "And only yesterday, this great vessel of wisdom was sent to my chambers at the exact moment I was to die," Redstar said. "The voice of Iam on Pantego sent to save me, the voice of Nesilia—as if it were fated. That after all these long centuries of fighting, we might come together once more, as was always intended."

"Lord Redstar s-s-speaks the truth," Wren said, stammering.

Torsten grabbed hold of the window-sill and squeezed. Something was very wrong with the High Priest. He'd only just been a part of planning the assassination of Redstar, yet now was supporting him and speaking with a stutter he'd never had before. As if this were his first time speaking in front of a crowd rather than the ten-thousandth.

"I see now how foolish we've been," Wren continued. "T-t-torn apart by unknown grudges when it is so clear. The light of the sun cast upon Pantego is worthless without the earth to bear its warmth. We must come together."

"And we shall." Redstar stood and approached the edge of the wall. "The Goddess below and the God above shall be together once more. In the name of our King, Pi Nothhelm, the Miracle Prince, first of his name and son of Liam the Conqueror, we beseech you, therefore, brethren, today, shed your hate and see what we can become. Nesilia, the Buried Goddess stands with you. Iam, the Vigilant Eye stands with you. Your King stands with you!"

Redstar pointed back at Pi, and the crowd erupted. Torsten hadn't seen anything like it in many, many years. All those loyal servants of Iam, roaring in approval. They probably had no idea what they were even celebrating, but it was clear now that Redstar's silver tongue made even Whitney's seem like mere bronze.

Pi stepped forward. "Together, we will finish what my father started," he pronounced. "I know now that this is why the gods brought me back." He wasn't enthusiastic, and nowhere near as florid as Redstar's speech, but his voice carried. More cheers rained upon him, and when he opened his arms, the soldiers in the bailey marched out. Drav Cra, Glass soldiers, and Shieldsmen marched out side by side through the parting crowd.

"Rebellion still rages in the Southern sands," Pi said. "I

hereby name Sir Nikserof Pasic of the King's Shield and Drad Mak the Mountainous of the Drav Cra, Co-Wearers of White. They shall lead our armies under a single banner in bringing Afhem Muskigo to justice."

That was when Torsten noticed. The White Helm he'd worn now resided on Nikserof's head. His cape and a single pauldron were fitted snugly over the Drav Cra chief's patchwork of fur armor. Nikserof had only just been with Torsten and wore no such thing, which meant all this had just happened down in the bailey. The most experienced Shieldsman, and likely the only one with the pull to stand up to this new shifting of power, was being sent far away to war where he could do naught but serve his kingdom through blood.

No other Shieldsman deserved the honor more, but Torsten knew it wasn't intended to be one.

"Let Iam's light s-shhine upon our brave soldiers as they bring peace to this world," Wren the Holy exclaimed, lifting his cane, so the eye of Iam atop it caught sunlight and refracted a rainbow of colors.

"And let Nesilia bring them swiftly across the earth, from here and back again." Redstar grasped the cane right above Wren and raised it higher. King Pi stood before them, still calmly taking in the revelry of his subjects.

Redstar glanced back over his shoulder, looking directly up at the window where Torsten stood. Then he grinned. Torsten's blood boiled. All the most experienced King's Shieldsmen he might be able to trust in—many of which had fought at his side in Winde Port—were being sent away to finish the war. And all that'd be left behind would be green Shieldsmen and men like Mulliner whose loyalties could be more easily swayed by the promises of survival or glory.

There's no time for patience.

Torsten whipped around, remembering his intent to free

himself, take Redstar down, and end his influence over the impressionable young King. Freydis stood directly in front of him. He went to swing at her, but her hand dripped with blood, and her magic held him back.

Before he knew it, more Drav Cra warriors flooded into the room, and he was hauled back to his cell, deep below the castle, damned to do nothing while Iam's kingdom was usurped from within.

XVIII

THE MYSTIC

Sora lifted her hands off her ears and peered through her eyelashes at the window. A series of softer pops followed the booms. A sickly green glow emanated through the window, then morphed to blue.

She drew her knife and crept toward the opening, keeping the blade against her palm just in case. A few more blasts on the way made her wince, but when she got close enough to peer over the sill, she saw their source. It left him breathless.

High above the Red Tower and all across Lake Yaolin, flames burst in the night sky like fiery paint on a dark canvas. Only they were all types of colors, not just the orange of fire—blue, purple, green. She also realized that the shouting which proceeded every blast wasn't frantic, but instead, celebratory. A grouping of people stood downstairs on the patio overlooking the lake.

"What in the name of Iam?" she whispered just before another splash of color painted the sky red. Finally, she didn't flinch at the sound. She was just glad nobody had been around to see her hiding from something that didn't seem to be hurting anyone.

She found herself in the lobby of the Emperor's Quilt,

approaching the crowd of people appreciating the light show. She'd planned on staying in her room all night, waiting to hear from Lord Bokeo again, getting much-needed rest, but her heart raced too fast now.

She tapped someone on the shoulder, but they ignored her. She nudged another. The man leaned back but didn't remove his eyes from the spectacle.

"What is that?" she asked, nearly forced to shout over the noise.

"What's what?" replied the man.

Sora leaned in and pointed over the man's shoulder. She'd never seen anything that could compare. Perhaps the mystics were in hiding, but magic was surely not absent from this place.

"You serious?" he asked. "They're fireworks. This your first Festival of Ghosts?"

"No, of course not," she lied. "I…" She was trying to think of something to say when she realized the man was no longer listening anyway. Then, as suddenly as the fireworks started, they stopped, and everyone cheered, hooting and hollering, clapping their hands. As one, they turned and walked straight by Sora as if she didn't exist.

"Time for the fun!" said one woman as she passed.

"Let the trouble commence," said another.

Sora turned and watched them leave, wondering what manner of "fun" and "trouble" they were talking about.

A pit formed in her stomach. Both of those words reminded her of Whitney in the worst way. There was nothing he loved more than fun and trouble, and here she was, running off toward it alone. She was so out of her element, lost in a world she was unfamiliar with, and confused about everything, down to the question of who she was.

She shook her head. "How often are you in Yaolin City?" she

asked herself, since Aquira wasn't around to listen. "You can sleep another night."

So, she decided to treat herself to a night out in this strange new city. With the autlas from Gold Grin and Aran Bokeo, she could do whatever she wanted short of buying a mansion and still be fine for a very long time. She'd see what this Festival of Ghosts was about, sample the local cuisine—now that it was quieter she couldn't help but hear her stomach grumble—clear her mind, and maybe even learn something about her people. She deserved it after the mess this week had become, and tomorrow, she'd storm back to Lord Bokeo's shop and demand they get started.

The Emperor's Quilt was off the beaten path, perched on a cliff on the east side of Yaolin. Although the din of celebration seemed to fill every corner of the city, it wasn't until she reached Xiahou Boulevard that she saw the sheer magnitude of the event.

People were everywhere, parading down the streets dressed to the hilt in costumes. She saw lich lords and wraiths, skeletons and walking dead. There was even a group of four, all wearing the same zhulong costume, dancing about, knocking into people and causing a ruckus.

She pushed through the crowd, and no one seemed to mind. The shop stands she'd seen the guards remove earlier had returned, now gathered into squares adjacent to Xiahou Boulevard. The scent drew her to the one selling something called dumplings, and her stomach did the rest. Next thing she knew she'd purchased one, devoured it, and then brought another back to the street. In the West, they'd never wrap meat in dough in such a manner, but they were missing out. And the spices... Sora's taste buds had never been so grateful.

On the way out, another salesman offered for her to buy a carafe of liquid. She didn't have time to ask what it was before he pushed it on her. It was both sweet and a bit tangy, going down with a bite. She couldn't say she enjoyed it, though she couldn't help but wash down every bite with a sip.

Filling her stomach improved her mood. All the street performers doing their tricks were far more enticing, juggling balls of fire or swallowing swords. A line of revelers passed her, each wearing a part of a dragon costume and moving in a serpentine, so they appeared like one of the great, ancient beasts. They wrapped a tight circle around her, the reptilian face swaying right in front of her, then spun away to circle someone else.

A blast of fire at her back sent Sora spinning again.

"Experience the breath of dragons!" shouted the old, bearded man responsible for it. Before him stood a table with many jars and glass bottles. "Feel the heat of their flames and the roar of their bellies!"

Sora scrutinized the setup.

"Come to see magic?" he asked her in a loud, booming voice.

Sora stared at him as he absentmindedly poured two liquids into one vial.

"Come on, girl," he whispered, "just play along."

"Sure… show me." Sora moved in closer and nodded at him. He cleared his throat, and Sora noticed a few more people sidle up next to her while she pretended to be interested. With that, the man feverishly began mixing various potions and herbs. She couldn't help but be reminded of old Wetzel as steam rose from one of the vials.

"Long ago, a strapping, young man, with only the leather on his back and his father's old, rusty sword, set out on a trek into the cold, unforgiving Dragon's Tail Mountains," the man said, emphasizing every word with his hands as any good performer would.

He grabbed hold of the vial, tipped his hand, and poured out the contents. It was a slow, agonizing drip, flowing like tree sap.

When it touched the man's hand, it turned into a fine powder. He threw it, and it hit the crowd, cold as ice.

They all laughed and brushed the snowy substance off their cloaks.

"The snow beat down upon him," the man continued, "but he pressed forward, sure there was treasure within the many caverns." He reached beneath the table and brought out a thin, brown leather mat which he laid upon the surface, flattening it with his palm.

"One such cavern called to him." He covered his mouth with his hand, and a voice came from behind Sora.

"Hello!" it said, almost seeming to echo. She spun, as did the others. There was no doubt it was the performer's voice, but how he'd managed to send it behind them, Sora had no idea. She turned back to the man and clapped. The others joined in.

Maybe he isn't just a trickster.

"As he entered, his footsteps echoed within the high ceiling." The performer carefully set small piles of gray rock at varying intervals on the mat. With a finger, he tapped the edge of the mat and the stones popped in series, sounding like footfalls against the leather.

Sora found herself enchanted by the man's story.

"Darkness surrounded the young man," he continued. "A darkness fell unlike any he'd ever experienced, as if it blanketed his very soul, and a cold chill came over him, colder than any snowstorm could produce."

Sora could have been imagining it, but goosebumps rose up all over her body.

The old man reached into a pouch on his belt and produced an orange powder. He held it above a basin filled with liquid.

"That was when he heard it," he said, dropping the handful of powder. Sora jumped, and the now-large gathering cried out in surprise when the roar of a great beast sounded from the bowl.

"The dragon was awake. It was true, there was a vast treasure trove within that mountain, but there was, too, a guardian."

"He drew his sword, slowly approaching. One step, and then another." He tapped the mat again and the rocks leaped. "He could hear, in the darkness, a shifting, a rattle like metal on metal. He knew it was the beast's scales rubbing against one another. A mighty thwack, a dragon tail, rising and failing, over and over like a drum or the beating of a heart."

Sora was so caught up in the moment, she'd hardly even noticed the sound. Thump, thump. Thump, thump.

"He readied his sword, lifting it high above his head," the performer went on. His knees buckled, shaking like leaves on a windy day. Then, without warning, the reptilian nightmare unleashed a breath of fire that tore through the cavern, singeing even the man's eyebrows."

The performer quickly swigged a small vile, lifted his other hand to his mouth, tilted his head back, and blew a flame from his mouth that reached the rooftops.

The unified cry of fear and delight rose so loudly around Sora, she clenched her teeth together. The heat was intense, causing little beads of sweat to form on her forehead.

When the flame subsided, the crowd erupted in applause, Sora included. The old man bowed, then rose and waved his hands, encouraging his audience to be quiet.

"The young man was so frightened. You could imagine, could you not?" the performer said. The onlookers laughed and nodded. "He abruptly lowered his sword and turned to run. The rusty blade fell against his neck and carved a deep wound."

"Did he die?" shouted a man in the back.

The performer laughed. "What do you think?"

"The dragon ate him whole!" called a girl, so young Sora wondered why she wasn't in bed.

"Surely, it didn't. How then would the man know the tale!" said the child's mother.

"Right you are," said the performer. Then he reached up and grabbed the neckline of his tunic and dragged it down, revealing a long scar stretching from earlobe to collarbone. "I ran like Elsewhere had just unleashed her demon hordes."

A collective gasp sounded, then murmurs bounced around from person to person, many whispers and expressions of awe.

"I thank you, fair people of Yaolin and elsewhere, for listening to my story. If you enjoyed it, please help an old man who never did find the dragon's treasure." The performer shook a tin cup, a few coins scraping around on the bottom.

Men and women rushed forward to fill it with autlas, and the old man smiled, nodding his appreciation. Sora happily added a few bronzers. When the man gave a disapproving glare, she reached into her bag and added a silver piece, thanked him in Panpingese for his show, and turned to walk away.

"You know they're watching you," he said.

Sora turned back. "What?"

The man wasn't looking. He fiddled with his props, preparing them for the next show. She rushed to his side and took his arm. "What did you say?"

"Huh?" he said. "I said nothing."

"You said they were watching me. Who's watching me? The mystics? Are you one of them?"

"Look, girl, all this here is just a trick of alchemy. Anyone who knew a lick about real magic died in the war or is smart enough to hide from the Glassmen. Now please, leave me alone so I can prepare. Time is money!"

Sora released the man's robe, and he brushed the wrinkles away before returning to his bottles. She glanced around, looking for where the voice might have originated, but the performer's onlookers had dispersed, leaving only the costumed revelers marching down the street.

She hurried along, once again caught up in the parade. By the time she'd slowed down, she was nearly at a central square, which was more of a circle. It appeared to be the spot where all the statues, presumably of the Pinyun, which now looked vaguely like an army of Liam the Conqueror, came together into what felt like an arena. A series of repurposed, domed temples, now all dedicated to Iam, encircled the fireside.

"Sora!" she thought she heard a voice call out from somewhere within the parade. However, through all the costumed bodies, all wearing masks, some colorful, some terrifying, she couldn't find its source.

They're watching you. Those words echoed in Sora's head.

She whirled, and more costumed people surrounded her. It grew dizzying. She picked up her pace through the mob, fingering the grip of her knife as she moved. Her name filled the air again; then a hand grabbed her shoulder, the grip firm but gentle.

"Aye, lass!"

Sora turned, tearing her knife free and raised it toward the neck of whoever was following. Only there was no neck. Her knife hovered over a clump of messy, red hair, and she looked down to see Tum Tum with his hands in the air.

Tum Tum laughed nervously as he slowly brushed her knife-hand aside. "If ye're ever bein snuck up on by a dwarf, ye might want to aim lower," he said, able to make a joke out of anything.

"Oh, Tum Tum !" Sora laughed and threw her arms around him. When she backed away, she saw Gold Grin behind him, wearing a long robe and... the Glass Crown upon his head. Fortist and Hestor stood at his side, one dressed like a noble and the other a jester.

"Are you mad?" Sora asked.

"What? This?" he laughed, fingering the crown. "Might be the only night I get to show it off. No one would be crazy enough to believe it was the real thing."

He bowed his head and took her hand. "Dearest Sora of Troborough. It is a pleasure to see you again."

He pressed his lips against the top of her hand. It was only then she realized that for the first time in longer than she could remember, she wasn't wearing gloves in public. Thanks to Lord Bokeo there were no scars of her unlawful practice of blood magic to hide.

"And you," she said as he gently released her hand. The act of a pirate who seemed more gentleman than monster caused her to blush, which in turn made her punch Tum Tum in the arm to draw attention from her cheeks. Unlike Whitney, Tum Tum was solid as a rock.

"Oi!" Tum Tum yelped. "What that be for!"

"For making me inquire about The Ruby House," she said. "And my subsequent red cheeks."

All four men, Gold Grin, Tum Tum, Fortist and Hestor laughed, hands to their bellies, nearly doubling over for the effort. Judging by their red cheeks and the distant look in their eyes, they'd all had a few drinks already.

"I'm supposin you din't want a room there then?" Tum Tum said.

Sora reared back again, and Tum Tum flinched, but she was sure it was just for show. "No, thank you. I've got a room at the Emperor's Quilt."

"Oh, ye tired of the *Reba*'s modest rooms, did ye?" Gold Grin said, then hiccupped. "Wanted a taste of luxury?"

"I hear there be a stand nearby that sells rice wine that'll knock you out," Tum Tum added.

"It's nothing compared to the Winder's Dwarf," Sora said, but immediately regretted it. She'd wanted to compliment Tum Tum on his wonderful pub back in Winde Port, but considering she'd been the one responsible for burning it, and the rest of Winde Port to soot and ash, she lowered her head and said, "Sorry."

"Nonsense! Nothin to be sorry for. Had that bundle of sticks not gotten torched I ain't never've been able to experience *Gu —Guin—Gway—*"

"*Gyuan Jie,*" Sora helped, then shrugged when his brow furrowed. "I've picked up a few words already."

"Bah!" the dwarf cried. "The Festival of Ghosts. Law be to speak common anyway, ain't it? Say, where's yer dragon?"

"Wyvern," she corrected, "and it's a long story."

"We ain't got time for long stories, dwarf," said Gold Grin. "Not if ye don't want us to leave ye where ye stand."

"Guess that's me cue," Tum Tum sighed.

"What? I'm not invited?" Sora asked.

"Trust me, lass, ye don't want a part of it. Old Gold Grin wants to help me open a right western pub here in his namesake. First, we have to convince an old codger to sell his place."

"Right on the lake." Gold Grin tossed his arm around her, and she realized why he was acting so strangely. He was so drunk, he could hardly stand. Extending one arm as if gesturing to something grand, he said, "There be no more perfect place for Gold Grin's Grotto. Can you picture it?"

Sora chuckled. "Stunning."

Tum Tum shrugged. "Pirates," he muttered to her. "Can't say no to me only investors though!"

"Come, Tum Tum!" Gold Grin slurred, stumbling a few paces after he released Sora. His arm no sooner left her than went around one of his men, though they were in no better state. "Leave this fair lady to her business. We have a shop to pillage —" His lagging gaze met Sora's, and he blinked. "Purchase. That's the word."

"I'll see ye around, aye?" Tum Tum said to Sora. "Ye know where to find me."

"If you think I'm going to come calling for you at the Ruby House like some desperate damsel..."

Tum Tum chortled. "I'll be findin you then. And the moment I've got me own place up and running, first drink's on me."

"I look forward to it."

Gold Grin shot her an awkward, crooked smile, then he, Tum Tum, and the rest staggered off. They were quite the sight, hulking man the pirate king was, shoulder to shoulder with the small, stout dwarf. Sora couldn't help but chuckle.

They were barely out of view when Sora heard a screech and saw a familiar shape zip by her face. At least, she thought she did. She wondered if she'd accidentally tried some of that strong rice wine Tum Tum referred to and that's why she was hearing and seeing things.

"Excuse me," she said, running. And, "Pardon," then finally, "Move!"

She didn't even care that she'd knocked several people to the ground, all of them berating her verbally as she put them behind her.

The line of people in their dragon costume passed in front of her, and she slid beneath their shuffling feet. She heard another cry, looked up, and saw Aquira. The wyvern flapped her wings and soared overhead, swooping in and out of a grouping of revelers with flags on posts, waving them to and fro.

"Aquira!" Sora shouted. She followed her wyvern friend up a flight of stone steps. If Aquira had heard her, she was ignoring her, which was very unusual.

Something is wrong.

When Sora reached the top of the stairs, Aquira was nowhere in sight. She searched, frantic, but there was no sign of her, nothing to clue her into where Aquira had gone until…

A frightened screech rang out. Sora dug her heels in and pushed off toward the sound. She slid around a corner and gasped.

She was before an open, circular temple with a domed roof held upright by marble columns, Eyes of Iam dangling from gold chains between them.

The seven mystics from earlier stood around a young boy lying horizontally on a stone slab in the center. He was tied down, struggling to wriggle free as he cried. The mystics' faces remained shrouded by the loose-hanging hoods of their robes. The Ancient One, Aihara Na, wielded a crude weapon, little more than a sharp rock, and had it raised above her head. Aquira hovered, watching but not interfering.

Aihara Na spoke words in Panpingese, words that Sora wouldn't have understood the day before, but now they met her ears with clarity. She wished she didn't understand.

"Blood of babe, bone of child, bring forth the power of Elsewhere's fire." Aihara rotated the weapon so that the razor-sharp edge was facing the boy's chest. Sora's mind instantly drew on rumors she'd heard from passersby and even Torsten in the Webbed Woods, about how the old mystics used to experiment on their people in the name of magic. She'd thought them to be exaggerated stories like everything else, but she'd thought the same about Nesilia.

Sora didn't think, she just reacted.

"Aquira, move!" she said as she sliced her arm with her knife. Blood flowed, and Sora barely noticed the pain. She entered the temple and raised her hand, knowing that she needed to be careful not to harm the boy she was trying to save.

Aihara Na and the other mystics turned to face her, Aihara lowering her shiv. All their expressions remained hard as stone, unfazed by her arrival. It was then that Sora realized how gravely outnumbered she was. But it didn't matter.

All manner of thoughts passed through her mind in the moments it took to call upon Elsewhere, turning her hand into a deadly, fiery war-machine. Fear gripped her at the thought of turning another city into cindery ash, but she had to do something to save the child.

"Lower your hand, girl," Aihara Na spoke, her voice like thunder. "The boy's life is the sacrifice to commune with the other side. With Elsewhere. It must be done, lest we fade to ashes."

Elsewhere. Sora froze, flame wreathed around her hand. Of all the places for Aquira to lead her, it was to this clandestine ceremony where the Secret Council sought to connect with Elsewhere.

"Aquira led you here with reason," Aihara Na said as if reading her mind. "Breaching the other side is the key to unlimited power. To eternal life and resurrection! It can be yours as well. For that is why you sought us out, is it not?"

Sora found herself unable to reply. The other mystics returned to the ceremony, surrounding the struggling child, chanting in Panpingese and other languages. Every language. They blended, one beginning where the other took off, overlapping. Their voices hummed, and the air crackled as air swirled around the temple. In fact, now she realized that around that structure, all she could see was darkness as if Yaolin City had disappeared.

"Come, Sora," Aihara beckoned. Before she knew it, Sora had lowered her hand and approached the boy. "Fulfill your destiny and join us. Rip open the fabric of this world as the gods did so long ago, and become as powerful as a goddess yourself!"

Sora felt Aihara Na place the stone in her hands but didn't see her. All she could focus on was that boy, thrashing, begging to survive. Fire closed in over the weapon as Sora gripped it. From within her, she could feel her power bubbling to the surface, her very soul drawing upon the world between worlds, on Elsewhere. Only now it was different, the sensation stronger. It was like a dam she didn't know existed broke open, and her power flooded through her.

She raised the stone over the boy. The blackness around them took shape, and again she could see Whitney in a realm of shadow and obscurity. He called out to her, so near yet impossibly far. All she had to do was complete the ritual, and she could tear him free from the torment she'd exiled him to.

Only, he wasn't alone.

She also heard Nesilia, whispering her name, her voice both matronly and seductive. She could see her pale, colorless eyes reflected in those of the boy. "I know you," she whispered. "I've always known you."

"Sora!" Whitney called out.

Sora's hand's shook as she gripped the weapon. Her fire was intense now, the stone itself glowed. She struggled to focus as more power than should have been possible through her bleeding hand crackled on her fingertips. And then, in the faintest whisper, she heard the boy's cries again.

"Please don't hurt me…" he whimpered. "I'll do anything…"

"No!" Sora screamed. She brought the stone around and stopped it a finger's length away from Aihara Na's throat. The darkness surrounding her whisked away, and the city and the temple grew visible again along with the other yellow-clad mystics.

"I'll die before I hurt an innocent child," she said.

Aihara Na stalked forward, unperturbed by the sharp object at her throat. Her hands were folded in front of her chest as if praying to Iam. Sora backed away but kept the blade raised.

"Don't touch him!" Her anger fueled the flame along the stone, and its tendrils now lashed out at Aihara Na. The mystic's skin should have been boiling, but it didn't appear to harm her at all.

"Brave," Aihara Na said. "It appears the Will of Fire is true." She waved her hand toward the boy, and all his bindings came undone. "Go child. And remember that we are not lost." The child didn't wait for her to finish speaking before he scurried away.

"What are—"

Aihara whipped suddenly around and placed her finger against Sora's forehead. She whispered something in Panpingese, too quiet for Sora to understand, and Sora's fire extinguished in an instant. Her vision blurred.

Before her world went black, she realized that she'd rejected the chance to open Elsewhere and save Whitney in exchange for a child she didn't know. She wondered if she'd missed out on her only opportunity, but she didn't regret it. No matter what happened in the Webbed Woods or Winde Port, no matter what she really was, she knew one thing—she wasn't a killer like Kazimir or Muskigo.

XIX

THE DESERTER

"Are ye sure this is smart?" Sigrid whispered into Rand's ear as they followed Valin Tehr and his cronies through the winding Dockside streets. Night had fallen upon Yarrington. While clouds obscured Celeste's normally bright glow, snow blanketed the streets, making it more like home for the Drav Cra.

"We need to disappear, and nobody does it better," Rand said.

"But still, Father always said he was a man never to get in bed with."

"The King's Shield deals with pretend-lords like him all the time. I know enough about his operation to keep us safe."

"Keep up, Shieldsman!" Valin hollered back. "I shouldn't be able to outpace you on this leg."

Sigrid took Rand's arm. "I trust ye; ye know that. And I missed ye."

"I've been with you this whole time," Rand said.

Sigrid leveled a glare at him. The kind that said, 'No you haven't,' and he couldn't deny it. Perhaps in body, but his mind had been absent for far too long. He put on an abashed smile. All things considered, she seemed to be handling her first kill well.

"I'm with ye now," he said, his Dockside speech returning, if only for a moment. No matter how badly his head ached or his body sweat as it longed for a sip of ale, he vowed silently, staring upon her face, never to touch the stuff again. He'd broken the vows he'd made to the King's Shield, but one made in her name, he'd keep.

"I hope so."

"You don't have to worry about me anymore. What about you? I know what it's like to take a life. Better than most. I—"

"I'm fine brother. It was him or watching ye die, and I'd do the same every time."

"You're stronger than I am."

"Yer finally noticing?"

They exchanged a smile and a nod, then caught up to Valin who crutched along the docks. A line of Drav Cra longboats swayed in the water. A group of them sat outside a tavern, drinking with no signs of stopping. They remained outside as if the worst winter Rand had known in his life were summer. They even had some of their animal-skin tents set up in the yard.

"Look at them, Rand Langley," Valin said. "They flood the district, autlas like trinkets to them, our women like toys. They pay for nothing and intimidate inns for ale and lodging. Some have scared my people from their homes and taken them for their own."

"They have no respect for us," Rand agreed.

"They have no need for that kind of respect. I don't fault them for how they treat this city. In the North, survival is all that matters. But they're bad for business." He stopped and pointed to the tavern's owner. The man poured them another round, shaking, braving the cold instead of making them come inside. "I control that tavern. I decide what everything costs. Jipper there is a good fellow, always pays on time. But when my people are more frightened of the foreigners than me… that's when I have a problem."

"Then why don't ye drive them off?" Sigrid said. "Yer owing them protection, just like yer owing it to Trapp. Ain't that how it works?"

Valin scowled. "It isn't so simple, girl. After they returned victorious from Winde Port, more came. There are now more than twice as many of them here than men on my payroll. The depravities Old Yarrington shirks as being for us poorer souls, the Drav Cra adore. I can't protect it all now."

"Only your drugs, huh?" Rand glanced back at the crate one of Valin's men grabbed from the basement of Maiden's Mugs before leaving. People all over the city used manaroot, the powerful sensory amplifier Valin smuggled into the city from the far east—the perks of owning the dockworkers. Rand had even found some in the castle kitchens once. The chef swore he was trying a new dish.

"Careful, Rand. You may wear that armor, but you're an outlaw, now, in the company of outlaws."

"Trust me, I know."

Valin started walking again, and everyone kept to his leisurely pace. "In the end, the Drav Cra are bad for us all," he said. "But make no mistake. If they came down here with gold instead of furs and relics, I'd have handed you over to Redstar already."

"Some champion of Dockside," Sigrid murmured under her breath. Rand nudged her.

"Did you know that some of the servants your brother executed for the Queen were from here?" Valin said. "Rose to the highest place a man or woman from Dockside incapable of fighting could rise, only to be cut down at his hands."

"She didn't leave him a choice."

"My dear, there is always a choice. I merely have the means to see mine through."

Sigrid grunted but kept quiet. Rand focused on keeping the memories of those executions at bay. He hadn't known any of his victims were from Dockside, but why would he? Neither he nor the Queen gave them a fair trial. All he could do was wonder if her beautiful, sweet, handmaiden Tessa had grown up right down the street from him, or if they'd played on the docks together as children, angered old Gunter together.

"Spare a coin, Lord Tehr?" a beggar asked. He kowtowed on the street, hands upturned, an Eye of Iam etched in the snow before him. A group of others doing the same had gathered on a lane down to Fortune's Landing, the small, well-off part of Dockside, if any part of it could be called well-off.

Rand knew the place well and knew that The Vineyard—the brothel Valin made his headquarters—would be just down the way. There was no sign on the door saying that was where to find him, but everyone in Dockside knew it.

Rand and Sigrid fell back a bit while Valin reached into a coin purse and removed a handful of silver autlas. He placed them in the beggar's hand, and before the man could run, grabbed him by the wrist.

"Share this, or it is the last that shall come," he said.

"Yes, me lord," the beggar said. "Praise Iam."

"There is no Iam here."

Valin continued walking by as the filthy beggar handed out alms for him. He'd made the man an employee without him even realizing, and all the others stroked Valin's arms and praised him as he passed, like he was Wren the Holy himself.

"Valin, we discussed this," Codar, his Breklian advisor said, speaking for the first time since the Maiden's Mugs. "The more you hand out to these people... they'll keep coming back like stray cats."

"Oh, Codar, have a bit of fun," Valin said. A dirt-coated woman took his hand and shook it in gratitude.

"So long as the Drav Cra are here, we can't afford to give—"

"Codar, do you know why you have stayed here all this time, instead of returning to Brekliodad to handle the coffers of one of your fancy oligarchs?"

"Because you pay better than anybody else."

"Exactly. And if, or when, all these poor souls are forced to rise and take iron to the Drav Cra, they'll do it for me. Loyalty, old friend. That's all that matters in this life."

"Valin Tehr!" a husky voice barked. "Just the man I've been looking for."

Rand saw the sheen of armor first, then grabbed Sigrid and ducked into the shadow of the nearest overhang. Captain Henry of the Dockside guard stood outside of the Vineyard with a few other Glass soldiers.

He was an unimpressive man, as one would expect for the soldier tasked with keeping Dockside safe. Rand didn't know him well, but having been a city guard before The King's Shield took him in, Rand had spent a year serving beneath Henry.

"Captain Henry," Valin said, leaning on his good leg so he could bow with a flourish. "To what do I owe this great pleasure?" He strutted right up to him, seemingly without concern that being carried behind him was a crate of outlawed manaroot as well as the most wanted man in Yarrington.

"What do we do?" Sigrid whispered into Rand's ear.

"Just wait," he answered. He kept his head low, hoping the darkness and the falling snow would be enough to conceal him.

"Crazy happenings down by the castle," Captain Henry said.

"Are there?" Valin replied. "I haven't heard of anything."

Captain Henry's fat lips went straight. "What's in the crate, Valin?"

"A cake from my favorite baker. It's Codar's birthday, you see."

Henry and his men circled him, stopping by the thug carrying the crate. Valin and Codar watched calmly.

"I love birthdays," Captain Henry said. He slapped the top of the crate. "You wouldn't mind if I crack it open, try a piece?"

"I would prefer you didn't," Valin said.

Captain Henry started to lift the lid, but the brute holding it glowered down at him and he backed off. Rand also noticed Codar's hand wrapped around the blade of a dirk sheathed behind his back.

"I'm full anyway," Captain Henry grumbled. He went to turn, and his gaze froze upon Rand. "Got Shieldsman working for you now, do you?"

"One can't be too careful in these days," Valin said.

"Ain't that the truth. Thing is, the Crown has us all keeping on the lookout for a traitor to the Order. One of them took a shot at our new Prime Minister, the hero of Winde Port and the King's own uncle."

"Why, that is awful."

"You wouldn't happen to know anything about that, would you?" Captain Henry started toward Rand, but Valin was unexpectedly quick on his cane and got in front of him.

"Nothing at all. But we'll keep a weather eye out for the traitor, in the name of the King. To kill the royal uncle, no matter what he did in the past... why, that I cannot abide."

Rand thought he saw something pass quickly between their hands. The captain looked Valin over once more, then grinned.

"Long reign the Miracle King," Captain Henry said.

"Now," Valin guided him back the other way, "why don't you go make sure your armory is secure before the savages take everything? Leave our busy streets to me."

"Aye boys, I think we will." He waved his hand in a circle for them to move along, then grabbed Valin by the collar. "You're up to something, Tehr," he whispered. "Whatever it is, I want in."

"I assure you," Valin said, removing the man's hand with two fingers, "I only mean to celebrate the life of my dear friend Codar amongst good company."

"I want in," Captain Henry whispered again before catching up to his men. He offered Rand a salute on his way by, a few of his men chuckling, then seized one of the beggars and shoved him along. "Clear the streets, ye filth. No begging beyond the church grounds. All of you!"

Rand rarely thought about it, but now he remembered why he was so eager to get out of the Dockside guard. Most of them were less honorable than Valin's thugs, and they did a hell of a lot less for Dockside. Rand also knew he should've been concerned that the guard captain recognized him, but he wasn't. So long as Valin kept the man's mouth full and his pocket's stuffed, serving the Crown came second.

"I detest that man," Codar said, releasing his weapon.

"Now, now, old friend, don't bite the hand that appeases us," Valin said.

Codar didn't respond.

Rand hadn't known many people from the mountainous lands of northeast Pantego, with their hair as white as the land and accents just as harsh, but all those whom he'd ever met were equally short with words.

"Come along, Shieldsman," Valin beckoned. "There are others who would take justice into their own hands, even if Redstar is a bloody savage."

Rand retook Sigrid's hand, and they followed Valin. Only two structures in Dockside were more prominent than The Vineyard—both were churches, both were on either side of Fortune's Landing, and both were in far worse shape. The chapel of sins, which made Valin Tehr the wealthiest man in Yarrington outside of castle halls, sat like a jewel within a field of gray stone. A balcony lined the second floor, oak railings sculpted to appear like grapevines and big-bosomed women. On warmer days, the terrace would be packed with wenches and rich, old men.

Rand never imagined he'd be bringing his sister anywhere near the place. He'd never been there himself. One step inside reminded him why he'd never had any desire.

A wall of hot, humid air accosted him. He was grateful for the warmth, but not the stench—sweat, ale, sex, and Iam knows what else. It was enough to send the aches of withdrawal soaring to the front of his mind and make him want to vomit. He found himself squeezing Sigrid's hand with a sweaty one of his own.

Whores strutted around in every direction, wearing naught but beads and frills. They chatted with men of all types and classes, feigning laughs and interest. A group of off-duty guards sat in the corner. A man dressed as a noble lounged in a booth by the bar, three women all over him.

It was like they'd left Pantego itself.

A single hearth gave the big space a hellish, red glow. The outside balcony was mirrored inside with the same oak railings. Rand followed a Panpingese man with his eyes as a whore led him behind one of the many curtains. Back on ground level, a musician troupe kept the racket of the upstairs dealings quiet, playing eerie tunes on stringed instruments Rand hadn't seen before. They appeared Shesaitju in origin but weren't loud enough to completely mask the loud moans and grinding bodies echoing all around like a percussion line.

Valin held out an arm. A bulky man crashed through the second-floor railing and hit the floor in front of them. Rand jumped back, Sigrid yelped. Men Rand recognized as more of Valin's thugs rushed down the stairs and grabbed the fat man. A young, Glintish girl burst out of a room upstairs, covering her breasts as she shouted in her language. She had a cut on both her chin and brow. Rand caught himself staring at the girl from Glinthaven and hoped Sigrid didn't notice. Their strange beauty had always enraptured him, skin the color of dark chocolate like Torsten's. The music paused, only momentarily, as Valin's men grabbed hold of the fat man and heaved him through the open doors and onto the Dockside streets. Not a moment later, everything returned to business as usual.

"And that is why I'm glad I never had a daughter," Valin remarked, brushing dust from his sleeve. "Clean this shog up. Now! It's bad for business."

"Rand, I have a bad feeling about this," Sigrid whispered.

"It's fine," Rand replied. He drew her close, then noticed a booth with at least a dozen Drav Cra warriors crowded around. A naked woman danced in the middle of them, and they all gawked, motionless.

"Manaroot," Valin said as if reading Rand's mind. "It makes the simplest things appear like magic, and it keeps the savages from tearing this place and my girls to pieces."

"A costly solution," Codar added.

"And a temporary one."

Valin snapped his fingers to two large men guarding a door behind the bar. They stepped aside to reveal a dark stairway. The sounds of merriment and stringed instruments were replaced by pounding. Rand saw light filtering through a curtain at the end of a long passage. The people beyond went silent, then half gasped and half broke out into raucous cheering.

One of Valin's men opened the door to their right and beckoned them in before Rand could see what was beyond the curtain.

"Weapons," the thug said, offering a hand. Rand glanced at Sigrid, who was busy looking to him for what to do.

"I assure you, it's merely a formality," Valin said. "I can't tell you how many people want me dead. It gets exhausting."

"I could say the same for myself," Rand replied. "How do I know you won't tie me up and hand me over to Redstar?"

"Do you think that sword of yours is all that's stopping me?

Stop being a fool like all the other sanctimonious Shieldsmen. You aren't one any longer."

Rand regarded his sister again. He could tell she didn't like where they were, but it was too late now. He nodded her along, then unbuckled his sheath and handed it over. Sigrid did the same with the Drav Cra shortbow and bone-tipped arrows she'd taken from the Maiden's Mugs.

The guard stepped aside. Everyone else but Codar stayed in the hall. Rand guessed they were now in Valin's personal office, judging by the fine mahogany desk stacked with writs and pay logs. Men like Valin didn't stay rich without keeping track of everything.

Months back, the Shield would have killed to be in this room, with access to enough shady dealings to wipe Valin Tehr and his gang from the face of Pantego for good. Valin didn't care to blend in or lay low like the other gangs of Dockside or South Corner. He was happy to flaunt his debauchery and wealth, and Rand was starting to wonder if the Shield ever even wanted to take him down.

A raid on The Vineyard wouldn't cost many lives, and few within its walls were innocent. But a number of gangs vying for Valin's underground kingdom, eager to make a name for themselves, sounded far worse than organized chaos beneath a self-proclaimed king. And if Rand previously had doubts Valin viewed himself that way, now he was sure.

Valin's self-portrait donned the wall behind his desk, an image of him leaning on his cane. It wasn't exactly the same as the portraits of Glass Kingdom monarchs lining the Glass Castle halls, clutching a scepter topped with the Eye of Iam, but the parallels were clear enough. All around the room, more stunning works of art and foreign trinkets covered walls and filled shelves. There was a fishing spear with a shaft of Shesaitju blackwood and a stone point—it had to be centuries old. Across from it was a dwarven helm centuries older, patterns etched into the bronze with such precision craftsmanship, only gods seemed capable of crafting it.

The room contained enough wealth for Valin to build a castle for himself, which had Rand questioning why he chose to remain in his underworld kingdom of shog-stained streets.

"Codar, please fetch our guests here some of that Breklian brandy I love so much," Valin requested, taking a seat behind his desk. He lifted his malformed leg onto the mahogany, groaned, and rubbed the knee.

"I shouldn't," Rand said, a hint of desperation in his tone. Valin must have noticed it because his brow raised.

"Ah yes, a man battling his vices," Valin said, waving Codar to stop. "You'll find few who understand better than I."

"Or how to get rich off them," Sigrid remarked. Again, Rand nudged her to stay quiet. She'd always been the more rebellious of the two. The one to want to explore the streets after their parents put them down for bed. All her pent-up anger dealing with Trapp, just to have a place to live, clearly bubbling to the surface. The guilt of having to kill a man likely wasn't helping either, even if she thought she was 'fine.'

"See what we get for offering our hospitality?" Valin said to Codar. The Breklian merely shook his head in disapproval. He remained by the door, hands crossed behind his back, eyes on everything. "One can only profit off what he knows best, dear."

"Those girls upstairs—"

"Those girls live better than half the louts in Dockside. And you saw what happens when a visitor doesn't treat them like they're my own flesh and blood."

"Then why don't ye take one of their places on a bed."

"Siggy, stop," Rand snapped.

"I heard about more than just manaroot working for Trapp," she continued, ignoring Rand.

"All lovely things, I'm sure?" Valin said calmly.

"Now there's a word for it."

Valin laughed and clapped his hands. "Your sister has fire, Rand Langley. Eyes closed, and I'd question which one of you was the knight. A woman like her could—"

Now it was Rand's turn to step forward and grit his teeth. "Don't you dare."

Valin shrugged. "Your loss. Men come here because they think they want a chance to control something for once in their gods-forsaken lives. They stay so they can lose control of everything in the arms of a goddess."

Rand lost his train of thought. Sigrid's cheeks turned the same color as her ginger hair. Valin swung his leg down, then came limping around his desk toward Sigrid.

"Yes, I see it now," he said. "Gideon Trapp was a fool to keep you all to himself in that dump." He circled her and drew back her messy hair to accentuate her features. She shrugged him away. "Just a little polish, you could rival the Queen of Glass herself."

"Yer disgusting," Sigrid spat.

"Please, Mr. Tehr." Rand stepped closer and took Valin by the arm. Out of the corner of his eyes, he noticed Codar's forearm tense out of reflex, ready to draw his dirk. Rand released Valin quickly and backed away. "You brought me here to discuss removing Redstar. We can't waste any more time."

"By Iam, you're right." Valin turned back toward his desk. "These young ones do hate conversation, Codar."

"A shame," Codar remarked.

"Always wanting to get right to the destination when the riches are in the journey." He plopped back down into his chair, and again, stretched out his leg. "So, tell me, Rand Langley. Why should we work together rather than fetch the hefty price your head is worth? Enough to buy your fair sister a farm of her own."

"Because together we can free the kingdom from Redstar's grip."

"And why would you want that? He's not hanging anyone like his sister. All he's done is root out a traitor in the Royal Council, and drive a rebel army away from Winde Port."

"But… you said you wanted to get rid of him." If Rand wasn't nervous already, he was now.

"I said I wanted to get rid of the Drav Cra. Tell me, have you considered what happens when you murder their Arch Warlock in cold blood? When their people go rampaging through the streets out for revenge?"

"I…"

"See, Codar? Even the deserter is like any other knight. Short-sighted. Charging ahead like a starved boar."

"If you don't want to help, why did you invite me here?" Rand questioned.

"I simply want you to understand what you're asking. Removing the Drav Cra now, while much of their army is off fighting the Crown's war, is the sensible decision. I can live with the carnage; chaos is profitable. Can you?"

Rand turned to Sigrid. She bit her lip, deep in thought, her eyes dull with sorrow. Rand knew why. They'd always been able to tell what the other was thinking.

More death on my hands.

He took Sigrid's hand and nodded. Her head sunk.

"The longer we give them to drive their roots into our streets, the more fighting there will be," Rand decided. "My Wearer, and the very mouth of Iam asked this of me. If I hide again, what am I?"

Valin chuckled. "A smart man. But, assuming you're insane, what is your plan to eliminate the imposter?"

Rand drew a deep breath. "We free Sir Torsten Unger from the dungeons. I know what cell he's in. Wren the Holy believes he still has enough support to get the King's Shield back on his side."

"Torsten Unger?" Valin's brow furrowed.

"Yes, he is the rightful Wearer of White, Commander of the King's armies, and one of the greatest warriors alive. I've faced Redstar alone and failed. Torsten is strong, experienced in fighting him, and together we can—"

Valin erupted in laughter until tears rolled down his cheeks. Even Codar let a slight snigger slip through his lips.

"What's so funny?" Sigrid questioned.

"Torsten yigging Unger? That is what you're offering? The location of another disgraced Wearer?" Again, Valin stood and limped right up to Sigrid. "Do you fools think I don't have people that can tell me where Torsten is?"

"They don't know the castle," Rand said.

"They sweep up the damn shog!" He slammed his cane on the ground. "All the kingdom knows that Torsten is a traitor who murdered one of their own. Who do you think would help him? Sir Nikserof Pasic was sent off to war. Who else is there from Uriah's old guard? Wren the Holy just stood beside Redstar and the King and declared Iam and Nesilia kin."

"What? No," Rand said, incredulous. "That's impossible. Wren came to me. He sent me on this quest."

"An imagined visit. Brought about by the drowning of your sorrows, I'd wager."

"He was there! And he saved my life from Redstar when he unleashed his dark magic by summoning a shield of light. It was as if Iam worked through him just to keep me alive."

Valin scoffed. "Are you so desperate for a purpose to believe that?"

"Iam chose me!" Rand screamed. He didn't care who he was talking to, but the harshness in his tone caused Codar to reach for his dirk again.

"Don't hurt him!" Sigrid shouted, but Valin slammed his cane again, and she froze.

"He chose me!" Rand's knees went wobbly, and he had to crouch to keep from passing out. Shouting made his head hurt so bad, it felt like someone was dragging a knife around the rim of his skull. "I have to fix what I started..." he said weakly. "I executed all those people for her. Drove away anyone who could stand up to Redstar."

"Get up, you sniveling fool." Valin placed his cane under Rand's jaw and lifted.

"Rand." Sigrid wrapped her arms around him and helped him to his feet.

"It seems power isn't for everyone," Valin said to Codar as he clacked back to his desk.

"Please, Mr. Tehr, you have to listen to me," Rand said. "I don't know why, but I know now that only Torsten can kill Redstar. Whatever they started in the Webbed Woods, it has to be him. I tried to do it myself, but Wren the Holy is right."

"Codar, come here." The Breklian lifted his dirk away and moved to Valin's side where they held a private conversation. The former remained staid as ever while they talked. Valin, however, couldn't help but glance over and grin.

"He's not lying," Sigrid said to them. "I was there, too. I saw Wren come to my brother after he tried to..." She regarded Rand mournfully. "All that matters is that he was there."

Valin seemed to take what she said to heart. Eventually, Codar stepped aside and calmly folded his hands behind his back.

"Okay, Shieldsman," Valin said. "We're going to help you break Torsten out. I miss my feuds with the stubborn, former Wearer. No matter how hard I tried, he remained... incorruptible. You have to respect that sort of blind obedience."

"Thank you, sir, I— "

Valin raised a hand to silence him. "Who am I to strike down a man chosen by Iam Himself? But this isn't charity anymore. If I do this, you're going to help me with something. A task worthy of a warrior of the King's Shield."

Rand swallowed. "What do you need?"

Valin leaned forward, steepled his fingers, and smiled. "Isn't that always the question?"

XX

THE MYSTIC

It wasn't exactly that Sora woke up; she hadn't been sleeping. She'd experienced the whole journey after whatever Aihara Na did to her, eyes wide-open. The problem was that although she saw everything, she couldn't process anything. It was as if she was under the influence of one of Wetzel's potions for some life-threatening malady, one that would require the patient to be relieved from the very feeling of existence.

That was how she felt, like she was relieved from feeling anything at all. She'd felt cobbled roads, and seen water. She remembered climbing stairs and seeing people—but all those things might have been true of any place in the city.

She was hopelessly confused.

A finger pressed against her forehead, same as before, and she snapped to. Her fists waved around as if trying to punch out an army by herself.

Sora's vision became clear again. She stood alone in a room with Aihara Na. Unlike most of Yaolin City with its wood and sweeping tile roofs, this room was hard, cold, red stone. The ceiling extended high above, braziers of fire hanging at varying intervals.

"There you are," Aihara Na said. "Everything is all right." For the first time, the woman had her hood drawn back, and Sora could see the details of her face. High, proud, cheekbones and a long chin creased with wrinkles at the point. She wasn't ancient like Wetzel, despite the title Lord Bokeo gave her, but it was evident she'd seen much of the world. Her expression spoke of decades of disappointment, exhaustion.

"What are you doing to me?" Sora was instantly reminded of the time, not too long ago in Winde Port, that Kazimir had her chained up in the steeple of a church. But this time, she realized, she wasn't chained up. Aihara Na wasn't even looking at her. Sora was completely free and uninhibited, yet still found incapacitated. It was like her mind had to relearn how to operate her body.

Aihara Na moved toward Sora, and Sora would have shrunk back if she could've. "We've already told you what we will do. We are going to train you in the mystic arts."

"Train me? I want nothing to do with you or your wicked rituals. You're no better than the Drav Cra, sacrificing life to get what you want."

Aihara merely smirked in response.

Just then, Aquira crawled out from behind a column.

"Aquira," Sora said. Her foot finally budged, and she stomped forward hard without meaning to. Now it was Aquira's turn to shrink back. Her eyes blinked fast, and Sora recognized a look of sadness when she saw one.

"How could you lead me to that?" Sora asked. "I... I"

"Stop," Aihara Na said. "Do not blame her. She may understand your words, but she is still a beast and knew not what was done. She only followed the command of those she knew cared for her."

Sora slowly crept forward and knelt before the wyvern. "You have no love for her if you'd treat her that way." She stretched out her arm for Aquira to climb up, but Aquira remained skittish.

"If it helps," Aihara Na said, "there was no real danger."

Sora turned, slowly. "Excuse me?"

"It was a test. You passed."

"A test?" Her brow furrowed, and as she went to stand, Aquira finally hopped onto her arm. One of her claws scraped Sora's arm, making her yelp. The wyvern flapped away again, fearful.

"What if I didn't try to stop you?" Sora asked. "You mean to tell me you wouldn't have killed that boy?"

"He was inconsequential, just an orphan."

"*Just an orphan?*" Sora took several steps toward her, cheeks hot with rage. "I was just an orphan."

Aihara's laugh was as hard and rigid as her face.

"That isn't funny," Sora said.

"Girl, you have no idea what you are," Aihara Na said. "Who you are. Of what you are capable. But we do, and we want to teach you."

"If that means sacrificing more people, I'm not interested." It took all her effort to force that ultimatum out, knowing it meant there would be no second chance for saving Whitney, but she had to believe he'd feel the same way. She hoped. There was a big heart hiding somewhere behind that selfish shell.

"As I said, it was a test. We are not savages. I apologize if our current way of living has made us numb to your value of life. You can remain upset that a nobody might have died, but we were confident in your resolve. You proved us correct. You saved his life."

"Correct about what?"

"That you would not sit back and watch as we opened a porthole to Elsewhere. That was the true test. In that, you passed."

"So, what? You were going to open up a gateway to Elsewhere by killing that boy?"

"Of course not. That was not a real spell. Could you imagine? It was just a silly limerick meant to test your fortitude."

"But the things I saw there…" Sora hung her head, and Aquira must have noticed her heartache because she returned to Sora's shoulder and nestled against her face.

"Only visions. We can, all of us, peer into Elsewhere, but the one thing that must never be done is creating a portal. You didn't even know that, and your intuition persevered."

"I only cared about saving that boy," she grumbled.

"It matters not. You have seen what evil it is to open a bridge to the source of our power."

"But it can be done?" she asked impulsively. It was hard to hold back. Opening Elsewhere was the truest reason she'd been so eager to meet with mystics.

"Can what be done?" Aihara Na responded slowly.

"A gateway, a portal to Elsewhere."

"Yes."

"And you can do it?"

"We guard that ability with our very lives. It is why the Order was founded in the first place. To keep those with the gift from undoing our world with power they scant not understand."

"But I thought you all hid from the Glass Kingdom there, in Elsewhere. Isn't that how you survived?"

"So those legends reached even your ears. Lies told to appease a murderous foreign king. To make him stop his search for us. Once there were thousands of our kind, but we seven of the council who remain do so because we draw on every ounce of our power to stay hidden."

Aihara approached Sora, extended her hand, and gestured toward it.

Sora hesitated, though, she wasn't sure why. For so long she'd longed to meet the mystics, but seeing them test her with the feigned sacrifice of a child was difficult to pass over. What if all the awful rumors about them weren't just lies spread by their conquerors.

"Go on, take it," Aihara Na said.

Sora finally gave in, but her hand went right through Aihara Na's as if the woman were little more than air. Her eyes darted between her hand and Aihara's, words stuck on the tip of her tongue.

"To draw on Elsewhere's power so fully nearly destroyed us," Aihara Na said. "But it was necessary for the Order to survive. We remain, not in Elsewhere, but in-between. Tethered here barely of body, but eternal."

Now Sora understood what Aran Bokeo meant about them being close to immortal. "Couldn't you just have hidden in Elsewhere and returned?"

"No!" Aihara Na bellowed, making the very walls shake. Sora winced. Aihara drew a long breath to calm herself, and Sora wondered if she even needed to breathe in her form, or if it was a habit, leftovers from when she was human.

"Elsewhere is the realm of more than fallen gods," Aihara Na said. "It is the well of our magic in this corporeal realm, and in that power, there is more than fire. To open Elsewhere, we invite demons, lesser gods, and dead men who refuse to believe their time here is through. If those with our gift traveled there and returned, it would not be as themselves."

"What would happen?"

"What is this about, Sora?"

"Curiosity," she lied. "It's just that… when you gave me that vision back in that chamber with Lord Bokeo, I think I saw—"

"What you saw was only what lies within, nothing more. And a connection to Elsewhere lies within all mystics. It is the gift with which we are born. What makes us special. And it is that connection we seek to sharpen into a razor's edge here on Pantego."

"But it felt like I was there. I saw—"

"You were not there." Aihara Na interrupted again, staring straight into Sora's eyes. "Listen to me Sora, and listen closely. I have trained many mystics in the centuries I've lived. Some, promising, living within these very walls. But far more perish, and there is no fate ghastlier than when a rebellious or clumsy soul finds itself possessed by a being of Elsewhere. That which goes there must stay. Too many born with the gift have come to us seeking training, driven by the desire to bring back those who have passed on from Pantego. We mystics are capable of many great feats."

Aihara Na flicked her hands and murmured in that same manner of mixed languages she had in the temple. Her words flowed as gracefully as her body, which whipped around in a dance of martial arts. A powerful gust of air zipped by Sora and swirled around the mystic, then turned into a globe of water over her hand. She swept it in a wide arc, and the water turned to ice. Then, slamming her fist into the floor, a circle of cracks spread wide. One zigzagged beneath Sora's feet, but as the mystic rose again, the cracks reversed and vanished.

"We can manipulate the elements that bind this world, mend wounds, extend our lives beyond comprehension," Aihara Na said. If Sora wasn't paying attention, she wouldn't have noticed the mystic was panting. "We can even see beyond this realm, but we do not travel there, and we do not bring the fallen back. We mustn't. I know the temptation might be strong. What is dead must remain dead. We have all lost, or will lose loved ones, but it is far too dangerous. Do you understand?"

Sora managed a nod. She couldn't tell Aihara that she'd just revealed that the mystics were capable of the very thing she'd come to Yaolin City to learn. If it would bring Whitney back, she didn't care if it was dangerous, as long as nobody had to die to do it.

"Where are we, Ancient One?" Sora asked Aihara Na, deciding it was time to stop resisting and play along.

"You do not know?" Aihara Na replied. If she was pleased with Sora's use of her formal title, her seemingly always staid façade didn't show it.

"How could I? You did that… thing… and then I was here."

"Yes," the mystic said, now standing with her back to Sora. "I do apologize for that. I had to be sure you'd come, and I wasn't sure what kinds of lies you've heard of this place. Liam spread so many after he destroyed the Council."

Aihara Na placed the palm of her hand against the wall, and the stones shifted, overlapping one another, some moving out and creating a platform on the exterior of the building, others folding inward. When it had finished, Sora was looking out over Lake Yaolin, enclosed on all sides by the city.

She approached the new opening, breathless. They were twenty stories above the water. Perhaps more.

"Welcome to the Red Tower," Aihara Na said.

By now, Aquira was comfortably perched on Sora's shoulder, purring softly. Sora stroked her beneath the chin. She couldn't help it.

"I thought Liam made you seal this place up?" Sora asked.

"He was a fool to believe we would use our own magic to keep us from the place where all magic is born. He also thinks us all dead. He grossly underestimated the lengths we'd go to protect the knowledge of proper magic on this plane."

Aihara Na turned to walk away from the window, and her body passed through Sora. Sora clutched at her heart, such cold stealing over her she thought she might pass out. The feeling left her nearly as soon as it had come.

"Come, Sora," Aihara Na said. "Let me show you around. This will be your home until training is complete."

"How long will that be?"

"As long as it takes. Not a moment less or more."

Sora thought to retort, but the truth was, she had nowhere better to be. Troborough was gone, as was everyone she ever loved or loved her. In his own demented way, Wetzel loved her, and he was now ash. Her feelings for Whitney confused her, but vexing others was Whitney's goal in life. She longed to be so frustrated by him that she had to punch him in the arm, yet at the same time, wanted to wrap her arms around him and squeeze. This was her only chance to have that feeling back.

Aihara Na led her down a spiraling flight of stairs, and then another. As they descended further, Sora couldn't believe she'd climbed all these steps while under the influence of Aihara Na's magic. She didn't remember any of it.

When they reached a landing, she had lost count of how many flights they'd gone. She breathed heavily, but Aihara Na wasn't affected in the slightest. The perks of having an ethereal body.

"This way." Aihara rolled her fingers, and a light bloomed in the center, revealing a hallway with rooms along the outside. They made their way to the other side of the tower, passing dozens of empty rooms until Aihara Na stopped at one, completely nondescript.

"It is not The Emperor's Quilt, but it should do," she said.

"It is lovely," Sora said as the door opened, and she meant it. The room had a window, and even though it was little more than an arrowslit carved into the stone, it was a vast improvement over Wetzel's basement where she'd grown up or even her bed on Gold Grin's ship. There was a bed as well, instead of a pile of hay, and it looked comfortable enough.

"What's through that door?" Sora asked.

"A space for you to take a bath and clear your mind. The

Glassman see no value in a clean soul, but you're in Panping now. We can finish the tour after supper if you'd prefer. It has been a trying day."

Aquira flapped her wings and soared toward the large, plush bed. She turned a few circles, then curled up and closed her eyes.

"No," Sora said, not wanting to waste any more time. Whitney had been trapped in Elsewhere with Kazimir for long enough. She didn't deserve rest yet. "Let's continue."

"As you wish."

Aihara continued to lead her down the stairs.

"How will I know how to get back to my chambers?" Sora asked.

"It will not be difficult."

Sora realized she would need to get used to terse responses from everyone in this strange place. Living such a secluded life had clearly left them cold. Sora could understand that. Being cooped up with Wetzel every day gave her a tendency to be short with him as well.

"You will do most of your training here," Aihara said, stopping at a floor a long way down containing a single, rectangular room that was far too large to fit within the tower. The walls, ceiling, floor; everything was white.

"How can—"

"We don't rebuild the world," Aihara responded before Sora could finish. "We are now beneath the waters." She gestured to the walls, emphasizing the size of the room. "Madam Neelangam Jayasin will handle much of your teaching."

Sora hadn't even noticed the yellow-robed woman seated in the middle of the room, one of the seven remaining mystics. Seeing her there brought a sense of wonder at the immensity of the place. It was bigger than any room she'd ever been in, except maybe the Throne Room in the Glass Castle.

The woman rose and joined them by the entrance to the room.

She bowed, and said, "Greetings Sora. You may call me Madam Jaya."

"Madam Jaya," Sora said and returned the bow.

"It is a pleasure."

"The pleasure is mine, I'm sure."

"When will she be starting?" Madam Jaya asked Aihara Na.

"First thing in the morning," Aihara Na replied. "Time is always of the essence. Are things prepared?"

"As they'll ever be."

"Excellent," Aihara said with a bow. "We will see you at supper."

Their next stop was just a few floors down, but at the end of the stairwell, the bottommost level. A large pair of stone doors stood before them, the image of a lush tree carved onto them and glowing blue.

"Beyond those doors is something few have ever seen," Aihara Na said. "Power beyond fathoming. Are you ready?"

Sora nodded.

Aihara Na had been locked up for a long time, but Sora was sure nothing could be worse than facing Queen Bliss or Afhem Muskigo's army. The mystic waved her hand, muttered under her breath, and the doors opened.

Bright blue light poured out, forcing Sora to raise her hand to shield her eyes.

"Come," Aihara said, walking forward.

"What is it?" Sora said, wonder filling her every fiber. A pool of blue liquid bubbled within, steam rising from it. Inside the fluid, floating on the surface, were hundreds of flower petals.

"This is the Well of Wisdom." She led Sora to its edge. "This place is the beginning and end of all of our journeys."

"What does it do?"

"Everything and nothing. Everything for the one who truly desires its gifts, but nothing for him who thinks it a weapon."

Another cryptic response.

"I see that answer doesn't satisfy you?" Aihara Na said.

"How could it?"

"As you'll see, there are no books in this tower. We have no library of records like kings keep locked away. The Well of Wisdom contains the collective memories of our Order since the first Mystic Council and visions of those who've looked beyond. It is here we learned you would return to us after the passing of poor Tayvada Bokeo, that you would be one blessed enough by the Gift to help us rebuild our fractured Order. The one with the Will of Fire."

"You wish to use me?"

"Is a blade demeaned by it being used to draw blood? To be used for that which you were created is a gift from the gods. Tayvada accepted his fate long before you knew of your power."

"You knew so long, but didn't save him?"

"For all our power, we cannot control fate. He is an example of what can happen when one accepts who they are. He lived life to the fullest, knowing the end was imminent, and helped so many of our people abroad, as you have seen."

Sora's lip twisted. *He died a hero to them,* she thought, but couldn't manage to say out loud.

"When you are done with your training—and only when you are done—you will enter and see what the gods would like you to see," Aihara Na said.

The liquid looked as if it would burn Sora alive, bubbling as it was. She couldn't imagine going into the pool and found herself glad it would be a matter for another day.

"Are you hungry?" Aihara Na asked, abruptly. "I apologize, it has been a long while, and I sometimes forget what hunger is like."

Sora nodded.

Aihara Na guided her back up to one of the ground levels

where many Panpingese men and women gathered in brown and gray hooded robes. Sora couldn't help but remember Redstar's cultist haven in that dwarven ruin south of Oxgate.

"Who are all these people? Trainees as well?" Sora asked.

"Servants."

The word didn't sit well in Sora's belly, like foul food curdling in the acids. "Slaves," she muttered, thinking about Winde Port and the Ghetto, about Darkings and his 'servants.'

"*Willing* servants," Aihara corrected.

"I hope so."

"Many wish to see the return of the mystics as a governing power within the Panping Region; those who are not so blessed with the Gift as you will take decades to see it manifest within them. They have chosen to hide in this place with us and serve our wills, never to leave unless commanded to. Lord Bokeo is among them, and his late son." Aihara stepped toward Sora. "I know you do not yet trust us."

"You were going to kill a boy just to test me," Sora retorted before she could help herself. "Now you force people to stay locked in here?" The thought of Tayvada dying for their vision had her frustrated. A handful of servants within earshot spun, now staring at the two.

Aihara's hand lashed out, slapping hard against Sora's face. Sora pawed at her cheek, not sure how the mystic had suddenly become corporeal again.

"You may not yet understand our ways and methods, but you will not question them here," Aihara Na said sternly, anger contorting her features. She glared around the room, and the servants turned away. "We are, you are, this place is so much bigger than some poor street urchin roaming around Yaolin City. You have looked upon the Well of Wisdom, seen beyond our veil. You are an apprentice of the Mystic Order now, and while you are here training, you will keep your opinions to yourself. Is that understood?"

Sora expected to feel Elsewhere rising inside of her, but she felt nothing. She just narrowed her eyes, staring into Aihara's.

"Yes," she said.

"Yes, Ancient One," Aihara prompted. "I am your master now."

"Yes, Ancient One," Sora said through gritted teeth.

"Understand that I have known lifetimes worth of opinions. I have seen things you could not possibly imagine. When I am passed, and you sit upon the council, then, and only then, will your opinions on this world matter. And when that time comes, I am certain you will see the world as we do."

"And how is that?"

Aihara Na continued staring for a brief moment in silence, then turned and walked away. Only then did Sora realize the mystic's steps made no sound. "Enjoy a meal," she said. "You begin training in the morning."

XXI

THE DESERTER

Valin opened the door back into The Vineyard's downstairs hallway, inviting Rand to follow. He barred the opening with his cane when Sigrid tried to do the same.

"Where we're going is no place for a lady such as yourself," Valin said.

"Ye don't know nothing about me," she bristled.

He sighed. "A young girl from Dockside with parents who loved her. She didn't like that her brother got all the attention, taught to fight and drink like a man of Dockside should, so she tagged along and learned some herself. Her parents died young, as they often do here, and she and her brother were left alone for years. He looked out for her when lechers like Trapp would have sold her skin until he left her for greener pastures. So, she learned to look out for herself, and then when he came crawling back and needed her, she started to learn how strong she truly was..."

"Enough," Sigrid said, refusing to look at him.

"I've seen every story Dockside has to offer one hundred times over, girl. Neither of you is special. Understand that. My only care is to make sure those stories don't end before they're meant to."

"Ain't ye such a hero?"

"This isn't a place for heroes. But even a lawless land needs someone to keep the order. We're animals deep down, and without them we'd rip each other to shreds the first chance we got."

"Says only those who turn their back on Iam," Rand said.

"And how has that faith worked out for the King's Shield, good knight?"

Rand bit his lip. He regretted thinking Valin was a worthwhile ally with a sincere heart for Dockside. Perhaps his grim vision of the world was the necessary evil Dockside needed to survive, or maybe it was men like him keeping the district from bathing in the light of Iam like the rest of the capital. For now, he was a tool only to help reach Torsten.

"We've wasted enough time," Rand said. "You said we could make a deal, so let's make one."

Valin laughed. "There he is! Not a meek little deserter hiding from the wicked Queen anymore, are you? Still, I must insist that your sister stay behind for now."

Rand was about to protest when Sigrid took his hand. "It's fine, Rand," she said. "I need a break from this bastard anyway."

"Excellent," Valin said. "You'll be well guarded here." He turned to one of his thugs. "Fetch her a drink and some hog's head broth. Best in Dockside."

Sigrid grunted a response, then returned to Valin's office.

"Codar, bring the bounty and meet us," Valin ordered. His Breklian aid bowed, then hurried off. Turning, Valin led Rand down the hall toward the curtain, flanked by a few cronies—most of whom were missing teeth. Rand tried not to stare, despite the fact they didn't return the favor. He imagined how ridiculous he must've looked, donned head to toe in Shieldsman armor in a place where Iam's Eye wouldn't dare glimpse.

"Your sister will be fine," Codar said. "Bloodsport has a way of... riling men. It's no place for women."

"Bloodsport?"

Valin grinned in response. It was then that Rand noticed the discolored stone of the walls as they went deeper into the passage. Red in places, bleached in others from trying to wipe the red away. And with every step, cheering grew louder. Dust poured down from the ceiling now as feet slammed in thunderous unison.

Valin pushed the curtain aside with his cane, and Rand saw the source of the tumult. An arena was sunken into the earth, surrounded by rows of wooden stands. Every inch was filled with patrons, screaming and spilling their drinks—hundreds of them. Rand had never seen an arena like it in all his life. Supposedly, there was a great coliseum built onto an island off the coast of Latiapur in which the Shesaitju warlords proved their mettle, but he'd never traveled so far. Yet this was right in his hometown.

On the sands of the arena, a man lay against some rocks, his weapon lying out of reach. A shaggy-bearded giant screamed to the crowd, the single eye in the center of his flat forehead open wide. Rand had seen giants before, mostly on construction crews in Old Yarrington. They were tall as most homes after all, with biceps the size of barrels.

The giant squeezed his massive fist, then drove it down into the combatant's arm with the force of a battering ram. The bone snapped like a twig, and the man rolled off the rocks, howling in agony. Rand had to turn from the carnage, but the drunken crowd went crazy. Autlas were passed around in bets, Valin's cronies collecting around the top of the arena. Rand couldn't imagine anyone would bet against the giant.

Two men entered the arena from a metal portcullis to drag the loser out.

"If the Shield knew about this..." Rand said as he followed Valin around the concourse.

"Do you imagine the former Master of Coin didn't take his cut?" Valin said.

"The traitor, Darkings, you mean?"

"From the mouth of a traitor? I assure you, Mister Langley, not a soul enters that arena who doesn't know the cost. And nobody gets killed… mostly."

A narrow stairwell led up to a private promontory looking out over the arena. Valin collapsed onto a plush couch that was severely out of place around so much stone. He winced in pain as he stretched his leg out beside a platter of luxuriant fruits from all over, places where it didn't winter.

From their vantage point, they could see everything within the arena, but nobody could see them unless they craned their necks. Rand moved to the edge and looked over. An announcer called out the giant's next opponent, and more bets flew around the crowd. A warrior entered the arena, hoisting a battle-axe into the air and roaring. His pale skin, painted face, and many piercings made it easy to tell he was Drav Cra, but as tremendous and musclebound as the Northman was, the giant was as tall as two of him.

"I thought you said the Drav Cra cost you money?" Rand said, realizing just how much coin was being tossed around.

"People pay to watch the savages die for now," Valin replied. "It won't last long. My champion, Uhlvark, never loses anyway."

"How is it fair to pit that against a man?"

"It isn't. But a desperate man will try anything, and get a few drinks into a Drav Cra, they'll claim they can slay anything. Unless you have an issue with thinning their herd?"

"I—"

Valin waved his hand in dismissal. "Spare me the sermon,

please. The people want what they want. I am here only to appease them."

"And what? You want me to fight down there, is that what this is? A Shieldsman in your arena?"

He scratched his chin. "You know, I hadn't thought of that."

"I won't spill blood for you."

"You will do whatever I ask if you want to see Unger freed."

The crowd roared. The next fight started, and the Drav Cra warrior circled Uhlvark, axe in hand. The giant spun in place, grunting indecipherable words. Their ilk were considered simpletons, and his battle-stance proved it. He had none. Without his size, the Drav Cra warrior, trained from birth for battle, would have cut him to pieces. Still, the warrior was playing it smart, keeping his distance and slashing at the giant's hand's every time he tried to grasp him.

"So, what do you want?" Rand asked.

Just then Rand heard chains rattling behind him. He turned to see Codar returning, and he wasn't alone. He had a bald man in tow, wearing naught but a loincloth, with chains around his wrists and ankles. His gray skin screamed Shesaitju.

"Valin, how long are you planning to delay this?" asked another man who entered behind the Black Sandsman, going silent when he noticed Rand. He had a thin mustache and large belly that his delicate, satin tunic couldn't hide. He looked like a noble and held himself like one too. Rand was sure he'd seen him before, though couldn't place where.

Codar sent the Shesaitju man to his knees, earning a few curses in Saitjuese.

"Who is this?" Rand questioned.

"The most important man in Yarrington," Valin said. "Until Redstar took over, that is."

"We had a deal, Valin," the nobleman said. "You dare hand us over to the Shield?"

"Relax, young Darkings. This is no mere Shieldsman. He's the deserter who sent your father fleeing for his life."

"The Mad Queen's Hangman?"

"The very same."

The nobleman grinned, teeth yellow and rotten despite how wealthy he appeared. That was when Rand put things together. He had seen that smile before, only on a grayer head belonging to the man's father. This was Bartholomew Darkings, son of the former Master of Coin, Yuri Darkings, who had fled the capital during Oleander's rage, then returned only to betray the Crown and conspire to aid the Shesaitju rebellion.

That means… "Is that?"

"Caleef Sidar Rakun, the embodiment of God of Sand and Sea, and the root of the war in the South," Valin pronounced. "There's that Shieldsman intuition I've become accustomed to. The mind works better minus the drink, doesn't it, Sir Langley?"

"How did you find him?"

"I didn't. A peculiar mercenary company led by a dwarf happened upon him on the road. Wouldn't you know it, that one of them knew I'd pay better than the Crown. I thought about selling him back to young King Pi, and then Yuri Darkings offered so much more."

"And the rest comes when you get him back to Latiapur, Valin," Bartholomew Darkings said. "Remember that."

Valin rolled his eyes. "Like you'd ever let me forget."

"This man started a war," Rand said, a harsh edge to his tone.

"Your King started it," Caleef Rakun snapped. "I came in peace, offered my help in what ways I could. He locked me in a room and expected my afhems to sit on their thumbs?"

"Quiet." Codar yanked on his chains so hard the Caleef fell forward onto his face.

"It does not matter to me who caused it," Valin said. "The Caleef is mine now, and he will be sent to the party which has shown they desire him more. War has already started." Valin grabbed a bellot from a platter set before his couch and took a bite. Juice from the yellow melon grown only in southern Panping ran down his chin. He offered the fruit to Rand, then continued with a mouthful.

"Tell me, Rand, what good is having him here as prisoner inspiring more to Muskigo's ranks?" Valin said. "More fighting so that more fine people of Dockside can be conscripted to march off to their deaths."

"That is the King's decision," Rand said, stewing.

Valin threw his hands up in frustration. "You Shieldsman astound me. You want help removing Redstar, yet you would judge me for this?"

"It's not the same. Redstar is—"

"The King's uncle and Prime Minister of all the Glass," Valin finished. "Ridiculous as that may be. And you would be remiss to know that Torsten Unger, the very accused traitor you wish to save, advised against imprisoning the Caleef in the first place."

Rand looked to the gray-skinned Caleef, stripped and disgraced. He was usually painted entirely black from head to toe, and now only a few smudges remained behind his ears. His sad eyes told the truth in what Valin had said, leaving Rand without a response.

"So, Rand Langley, this is what I need from you." Valin stood and limped around Rand's back. He tossed the bellot pit into the sands below where the Drav Cra was still taunting the big giant. "In two days time, the Dawning will be upon us, and the King's Shield in the Glass Castle will be lax. We have always respected the Dawning as a solemn day of reflection, but foreigners are amongst us. We can't play by the rules either."

"The Dawning," Rand mouthed to himself. He hadn't even realized it was coming up. For Iam's followers, there was no day more sacred. It was at the heart of winter, the tenth day of

Freefrost, when Pantego's two moons passed across the sun at dusk, forcing an early, fleeting night. Celeste, matching its path across the sky, kept the world in twilight until it fell behind the horizon for the night. A time without Iam's light, when his flock was forced to look within for it.

Rand was surprised Valin Tehr, and his underworld would respect such a day. He also knew, from experience, that he was right, the guard would be light. Most people didn't work on the Dawning. They spent the day in sermons and amongst family, then the night in prayer and fasting, waiting awake to see the first dawn of the new year. Even children endured the long, quiet night. Most of the Shieldsmen and castle guard would be given the day off, with a skeleton crew left behind of the greenest among them—those who hadn't yet earned respite.

All gates and entries to the Glass Castle would be sealed off as the Royal Council observed the holy day. Then, the King and Wren the Holy—If Wren was even still alive—would walk outside the next morning, side by side, and declare the new year.

"Even if there are few Glassmen, the castle will be swarming with heathens," Rand said. Even if the worst Glassmen, like Valin, recognized the Dawning as a day of peace, Redstar wouldn't.

"More of their herd to thin then," Valin said. "I cannot promise Unger's freedom without spilling a bit of blood, but at least on that day, it will be savage blood alone."

"The castle will be sealed off."

"Dwarves don't celebrate the Dawning. The hairy bastards always live in darkness." He laughed, drawing a smirk from Codar and Bartholomew. "You and my men will enter the dungeons through the damaged Royal Crypt. The ceiling is nearly rebuilt, but there remains one opening."

"They'll keep heavy guard there to keep the pilgrims and

crazies out," Rand said. "Especially during the Dawning, people will crowd Mount Lister for sermons."

"This is the man you claim will help us?" Bartholomew said. "He questions everything."

"You are in no position to be picky, Bartholomew," Valin replied. He turned back to Rand. "Yuri Darkings knows the dwarven foreman performing repairs, and he'll let us through."

Rand regarded the revolting son of the traitorous Master of Coin. "I don't feel comfortable leaving this in the hands of a Darkings. They're traitors. What would stop them from having us gutted the moment we get in?"

"You would be wise to look at the company you keep, knight," Bartholomew snapped.

"Even I have my limits." Rand took a hard step toward him.

"Enough!" Valin barked. He distracted half the crowd downstairs from the fight, and the warriors as well. The Drav Cra man glimpsed up toward Valin's private viewing chamber, and at that moment the giant got his hands around his waist. The savage hacked at Uhlvark's enormous forearm, but the giant raised him above his head and pulled with both hands. The crunch as the Drav Cra warrior was torn in two made Rand's stomach turn over. The crowd went into a frenzy.

Uhlvark tilted his head back, letting the savage's blood pour into his mouth. The giant spit the blood in a spray above his head, and the mist carried into the crowd. It only made them cheer louder.

"He put up a good fight," Valin remarked, as if he'd been somehow keeping an eye on the battle the entire time, then he returned his attention to Rand. "Yuri Darkings speaks only one language." Valin rubbed his thumb and forefinger together. "The dwarf will be paid amply to get us through."

"No small price, indeed," Bartholomew said. "Greedy

buggers, as if our coins aren't made of the very rock they sleep on."

Rand breathed in through his teeth. Knowing the people he was plotting with was more sickening than watching a man torn in two, but he had to trust in the path Iam placed him on. "So, we get into the crypt, then what?"

"The rest is up to you. You'll sneak or fight your way through the catacombs to the castle's lowest dungeon. Codar and a few of my most trusted men will accompany you in case it comes to fighting."

"No killing Glassmen," Rand said.

"We will try our best. I may not look it, Rand, but I am a pious man. You think I want my hands stained with the blood of our people on the Dawning?"

"You're right," Rand said, finally picking up a bellot and taking a bite. "You don't look it."

Valin grinned. "And that's it. We will free Unger, and then you'll have your chance to repay me."

"How?"

"The distraction Torsten causes along with the Dawning will be the perfect cover for the Caleef to be escorted out of the city that very night. You will lead a company of men along with Bartholomew, and deliver him back to his people as promised."

Rand was mid-bite, and the bellot nearly slipped through his fingers. "You want me to guard a rebel king?"

"Look at him," Valin pointed to the Caleef. The man had a soft body and his old, gray eyes brimmed with fear. His were a race of renowned warriors, but it was clear the same could not be said for their ruler. "Who better to guard the god-king of the Shesaitju than a Shieldsman of the Glass? In your armor, no one will question you at the gates on the Dawning. And bandits or worse will be less apt to attack."

"And what of Redstar?" Rand questioned. "Even if I agree to

that. I can't promise that Torsten and I will be able to handle him by the end of the night."

"Who said anything about Redstar? We arrange to free Torsten Unger so that he may handle the imposter. That is what you agreed to in exchange for my help."

"So, what? I open Torsten's cage and then leave him in a castle full of enemies to fend for himself?"

"In simpler terms," Valin agreed.

"So that I can help you commit high treason alongside a family that has already done so? I heard men say that Yuri Darkings killed Sir Wardric Jolly. He was a good man who helped train me. Loyal to the Crown and I am."

"Is that the name of the Shieldsman who tried to stop us?" Bartholomew said. "Squealed like a pig when I sliced his gut open."

"You son of a—" Rand charged at him, but didn't get far before Codar's dirk was at his throat. Rand had the satisfaction of seeing the cowardly nobleman flinch, however.

"Codar, if this worm makes another move, cut out his throat." Valin's cane clicked behind him as he made his way around. Gone was the calculating, visage he usually wore. Replaced instead by the controlled rage that was the reason he was the most feared man in Dockside.

"Now is not the time to be brazen, boy," Valin said. "I could just as easily tear that armor off your body and give it to one of my men. It doesn't belong to you anymore anyway. But in open battle, a Shieldsman is worth his weight in glaruium, and I'm feeling generous toward a fellow Docksider who rose so high and fell so spectacularly."

"You said..." Rand cleared his throat. "You said you wanted Redstar and his people gone. Leaving Torsten alone in a castle where he has no allies left is murder."

"I consider it a calculated risk. I won't have my people seen assassinating a member of the royal family. Necessary or not, that kind of attention is bad for business."

"Then let me help him. Together we can see an end to this silent invasion, and then I'll do whatever you need. Even if it means helping this worthless sack of shog." He pointed to Bartholomew, who seemed amused at the title.

"And risk my opportunity to move during the Dawning while the castle is distracted?" Valin said. "Or losing you?"

"I'll give you my yigging armor!"

"Do not think for one second that this is a negotiation, Mister Langley."

"Isn't everything you do?" Rand replied. His head turned, and the point of Codar's blade pushed gently into his jaw.

Valin wasn't entertained. "Bartholomew, make sure his highness doesn't scamper away." Everyone glanced over to find Caleef Rakun crawling to the exit, hoping nobody would notice him. Bartholomew stomped down on his ankle. The Caleef cried out, then whimpered.

"Bring him." Valin waved them forward to look down upon the arena. Codar didn't leave Rand much choice but to follow.

A cleaning crew was busy dragging away the two halves of the Drav Cra warrior's body. Nobody cared to swab up the blood or entrails. The crowd trickled out, seeing as how the foreign warrior perishing was likely the main event. The giant, Uhlvark, sat on some rocks, chomping on a cow's thigh as if it had once belonged to a chicken.

"I think it is time you understand exactly where you are," Valin said. "You've spent too much time away in grand castles, you forget who owns this district. You think I don't know the threats you made to poor Gideon Trapp about exposing my shipments there?"

Codar shoved Rand against the rail, then pressed the point of his dagger against the weak point at the base of his skull. Valin leaned over next to him.

"My friends!" Valin called down to the dwindling crowd. "Why do you leave? I have a special performance for you. I give you a traitor's sister, and the only one who can save her would rather keep his pride!"

There was motion down by the lower entrance to the arena. Rand extended his neck to get a better view and saw Sigrid shoved out by a group of thugs. Her clothes were shredded beyond recognition. Whistles sounded all around the arena as the crowd returned to their seats. Ale showered down from flagons and drenched her wild hair.

"Rand?" she cried out as she spun, voice cracking. "Rand!"

"What is this?" Rand asked. "What in the name of Iam are you doing!" The angrier he got, the harder Codar pressed the blade into the back of his neck. Too fast a move and he'd be dead before he got a finger on Valin.

"Teaching you some respect." Valin flicked his hand. One of his men in the stands tossed Sigrid her Drav Cra bow and quiver.

The giant finished his meal at the same time and noticed her. The single eye in his pear-shaped face went wide. "Prettyyy giirl," he said, enough drool to fill a tub dripping from his lips. The ground shook as he stood, then more as he lumbered toward her. The quake sent Sigrid staggering, but she grabbed the bow and arrows and found her footing.

"Please, let me out of here!" she screamed. "Rand!"

"Let her go, Valin!" Rand felt a kick and dropped to his knees. Codar's blade slipped around in front, pointing at his trachea. One of his arms was wrenched behind his back and Codar's boot pressed against the back of his legs. The Breklian was extremely well-trained.

Valin leaned in and whispered into Rand's ear. "I need you to listen and listen close, boy or your strong, pretty sister will be split in half by that oaf in ways you don't want to imagine."

"Please, Valin, be reasonable. She's a good Docksider. Please."

The giant grasped at Sigrid, but she rolled out of the way, tearing a bit more of her dress. The crowd yapped in delight.

"Reasonable?" Valin grabbed Rand's jaw and pulled it so near Rand could smell the wine on his breath." I trade in favors and gold. You come here, with nothing to offer me but your sword and your identity. And you dare try to push away my generosity?"

"Whatever you want, I'll do, just let her go. I'm begging you."

The giant charged again, and Sigrid struggled to thread her bow. Rand now knew how well she could do it, but nerves had her hands shaking like Rand's had his first day of training under Sir Torsten and Sir Wardic. She got a shot off, and it slashed the Giant's shoulder on the way to stabbing into the stands, right next to a drunkard's head.

The giant grabbed her. She stabbed an arrow into his wrist, and he flung her aside. The fall wasn't far, but the magnificent creature didn't know his own strength. Her side hit the sand, and she rolled all the way across, slamming hard into the wall. The giant's eye narrowed with rage, and he roared.

"Valin!" Rand screamed.

The giant took two clumsy steps, then Valin raised a hand. "Stop, friend Uhlvark," he said, barely needing to raise his voice. "Please, return to your room."

The giant did as commanded and looked up toward them. "Yes, Papa..." he said. Then he grabbed the stripped cow bone and ran off through the lower gates. The crowd moaned in disapproval as if watching the ravaging of an innocent woman was worthwhile entertainment.

"That is but a taste of what will happen if you betray me,

Rand Langley," Valin said. Codar released him and stepped in front of his leader, leaving Rand hanging onto the railing to keep from collapsing. He could barely feel his legs. Some of Valin's men ran out and grabbed Sigrid. She got a swing in at one with an arrow, slicing his calf, but he slapped her. Her gaze found Rand's as they dragged her away, and all he could do was wish he'd listened to her and they'd run.

"You're worse than any of them," Rand whispered once she was gone.

"You're going to hurt my feelings." Valin clacked toward the other end of the room. Bartholomew wore a smirk, but the Caleef looked horrified. A foreign rebel, the most human of them all.

"Now, you are going to help Codar free Unger so that he may cause all manner of chaos for the city guard in his mad quest for vengeance," Valin said. "Then, you will meet Bartholomew and the Caleef at the South Corner gates, and help transport him south to his people. If you are discovered, the Crown will blame you, the deserter who tried to kill the Prime Minister and you will not say otherwise. If you do this, your sister will come to no more harm, and you will find a fruitful place in my employ."

"I'll never work with—"

Valin clicked his tongue and wagged his finger to silence him. "If you fail in any of this, your sister will taste all the rotten men of Yarrington until they've had their fill. Only then will I allow her to die."

Valin turned to leave, and before Rand could shout at him, Codar smashed him in the side of the head. He hit the floor like a sack of dirt, his vision blurry and blackness closing in.

"You went off to serve in the King's Shield, and you forgot where you're from," Valin said. "Now, boy, I hope that you remember."

Rand looked down into a full mug of ale. He didn't drink from it, only stared until the foam dissipated, and he could see his pale reflection in the amber liquid.

"You may as well have one," someone behind him said. "Codar says his people drink their full before every battle. It takes away their fear. Dulls their pain."

Rand glanced back and saw Valin limping toward him across The Vineyard, wearing a warm smile. His brothel was mostly empty now that it was the morning of the Dawning. A few stragglers remained, unable to spend even a day avoiding sin.

"I want to feel everything," Rand said, squeezing the mug so tight his fingernails made marks in his palm. He'd been kept in a small room below The Vineyard for two days, forbidden from seeing his sister or talking to anyone.

Now Rand knew he'd led them straight into the house of a snake. Their father always told them to stay away from Valin because before you knew it, you'd be working for him. It was a slow end, like the venom of a Shesaitju sand snake, breaking you down piece by piece until your body seized.

Valin had his fangs in Rand now, and there was no wriggling free. He just had to focus on the task at hand. Torsten was a mighty warrior, and there was no man in Pantego closer to Iam. If anyone could end Redstar's insurrection, it was him.

The legs of a stool screeched. Valin lifted himself onto the velour seat, wincing. Codar stood a short distance behind, just out of sight and easy to forget about, ever vigilant.

"I hope there are no hard feelings between us," Codar said.

"You threatened my sister's life."

"I threaten lives daily. Don't take it personally."

Rand squeezed the mug harder until he could feel the area under his thumb ready to crack. "Don't you have more fights to put on?"

"Even I take a little break this holiest of days."

Finally, Rand decided to look at Valin and noticed the luminescent paint under his eyes. All the children of Iam wore it on the day of the Dawning, spread onto their faces by priests during morning service. It shimmered with Iam's light and also allowed people to observe the eclipse of the sun without winding up as blind as the priests themselves.

"You don't deserve to wear that," Rand bristled.

"Is it my fault you were too stubborn to see the right path in front of you? You'll thank me in the end. A man like you could do far more for this district at my side than in the King's Shield, and get rich doing it."

"Gold isn't everything."

"Now that's where you're wrong," Valin said, slapping the bar. "The only reason places like Dockside exist is so the pampered ingrates on the other side of the fence can feel better about what they have. We're a frame of reference, kid. A novelty."

"And men like you will keep us there forever."

Valin chuckled. "Ah, the eternal battle. Pragmatist versus dreamer. I've met countless men like you who thought the same, yet I'm still here, and men like you end up dead or in a gutter more often than not."

"Is there a purpose to this conversation?"

"I have every right to check up on my investment before he leaves. But really, I came to invite you to see your sister one last time before you go."

Rand turned so fast he knocked over the mug, ale quickly spreading across the bar. "If you hurt her anymore."

"She's fine, I assure you. I have no desire to harm her or to see you fail—on the contrary, I root for all my people to rise as far as they can."

"We aren't your people."

"Such the perfect little Shieldsman." Valin slid off the stool and made his way to the stairs. "Come, I'll take you to her."

Rand followed him up to the second floor overlooking the lobby of The Vineyard. Curtains leading into semi-private rooms lined the walls, usually all full, this morning they were mostly open. They did pass one with deep moans emanating from within. A thug stood guard out front. Rand's heart fell to his feet, thinking Sigrid was inside, but Valin continued past.

He turned down a hallway running along the empty, outdoor balcony. It was a quiet day, snowflakes fluttering about from a patchy, blue sky. A perfect day for the dawning. Too many clouds and the eclipse would have been barely visible.

They turned again and reached a door guarded by two thugs. All that was beyond it was silence.

"Let him in," Valin ordered.

"The screaming wench finally got a client?" one of them joked.

Rand had his forearm against the man's throat in a heartbeat, pinning him against the wall. "If you touch her, I'll rip out your tongue."

"Relax, Rand," Valin said. "I said she would not be harmed unless you betray me, and my word is my bond."

Rand backed off, then noticed Codar in his peripherals. The mustached Breklian stood directly behind Valin, his weapon-hand, whether full or empty, was concealed behind his back.

The thug coughed and rubbed his neck. "Someone ought to teach this knight some manners," he rasped.

"A lesson I am certain you wouldn't survive," Valin said. "Now, let him in."

The other guard rattled through some keys and gave the door a push. It creaked open, and Rand saw his sister curled up on a bed, a metal cuff around her ankle that kept her chained to the bedpost. A ratty dress was draped over her body, but at the very least, this one wasn't ripped and adequately covered her.

His whole world melted away, and all that remained was her. Rand ran in and wrapped his arms around her. He could feel her shaking like she probably had been since a giant tried to have his way with her. She had a few scrapes on her forehead from falling in the arena, and her hands were cut up far worse.

"Are you okay?" he asked. "Did they lay another hand on you?"

"Not since the arena," she replied, voice shaking.

He squeezed her again, then held her at arm's length. "I'm so sorry for letting us come here. I should have never trusted him."

"No, ye shouldn't have." She forced a smile. It stung Rand's heart to see how difficult it seemed for her to do.

"And I was always so good at listening to Father, too."

"He'd be so disappointed."

Rand laughed, then his features darkened. He would've been. The day he died in a riot at the docks, crushed by fallen debris, was the day Rand promised to help fix Dockside. He'd failed in spectacular fashion. He couldn't even protect his own sister.

"I'm going to get you out of here," Rand said.

"I'll be fine," she said. "Ye've got to finish what ye started."

"You're not fine. Valin is a monster, and if I don't do what he says he'll... I won't let him hurt you anymore."

"I'm tougher than I look."

"I don't know... you look pretty tough." This time he got her to actually smile. It was a sight he'd missed more than anything. All his wallowing, he'd forgotten how much he enjoyed being around her. Sigrid was his best and only friend.

"What's he makin ye do?" she asked.

Rand bit his lip and looked to the floor.

"That bad?" She took his hand and pulled it to her face. Her skin was cold, like the empty room. Everything was freezing these days. "Don't tell me, just promise me something."

"Anything."

"Don't let this city fall to the Drav Cra for me. I can handle whatever Valin throws at me; I been practicing with Trapp for years. But I can't handle ye being crushed again."

Rand held his head high. "By the morning, after the Dawning, Redstar will no longer be poisoning the ears of the King. He and his people will return to their frozen tundra where they belong."

Or Torsten will die trying. He didn't add that last part, but it was the truth. A part of him felt like he might betray Valin, help Torsten, and rush back to kill Valin and save Sigrid before the king of the underworld knew what hit him. But now that he saw her, frightened and alone in a room meant for Valin's whores, he knew exactly what he had to do.

There was a hard knock on the door. "All right, enough," one of Valin's thugs grated.

"I'll be back for you before you know it," Rand said. He took Sigrid in his embrace again, wishing he didn't have to leave.

"Just come back the same man ye are now," she whispered into his ear. "I missed him, and I don't want to lose him again."

"You won't." Rand kissed the top of her head. "Ever again."

Two sets of hands grabbed him and pulled him from her. He didn't fight it. Not with her life in the balance. Instead, he held her gaze until the door slammed shut. Just before it closed, he could see the stark terror in her eyes. Worse even than when those Drav Cra monsters had her by the neck.

"We have our opening," Codar said. "Time to go."

Rand allowed a final wave of sadness to wash over him, then turned. Valin was gone, leaving only Codar and three thugs behind. Their grand raiding party to break Torsten out of his cell.

"No farewell from your boss?" Rand questioned.

"None required."

He set off down the hall, and Rand followed. They headed downstairs to the exit where another one of Valin's cronies handed Rand's sword to Codar.

"Try anything, and it will find its sheath in you," Codar warned, then presented the weapon.

"I wouldn't dream of it," Rand said as he took it.

"Walk straight, head down. Remember, you are the most wanted man in Yarrington, but the people are distracted, the guard is light, and few would know you at first glance." Codar snapped his fingers, and a man dressed in rags stood from the bar and shuffled over. His eyes were burned out—as were any priest's, but he banged into every table on the way over. Most went through enough training at the convents to move fluidly despite lack of sight, learning how to rely on faith and senses. He held a bowl filled with luminescent paint made from the poppies that grew on the banks of Mount Lister, and it sloshed over the rim as he swayed.

"He will help," Codar said.

"Always happy to serve." The blind man bowed, hiccuped, and almost spilled the bowl. Codar had to keep him upright.

"Get a hold of yourself, Father," he hissed.

The blind man wriggled himself free, then took Rand's face and went to paint it. Rand pulled away.

"Only priests are meant to do this," Rand protested.

"I am one!" he slurred. "Father Morningweg of Fessix... or I was before those filthy savages razed it a few years back."

"Many combatants won't enter the arena before unburdening their souls," Codar explained.

"And I'm a gr... great listener."

The Father grasped Rand's head, then nearly toppled over. Rand wound up holding the man upright while he spread the paint around his eyes. It was sloppy, dripping down Rand's cheeks and over his nose in a way that masked much of his features. By the time he finished, Rand figured he looked more like one of the Drav Cra heathens than a Glassman on the Dawning.

"Priase Iam, my son," he said when he'd finished. His breath reeked as Rand imagined his own had for so long. "May His light always be with you. Praise be the Vigilant Eye." Father Morningweg circled his vacant eye sockets in the gesture of prayer. "Good'nuf for you?"

"We're all going to Elsewhere," Rand said.

"Not where I'm from," Codar said. The drunken priest then painted his face, along with the three of Valin's thugs accompanying them. Rand didn't bother learning their names.

"All right..." the priest said. "Good.. uh... luck boys. May Iam watch your feet or whatever." He took a step, stumbled into Rand's chest, then put on a nervous smile as he patted his arm and went to pass.

"No, you don't." Codar grabbed the priest and shoved him out the door. "Valin is paying you well enough. You'll escort us to the mountain."

One of the thugs nudged Rand in the side. "Ain't nobody gonna question a priest's party on the Dawning. Valin's a genius."

"That's a word for it," Rand mumbled.

Rand watched as the cold air greeted the priest's face. His cheeks went green, and he leaned over on the patio to vomit. The sight sent a shiver up Rand's spine. Sorrow had sent him on a similar path of sin. If a priest, willing to burn his own eyes out in the name of Iam, could fall to vices so severely, he couldn't have imagined what would have happened to him had Wren not shown up...

I would have been a corpse swinging from the ceiling, he reminded himself. Just like Tessa and the rest.

"Keep your eyes up," Codar said, forcefully tilting Rand's head back toward the door. "No distractions. You are a Shieldsman from the moment we step out that door."

"You told me to keep my head down," Rand said. "Make up your mind."

Codar wasn't amused.

"Do you think this is my first mission?" Rand questioned.

"It is your first with me." Codar folded his hands behind his back and headed outside, giving the priest another shove to get him moving. The thugs sneered at Rand as they all followed.

The air was warmer than it had been in many weeks. It still snowed lightly, but Iam's mercy was upon the city for the Dawning. The street was empty. No line of beggars waiting for handouts from the richest man they knew of. Everyone was off to church, nary a guard in sight.

Valin was right about something. It was the perfect day for Rand to walk the streets without drawing suspicion.

"Today's your lucky day, my son," Father Morningweg said, wiping his mouth with his sleeve.

"Why is that?" Rand asked.

"Not everyone gets to die on the Dawning."

XXII

The steel doors of Torsten's cell flung open, slamming hard against themselves. He jumped up, not even realizing he'd fallen asleep. So deep underground, it was impossible to know night from day. His sleeping came in spurts whenever exhaustion finally took him. After seeing Redstar's plans further unfold, he was trying his best to stay awake. He had to keep his eyes open, searching for a chance to escape and put an end to the Arch Warlock.

Torsten heard a commotion as Sir Austun Mulliner stormed in, grabbed Torsten by his dirty tunic, and chained his wrists while another unlocked his ankles.

"Come on," Mulliner said as they hauled him out of the cell.

"What is this?" Torsten questioned. Out of his peripherals, he saw two warlocks leering from the darkness. "Another of Redstar's tricks?"

Nobody answered. Mulliner simply dragged him along while the warlocks followed in their shadows. With Nikserof gone, Torsten had seemingly lost his greatest potential ally in the castle. His only potential ally—just like Redstar wanted. Nearly all the distinguished members of the Royal Council were strangers after Oleander chased so many away or hung them, and while he knew the Queen Mother better than anyone else alive, she was unpredictable. She'd fetched Wren for him as was his last request, and there was that moment outside the throne room when she seemed eager to ask him something, but when last they spoke she remained furious with him for not killing Redstar and refused to support his position with Pi. Her fury rarely waned.

Mulliner took him out of the dungeons, through the courtyard, and then down dark castle halls until they were at the entrance to the royal stable. The ground was splotches of white and brown. They dragged him through the snow, not caring to avoid puddles or piles of shog, throwing him down in front of a stable gate.

"Thank you, Sir Mulliner," Oleander said. She turned from brushing the mane of her beloved horse, a trim, Panpingese Whitehair gifted to her by Liam after the last war in the East. The beast came from perfect stock.

"You can leave us."

"Your Grace, he is a—"

"A criminal?" she interrupted the Shieldsman. "A killer? I've been called the same thing. Now leave us, or you'll find out why."

"Right away, Your Grace." He didn't seem pleased, but Oleander either didn't notice his insolent tone or ignored it. "We'll be right over there with them. Prime Minister's orders." Mulliner pointed to the warlocks, standing on the opposite side of the grounds in their ratty cloaks, watching their every move.

Oleander exhaled and clenched her jaw. "What joy."

Mulliner released Torsten.

"Do you know why I prefer horses to men?" Oleander asked.

"What is it, Oleander?" Torsten said. He'd always been proper around her, even diffident, but now that his arms were chained and he wore rags he couldn't find a reason to be. All he could think about was her silence back in the Throne Room when he needed her help more than ever.

She ignored him and continued stroking her horse's mane. "They cannot speak, or lie, or cheat. I hated this horse when Liam brought her home to me. I knew what it meant when Liam gave me an extravagant gift. Now, I have nobody else in this gods-forsaken castle."

"Oleander, what do you want?" Torsten took a hard step toward her and heard the rasp of Mulliner's blade sliding from its sheath. Torsten acknowledged the threat and gave her space. Oleander didn't let it stand. She turned all the way from her horse to take Torsten's hand and drew herself closer.

"Must the Queen Mother have a reason to call upon a knight?" she asked.

"I'm a prisoner now, no thanks to you."

"Oh, Torsten, don't be so dramatic."

"Dramatic? I stood by you, after everything you did. Not just hanging those men. For a year you ruled this kingdom in Liam's sickness, and you ran our coffers dry with parties you barely wanted to attend, let our streets and trading agreements wither, our armies rust."

"Sounds like you weren't a very good advisor."

"Advisor? That's never been my job. I was simply the only one on the Royal Council who wasn't terrified of being near you. Even Yuri Darkings chose to keep his distance and now… he'd rather betray the kingdom he's served loyally for decades."

As it had in the dungeons, the back of her hand lashed out. Torsten winced, but she stopped just short of his face. He couldn't say he didn't deserve it, but he'd had far too much time to think in his cell—about every little thing that had happened since the day Liam's sickness had become known.

Oleander lowered her hand. "And I asked you to do one thing as Wearer," she growled, keeping her voice low so as not to be overheard by their watchers. "More than ending the rebellion or proving the might of your arms, I demanded he not return home."

"I guess we're both inspired failures."

He could tell she was about to continue scolding him when she heard what he said. Torsten noticed a grin pull at the corner of her lips.

"I suppose we are," she said. She sauntered to the other side of her horse and continued brushing. "Why were you never so honest with me before?"

Torsten rolled his shoulders. "Chains have a way of bringing it out."

"I like it."

"I'm glad someone does."

A long moment of silence passed between them. All he could hear was the sound of her brush against coarse fur.

"Thank you for sending Wren," he said.

"I'm sorry, Torsten," she said softly at the same time.

His brow furrowed. Those were words he wasn't sure he'd ever heard her speak, let alone sound genuine saying them.

"My Queen?"

"After Liam grew ill, I had no idea what to do," she continued. "I knew what everyone called me. How they looked at me—the Council like I was an imposter, you and the other soldiers like they were all keeping secrets about my husband. I was just so…"

"Angry?" Torsten finished for her. "It isn't too late to make amends."

"Just because your prison has a name doesn't mean you're the only person in one. They watch me everywhere I go. I had to ask my brother's permission just to speak with you outside of that foul-smelling dungeon, like I'm a child."

"And why did you invite me here?"

Her brush got caught on a knot in the horse's mane. The horse snorted, and frustration twisted Oleander's features, but she kept her composure as she calmly smoothed it out. "Would it sound unqueenly to say I just wanted to talk?"

"Not at all."

She inhaled deeply. "I was getting through to Pi while you were off to war. I know it. And the moment Redstar returned, it all vanished. He's not even cruel anymore, Torsten. He just ignores me so he can spend every waking moment with the beloved uncle who destroyed his childhood. They're out joining the hunt for the Caleef right now as a 'lesson.'"

"I should have left him to rot on the cold dirt of the Webbed Woods. Maybe we would have lost Winde Port without the Drav Cra at our side, but we wouldn't have lost the throne."

"Every night, as my head hits the pillow, I find myself wishing Liam were here. Even after his mind started to go, or as he screamed at me for not bearing him a son. I wonder what he'd think of his heir now?"

"A child who's been through what King Pi has needs a father. Redstar saw that and took advantage of it. We were always a step behind."

"It should have been you."

Torsten choked on his next breath. "Your Grace?"

"To help bring him up strong like his father. Guide him. You're the closest man to Liam I've ever known, the good parts at least."

"I'm barely a shred of him." He stared up at her and saw her nose twitch like it always did when she was annoyed. He hadn't ever realized he knew that about her, but he'd spent a lot of time watching over her; listening to her rants about every 'worthless wretch' living in the castle.

"Thank you, my Queen," he said softly. At the same time, he reached around the horse with his chained hands and took hers. "We've had our differences, but I know you did the best you could. To live in the shadow of so great a leader for so long; none of us were prepared to take the reins, even knowing his days were numbered. It is all our failings."

"No, it is him." She released Torsten's hands and glared at the warlocks. "My vile brother."

"I wish that were true. I've had a lot of time to think down there, and I'm certain about a few things now. Redstar cannot stay, but we gave him the power he now possesses. We let the people feel scared and neglected in the absence of their King. Pi's rebirth comforted them for a short while, and then he kidnapped the Caleef. They grew fearful of the cold, of rebellion, of—"

"Of me." Oleander turned her gaze to the floor. "No need to be coy, Torsten."

Torsten reached out further and lifted her chin. Mulliner cleared his throat, and Torsten ignored him. "I threw blame around for a long time. Now we're both killers. Redstar isn't a plague destroying us; he's a symptom of what was already here."

"Then enough of us wallowing. End him like you were supposed to. I'd kill him myself at this point if I ever had a moment alone. Anything is better than this."

Torsten rattled his chains. "As would I. But it's been left in the hands of Iam now."

"You're blind as a priest, aren't you?" She patted her horse on the back. "She's the fastest steed in all the West." She leaned close and whispered. "Take her. Find a blacksmith to break your chains, and do what the assassin you sent failed to. I'm sure that oaf in the castle, Hovor, Hovom? No matter, I'm sure he would do it. I hear him muttering incessantly about having to repair weapons for the savages who raided his home when he was a child."

Torsten repositioned himself in front of Oleander so their watchers couldn't read her lips. "You can't be serious? Who knows what he'll do to you."

"He's robbed me of the love of my only son. There is no worse he can do."

Torsten swallowed and looked down at his bindings. He remembered when Redstar enraged him enough to kill one of his own men, him posing as Sir Uriah Davies in the Webbed Woods, ready to murder Torsten and his companions. "Trust me, my Queen. There are no limits for him."

"Am I not still your Queen?"

"Always, Your Grace."

"Then you will steal this horse and escape. Find your assassin. Band together. Do it whatever it takes to get back here and take our city back before his lies spread too deep."

Torsten glanced down and saw that Oleander had unlatched the gate—the only thing between a mounted horse and freedom. The impressive beast took one step forward, and soon he'd have no choice but to mount her before she trotted out onto the grounds alone. He looked back to Oleander. Happy was never a word he'd used to describe her, but she seemed content in her decision to openly defy her brother. He then glanced back at Mulliner and the warlocks. They watched, but the stables were too darkened for them to be able to see what was happening.

"No more fear of false gods?" Torsten asked.

"Let them smite me," Oleander sneered.

"Then this time I will not fail you."

"I hope not. I don't know how many more times I can bring myself to forgive you, my dear, sweet Torsten."

The horse took another step, and Torsten grabbed a handful of her mane.

"At least once more." Torsten smiled.

The wall into the castle gardens was low enough for a Panpingese Whitehair to jump. After that, using a few secret doorways groundskeepers used so they could keep out of sight, he could traverse the outer fortifications toward one of the main gates and escape through the guard exits. If he was fast enough, all he'd have to do was barrel past a few sleepy guards. Nobody would even need to die. There were blacksmiths in South Corner or Dockside who would break his chains without question. Then he could return and do what Rand couldn't.

He didn't blame the kid. He had no idea what he was up against, but Torsten knew all Redstar's tricks. And he knew the castle better than anyone. He'd grown up in it. He could find Redstar when he was at his most vulnerable, fulfill the will of his Queen, and let Iam decide where his actions would send him.

"I will help your son, my King, see the light again, and you will know his love once more," Torsten told her. He pulled on the mane to yank himself up onto the horse and then raced by Oleander, the wind brushing back her exquisite dress.

Mulliner and the others had grown lax and scrambled after him. Torsten kicked the horse and set his sights on the garden wall. He went to spur it a second time when suddenly, the horse stopped in her tracks and flung him off.

He skidded through the snow so hard his head rebounded against the stable wall. The horse whinnied and reared back, and as he gathered his bearings, he noticed the vines growing from the frozen dirt now wrapped around her back hooves so tight she was rendered immobile.

Oleander sprinted down from the stables. "What is this?" she shouted.

"Redstar hoped you could be trusted," Freydis said, emerging from behind the stables. Her sliced hand dripped blood into the fresh snow, turning it pink. "He hoped there was a bit of the tundra left in you. I let him have faith for his sake, but I knew you'd betray him. That you would choose lust over blood."

Oleander pointed to her horse with a long finger. "Let her go, you filthy daughter of a—"

"Silence." Freydis ran a bloody finger across her lips and Oleander's sealed shut.

"You will release your Queen!" Torsten hopped to his feet and charged at her, but Freydis slid a knife out and swung it toward Oleander's stomach. It didn't cut her, but she kept it close enough to make an incision in her stomach should Torsten come nearer.

He froze.

"Careful, Redstar may have a soft spot for her, but accidents happen when criminals try to break out of their holes." Freydis clicked her tongue to the guards, and they hurried over like trained pups. Mulliner and the other Shieldsman seized Torsten while the two warlocks drew their daggers and watched.

"Let her go," Torsten said, seething. "I stole the horse. She had nothing to do with it."

"I heard everything." Freydis placed her mouth right against Oleander's ear. "All your *scheming*."

"Freydis, I'm warning you. Release her."

"The ex-Wearer is right," Mulliner said, reluctant. "The Queen Mother must answer to the Prime Minister and the King for her actions. We will bring him back to his cell, and she should be returned to her quarters until they return from the hunt."

"But what punishment befits such betrayal of blood?" Freydis asked, circling Oleander. The Queen grunted, but her lips remained magically sealed. "I have no tundra to abandon her in with nothing but a broken clan like she did to us so long ago."

"Sir Mulliner, she is the Queen Mother," Torsten said, desperate to appeal to the Shieldsman's better nature despite how he might feel about him. "You have to see reason. This is wrong." Torsten felt the grip on his chains loosen. A little more and he might be able to pull free and do something before any of the warlocks could assail him with blood magic.

"That's it," Freydis said. "I'll leave her alone. More alone than she's ever been." She strolled toward the Queen's beloved horse and raised her dagger to its neck. Oleander's muffled screams resounded as she fell to her knees, unable to even beg.

"That horse is the property of the royal Nothhelms!" Torsten shouted. "You will not touch it!" Mulliner's grip on him loosened a little more. That's it, a little more doubt. Torsten was about to break free and charge when the castle doors swung open and Redstar strolled out.

"Now, now, Freydis," he said. "We mustn't blame the beast for the faults of her master." He approached the horse with Pi in front of him, hands on the boy's shoulders like a proud father teaching a lesson.

"Such a fine specimen," Redstar went on. "Panpingese? A gift from your late husband, no doubt. He kept you locked up here tighter than these noble beasts. I wonder what the whore he was apologizing for looked like."

"Shut your cursed mouth," Torsten said.

Redstar ignored him. "Perhaps I will ride her in celebration after we defeat Muskigo. What do you think, my King?"

"My father's gift would get far more use than standing around here," Pi said. He glanced at his frantic mother, not a hint of worry in his eyes. His lips, straight as an arrow.

"My thoughts exactly."

"Drad Redstar, it was as I warned," Freydis said, reeling her dagger back to her side. "Your sister tried to free the traitor. She is not one of us."

"She hasn't been for a long time, but still, she is the Queen Mother," Redstar scolded. "While I am ever thankful for your loyalty, you will take her to her quarters. I will deal with her betrayal shortly."

Freydis regarded Oleander, bit her lip, then said, "Of course, Arch Warlock." She grabbed Oleander's arm and shoved her along, still keeping the Queen Mother from speaking. Torsten locked eyes with Oleander as they left, holding her gaze until she was out of sight. The vines around the horse's hooves, withered, and the Whitehair ran back to her pen.

Redstar leaned down, close to Pi's ear. "My King, perhaps it is time for you to rest as well? It was a trying day, hunting for the lost Caleef. Alas, the search continues."

"Yes, Uncle," Pi replied. "I should rest if I want to stay awake through the Dawning."

"Ah yes, how could I forget? Soon, when the moons cast out the light, all will be illuminated." He rustled Pi's hair, and the boy strode off with perfect posture. He didn't even acknowledge Torsten's existence as he turned to leave.

"I'm disappointed in you, Torsten," Redstar said. "Using my sister to get to me?"

"I'll do far worse when I get out of these chains." Torsten lurched forward, and the knights reeled him back. "You'll handle her? What exactly does that mean? Please, tell these fair knights who believe you to be a hero."

"They serve their King, just as I do." Redstar bowed in their direction. "And he has already made his decision on you. Take him away. And you two." He gestured to the two warlocks. "Do not leave his sight and allow no visitors but me. Especially not the Queen Mother."

The two knights started pulling Torsten along, but he noticed something before the metal chafed his wrists again. Hesitation. Maybe it was little more than hope beyond reason that with Nikserof gone, there was still someone in the Shield he could get through to, but he swore he felt it.

"Rand already took a piece of you," Torsten snarled. "I look forward to taking the rest."

Redstar stopped them. He raised his arm so his sleeve fell back and fully revealed the stump he had for a right hand. "He took nothing, Torsten. I did tell you that you would help me discover the secret, and so you did. The power I felt when the deserter you sent for me took this… the connection to her. You showed me why we failed to bring her all back in fullness."

"You failed because she's gone. Defeated as you will soon be."

"I failed because I wasn't willing to sacrifice everything. Now I understand." Redstar waved for the men to continue dragging Torsten away. "Enjoy the Dawning from below the Earth, Torsten," he said as they passed. "It's the last time My Lady will ever have to. Soon she will wake, and the world will know the truth."

XXIII

THE MYSTIC

The next morning came and with it, a fresh blaze within Sora. She rose, leaving Aquira asleep on the bed in her room inside the Red Tower. She stared through the arrowslit window at Yaolin City and the lake surrounding them. Dark, gray clouds loomed high above, casting shadows. Although, compared to Winde Port, life seemed to be pretty good here for her people, she tried to imagine what it would have been like when the mystics ruled, before King Liam brought his army and drove them into hiding.

Then, she recalled—as if she could forget—that poor boy Madam Aihara was ready to slaughter for the sake of a lesson. She thought of the repurposed temples now serving Iam, which the locals happily attended. She remembered how that clairvoyant kowtowed at the sight of Sora, thinking her a member of the mystic's Secret Council.

It wasn't only men like Liam and Torsten who feared their power. Whitney had tons of lessons, but none of them involved willfully murdering anyone to make a point. Maybe the mystics needed governing, needed to be chased away.

No, that can't be.

Mad as they might seem, their rule had to be better than living under the control of a far-off king, forced to worship a God that was not their own and serve a Crown they barely knew. She simply didn't understand the mystics yet, and Wetzel had taught her never to discount anything without first studying it.

A knock on the door startled her. Aquira nearly flew into the ceiling before growling toward the disturbance. Sora quickly threw on a Panpingese dress she'd heard called a kimono.

"Come in."

The heavy door swung and in walked a young Panpingese man. His brown robes looked worn and old, although he couldn't have been long past adolescence.

Aquira swooped down to a dresser near the door and continued growling. The man didn't seem frightened in the slightest.

"Aquira, it's fine," Sora scolded as she hurried over to grab the wyvern and place her on her shoulder. "Sorry about her. She's protective, even though she's a liar." Sora shot Aquira a smirk, and the wyvern features darkened. Smoke billowed from her nostrils as she huffed.

"I'm sorry, Miss," the man said. He carried a tray. "The madams wished me to bring you this breakfast. They didn't want you hungry for your first full day of training."

"Thank you…"

"Kai, Miss."

"Thank you, Kai. Would you please put it down there?" She pointed to a table by the bed.

After placing the tray down, he turned, bowed, and went to take his leave.

"Kai?" Sora said, stopping him at the door.

"Yes, Miss?"

"First, my name is Sora. You may call me that."

"Yes, Miss Sora—"

"Just Sora."

He blushed and nodded.

"Could I ask you a question, Kai?" she asked.

"Oh, uh—Sora, you are permitted to ask anything you'd like of me," he said.

"How do they treat you?"

"They?"

"The mystics. Aihara Na and the rest."

"I live to serve," he answered. "That is why we are here. To assist the Secret Council with all of our beings."

She noticed his eyes wander toward the red, stone floor.

"That is not an answer to what I asked," Sora said.

"Miss Sora, please, I have much to do this morning and time is dwindling."

His face betrayed something his words did not; that the mystics were listening and he couldn't speak freely. Or at least that's what she thought his face said. Considering they could seemingly appear at a whim in their spirit-like state, Sora wasn't sure how she'd slept so soundly the night before.

"Thank you for the breakfast, Kai." Sora bowed, and Kai returned the gesture before hurriedly exiting the room.

Left in silence, Sora sat down and pulled the lid off a delicious looking fried turnip cake and orange dumplings. She ate it all, washing it down with a large cup of rice milk.

She looked around the spartan room. A storage chest sat in the corner, a desk by the window, and the bed in the middle. In the far corner, she saw something she couldn't believe she'd forgotten. She slid open the semi-transparent paper door and was greeted by a bright room, though she couldn't find the source of the light. Steam rose from a tub in the center but there was no room to fan a flame beneath it—a self-heating bath.

Sora nearly tripped over herself in her haste to remove the

clothing she'd only just put on. She hadn't had a hot bath since she'd been a guest of that brute Muskigo in Winde Port, and that had only been her first time experiencing one. She shuddered at the thought of the afhem.

Evil like Kazimir's, she could understand—his thirst made him wicked and forced him to see other human life as little more than cattle. Muskigo's evil she could not. He had been kind and hospitable to her, as well as his handmaid Shiva, yet only moments before had led a massacre of innocent people in Winde Porte. And not long before that, had razed Troborough and so many other villages.

Sora had experienced more in the past couple of months than nearly her whole life combined, and so much of it was evil. Sure, she'd survived a war she didn't remember, traveled across Pantego in a refugee wagon, lived within a crazy old man's house who happened to have an interest in the occult, and gotten into her fair share of mischief with Whitney, but that was nothing.

If she closed her eyes, she could find herself back in the Webbed Woods, listening to Whitney poke egg sacs of monstrous spiders that he didn't know were egg sacs. She'd seen creatures she didn't know existed. She'd be lying if she said she hadn't woken up in a puddle of sweat after a nightmare over the demonic satyrs or Redstar's dire wolves.

But right now, all she wanted to think about was hot water.

Sora drove the memories from her head and tried to enjoy a moment for once. She climbed the stone steps of the bath and tested the waters with her toe. It was hot, but not scalding—the perfect temperature. Soon, she was waist deep. She hadn't even realized how her bones ached until they found relief. She dipped below the surface, allowing the hot water to soak her hair and face. Eyes closed, she blew bubbles, slowly releasing the lung of air, then came up for air, pushing her hair back.

"Better than a pirate's cabin, isn't it?" she said to Aquira who flapped into the room and perched on the rim.

The wyvern screeched in response.

"Yeah. Maybe we won't burn this one down."

Sora stretched her arms out, extending one toward the creature. Seeing smooth and not scarred skin on her limbs surprised her once again. She'd grown so used to water making the fresh cuts on her hands sting. Aquira nuzzled her warm nose into Sora's palm, the steam pouring from her nostrils making the hot water seem cold.

"Friends again?" Sora asked.

Aquira chirped. Sora smiled ear to ear. They had been apart for less than a day, but she missed her tiny friend. All the deception wasn't her fault. Even had she'd been told Tayvada was going to die in the process of sending Sora to them like they somehow foresaw, Sora wasn't sure she truly understood what death meant. The permanence of it that even the mystics apparently couldn't undo. Or rather, refused to.

"Sora, report to training room posthaste," someone said suddenly. The voice echoed like it had been shouted in the Pikeback Mountains—not that Sora would've known what that sounded like, not really. She searched the room, but it was empty.

Then Sora recognized that the voice belonged to Madam Jaya, her new teacher, as Aihara Na had called her. She reluctantly exited the bath. She didn't see a towel, so she pricked her thumb on Aquira's tail to summon warmth from within. Once dry, she slid on her kimono again and slipped into her heavy boots.

She considered bringing her knife, then decided against it. If she needed weapons, she was sure Madam Jaya would provide them, plus she wanted to seem open to their instruction rather than nervous. It was her first day as a mystic acolyte, after all, and she had no idea what training even entailed.

"Aquira, are you coming?"

Aquira, who had already made herself comfortable on Sora's bed, cracked one eye open and released a mouthful of air as she yawned. Then she turned her head and trilled her tongue.

Sora took it as a 'no' and left the room.

She reached the level of the tower below the lake without incident. Staring at the door to the training facility, she took a deep breath, then knocked. When no answer came, she decided to push her way inside. When she'd come with Madam Aihara, she hadn't had the time to take in the room. It was massive; she knew that. She didn't, however, notice how high the ceiling was.

There were no windows or secondary doors, just the exit behind her and the white walls before her. Sora took a few steps toward the center of the room. An overwhelming sense of its magnitude washed over her. She felt vulnerable.

"Hello?" she said, listening to only her echo as a reply. "Madam Jaya?"

The sound of metal scraping metal bounced off the walls. Sora spun but still saw nothing. Footsteps pounded behind her, but again there was nothing.

"Who's there?" she asked, her voice shaking.

Sora felt a dull thud against her lower back, followed by pins and needles up her spine, and then a hard crack as her face hit the floor. Stunned, she barely managed to roll over before a familiar face bore down on her.

Muskigo's gray skin and tattoos were unmistakable.

Sora scrabbled backward, kicking with her feet at his impossibly hard abdomen. She rolled over and drew up to her knees. Her heart sank as she reached for her knife. *Why would I leave it behind after everything?* The better question would have been how Muskigo entered the Red Tower, but she was too distracted to give it much thought.

Not daring to take her eyes off him for more than a split second, she used her peripherals to search the room, hoping to see a weapons rack she'd missed, something that might help her fend off the afhem. There was nothing. Just a stark, empty room with supernaturally tall ceilings, and no exit beyond the one she'd come in. And now, Muskigo stood squarely between her and it.

"What do you want?" she huffed.

His scimitar glistened, reflecting the light of a burning brazier. Elsewhere begged her to draw on its power, sacrificing her blood, but there was nothing to be done without a blade. Muskigo charged her, rearing his weapon back and preparing to slice down. She sidestepped so the sharp edge of the blade would gash her arm. If he drew blood, then she would rain fire down upon him, delivering him swiftly into the arms of the fallen gods.

He rotated the scimitar just in time to slap her hard with the flat of the blade. It would be sure to leave a bruise, but it drew no blood.

He lashed out again, but Sora rolled out of the way.

"Stop this!" she panted as he pursued again. "The mystics will be here any moment, and you'll be killed. Stop now, and they might spare you."

He only smiled and pressed again, that debonair grin that hid the monster he truly was. Sora punched him, but Muskigo palmed her fist and forced her to the ground. He dropped the scimitar, and it clattered against the stone. Straddling her, his gray hands wrapped tightly around her wrists, he leaned in, breathing into her ear. She squirmed, but couldn't move, couldn't break free.

"Without blood, you are useless." She heard the words, but they weren't in Muskigo's smooth, accented voice.

"Madam Jaya?"

"See me now for who I really am," she said.

Before Sora's eyes, Muskigo's visage changed, color coming into his skin, tattoos disappearing. The muscles disappeared, giving way to a pair of unclothed breasts. Suddenly, the weight of the mystic's body vanished as well, and she rolled over, her limbs passing through Sora to quickly find her footing. Sora remained, back on the ground.

"Wha… Why?"

"Tell me, child," Madam Jaya started. "What did you see?" She rolled her hand, and her yellow robe materialized out of thin air. As she dressed, Sora climbed to her feet.

"I saw Afhem Muskigo of the Black Sands. How did you…"

"Curious. Very curious."

"I'm sorry, what's curious?" Sora asked.

"The spell I used was designed to show you the image of that which you most fear. Most people see themselves or their parents. Who is this Muskigo, and why do you believe you hold such fear in your heart for him?"

The question gave Sora pause. If asked who she most feared, she'd have thought Kazimir would have been the obvious answer. The upyr had terrified her, nearly killed her, held her captive, and tortured her—mentally if not physically. But as she heard this, she realized the truth.

"He destroyed my home. Killed the man who raised me, everything I loved." Even Whitney was gone because of Muskigo, though she didn't say that part out loud. If not for Muskigo's rebellion, they'd have passed right through Winde Port. They wouldn't have needed a ship, leading Bartholomew Darkings to find them and sic the Dom Nohzi upyr on Whitney in vengeance. Which meant Tayvada wouldn't have been killed to serve as prey for them…

He wouldn't have been killed.

Her eyes went wide. She'd never even thought of that, how even Tayvada's death could be traced back to Muskigo. Kazimir was a wolf on a hunt, but Muskigo's very existence had sent her life hurtling toward this place like it was fated for them to meet.

"For all our power, we cannot control fate." Sora couldn't help but recall those words from Aihara Na.

"Interesting," Madam Jaya said. "Did he harm you?"

"No," Sora said. "Even after I attacked him, he never did."

"But others have?"

"Many." She grimaced. "Too many to count."

"Family and friends, they mean the most to you, do they not?" Madam Jaya circled Sora. Sora's gaze followed until it could not, then she turned her head, her body.

"I never had a family," Sora said.

"Oh, but you did. Blood is not everything—as you have learned today. You were completely at my mercy. It is a wonder you've survived as long as you have." She raised her hand to stop Sora's retort before it started. "Do not misunderstand, child, you've done well—but it is time you stop relying upon spilled blood like a common bloodfiend."

"I survived no thanks to this place." Sora couldn't help herself. "I always thought Panping was going to be some godsforsaken, desolate place where people murdered each other for food. The way I was abandoned and shipped off to the Glass, you'd have thought there wasn't a street to spare. But everyone here seems to be living peaceably. Why did I have to grow up in a place only to watch it burn."

"You were left in good and necessary hands to keep you safe until you were ready. I know it is difficult to see, but there is no teacher like the open world. You've been training for this all your life, Sora of Troborough."

"What do you know of Troborough?" Sora questioned. "Do you know of its ashes? Of the lives lost? Most of the people there may never have cared much for me, they barely even noticed me, but not one of them deserved what they got."

"I know many things, and you would be wise to remember that. Do not forget your role, even in your anger." Madam Jaya stopped in front of Sora. "I know that Wetzel never made it past meager blooding. He died tragically before he could try, but without being a true mystic he never would have been able to."

"If he wasn't a mystic, then what was he?"

"A servant of our Order, looking after one strong with the Gift. Like Kai, or the Bokeos."

"Why do you call them that?"

"What?"

"Servants. If they're so willing to be here, the word seems…"

"Harsh?" Madam Jaya finished. "You will find that some words do not translate well from Panpingese to common. The definition may remain the same, but here, to be a servant is not considered an insult. Perhaps, acolyte is a more apt term, but there is no greater calling than to choose to serve that which is greater than you." She began to pace the room.

"You will come to find that there is no logic to those that are chosen by fate to wield the Gift," she continued. "Some never even realize the font of power growing within them. Some escape our gaze and the Well of Wisdom; even the most attuned clairvoy-ants. Only the gods decide, but that does not mean the lowliest member of our Order is of no importance. We are not all seeing, and the nature of this world is relentless even to those given the ability to change the rules. Without cleanliness, we could be taken by disease beyond healing. Without farms, we would starve."

"So, everyone in Panping exists to take care of the few people within this tower?"

"Existed. And I may not be as strict as Master Aihara Na, but consider your tone." She turned quickly and glowered at Sora, her robe snapping up behind her. "You explain the nature of our very world. Did the vassals of King Liam not serve him and his king-dom? Did the warlords of Latiapur not serve their Caleef? Yet they cannot summon rain in the driest summer, nor will crops to grow in stubborn dirt."

Sora lowered her head. "No, they can't."

"Precisely. Ours is a world of give and take. The masses provide for their lords so that they may be kept fed, safe. The lord provides for the masses, so he is not massacred out of desperation and hunger. It is the same with magic. Wetzel spoke to you about sacrifice, and so you scarred your body. We will teach you how to channel your blood from within in order to bring the magic of Elsewhere to bear."

"Is that what you do? Sacrifice blood from within?"

"In a way. It takes many years to learn the channeling in a way that will not leave you clinging to life even with the most tenuous of spells, that is why we have this." She produced a necklace from the folds of her robe. A periapt hung from it, a golden disc surrounded by six small, stones, each etched with a unique, symbolic marking. They seemed like characters in a written language, but Sora had no idea which.

"What is it?" Sora asked.

"Turn."

Sora hesitated.

"If you are going to be here, you must learn trust. Go on."

Sora conceded and turned her back to Madam Jaya. She felt the unnaturally cold metal against her skin and heard it clasp behind her. It hung heavy around her neck, yet it was oddly comforting.

"This is a bar guai," Madam Jaya said. "It will help you in casting without mutilation until such a time that you learn to channel from within. We must bind it to your blood. Please be still, this will only sting for a moment."

Sora was used to pain, but she did not expect what came next. Madam Jaya pressed her finger to the front of the flat disc and said a phrase in a language that wasn't precisely Panpingese. It sounded older, rougher.

A sudden, stabbing pain—no, not one, but several sharp stabs broke the flesh beneath the disc. It felt like she was being branded. She looked down and saw the round disc boring into her skin. Blood poured down her front, soaking her clothes.

She tried to cry out, but no sound would come. Then, as quickly as it started, it stopped. The pain stopped. The sharpness stopped. The chain fell from the periapt, but that didn't matter, the disc and the connected stones were now firmly embedded in her skin.

"It is not like true channeling, and it is far more limited, but you are powerful Sora—more than you know," Madam Jaya said. "Your blood is unique and strong in its bond to Elsewhere. Perhaps that is why, in the vision Aihara Na gave, you saw that realm in detail. The bar guai will allow you to use that power, harness it."

Sora touched the disc. She wiggled it, but it wouldn't budge.

"The bar guai will not come free except by my word when you are ready for channeling," Madam Jaya said. "You will come to appreciate it and what it can do for you."

"You did not..." Sora gasped. "I did not..."

"What? Ask your permission? I am your teacher now, Sora of Troborough. I need not your permission, and you need not worry about anything other than proving to me that you are ready to be more than a simple blood mage. Someday, when the Order is rebuilt, you will be a mystic, and you will understand the weight that comes with the title."

Her words, although harsh, did not come across that way. There was a softness to her tone, a gentleness that put Sora at ease.

"Why me?" Sora asked.

"Why not?" Madam Jaya replied.

Sora rolled her eyes, a bit of Whitney's influence coming through.

"Do not speak with your eyes, child," Madam Jaya scolded. "If you've something to say, use words."

"Fine. I didn't ask for any of this. I was practically kidnapped and brought here, and although I enjoyed two lavish meals and a hot bath, I've also been attacked by a man I hoped never to see again. I think it's time someone explains something, anything."

"After you learn to use your bar guai, you will have all the answers you will ever need."

"I'm not asking for all the answers, only—"

"Sora, the process you are about to go through has taken all the mystics, including me, decades. We have all gone through our period with the bar guai. In the time of the Mystic Order, some apprentices never grew beyond its crutch. Some were consumed by the power it unlocks. If patience was our first lesson, you are failing."

Hearing the word 'lesson' reminded Sora why she was doing this in the first place. She considered all Whitney must be going through, all the suffering. She had to do whatever it took.

"I am sorry, Madam Jaya," she said. "Please, teach me. Teach me everything."

XXIV

THE DESERTER

Rand and the others kept to backroads on their way up from Dockside, avoiding churches, where people were gathered in great numbers, waiting to receive their blessings for the new year. Even the Drav Cra set up camps to watch a phenomenon probably as strange to them as summer. A day without labor, Rand imagined them saying. In the harsh lands they came from, that would probably spell certain death.

Father Morningweg had sobered up a bit in the frigid air, at least enough that his swerving could be chalked up to a blind man walking without a cane. Codar kept him moving briskly, however, and he only stopped once more to clear out the contents of his stomach.

They were headed northwest of Yarrington, for the base of Mount Lister where the royal crypt's ceiling had broken open months back on the day of Pi's rebirth. The magnificent stone spires gleamed in the low winter sun, and the glass Eye of Iam atop it painted a rainbow across a vast crowd. The faces of those who'd already been blessed with the luminescent paint of God reflected the vibrant colors.

It was a magical sight; one Rand looked forward to every year… until now. For standing before the tall open doors of the cathedral wasn't just High Priest Wren the Holy and his circle of bishops, but Redstar and his warlocks too. Their faces were painted white on the bottom, their mouths and chins, and black across their brows as usual as if mocking Iam's own followers. The petrifying, female warlock beside Redstar was the one Rand had knocked out in the castle. If only he'd known how important she was, to stand directly at the Arch Warlock's side, he wished he'd killed her instead.

The sight gave Rand pause. Not long ago, he'd watched Wren stand against Redstar with a shield of light, proud and mighty. Now he looked like nothing more than an old, tired man, leaning on his cane more than ever before. His wrinkles were deeper, his cheeks saggier, and his hair somehow whiter, wispier. Gone was the man who appeared as Yarrington's all-loving father, replaced instead by the visage of a vagrant.

"Long has this kingdom stood alone in the light of Iam!" Redstar announced. "And on this day, year by year, you stand in the absence of it, looking within. No longer." He took Wren's cane and raised it. "Today, as the light falls away, know that Nesilia is with you. Her love is eternal, always within us and the earth, buried but not dead. After all these long centuries, you may be open to it again."

"Buried, not dead," the warlocks alongside him chanted. Buried Goddess cultists and Drav Cra civilians in the crowd repeated the words as well. Rand only then noticed how many of the former there seemed to be with their chilling, expressionless white masks.

"The light of Iam never leaves you, for you cannot have light without shadow," Wren said, voice weathered and raspy. Rand had heard him give sermons before, and he usually spoke with enough verve to inspire a stone to the faith. Now, he could barely be heard. "Praise be the Vigilant Eye." He circled his burned eye-sockets, hands trembling as he did. The Glassmen in the crowd mimicked him.

The female warlock handed Redstar a horn. He scooped out a glob of black paint and ran it over Wren's sightless eyes in the very same manner as his warlocks wore it.

"There is no more time for spectating," Codar said, taking Rand by the arm and tugging him along until the Cathedral Square was out of view.

"How can they stand there and watch that... atrocity?" Rand said.

"Their king accepts Redstar. Their High Priest now does as well."

"Sheep will always follow the shepherd," Father Morningweg said, burping. "Even to the slaughter. That bastard was there when they ravaged my home. Now he's up there, and I'm down here."

Rand yanked his arm free. "Whatever he did to the High Priest, getting him to speak like that, he can't get away with it."

"That is not for us to decide," Codar replied, still hurrying them along.

"You can help us end it. Valin won't even have to know. You have to realize that there won't be a Glass Kingdom anymore if they win."

"I do not serve the Glass Kingdom."

"Then there won't be anything left for you to exploit!" Rand shouted, stopping.

Codar stopped and glared daggers at him. "Keep trying to persuade me to betray Mister Tehr, and you will do so without a tongue."

"Gentleman," the Father slurred. He slipped his way between them, then beckoned them along. "This way. I was promised revenge on Redstar too."

They continued skirting around Old Yarrington, along bridleways toward the northern gates of the city which stood a short distance directly behind the cathedral. The road led straight to the trails up Mount Lister. A group of guards passed by, offering Father Morningweg a circle of prayer. They didn't even give Rand a passing glance.

"See, just follow my lead." The priest started walking, then stopped to dry heave and nearly toppled over.

"Is there no depth Valin Tehr won't sink to?" Rand asked. "That man needs help."

"That man lost everything," Codar said. "His home, his flock. All to Redstar and his horde of savages. Mister Tehr gives purpose to those who would otherwise hang… like you."

"How did you wind up working for the bastard then? A resourceful man like you, I'm sure you could make a fine living back home."

"Have you ever been to Brekliodad?"

Rand shook his head. He'd never been to Winde Port, let alone beyond the Dragon's Tail to the Pikeback Mountains of Brekliodad and their colorful palaces.

"Then do not assume what I could do back home," Codar said.

"Did he take your sister hostage too then?"

"He gave me purpose when I could no longer return home. And now my purpose is to help you get what you want." He touched his temple with his forefinger. "You would be wise not to forget that, and maybe, one day, if you return from your duty in the South, you will see that there is as much work to be done in the shadows as there is in the light."

"Praise be! Light shines brightest in the shadows." Father Morningweg cheered, pumping his fist in the air.

He rounded a corner and fell in with a line of citizens headed out to the base of Mount Lister. Every year, people camped around it, for there was no more splendid a place to watch the Dawning than the site where Iam brought an end to the God Feud. The most faithful would climb to the flattened peak of Mount Lister itself for the event. After sermons throughout the city, Wren the Holy and the King would ride up to join them. Rand had never been, as he was still in training at the last one.

So much had happened in just a year.

The slope started off shallow and smooth, stairs weaving back and forth until the angle sharpened at the center and they had to wrap the mountain. Areas around the entries to the glaruium mines were known to be unstable, and the rock toward the top was so thick the path grew thin enough to be traversed only in a single file.

Anyone seeking to reach the flat peak by foot before the eclipse had to start the climb in the morning, and there were already Shieldsmen and warlocks doing so as the sun crept over the horizon. Rand didn't spot any civilians making the climb this year, however.

Once within the flow of the river of the faithful, Rand and his odd party were rendered nearly invisible. Only the fur-covered Drav Cra and masked cultists sprinkled throughout the throng drew any real attention. The base of the mountain had become a Drav Cra trading camp, the savages hoping to take advantage of the pilgrims, hawking their thick furs. On the trail, priests stood at intervals, praying out loud.

"They're using us," Rand said, then he remembered to whom he spoke.

"Everyone is using someone," Codar said. He nudged Rand in the arm, then pointed through a mob of sojourners to an area at the base of the Mountain that was blocked off by a low, spiked wooden wall and a line of Glass soldiers. "Crypt is through there."

"It'll take us an hour to shove through," Rand complained.

Codar turned Father Morningweg toward the crypt entry. "Act convincing for once," he said.

"I'll have you know, there wasn't a soul in Fessix who missed my sermons," the Father replied.

"Then pretend they aren't all food for worms somewhere up north."

The priest's cheeks went from a pale green to white. His gaze grew distant, and it was a look Rand recognized. He wore the same one every time he pictured Tessa and the others hanging from the walls of the Glass Castle. He then realized that it'd been some time since he last thought of that. Now, when he closed his eyes, all he saw was what horror might befall Sigrid should he fail.

"Come on, Father," Rand said. He took him by the arm and helped him walk. "Just because you don't have a church any longer, doesn't mean you aren't a priest. Every man and woman of Fessix looks down upon you now from the Gate of Light. You mustn't disappoint them."

The crowd parted easily, and after a short while, the Father's gait was brimming with renewed confidence. "Bless you, my son," he would say as the people shifted. "Iam watch over us," he said to another. "May His light shine eternally upon you."

By the end of the walk, he no longer swayed. Reminding him of what he used to be seemed to sober him up, and it got them through the dense crowd faster than Rand could have wished for.

"Tell Valin I'll take double," Father Morningweg said when they stopped a short distance from the crypt's guards.

"You'll take what was agreed upon," Codar said.

"Yeah? Why don't I mosey over to those guards and tell them what you're planning then?"

Codar's hand shot forward, fast as a crossbow bolt, to clutch the father by his robes. Murmuring broke out around them just as quickly. Rand didn't need to hear the words. A Breklian grabbing a priest in obvious anger on the day of the Dawning... it was bound not to go well.

"Valin wouldn't hurt a priest now, would he?" the Father said.

Codar's bushy, white mustache wriggled as he grit his teeth, and he released him. "You god-worshippers are all the same. He reached into a pouch and drew a few gold autlas. "For your trouble, Father," he said as he pulled the man close and slipped them into his hand.

Father Morningweg bowed and circled his eyes. "Bless you, child of Brekliodad," he said. "May the light of Iam guide you on your journey in sending that bastard Redstar straight to exile." He flashed a grin, then strutted off.

All the pride Rand felt at helping the priest regain a fragment of his poise instantly melted away. Men who took the vow of sightlessness swore off all wealth and finery, and evidently, Morningweg had been changed too much by the horrors of war. Or perhaps, he had always been corrupt, and Valin Tehr was there to feed that darkness, to prey on his weakness to accomplish his goals like he had with Rand.

"Did you hope his kind was above greed?" Codar asked.

"I hoped many things weren't as they are," Rand replied.

"The old gods have abandoned us. Soon, you people will see as mine have, that all we are is flesh and desire."

"How much is Valin paying you to try and coax me toward loyal service to him?"

Codar didn't bother responding. "Come. Tell the guards you are here to see Foreman Orebreaker. That we are more masons to help finish the job." He gestured to Valin's three thugs accompanying them.

"And if they recognize me?"

"The Rand they knew wasn't a drunk with a beard patchy as a goat with mange." Codar again poked Rand's jaw to lift it. "Head up. Avoid their gaze like you're above them. Breklian emissaries are not renowned for being on the winning side of deals because they are special, but because everyone thinks they are."

Codar continued along with Valin's men. They strolled right up to the guards at the fence as if they were invited in until two spears closed before them.

"Sorry," one of the guards said. "All revelry is to be kept east of the break."

"We are here to help with repairs," Codar replied.

"On the Dawning?"

"I'm not a Glassman and they're masons from east of Crowfall. Wouldn't know Iam from Meungor."

The guards exchanged a confused look. "Sorry, we have orders."

Rand took that as his cue to step in or risk failing. They'd given him a loose sense of the plan, but Codar didn't speak much when Valin was around.

"Now you've got new ones," he said, stepping forward. He did his best to sound commanding, drawing on his memories of Torsten and Wardric.

"Sir," they both saluted.

"The Crown doesn't want construction to stop on account of the holiday, and there aren't enough dwarves alone," Rand said.

"I ...uh... we heard nothing about it," one of them stammered.

"And that's why you're out here. Now let us through to the foreman."

"Yes, sir... right away, sir."

Their spears parted, and Rand walked through first. Codar and the others followed. He knew the way many Shieldsmen spoke to their underlings even if it had never been how he treated other men of the Glass. He'd been a meager guard before, been spoken to the same.

"Well done, *knight*," Codar said, the title oozing with mockery.

"Keep walking."

Inside, a barricade retained massive hunks of fallen rock on the mountain-side of the trail. On the day of Pi's rebirth, it was said Mount Lister split open as if bearing him from her womb. The metaphor was apter than Rand expected. A gash ran down a portion of the mountainside all the way to the base, ending directly above the buried Royal Crypt.

They climbed over and through a pile of boulders, then arrived at the construction site. A handful of dwarves stood in a clearing surrounded by piles of rough, jagged stone, the size of which made the dwarves seem even smaller. A few of their construction machinations sat beside the gap in the earth leading down to the Royal Crypt—huge contraptions able to lift stone into place with a system of pulleys and levers. A few more Glass guards stood around the area, making sure no curious pilgrims tried to sneak in and disturb things. One of them wore glaruium armor, a Shieldsman Rand didn't recognize.

"For such small folks, everything they build is huge," Rand remarked.

"Whatever it takes to prove they're better than us," Codar replied.

"Aye, who let you pass!" the Shieldsman called, rushing over. The two Glass soldiers took their time following.

"They're here to help with construction," Rand said. He purposefully turned his body and head to face Codar, and never turned all the way back.

"Today?"

"No delays."

A lift rose to the surface out of the maw, a burly dwarf perched atop, chest thick as an iron keg and beard full as an oak in summer. He noticed Codar and the features on his grime-covered face lit up.

"There ye be, lazy bugger!" he exclaimed. "Been waitin for you."

"Why didn't you mention anything?" the Shieldsman asked.

"Last I heard, I report to the Leuvero Messier, Master of Masons, who reports to the Prime Minister," the foreman said.

"You report to the Crown, of which I am an extension."

"So is he." The dwarf stuck one of his stubby, calloused fingers toward Rand. "Found him this morning and sent him to fetch this crew by the gates. Barely a soul working today, festivities tomorrow; you lazy flower pickers hate work." He and his crew burst out in laughter.

The Shieldsman wasn't entertained. "We don't fall behind on our work."

"A mountain filled with metal makin iron seem like parchment split open and collapsed on a crypt. Ye try stickin to a deadline."

The Shieldsman groaned. "Fine, get them working. But anything goes wrong, and it'll be your head on the Prime Minister's spike."

Even the Shieldsmen are recognizing Redstar's new position, Rand noted.

Codar approached the dwarf, and they exchanged some quiet words as the dwarf invited Valin's men onto the lift. Nothing passed between hands like with the priest, but that arrangement was likely already taken care of.

Rand took a step toward them, but the other Shieldsman did the same and got in between them. "What are you doing, *knight?*" he questioned.

Rand stopped. He kept his gaze fixed on Codar, refusing to look the Shieldsman in the eye. "Taskmaster Lars asked if I could fill in at the dungeon today," Rand replied. Lying wasn't his forte, and with all the turnover he wasn't sure that the old scribe in charge of organizing the day-to-day affairs of the King's Shield barracks was still in place. The name didn't appear to surprise the Shieldsman.

"There may not be a new wearer yet," Rand added, "but we still have to work, right?"

"No new Wearer?" the Shieldsman's brow furrowed. "They named Sir Nikserof co-wearer just the other day."

Rand's throat went dry. Codar had mentioned that in their prep over the last few days and it completely escaped his mind. "Sir Nikserof? Really? I just transferred down from Crowfall, and nobody bothered to tell me?"

The man gave him another look over, then sighed. "Not surprising. It's been a mess since Sir Unger lost his mind."

"Were you there?"

"Aye. He was like a mad bull, never seen anything like it. Would have killed me if I were in the way but I was lucky to be behind the giant."

"By Iam..."

"These are strange times sure. Rebellion, warlocks on the streets, a Wearer sharing the white with a barbarian..." Rand nodded along with the man until his train of thought seemed to end. "Anyway, what were you saying?"

"I was hoping to pass through the crypt. Just got stationed back here so I've got dungeon duty on the Dawning of all days."

"Well, that's an active work zone," the Shieldsman replied, pointing. "Only masons allowed while they finish the dome. You'll have to head back to the castle the long way."

Rand gestured back to the northern gate. "Back though that crowd? It'll take me all day."

"You should've thought of that before taking on an escort that any guard in Yarrington could have handled."

"C'mon Sir..." Rand made the mistake of locking eyes with the man momentarily as he lingered on the word, waiting for a name.

"Childress," the Shieldsman said.

"Sir Childress. I didn't even know about the new Wearer, let alone how best to get around the city these days."

"And you didn't think that the Royal Crypt might still be dangerous?"

"To be honest, I figured it was done by now."

The man grimaced. "Then you haven't worked with dwarves. Only thing that gets those short runts to move is gold, and the war in the South has the coffers low."

Rand thought back to the man's earlier conversation with the dwarven foreman and remembered the constant butting heads between the Glass and the dwarven kingdoms. He wasn't used to his mind being so sharp as it was of late. He could get used to it.

"You're telling me," Rand said, acting exhausted. "It's amazing any of us in Crowfall has a bronzer to spend with how many of the little-men live near there."

Sir Childress' stance appeared to relax. "Fine, I'll let you through just this once, but don't tell anyone."

"Thank you, Sir." Rand saluted and took a step, but the Shieldsman wasn't done talking.

"How is the old snow city?" he asked. "I grew up there myself."

"Did you, now?" It wasn't hard to feign the excitement in his tone. Of all the cities in the kingdom he could've picked, of course, he chose the one where the Shieldsman grew up.

"Aye." He snickered. "You probably came up a few years earlier than me, green as you are, but I'm Crow through and through. Trained under the Sir Barvadi. He still up there?"

"Still a pain. Barely made it a day in training without him screaming at me."

"You sure it was him? Sir Barvadi lost his tongue to Drav Cra raiders."

Rand cursed himself inwardly. Another slip up. All he needed to do was get out of this conversation. "Of course, figure of speech. His glare was worse than words."

Sir Childress took a step forward and looked Rand straight in the eyes. "What did you say your name was?"

"I didn't." Rand forced a smile to mask how hard he swallowed next as if all moisture left his mouth. "I really ought to be going. Thanks for letting me through. Always a pleasure to meet a fellow Crow." Rand banged his chest-plate in salute again, then moved for the lift. Childress grabbed his arm.

"Wait, I know you, don't I?" he asked, leaning in close.

"Maybe we trained together one day up there?"

"No, that's not it, I... wait. You're..." He didn't get a chance to finish his sentence. A knife stabbed through the back of his neck, the point dripping red through his throat. As he fell, Rand saw Codar, arm outstretched, hand open like he'd thrown it.

The two soldiers in the clearing reached for their weapons, but Valin's men bolted into action. Rand wasn't sure where they drew knives from, but two of them gutted a soldier so fast he collapsed at Rand's feet before he could step back. The other was able to get his sword from its sheath in time and cut open the third thug's belly. Valin's man crumpled, pawing to hold his innards in before toppling over.

In the confusion, Rand nearly betrayed his feelings, thrilled to see the brute get cut down.

"Traitors!" the soldier barked. He charged at Rand, but Codar slipped between them. He was both incredibly quick and elegant, like a dancer in a southern troupe. He deflected two blows, used the guard's weight against him to affect his balance, then spun low and kicked out the soldier's feet. In the same motion, Codar brought the tip of his blade around and shoved it through the soldier's eye.

The Breklian wiped his blade off on the end of his tunic as he stood.

Rand was stunned by the carnage. Foreman Oarbreaker and the other dwarven masons were similarly dumbfounded. The Shieldsman still gurgled, somehow having risen to his hands and knees. One of Valin's men kicked him over and released a chuckle.

Rand shot forward, seized Codar, and threw him to the ground. "We said no killing Glassmen!" he roared. He heard metal scraping, then felt something sharp at his belly, but it didn't stop him.

"*I* didn't," Codar replied.

"Your boss did."

"But I didn't," he repeated. "That man recognized you. We do not have time for this."

"Time for this? You murdered a Shieldsman. He never even reached for his sword, he might have just thought I was someone else."

"Well, next time you try to deceive a well-trained man, don't slip twice. Now release me before it's too late."

Rand's fists squeezed tight, then he shoved Codar down for good measure and stood. The Breklian kicked back up to his feet and pointed at Foreman Oarbreaker. "Get these bodies down into the crypt. I don't care where you bury them."

The dwarf remained frozen, staring at Sir Childress' now twitching body.

"Now, dwarf!"

Foreman Oarbreaker shook out his head. "Aye lads, ye heard him. It'll be our heads too if these're found."

The dwarves grabbed the bodies of the soldiers and Valin's fallen thug and dragged them onto the lift, grumbling to each other the whole way. Codar hopped up some rocks to take a look beyond the construction site.

"Nobody saw," he said. "You're lucky, Glassman."

"Lucky that you killed these men?" Rand said.

"*We*. Like it or not you're one of us now, and it was them or us."

"I…" Rand lost his train of thought. He wasn't sure why he was shocked that foul men like these would do something so horrid beyond the gaze of their equally monstrous boss. "You could have knocked them out."

"Incapacitation is a risk. Death leaves no room for regret."

Codar backed onto the lift alongside his men, the dwarves, and the bodies. Rand had no choice but to join them. He was in too deep now. All he could hope was that saving Torsten would be enough.

One of the dwarves climbed onto the pulley, and the lift began its descent. Now that the initial shock was out of the way, the little men seemed peculiarly calm amidst all the death.

"Valin's gonna be payin a lot more for this," Foreman Oarbreaker griped.

"I'm sure he'll be happy to renegotiate," Codar replied.

"Renego... I'll be visitin him on our way out. Soon as yer through, this is the last time ye'll see us in Yarrington."

"What about finishing the Royal Crypt?" Rand wasn't sure why that was a concern at a time like this, but he'd only been down once before during training. Sir Torsten and Sir Wardric liked to show new recruits the incredible breadth of history they protected.

As they descended into the massive, domed space, it was impossible for its majesty not to overshadow Rand's anger at Codar. Caskets made of glass wrapped the walls, allowing the preserved bodies of former kings to be viewed. Every inch of stone was carved with imagery from both the history of the Glass Kingdom and Iam himself. Flawless work that only the greatest artisans in history were capable of. The very floor was a mosaic telling the story of how Iam ended the God Feud, took man under his wing, led them all those centuries ago from the wintery wasteland of Drav Cra, and inspired the first King of the Glass, Autlas Nothhelm, to found Yarrington at the foot of Mount Lister.

The damage from the quake which ruptured the Mountain above was nearly all repaired. Some scaffolding still lined the walls, as some of the low, arched openings within which the caskets were slotted had collapsed. A portion of the domed ceiling was ruptured, and an area of the vast hall encasing the space had its columns knocked out, supported temporarily by wood. The scepters of old Kings sat in alcoves along it, and some were now damaged and could likely never be replicated. Hallways shot out between them toward lesser crypts for the families of the kings, some of those blocked off by rubble.

"Good enough job for me," the dwarf said. "You humans want to keep burying people underground, maybe you should learn how to build down here."

"Quiet," Codar demanded. "Are there any guards in the crypt?"

"The softies preferred the fresh air until they got too cold." He glanced down at the Shieldsman's corpse and stuck his tongue out in disgust. "They'll be awful cold now."

"What about Drav Cra? Have you seen them in the castle tunnels?"

"This a quiz? I come, I work stone, and I go home. If ye wanted me spyin on the castle, ye should have made an offer, Breklian."

"Dwarves," Codar grumbled. The lift clanked to a stop in a cloud of dust, and he stepped off. "Hide them in one of the family crypts."

"Which one?"

"I don't care." Codar removed his entire purse of autlas and flung it at the dwarves feet. "Just don't let them be found, and consider that final payment."

Foreman Oarbreaker kneeled and pulled back his beard so he

could peak into the bag, then snatched it up. "Aye, boys. Ye heard him. Got one more thing to bury before we head off." He and his crew slung the bodies over their shoulders, two per man, like they were carrying logs, then headed off toward one of the lesser crypts.

"Those are sacred places," Rand said. "This is wrong."

"You wanted to get inside; this is the cost."

"Are you truly that cold? They didn't have to die. They at least deserve to be put to rest properly."

"Brek is cold. Those men, you're welcome to dig them out and do so after we're done."

Codar brushed by him, heading for one of the catacombs branching off from the Royal Crypt. A locked gate stood in the opening, each iron bar as thick as Rand's forearm, impossible to bash open. Codar grabbed a burning torch from the stone wall and raised it to the lock.

"You," he said to one of Valin's thugs. "Get to work."

The man cracked his knuckles, then knelt before the gate with a pin and started picking the lock. Rand wasn't sure where to look as he did it. He had to avoid facing the Royal Crypt where it felt like the eyes of every fallen king were watching, judging him. He couldn't face the surrounding colonnade through which he could hear the dwarves fumbling with bodies. He couldn't even stare at the wall or floors, or he'd see stories of Iam.

So, he closed his eyes. He felt ridiculous doing it, like a child who'd broken a rule down by the docks, but his entire life had become so absurd. The only thing he was sure of was that he wasn't doing the work of Iam any longer. That was up to Torsten. From being the Queen's hangman to this... his hands were covered in too much innocent blood.

The lock clicked, and the gate creaked inward. The thug rubbed his hands together. "Easy as a Vineyard wench." The remark instantly drew Rand's glower, and the man smirked. "Most of em anyways."

Rand pushed him aside and moved into the entrance. "Let's just get this over with," he said. "I think I know the way to the lower dungeons from here."

"Lead on," Codar said.

"Do you have another pouch of gold?" Rand asked. "What do we do if we have to buy someone else's silence?"

"A favor owed from Valin Tehr is worth far more than gold," he replied, without even needing to give it a second's thought, like he didn't sense the venom in Rand's tone.

"Then I hope we don't run into anyone else."

"Now you are learning." Codar slid his dirk back out of the sheath on the small of his back. Valin's two remaining men drew daggers as well and held them backward, concealed by their wrists and forearms.

Rand moved ahead. "I'll go first. My armor will make any guards hesitate. No more killing."

Codar grabbed Rand and pulled him out of the hall. Rand was about to protest when the Breklian held a finger to his lips. He gestured back down the tunnel. Two men passed by the nearest fork, a torch revealing their pale skin, furs, and leather armor. One spoke in Drav Crava, and the other laughed.

"And what about them, knight?" Codar asked.

Rand didn't dignify him with a response. Instead, they waited for the savages to pass, but they both knew the answer. They were here to help stop the spread of the Drav Cra into Yarrington, and if one of them got in the way, Rand wouldn't falter.

"Let's go." Rand took the torch and headed into the cata-combs. The light would give away their position, but any guard in the tunnels was required to keep a torch with them. He didn't draw his sword either, so as not to look threatening at first glance, but he held his hand on the pommel as they moved. The Dawning had cleared the passage out until they were all the way to the end of the catacombs. Down the passage, where stairs led up to the castle courtyard, stood two Glass soldiers.

Rand positioned the torch directly in front of his chest so the shadow he cast would make Codar and the others invisible. He walked straight, shoulders proud, and the guards didn't seem to care about his presence at all. He did appear to be a Shieldsman after all, and he was too far for them to distinguish his face. He stopped at an entrance to a more cramped tunnel that led to the lower dungeons and allowed Codar and the others to slip behind him unseen.

"Well done," Codar said.

"Just keep walking," Rand replied. "The Dawning has helped, but the dungeons won't be empty."

A warren of tunnels crisscrossed beneath the castle. Some said it was an old dwarven city before the first king, Autlas Nothhelm, had his capital built above it centuries ago. Rand followed the light, avoiding the corridors where he could see the shimmer of torchlight on the moist stone walls. He may have appeared a Shieldsman, but he didn't want to encounter anyone else unless there was no choice.

The longer route avoiding patrols took them through storage halls—food, supplies, everything the castle might need to withstand a siege for months if it ever came to that. They had to slow on their way through as two Drav Cra warriors were passed out on a mat after looting some of it and eating their fill.

A staircase led to the lower dungeons where all the most rotten criminals the Crown got their hands on rotted for the rest of their lives. That was where Torsten would be, like some sort of mad killer. He, a man who had so loyally served the Crown for so long and faced untold evil just to bring back a doll Queen Oleander thought would save her son. Considering that the very next day King Pi rose from his casket alive and well, Rand couldn't deny that she might have been right and that Torsten's actions, insane as they might've been, had saved the Nothhelm line.

Rand now knew all the rumors about what Torsten did at the battle of Winde Port; killing a Shieldsman in rage, failing to capture the rebel Afhem Muskigo on purpose. Rand knew it was all hogwash. Sir Torsten Unger had trained Rand to serve the King's Shield far better than he ever had, and there was nobody who cared more for the realm.

"Is this the lower dungeons?" Codar asked as they reached the bottom of the stairs. So far below the ground, the air was dank and stale. The narrow hall extended two ways, barred cells lining it on either side. There were barely enough torches set on the walls to see anything. It was quiet, save for the soft echo of madness and the occasional scream.

"I'm surprised you've never been here," Rand replied.

"Perks of serving Valin Tehr. Now, where would they keep you, Torsten Unger?"

"There." Two Drav Cra warlocks stood outside one of the cells and a Glass soldier at a desk in a nearby nook. He was the unfortunate soul forced to endure the smell of shog and the din of insanity in the lower dungeons while the city above celebrated the Dawning. That meant he'd be the one with the keys.

"Your move, knight," Codar said.

Rand drew a deep breath. Warlocks were dangerous, as he'd learned in Redstar's chambers, but Rand had them outnumbered, four to three. Any other day of the year that number might have been tripled, but Valin Tehr was brilliant as he was wicked.

"We take out the warlocks, then convince the guard to open the cell," Rand said.

"And if he doesn't?"

"We take the keys and leave him in Torsten's cell. He doesn't die."

"Then don't let him see my face," Codar said, shoving Rand. "Go. This has taken too long already, and we have a schedule to keep."

Rand stumbled forward, the clatter of his armor drawing the attention of the warlocks. He had no choice but to proceed. They turned to face him simultaneously, two men with their faces painted black and white. Their heads were shaved, the black continuing all the way over their skulls. Ragged furs hung over their bodies, stitched together from various animals, and bone trinkets rattled around on their necks. Luckily, they weren't the ones who'd been outside Redstar's room.

The guard scrambled to his feet and saluted as Rand passed. The warlocks slowly repositioned themselves, now facing Rand, side by side.

"What is it you require, Shieldsman?" they asked. Hearing them speak in synchronization gave Rand momentary pause.

"I have to speak with Sir Unger," Rand said.

"Only Drad Redstar can order that."

Rand lifted his chin. "I was sent by the King himself."

"And we serve the Arch Warlock."

"You are in King Pi's castle, in our castle," Rand said sternly. "You will obey a direct order, or you will feel the might of the Glass Kingdom."

"We are that might. The former wearer is not to be—"

A knife zipped by Rand's ear. The warlock it was aimed at somehow predicted the attack and was able to slide out of the way, the blade stabbing into his shoulder. Rand swung at the other warlock with his torch without thinking twice and bashed him across the face.

Reeling from the knife, the first warlock raised a hand, and suddenly, the flame on the end of the torch jumped onto Rand's arm. His armor was infused with glaruium yet it caught fire like a thistle in a drought. One of Valin's men squeezed around him in the narrow passage and leaped onto the warlock Rand had struck, plunging the dagger into his chest over and over. The warlock murmured in Drav Crava as it happened, calmly, as if he felt no pain. When Valin's man glanced back up, all the deadly wounds he'd inflicted in the warlock showed on his chest as well, identical. He toppled over, dead in an instant.

The Glass guard grabbed his bludgeon and swung at Rand, but Codar parried the attack. "No!" Rand shouted as Codar swiftly ducked around the man and got his knife to his throat. Codar stopped centimeters away from shredding the man's throat.

The injured, remaining warlock stepped forward, chanting in Drav Crava. His eyes were wild, gray but glowing like hot coals, and the fire he'd summoned wrapped like a serpent up Rand's limb. He could feel his skin boiling beneath his armor, the pain so intense he could barely move. Valin's other thug stood to the side, the one who'd picked the lock, too petrified by the dark magic to move. The fire leaped from Rand's arm onto the thug like a living thing, and without armor, the man's clothing caught quickly. He shrieked, falling to the ground and rolling.

Rand fought through the pain. The heat was on his neck now, the skin beginning to blister, but he drew his sword and charged. The warlock backed up and sliced his own wrist with a knife so deep blood instantly gushed out. The body of the other warlock flew off the ground, knocking Rand from his feet and crushing Valin's lockpicker's head against the wall.

Rand groped for his sword, but the fire only grew brighter, hotter. He caught a glimpse of Codar and the guard out of the corner of his eye.

"There is no choice," Codar said. He was about to slit the man's throat so he could join the fight when all of a sudden the fire dwindled. Rand found his sword and got to his feet, only to see the warlock with his back against the bars of Torsten's cell. A chain was wrapped around his throat, scraping the white paint off until the man's throat crunched.

"You'll never get away with this," the glass guard rasped as Codar choked him. Rather than answering, the Breklian bashed him in the back of the head with the guard's cudgel and knocked him out.

"Rand, is that you?" a gruff, haggard voice asked. It didn't sound anything like the booming voice Rand remembered, but it couldn't be anyone else in the cell but the man who'd left Rand as Wearer while he saved the kingdom, only for Rand to ruin everything.

Rand wasn't sure why he hesitated, but it took all the strength in his limbs to drag his body in front of the cell. It was Torsten inside, still tall and strong as an ox with skin like pitch. He had a chain in one hand which hung from the ceiling, the end around the Warlock's throat keeping him from collapsing in a heap of tangled limbs. His ankles were chained like common livestock for slaughter.

"Sir Unger," Rand struck his chest and bowed his head. "I received your message."

XXV

THE MYSTIC

Wetzel was a strict teacher. Sora could remember the feeling of his cane against her knuckles every time she messed up or didn't listen, but he often wound up more upset with himself for not being able to teach her correctly. Then he'd storm off alone, rambling like a madman that he couldn't do it.

Madam Jaya was calmer, which she made up for in both unpredictability and ambiguity.

For days, Madam Jaya forced Sora to meditate, to clear her mind—as if she could focus on anything other than Whitney and his torment in Elsewhere.

Finally, after days of solitude, Madam Jaya finally returned. Just when Sora thought she'd gain some reprieve, the mystic told her she couldn't leave the training area until she'd summoned flame without the drawing of blood. She left with no further explanation of the bar guai and sealed the door behind her.

Sora stared down at the disc embedded in her skin, puzzled. "I guess this is teaching me." She drew a long, beleaguered breath. "Okay. Summon fire. You've done it a thousand times."

She closed her eyes and reached inward how she always used to. Ever since the first time Wetzel's teachings had unlocked her powers, the presence of Elsewhere had always called out in return. But they could only ever communicate if she drew blood.

Presently, Sora heard only the echo of her thoughts. Eyes closed, she pictured fire, roaring, its arms reaching out to devour everything in its path. Then, she thrust her arm forward. Nothing happened.

She shook out her limb, took another breath and tried again. And again. And once more, until she wasn't only thinking about fire, she was consumed by it. She imagined herself back in Winde Port, tongues of flame licking all around her. She could feel the terror. She heard a laugh and spun around only to see Kazimir chuckling as he slid a bloody blade across his tongue. She tripped over her own feet as she scrambled backward and away from the upyr.

"My dear, you've fallen," said another. "Allow me." A gray hand extended to her, and she looked up to see Muskigo smiling down at her.

"Get away from me!" she yelled, jumping to her feet. When her heels hit the ground, she found herself in the training room again.

"What did… Madam Jaya?" Nobody answered.

Sora struggled to catch her breath, and once she did, she felt a sharp pain in the center of her chest. Painful memories often helped her fuel her power after she cut herself, and the bar guai seemed to enhance that sensation, to send her deeper into her fears and emotions until she was lost in them.

"It's this yigging thing," she said as she dug her fingers beneath the disc and tried to pry it out of her chest, but she couldn't find purchase.

"As I said, you are not yet capable of removing it," Madam Jaya said.

Sora spun. The door remained closed, but the mystic was suddenly standing before her again.

"You said I had all day," Sora said.

"You did. It is now night."

"What? How? I… I… I guess I lost track of time."

The woman's thin lips creased into a pathetic excuse for a grin. "Nobody casts through the bar guai on their first attempt. I told you that patience would be your first lesson."

Sora sighed. "Another test."

"All life is a test. I tell you this, so you do not blame yourself for not being able to do in a day without instruction what has taken others years, no matter who they were."

"It's just… I can feel the power of Elsewhere within me still, but it's like it's ignoring me. Telling me I must bleed."

Madam Jaya sat and folded her legs. She invited Sora to sit beside her, and now that Sora knew how long she'd been struggling to find her power, she was eager for the break.

"We spoke of sacrifice, and without it, Elsewhere remains blocked off for all of us."

"Then why can't I use my knife?" Sora snapped, her frustration peeking through. "Sorry, Madam, it's been a long day."

"I understand. It is rare for one of our apprentices to be so accomplished in blood magic before reaching us. Their comprehension of Elsewhere's power and what it means to sacrifice often winds up tainted. It can take time to retrain your mind."

"Time…" Sora sighed. "Madam Jaya, can I tell you something?"

The mystic nodded.

"I believe I have already opened Elsewhere, but there was no sacrifice."

Madam Jaya turned her head but betrayed no emotion. "Tell me."

"When I was in Winde Port, I was attacked, hunted by a

monster. He'd finally cornered me and, without knowing, I sent him to Elsewhere." Still unsure of what they might think about it, she decided to leave Whitney out of it altogether.

"How do you know that is where he went?"

"I..." Sora swallowed. "I saw him in the chamber beneath Lord Bokeo's bookstore when the Ancient One gave me that vision."

"Does this monster have a name?"

"He is an upyr," Sora admitted. "His name is Kazimir."

"Ah," Madam Jaya breathed out in relief.

"Why are you smiling?" Sora asked.

"The upyr are very different from us. Their powers come from an otherworldly attachment to Elsewhere, and at a high price. For an upyr to even close his or her eyes is to see Elsewhere. Each time they blink, there it is, waiting for them. It was not your power alone that cast him into that abyss. It was his already strong connection to the place that allowed it."

Sora felt something she couldn't immediately pinpoint. It might have been relief—relief that perhaps she hadn't been wholly responsible for Whitney's fate.

"Rest assured," Madam Jaya continued, "you alone will never open Elsewhere without sacrifice. In this case, the upyr already made the sacrifice long ago. For you, it remains blocked off and this," she motioned to the disc buried in Sora's chest. "The bar guai acts as a conduit for what we call a makros."

"A makros?

"It is when the power of a casting is stored within an object, making it able to be called upon at will without sacrifice. I know that amulet seems like nothing, but there is no object in this realm of greater value. For centuries, mystics have poured bits of their power into those stones, bound by runic magic, carved in the language of the gods."

"So, the sacrifice has already been made?"

Madam Jaya nodded, taking no effort to hide her self-satisfaction at triggering the realization. "Exactly. You failed because you called on the wrong place. Self-channeling through Elsewhere takes decades to master, so for now, you must channel through the stone as all new apprentices learn to do. Walk before you run, or so they say. Where once you could cast fire through thought, now you must call upon the rune by name."

Sora stared down at the six strange symbols glowing on her chest. "I don't know their names."

"You know one. The most gifted mystics are born with an affinity for a certain element. You've always been drawn to one."

"Fire." She didn't even have to think twice.

"Yes. The giver and the destroyer. It is the power that blossomed within you naturally, and that which burned your home to the ground. It saved you from certain death in the Webbed Woods, yet made you fear your own abilities in Winde Port. In you, the fire is two sides of the same coin, and its name lies on its ridge."

Sora was too overwhelmed to wonder how Madam Jaya knew about what happened in those places. She'd come to assume that her new caretakers knew everything about her past.

"I don't..." she stammered.

"Look within," Madam Jaya said. "The runes speak, but the language of the gods is unique in us all, as we were all made unique. I can show you the way, but only you can find the word. Imagine it like a flower, blossoming in spring—you are the flower. Within you holds the power of life, the seed that will grow into a great field."

Sora looked to her teacher, but the woman remained stone-faced. So, she closed her eyes again, and this time didn't allow herself to go to dark places. She searched inside herself, into her memories, until she felt that sharp pain in her chest again.

"Aquira!" She blurted the word out before realizing what could happen. Energy roiled beneath the surface. Her eyes snapped open, and air flooded her lungs. One of the bar guai's runes glowed blue like the door to the Well of Wisdom.

"Of course," Madam Jaya said. "Yours was a destined meeting. The fulcrum on which your future rests. Now, try again."

Sora stood, feeling like she'd just woken from an extended rest. She raised her hand and looked inward. She could always feel the presence of Elsewhere staring back if she searched deep enough, haunting her, tempting her to push beyond her limitations and sacrifice a piece of herself, but now she only heard the thumping of her heart.

She whispered the name of her wyvern friend, and a spark ignited at her fingertips. Then she spoke it louder, and flame wrapped her hand as it always had after blooding.

"Marvelous!" Madam Jaya applauded, showing enthusiasm for the first time.

Sora exhaled, and the flame extinguished. Usually, summoning fire left her weakened, as if her power were a muscle to be exerted. Thanks to the bar guai, she felt perfectly fine.

"Do not get used to how little it drains you," Madam Jaya said. "The makros imbued in the stones is limited. With practice, you will grow more efficient, but draw on them too much, and you will find magic as impossible to wield as a commoner."

"So then how do I learn to channel as you do?"

"By not getting ahead of yourself." Madam Jaya stood and guided Sora's hand to her side.

"I don't mean to be difficult. It's just, I don't understand how learning to use a crutch will help."

"It is a good question. A crutch, by any definition, is meant to help one who is weak become strong. Channeling requires extreme knowledge of oneself. Through blood sacrifice, Elsewhere responds, begs even, for you to unleash its power here on Pantego. It is why we admonish blood magic. For those without your natural gift, it can be impossible to control the rage it fosters.

Elsewhere can consume the host or turn them into vengeful husks bent on consuming all before them."

"Like an upyr," Sora remarked.

"In a way, yes. An upyr with no sense of what they once were. The bar guai allows you to see only your own reflection, and thus it is purer. More controllable. When you learn to channel, it is from within yourself you must draw. You will come to find that Elsewhere isn't a parasite you answer to, but a tool to be wielded."

"But I thought you said that using our abilities in Pantego meant a sacrifice is needed. Spilling blood, I understand. Other mystics, they gave their power to store in this stone. But if you can channel it through your own body, what is the sacrifice?"

"That, Sora of Troborough, is an answer for another time."

"Please, I'd like to know." And she meant it. She knew Whitney needed her as soon as possible, but these answers were why they'd set out from Yarrington in the first place. For her to discover her true identity. It was difficult to look away now.

Madam Jaya stared longingly in Sora's direction, through her. "With every spell, we give a piece of ourselves."

"What do you mean?"

"Not a piece made of flesh or bone, but a shred of who we are. Our personality, our memory, but not our sanity as with blooding. It is why the first of us created the Well of Wisdom. So that we may remind ourselves of who we are if we stray too far. Abuse your power, and who you are will cease to be in both mind and body. A spectre." Madam Jaya reached out to touch Sora's cheek, and her hand passed through.

The grief twisting her features was unmistakable. Since she found them, Sora had looked upon the mystics only with fear, awe, and disdain. Now, she pitied the woman before her who had been reduced to air.

"Is that why Aihara is so coarse?" she said, grinning impishly.

Madam Jaya looked shocked, then allowed a smile to show as well. *So, they do have a sense of humor.*

"I suppose," Madam Jaya said. *"The Ancient One,"* she stressed the mystic's title, "has been around for a long, long time. She clings to this realm for the good of our Order. Do you know why she speaks for us when there are seven of us who remain on our Council?"

Sora shook her head.

"For a mystic, there is no greater achievement than age. The focus and honing of the power it takes to exist here in Pantego for three hundred and six years is beyond comprehension."

"Three hundred and six?" Sora asked, jaw dropping.

"Before Liam the Conqueror was even a thought. When there was an Order of our people to lead, the eight eldest sat atop the Tower ruling over us. We are the Council now, only because we remain, waiting for our eight to restart our great order."

"How old are you?"

"Alas, I am only one hundred and fifty-two."

"Only…" Sora muttered.

"I see your spirits are higher now, Apprentice Sora, and I am glad of it. For next, you will find the god-word for another spell. Tell me, since your Gift first manifested, have you found a proclivity for another type of magic?"

"I've healed people, but it's always been much more difficult and drained me far more. There was a time with… well… I healed a rancher after a dire wolf attacked him and it nearly killed me."

"There is no art nobler than healing, but it draws on two of the fundamental elements in your bar guai. Power over flame, as you know, and over water. If fire is the life giver and the destroyer, water is the life-essence that flows within all of us and the land upon which we live. It is within your blood, within your flesh, as it is within the earth."

"Okay… I think I can do that."

"Many have thought." She snapped her fingers, and the door to the room opened. In walked two of what they called servants, carrying a table. Sora felt her stomach turn over. On the table lay Kai, stripped completely bare, with a gash cut across his chest.

"What did you do!" Sora ran directly through Madam Jaya to the men. She inspected Kai's wound. He was breathing well and had the muscle tone to ensure that the cut wasn't too deep, but it still looked incredibly painful.

"What did they do to you?" she questioned as she pushed the other servants away.

Kai took her hand and squeezed. His palm dripped with sweat, as did his brow. "I'm helping with your training," he rasped.

"Relax, Sora," Madam Jaya said.

"Relax?" Sora glared at her, Elsewhere in her eyes.

"The wound is not fatal, and in this place, it cannot get infected. It is only the pain he feels, and we must learn to conquer pain. Kai understands this."

"It is all right, Miss Sora," he said. "I trust you."

"This is wrong," Sora said.

"As I said, all members of the Order have their part to play. Not only us. Kai bleeds so that others who are at your mercy do not have to."

"You could bleed yourself."

Madam Jaya raised her hand and stared at it, longingly. "We no longer can. Now, eat." A bowl of lumpy soup suddenly appeared in her ethereal hand. She shoved it toward Sora's gut. "Maintain your strength and stay focused. I will return in the morning to see if you have healed his wound.

At that, Madam Jaya soundlessly exited the room, the two healthy servants at her side. "Wait, but I don't—" Sora chased after her, stopping when she noticed Alhara Na standing in the entry, appraising her. Her hard glare sent a chill up Sora's spine. Then, the door sealed shut.

Sora turned back to Kai. He seemed calm enough despite being treated like a test subject… *as* a test subject.

"You'll be fine, Miss Sora," Kai said. "Find the power within, and you'll be okay."

"I'm not worried about me," she said, softly. She returned to his side. "Is this what they do to you? Treat you like meat?"

"The Secret Council is in no need of training. I do this for you, and only you."

Sora swallowed. She extended her hands over his bloody chest and wriggled her fingers in preparation. "Then I won't let you down."

XXVI

THE KNIGHT

Torsten couldn't believe his eyes. He'd sent Wren to Rand's home to try and find an ally who hadn't yet been manipulated by Redstar, but it'd been so long he'd nearly given up. Especially after seeing Wren, broken and subservient, agreeing to Redstar's every word before the people of Yarrington.

"Rand Langley," Torsten said. He released the chain he'd used to strangle one of Redstar's warlocks, letting the body crumple. Stepping toward the bars, he said, "From Iam's Eye to mine, it's really you."

Rand raised his head to regard him. The young man looked even worse than the last time Torsten had seen him, weeks after he surrendered the white helm and fled the castle. His face was gaunt, almost skeletal, and a patchy beard sheltered a bony jaw. The luminescent paint around his eyes masked just how tired and dark they were.

"No warlock tricks, Sir," Rand said. "I came just as you asked."

"I was worried Wren never made it to you."

"He did. I... I tried to take down Redstar myself, but if not for the High Priest, I'd be dead. Whatever Redstar did to him, he's—"

"I know. I saw. He's another puppet to the deceiver's will now, just like our poor king."

"The reunion is over," said another who accompanied Rand. "Time to go, Rand Langley." The man stepped forward and tried a few keys in the cell's lock before its gate swung open. He was a Breklian, judging by his white hair and mustache, and the feathered muffin cap topping his head. Torsten swore he knew him from somewhere. It wasn't often Breklians came so far south outside of trading vessels.

"He's not free yet." Rand snatched the keys from the man's hand, then hurried into the cell. He kneeled before Torsten to unlock the cuffs chaining his ankles to the wall.

"What did he do to the High Priest?" Torsten asked. A cuff fell off his leg, and the stale air against his irritated skin stung. He welcomed the pain.

"I don't know, but he has to be stopped," Rand replied. "I maimed him, but it only seemed to make him more powerful."

"So that was you who took his hand?"

Rand released the second cuff, then stood and nodded. "Spilling blood only seemed to make him stronger."

"It is the font of wickedness his kind draws on. You've done well, Sir Langley. It won't be forgotten. Now, it's time we end this nightmare once and for all. Redstar said that on the Dawning, light and darkness would be one. Whatever he's planning, it must be stopped."

"He mentioned something similar to me."

"You Glassman would see all the wonder wiped from this world, wouldn't you?" the mustached Breklian interrupted. "Unfortunately, the young deserter has made a deal, and I take those seriously. You are on your own from here, Sir Knight."

"Rand, what is he talking about?" Torsten asked. "I can't do this alone. But together, two Wearers stripped of their honor—thanks to Redstar's treachery—we can win back the King's Shield." Torsten lay a hand on Rand's armored shoulder. "I may not know the faces of those who remain, but I know their hearts."

"The Crown is not everything to all of you. Move, Rand."

Rand glanced back at the Breklian, then Torsten, and then his gaze fell to the floor.

"I won't ask again," the Breklian warned, stepping into the entry of the cell. The burning torch, lying on the ground, cast light on his face.

"Wait, I do recognize you," Torsten said. "You're Valin Tehr's man, aren't you? Codar, is it?"

The Breklian bowed. "He sends his regards and says that he misses your squabbles. You were too good for us after you put on the White Helm."

"The whole world is too good for you lot." Torsten turned back to Rand who seemed heartbroken. "What do they have on you? I swear, help me now, and when the kingdom we once knew is restored, they won't be able to touch you."

"We don't need to touch him," Codar said. He scraped his dagger up one of the cell's bars, the screech causing nearby inmates to cry out in anger. "Let's go."

"Rand… what did you do?"

"Whatever it took to get you out." Rand bowed his head to Torsten. "You didn't give up on me, sir, when all the world's light seemed to go out. You don't need me. This kingdom never has. Now fix what I helped start."

Rand hurried past Codar as if he didn't want a chance to second guess his decision. The Breklian's mustache lifted with a grin. "Good luck, knight. We look forward to what happens next." The man sunk back into the shadow, and when Torsten rushed to the open gate, he saw their shadows fading down the dark tunnel.

"Rand!" he called out.

The young man stopped and glanced back.

"You had nothing to do with this," Torsten continued. "Whatever it is you think you did wrong, you are forgiven. Thanks to your strength we have hope again."

"If only you knew what I have done," Rand said softly. Then he and Codar headed upstairs and out of the lower dungeons. Again, Torsten was alone with the ravings of madmen asking why they too weren't freed.

Torsten knew well of Valin Tehr and his exploitation of Dockside. He'd grown up in the South Corner, just beyond the docks, where Valin's influence over the many cobblers and tailors dotting the clothing district were continually butting heads with his thugs. His years in the King's Shield consisted of many days cleaning up Valin Tehr's messes. However, the wretch always seemed to avoid a cell. Eventually, Torsten moved on to kingdom-wide concerns, but Tehr's gang remained a nagging pain in the King's Shield's side.

He couldn't imagine what Rand had offered in exchange for their help, but as Torsten crossed over into the anteroom, he whispered a silent prayer for him. Then he looked to the moss-covered ceiling.

"Not all of us have lost our faith, Iam." He fell to one knee. "Give me the strength on this, the holiest of days, to see Your will done. To cast Your enemies from this sacred land once and for all, and return light upon Your chosen kingdom."

He traced his eyes, noticing that for the first time in his life, he hadn't received the blessing of a priest on the day of the Dawning. And he wouldn't. For today, he planned to do the work of his kingdom, even if it meant he'd never reach the Gate of Light.

Whatever it took.

He and Redstar had danced for too long, and he wasn't sure why he'd expected it to end with him anything but alone. He grabbed the unconscious guard's cudgel, then headed for the exit. The other prisoners begged him to free them as well, but if he was guilty of killing one of his own Order, he couldn't imagine what they'd done.

He climbed the stairs and headed down the dank tunnels toward the castle. The Dawning would mean fewer guards to deal with, at least any Glassmen standing in his way who believed him a traitor. Any Drav Cra would face the unadulterated wrath of Iam.

Two Glass soldiers stood guard at the stairs leading into the castle courtyard. Torsten headed straight for them.

"Halt!" one shouted. "Who are you?"

Torsten didn't stop, didn't respond, just continued onward until the torchlight was enough to reveal his features. The sentry's eyes went wide.

"Sir Unger? You're not supposed to be—"

"Step aside," Torsten ordered.

Their hands fell to the grips of their swords. "We have strict orders."

Torsten closed his eyes. "Forgive me," he whispered.

"For?"

Torsten swung the cudgel and swept one of them off his feet. The other got his sword free and slashed, but Torsten grabbed his forearm first and bashed it into the wall, knocking the weapon loose. He drove his head hard into the bridge of the man's nose. As he turned, he brought his foot down on the other's face, knocking him out cold as well. They'd be fine save for some bumps and bruises.

He quickly dragged their unconscious bodies into a near-empty storage nook, used some rope from sacks of potatoes to tie them down, and covered their mouths with a shred of torn cloth. Checking their armor for anything useful, he found that only the chainmail hauberk of one of them fit his tremendous build, and even then, it was a tight fit. Ever since his days as a squire, he'd needed the castle blacksmith Hovom Nitebrittle to craft his armor specially to fit him even when such meager work was beneath him.

It wasn't the full uniform of a castle guard, but it would have to do. At the very least, the hauberk had the Eye of Iam painted in blue on the chest. One also wore a kettle helmet that Torsten could barely squeeze around his skull, but it would be enough to disguise his face at first glance.

As he stood, a flash in his peripherals distracted him. He rolled quickly. An axe struck the stone floor right behind him and sent sparks flying. A Drav Cra brute reeled back and swung again. Torsten grabbed one of the guard's longswords and raised it in time to deflect the blow. It still sent him staggering back into a row of storage barrels. The weapon was worthless compared to his claymore which now rested at the bottom of a canal in Winde Port.

"And they said staying in the castle today wouldn't be fun!" The mass of muscle came at Torsten again before he could get up, but he was all power. Torsten ducked out of the way of two more swipes until the man's axe crashed into a barrel and sunk through the wood. Grain leaked out as Torsten rolled forward and slashed up. Blood poured into the meal as the swipe severed the man's arm off at the elbow. Before the man could scream, Torsten covered his mouth and propelled him to his knees.

"Where is Redstar?" Torsten growled. He waited for the man to stop squirming before removing his hand, but received only a wad of spit on his chest. Before the man could curse him, Torsten cleaved his head from his shoulders.

"Your time in my castle is over," he said.

Torsten wiped the blade on the savage's furs, then headed upstairs into snow-covered grounds of the western courtyard. A now-bare cherry tree presided over the frozen dragon fountain.

Torsten could remember being in that very courtyard, holding Oleander on the night Pi threw himself from the tower just behind him.

He sighed and took a step out into the frigid air. He wasn't sure where Redstar would be. It was the day of the Dawning, and Redstar had intimated he would be spending it with Pi, but surrounded by the castle building and the sky brushed with clouds, he couldn't tell how late it was or if they'd have begun the trek up to the summit of Mount Lister yet. His former Wearer's quarters where Redstar made home seemed a good place to look first.

"Quickly, a prisoner has escaped!" Torsten shouted, noting two Glass soldiers patrolling the arcade bordering the grounds.

The guards sprung to action, running toward him without a second glance. Torsten stole one's sword as they raced by and slammed the door shut behind them. He jammed the weapon through the handles to lock them in. They shouted, banging gauntleted fists against the wood, but it was a long way to any other exit.

Not caring to hear their cries, Torsten headed toward the castle chapel adjacent the courtyard, facing northwest toward Mount Lister as all churches in the kingdom did. He peered in first. Although he couldn't see the whole room, the crystalline altar was empty as he expected. Anyone important would be traveling to the summit of the mountain for the Dawning.

Torsten swept in and made it a few steps down the aisle when he heard a cough. He looked left, hands squeezing the grip of his stolen sword when he saw Hovom, the castle blacksmith, seated on the far end of a pew all alone.

"Wren said you'd pass through here," Hovom said. "I guess the old man was right." Hovom stood. He had the longest beard of any man Torsten had ever known, nearly down to his waist. Burn marks from a smithing accident covered half his body, but there was no finer blacksmith in all Pantego, dwarves considered. It was said the secret to smelting glaruium to use in weapons and armor had been passed down in his family since the first kings. He was an odd, quiet man, who rarely left the heat of his irons for anything, even the call of food or drink—only for prayer.

Torsten set his feet and tensed. "Hovom, just let me pass, and you won't be bothered."

Hovom approached, sword held out in front of him. Torsten prepared to fend him off when the blacksmith flipped the claymore around and presented Torsten with the hilt, bowing his head.

"Relax, my friend," he said. "I have no quarrel with you.

Torsten let his shoulders loosen, but not his grip on his sword. After everything, he couldn't afford to trust anyone. There was no saying who had Redstar's claws in them. "I'm afraid I'm not 'friend' to many these days," Torsten said.

"Not all have lost faith in you or Iam." He ran his hand tenderly along the blade while he remained bowed. "Wren came to me days ago before the deserter attempted to kill Redstar. He spoke in riddles, but I think I understood."

"What are you talking about."

"He'd expected you'd be needing this." He shuffled forward, urging Torsten to take the massive claymore. That was when Torsten finally let himself observe the hilt and his eyes went wide. His stolen longsword fell from his grasp. The claymore's crossguard extended from a sculpture of the Eye of Iam, a grip of beautiful leather threaded with gold, and a pommel, silver and sculpted in the shape of a dragon's head. The sword had belonged to King Liam, buried with him in the Royal Crypt.

"That's..."

"Salvation. The sword of King Liam. The blade broke when the earthquake ravaged the Royal Crypt. Wren gave me very specific instructions to reforge it. He made me vow in the name of

Iam to tell nobody of it, not even the King, until you found me here on the Dawning."

Torsten reached out and let his fingers run across the handle. Then he pulled back. "I cannot accept this," he said. "The sword of Liam the Conqueror can find no home within the hands of a sinner."

"The sword's name says otherwise. Wren said you would need it."

"Wren is broken, you must have seen it from your quarters."

"Whatever his Holiness has become, the Wren we knew said you would pass through here at this exact moment." Hovom closed his eyes and inhaled. "What other proof do you need. I've always said, the sword chooses the man, not the other way around."

Hovom released the weapon, causing Torsten to catch it out of reflex. The heft and length were about the same as his old claymore, though this one was heavier. He turned it over and flicked the blade. "No glaruium?"

"Wren insisted I reforge the blade without it."

"It is perfect, nonetheless." Torsten's heart sank. "Still, I cannot accept this." He extended it for Hovom to take, but the blacksmith folded his arms behind his back.

"Then you must leave it on the floor. Its time with its maker has come to an end." He walked by Torsten, stopped, and picked up the rusty longsword he'd stolen. He spun it, and even through his thick beard, Torsten could see his heartbreak. "When all this is over, tell the King our men need new weapons. My children grow old."

"Wait," Torsten called. "Do you know where Redstar is?"

Hovom didn't look back. He pointed up, then continued on his way toward the chapel's front doors. Torsten stood, dumbfounded, staring down at the sword which once filled the hand of the greatest King Pantego had ever known. When he looked up again, Hovom was gone.

Torsten exhaled. *Who am I to question the will of Iam? Perhaps he hasn't lost faith in me yet.*

"With this sword, I will reclaim your holy kingdom, Your Grace," he spoke aloud to the sword. "Then it will find you at the Gate of Light once more."

Without another word, Torsten crossed the chapel to a side door that had direct access to the western tower, so the King could visit the chapel without being bothered. Hovom indicated that Redstar was above, so Torsten felt confident in checking his own quarters first. The door was locked, but no entry was built to withstand Torsten's frame. He rammed into it with his shoulder once, then the second time tore it from its hinges.

Drav Crava protests met his ears immediately. A white-faced warlock was descending the stairs and upon seeing Torsten's drawn weapon, immediately sliced his thigh. A stream of ice struck Torsten in the shoulder and thrust him into the wall. Even though it was ice, it stung like fire and was a spell he'd never faced from a warlock before.

Torsten fell back behind the turn of the spiral stairs, but the warlock shot ice across the landing between them, making it slick so Torsten wouldn't be able to pass.

"Stop!" A Shieldsman charged in from the other direction and aimed a spear at Torsten's chest. Not just any Shieldsman, but Sir Austun Mulliner. He wore the luminescent paint of the Dawning, apparently having attended service before his duty. "Torsten," he spat.

Torsten kept his new sword raised toward the warlock. "Sir Mulliner, you have to listen to me."

"How many times are you going to try this?"

"Then just walk away. You don't need to be a party to this."

Mulliner didn't flinch. His grip on his weapon tightened.

"Trespassers in the Glass Castle on the Dawning receive no quarter. Maybe this time, Sir Havel will finally get justice."

"He is a criminal," the warlock said. "Kill him, Glassman."

"Do you really believe that abomination speaks for the Crown?" Torsten asked. "I don't care what you saw in Winde Port, Redstar is no hero. He is a deceiver."

Mulliner's armor was so shiny and unsullied that Torsten saw in its reflection that the warlock had slit his hand. Ice shot forth from his palm, and Torsten grasped Mulliner's spear and turned them both, so the stream of magic hit the wood shaft. It froze solid in an instant. Torsten cracked off the spear end and threw it at the warlock, the point piercing his heart.

By the time the warlock hit the ground, he was already dead, with no ability to draw power from the mass exodus of blood. Torsten promptly used the railing and his sword to propel himself over the landing still slick from mystical ice. He turned back. Austun stood at the edge, and in his heavy Shieldsman armor, it would be difficult for him to get over with ease.

"You won't stop, will you?" Mulliner said, grimacing. "Until the King hangs our entire Order for your treason."

"Sound the bells of alarm," Torsten said, pointing his claymore toward Mulliner. "Don't find yourself on the end of a noose on my behalf if I fail." The knight remained still. "Trust me or not, I'm here for Redstar and Redstar alone. The King is in no danger."

Mulliner didn't answer, but he slowly backed away to find another way around. That meant Torsten wouldn't have long before the castle gates were sealed and the intruder alarms rang out. He took the stairs three at a time, all the way to the second highest floor below the King's chambers.

He slowed at the landing and sidled up against the wall. A single warlock guarded the door to the Wearer's chambers. Another stood a few meters off, staring in the opposite direction.

Two of Redstar's apostles sharing a floor meant to house members of the Royal Council and nary a Glass soldier in sight. What a disgrace. Torsten recognized neither from his previous encounters with Redstar, and no Freydis.

Torsten rested Salvation against the wall, knowing that if he cut but didn't kill either of these men, their magic would be unleashed. He quickly lashed out and wrapped his massive sword-arm around the nearest warlock's neck. With the other, he wrenched the warlock's hands so the man wouldn't be able to cut himself. He was growing more proficient at handling the blood mages.

"Move," Torsten growled. The warlock cursed back in Drav Crava, then called to his comrade. The other warlock pulled out a dagger, dragged it along his palm, and turned to face them. Fire bloomed around his hand, but he didn't throw it yet.

"Drop him!" he hissed.

"First, we need to talk!" Torsten answered. He glanced left, sensing motion. One of the chambers had its door open, and inside was the young Master of Scrolls who had been forced into the position after his master was hanged. He looked terrified, and as Torsten passed with the warlock in his grasp, the young Master of Scrolls slowly shut his door.

The castle bells sounded and drew both warlock's attention, distracting them just long enough for Torsten to throw the warlock he held against the wall headfirst and charge the other. A stream of flame shot over his shoulder, so hot his bald head immediately started to sweat. His shoulder slammed into the warlock and drove him to the ground. White-hot hands grasped his bicep, melting through his hauberk and keeping him from furthering his attack. The warlock muttered under his breath in Drav Crava, the whites of his eyes bright against the black paint surrounding them. Torsten fought the pain, grasped the skinny man by the throat and crushed his windpipe until his arms fell limp.

He jumped to his feet and retrieved Salvation from near the stairs. Then he positioned himself in front of the room he'd called home for over a year. He built up momentum and kicked through the door.

The splinters peppering his face were a bracing reminder of how much had changed. As was the sight that greeted him. Redstar's pieced-together mural remained on the floor, and strung up on the wall was the Queen Mother, Oleander. She was stripped completely bare.

"Torsten," she said. "By Iam, I never thought I'd be so glad to see you."

Torsten averted his gaze out of reflex as he approached.

"Grow up, knight," she said. "Have you never seen a woman before?"

He swallowed the lump in his throat and turned back. There wasn't a scratch on her, but Redstar had many ways to inflict pain. Her lithe limbs were spread wide by the ropes stringing her up, leaving little to the imagination. Someone had sloppily painted her face in the manner of warlocks, the black and white dripping down onto her bosom.

"Who did this to you?" Torsten asked. He had to raise his voice since the window was open and the castle bells continued to chime.

"Who do you think?"

"You're his," Torsten caught his breath, "sister."

"Apparently, I'm a 'foreign whore, and it's time I look like one.' Now get me down so I can rip that traitorous bastard's throat out myself!"

Torsten didn't answer. He could barely summon words. Seeing his Queen in such condition broke his heart. She'd never been good at ruling, and after the night she attempted to seduce Torsten, her figure had filled his dreams. But not like this. It was no way for the widow of Liam Nothhelm to be treated, no matter what the cause.

He started untying one of her ankles, then heard gurgling. A vine had crept in through the open window and wrapped around her throat. Her foot got free, and she pointed it to the doorway. The warlock Torsten had thrown against the wall lay in the threshold, stretching his bloody hand through the opening.

"Only Iam gives life," Torsten said. He lifted his sword, strode over to the man, and plunged it down into his back, straight through the heart. His magical vine loosened, allowing Oleander to cough, then crackled away into dust.

He was about to return to Oleander when Sir Mulliner and a host of Glass Soldiers appeared behind him, weapons drawn.

"Drop your weapon and surrender," Mulliner demanded. "I won't ask again."

Torsten backed slowly into the room, and as the soldiers followed him, they realized who was on the wall. "W—what have you done?" Mulliner stuttered.

"Stand down, all of you," Oleander rasped. "How far do you think your true Wearer has fallen that he would do this to me?"

"He killed one of our own!" Mulliner and the others kept their eyes fixed on Torsten, refusing to regard their Queen in such a manner. Mulliner edged forward until the tip of his sword was a hair's breadth from Torsten's throat.

Torsten lowered Salvation. "It's true Austun," he said. "I did. I didn't mean to, but it happened, and Iam will judge me for that. But I had nothing to do with this."

He pointed back to Redstar's mural telling a false version of the God Feud that painted Nesilia a hero. "Look upon that heathen's blasphemy, he and his horde of devils. He did this to your Queen, his own sister."

"Do you plan on letting me hang here all day?" Oleander spat.

Torsten took a step toward her, but Mulliner positioned himself between them. He gestured to two of the soldiers and sent them to untie Oleander.

"I have made many mistakes," Torsten said to Mulliner. "I should have been closer with you, with all of our Order. Then perhaps you all would see Redstar for what he truly is and not the savior he claims to be."

"Watch your hand, knave!" Oleander yelped and kicked one of the soldiers in the face.

Torsten smirked. He knew it wasn't the time, but he couldn't help himself. He was so used to being on the receiving end of her barbs, it was nice to hear someone else facing them.

"You dare laugh at a time like this?" Mulliner said.

"All my mistakes, but my loyalty to the Crown has never been in question. I would die for any Nothhelm, and that means now too. So, you have two options, Sir Mulliner. Try to kill me and fail, or watch me and the Queen walk away."

"Must everything you do be so dramatic?" Queen Oleander said as a soldier helped her down. She shook him away without even a 'thank you,' and strode across the room to the bed, taking no care to cover herself. The entire room went silent. She picked a dark blue dress off the bed and began dressing. That was when Torsten noticed one of her handmaidens lying over the side of the bed with her throat slit.

One of the soldiers went to help her with her dress, but she slapped his hand. "Don't dare touch me," she snapped. She got it on without tying the back, then yanked the blankets out from under the body of her handmaiden. The poor girl's corpse rolled off and thudded against the floor.

"You will stand down, and Torsten and I will walk out of here together as he said," Oleander said, using the blankets to wipe the paint off her face. "There are no options."

Mulliner didn't lower his weapon, but his hand started to

shake. "We were ordered by the King to follow only the Prime Minister. Not you."

"And after I rip out my brother's tongue, where would you like me to hang you for treason? I hear the sun is warm on the south side of the wall."

"Your Grace, I..."

"Unless your next words are an apology, I suggest you keep your mouth shut! Now, Torsten, dear, come and help me tie my dress."

"Yes, Your Grace." Torsten backed away slowly from Mulliner's blade until he was behind Oleander, then tied the back of her dress as he'd seen Tessa and her other unfortunate hand-maidens do so many times before. Hers was an uneven history filled with sorrow and actions Iam would never approve of, but Torsten had never been more grateful for her hard hand and the fear she instilled in men.

Mulliner drew a deep breath. "Come, men, there's nothing here for us."

"But—" one of them began before being cut off.

"I said let's move. You, silence the bells." He turned to leave, but stopped in the doorway and glanced back at Torsten. All his resentment dripped away and gave way to sadness. "You killed my friend, and I can't ever forgive that."

"You don't have to," Torsten said.

"But any man who'd be willing to do that to his sister doesn't deserve the King's ear. I hope I'm wrong about you. Otherwise, I'll see you in Elsewhere."

"You're a good knight," Torsten said. "You all are. Uriah Davies made sure of that. I never deserved to wear the White, but now I go to make sure that Sir Nikserof can do so with honor. He's worthier than I ever was."

At that, Mulliner left Torsten and the Queen behind, standing before the bed on which she'd once tried to seduce him. He'd been nervous then, but not anymore.

"My Queen, where is your brother?" Torsten asked.

"I thought you'd never be rid of them." She straightened her dress and strode away from him. "He's already on his way to the summit with my son for the Dawning, along with that useless ingrate Wren who now has decided he'd rather hold hands with Redstar. Said he planned to show him the true reason why the sun goes out today."

"More tricks, Your Grace."

"It doesn't matter. When I see Redstar again, I'm going to kill him as my husband should have decades ago."

"No." Torsten took her hand, turning her toward him, and stared into her fierce, blue eyes. "No more blood on your hands. As the light of Iam fades upon the Dawning, Redstar's games end with it. By my sword."

XXVII

THE MYSTIC

Despite her best efforts, Sora let Kai down.

Hours passed as she looked within, searching her mind for the answer to healing him, but all she found was fire. She forced herself to remain calm for his sake. After those hours, after he'd finally fallen asleep, Sora collapsed to the stone floor.

Not being able to summon fire was frustrating, but watching the blood trickling off the table, beginning to pool next to her on the floor made her feel like more of a failure than ever before.

Early on, she'd torn a piece of her kimono and laid it over the wound so she could keep pressure on it. Her hands were covered in blood now and shaking. She whispered, conversing with herself in search of solutions. A few times she looked too far inward and wound up encircled by her fears, thanks again to the bar guai. Kai's face became Whitney's, begging her to help him, asking why she didn't care enough about him.

"Sora," someone said. "Sora."

"I've always cared!" she screamed. Her head shot up. She glanced side to side in a daze, not even realizing that at some point, she'd fallen asleep with her head against the leg of the table. Madam Jaya now stood beside her. Sora sprang to her feet.

"I see you haven't found your answer," Madam Jaya said.

"Please, you have to help him," Sora pled. She turned and went to grab Madam Jaya's arm, but her hands slipped through. Her knees hit the ground again. "He's lost a lot of blood."

"What a disappointment," another, deeper voice spoke. Aihara Na strode into the room, arms folded behind her back. "I thought you'd find the bar guai simple to master."

Madam Jaya bowed to her. "She is a quick study, Ancient One, but she has not had much time."

"Time enough for one so gifted as she."

"I'll work harder, Ancient One. I promise," Sora said, still on her knees. Her legs felt like sand. She'd been standing a long time, and even with her short break, it hadn't done much to return the feeling to her lower extremities. "Just please, heal him."

"It is not for lack of trying that you fail," Aihara Na said. "It is a lack of focus. You wanted to be here with us, but you are not here with us, not really. You are distracted. Your thoughts are... *elsewhere*."

The way she said the word made Sora wonder if she knew the deeper desires of her heart. That she wasn't just here to find a place she belonged and an answer to her powers but to free Whitney. To do the one thing their Order forbade.

"Please, just help him, then deal with me," Sora said.

"Ancient One, she found the word of fire in mere minutes after I explained how the bar guai works," Madam Jaya said, stepping between them. "If she is distracted, it is because I revealed too much, filled her mind with thoughts she didn't need."

"We will discuss your tactics later," Aihara Na said.

"It has been so many long years since I had a pupil and I... my mind has not been the same since... this." She motioned to her incorporeal body.

Aihara Na stopped and placed her hand upon Jaya's cheek. Her hand didn't pass through. "You have forgotten more than most will ever know. I do not blame you for this."

"You are too forgiving, Master." Madam Jaya backed away, bowing low. Aihara Na stepped forward. Sora had never realized how tall she was.

"Tell me, Sora of Troborough," Aihara Na said. "In all your years practicing blood magic, have you ever managed to heal yourself of even the slightest injury?"

"Never," Sora said, her voice shaky. "Wetzel told me never to try, that it was too dangerous."

"It is indeed. It is the key to possession for a blood mage. To draw on the power of Elsewhere to use it on oneself. It is an ability few but the most powerful can accomplish without drawing too deeply and leaving themselves vulnerable to Elsewhere's darker side."

"Then I won't ever try! Just help him." Sora lifted her head, her eyes bleary from lack of sleep and budding tears. She saw Kai's hand hanging from the table, slack.

"With the bar guai, self-healing is difficult, but not impossible. The power and focus required will drain the makros faster than any other spell. To do so as a mystic, without sacrificing too much of oneself, is an ability few have accomplished, a power few have been found able to wield. It is that singular focus on oneself, in applied power and mind, that overwhelms even masters of channeling. Back when I was more than a shade in this world, even I could mend little more than a scratch on my own being."

"Why are you telling me this.?"

"Because if you are as gifted as the Well of Wisdom promises you are, then healing should be your greatest strength. Training a mystic apprentice to gain a full understanding of their abilities is a slow, tedious process. Each of our connections to

Elsewhere is unique. We are all born with natural affinities for different spells and elements. It can take years to uncover." Aihara Na grabbed Sora by the arm, now physical, and hauled her to her feet. "But sometimes, the best means of instruction is a push."

Sora's eyes darted nervously between Madams Aihara and Jaya. Upon those words, even Jaya's features darkened with fear.

"Ancient One, she is not re—"

Aihara Na took Sora's arm. Then, from the folds of her robes, Aihara Na produced Sora's own knife and slashed her wrist vertically. Sora had cut herself countless times, but never so deep, and never upward. That was one of Wetzel's first warnings.

Blood drooled onto the stone floor in puddles and Sora fell to all fours. She was too shocked to feel pain, but it had been mere seconds, and she'd never seen so much of her own blood. She could hear Elsewhere begging her to its waiting bosom; for her to give in, let the power overtake her.

It came in the form of Nesilia whispering her name now. But with the bar guai buried in her chest, she found she couldn't access the power through her blood as she once had. Every time her mind surrendered to Elsewhere, her chest stung and threw her back into focus.

"Fight the urge, Sora," Aihara Na said. "Don't allow your baser instincts to grab hold. Do not call upon your sacrifice, use the bar guai. Call upon the gods who built this world. Who built you. Call upon the mystics of old who sacrificed themselves so you may rise."

"I… I can't…" Sora whimpered.

"Yes, you can," Madam Jaya said. "It is your destiny."

"I can't!" Sora was on the ground now, eyes clenched shut. The shock waned, and the pain began to take hold. Her arm felt like burning flames. "I can't!"

"Do not be weak," Aihara Na said. "Do not be fractured.

Focus on who you are. Too much longer and you will die. Unlike the servant, your wound is fatal."

Sora could feel her heart beating faster, and as it pumped, more blood gushed from the wound. She drew a few long, steady breaths and remembered how she'd learned to use fire.

Calm, she told herself. *You must stay calm. Calm for Whitney.*

She ignored the urging of Elsewhere that was so present yet impossible to access. The wound burned. She thought she felt bubbles roiling around it. Whether it was blistering skin or her blood boiling from Elsewhere's fires, she didn't know, but she kept digging.

The inferno in her mind dwindled, and through it, water began to cascade, gurgling as it gushed over rocks and around bends. She saw the small homes of Troborough—the Julset twins, the Whelforks, Wetzel's shack. And she realized she stood in the narrow river running behind it. Her old caretaker was in the river with her, washing her messy hair. Only, she couldn't have been more than three or four.

She remembered that day, so long ago, like a memory grasping at the threads of her mind. Her refugee caravan had finally let her off into the arms of an old man. She was so grimy from the long trip, Wetzel dragged her right out to the river, and as he scrubbed her, a young boy strolled by, tossing a rock into the air again and again. He stopped when he saw her.

"What's wrong with your ears?" he'd asked, gawking. Then Wetzel shooed him, both hands flailing in the air like the town kook he was.

"Shellnak," Sora said the name of Troborough's puny river. She felt a rush of power again, starting in her chest. Her eyes opened, and another of the runes in the bar guai started to glow. "Aquira-Shellnak." She chanted again, the rune of fire illuminating as well.

The whole of her body tingled then grew numb as she focused

on the wound. The pain became unbearable, causing her to scream. It radiated to her chest, then pulsed, and as she fought to stay conscious, she felt the blood rushing to her gashed limb.

She squinted at it through the sweat coating her brow. Her arm and hand trembled, but the deep gash began to close. It went from a blanket of blood to sinew, to her skin threading back together as if made from strands of yarn on a loom. She embraced the pain until the flesh sealed, then released a mouthful of air. All that remained on her arm was quickly drying blood.

"I did it?" she whispered. A laugh snuck through her lips without her intending to do so. "I did it."

"Well done, Sora," Madam Jaya said, smiling.

"As I said, sometimes all it takes is a push," Aihara Na said. She extended a hand to help Sora to her feet, but Sora didn't take it.

Unlike summoning fire through the bar guai, healing herself left her so weak she felt like she'd just run from Troborough to Yarrington and back again. But she didn't care. She scrambled to her feet, ran through Madam Aihara, and to Kai's side.

She placed her hands over his wound and began incanting, focusing her mind on that key memory of water, on the feeling it brought her. Kai's injury started sealing just as hers had. It was nearly halfway closed when her legs wobbled, and she grasped the table to stay upright. The pain in her own chest grew so intense she stopped trying to breathe. Only after Kai's wound closed did she stagger back, dizzy.

She tried to say something to her masters, but her words came out in a garbled mess of languages. She caught the table for balance, then her hand slipped, slick with hers and Kai's blood. Kai sprung awake and tried to catch her, but was too late. She hit the ground hard, skull slamming against the floor.

XXVIII

THE THIEF

After Kazimir revealed to Whitney why he was really sticking around, Whitney returned to the Fierstown farm as promised. Never in his life had he thought mundane work would be exactly what he needed to keep him from doing something stupid. But focusing on the bugs biting him, or the sweat, or how tedious it was, it helped him ignore the misery of his situation. Helped the days go by while he waited for night to come so he could seek a way through his personal Elsewhere's barrier without prying eyes.

The spring harvest came and went, but there was never downtime as a farmhand. Pigs and cows needed constant attention, and the moment he finished fixing the roof of his childhood home, something else broke that required the hands of someone who could stand since Rocco couldn't.

Days turned to weeks. Whitney tried his best to keep quiet and disturb nothing. All he had to do was bite his lip around his father to avoid his basic instinct to battle with him. Perhaps it was his injuries, but the man was far more docile then Whitney remembered.

Weeks turned to months. Lauryn kept Whitney well-fed. Rocco ensured that payment was timely, and they even gave Whitney a raise when the fall harvest hit. Even though he couldn't leave Troborough, the people there still took autlas. The cost of a drink at the Twilight Manor was torturous—a week's pay alone, far more than in real Troborough—but it helped remind Whitney this wasn't the real Troborough.

In his off-hours, Whitney and Rocco constructed a wheeling chair to keep Rocco from complaining so much. Occasionally, Whitney would roll him down, and Rocco's condition earned a few free rounds, which made hearing his stories about what Troborough was like a decade ago tolerable.

Whitney even heard a few he'd never had before or had never paid attention to, like when conscript officers for the Panping War passed through. Rocco wanted to go off on an adventure like never before and serve his kingdom, but Whitney was born only days before, so Rocco stayed for him.

Whitney couldn't imagine his unworldly father ever wanting to set foot in a place that wasn't Troborough, but this version of him seemed to long for adventure. It was like losing his legs showed him everything he'd missed out on.

Sometimes Kazimir was around, quietly watching from the corner. He'd taken up residence in an apartment above the Twilight Manor. Mostly, Kazimir kept to himself, locked in his room, doing gods know what. From time to time the upyr helped on the farm, and since he had less need for autlas, because he didn't eat or drink, Whitney got the bonus. Maybe he hadn't needed food to survive, but Whitney had found eating to be a tough addiction to break and a soothing one. Though he did discover that he couldn't get drunk, not even a smidge.

Winter came and went.

It was a brutal one, and it battered the farm, which meant more repairs. The cold was worse than any Whitney had known before, and Rocco couldn't handle it. He passed away from his injuries around the time when the Dawning should have occurred but didn't, and they buried him in the cemetery behind the broken-down church.

Whitney couldn't say how he felt about watching Fake Torsten lay his father down, but even stranger was the fact that Whitney attended. He'd known this shattered version of his father for a few months, even shared a few laughs, and it seemed right considering he was part of the reason his back wound up broken. Lauryn wept, holding Young Whitney in her arms as he did the same. Although his father's condition and subsequent death was Young Whitney's fault, Lauryn's buried resentment toward the boy waned now that he'd became the only family she had.

Whitney was sure as shog his real mother never would have done that. In real life, a burned down barn made her regard him like a monster. Here, she hugged Young Whitney every time he came home, whispered to him that it wasn't his fault every time Rocco was brought up. She even allowed Sora over for supper almost nightly, treating her like a daughter.

Whitney took his useless food to the barn those nights. He knew being around Sora wouldn't be wise. It was easiest that way. Every time this Troborough got too strange for him, he just held his tongue and went to sleep. Sometimes Kazimir was there, and even if they didn't talk, it was comforting having someone around who knew he didn't belong. It helped him remember what he was waiting for.

Months turned to years, and Whitney never stopped hoping for Sora to find a way to reverse what had happened. He'd learned more about farming than he ever wanted to, and construction too. Things grew too somber around the Fierstown home with Rocco gone, having to hear his mother cry from time to time. Young Whitney stopped sticking around to help around the house during the day, barely showed up for dinner, and when he did, it sounded like Sora had forced him. When he misbehaved, Lauryn forced herself not to be mad, Big Whitney could see it in her eyes. And he got into trouble often, more so than even Whitney could remember doing as a child. Everyone else had, but Whitney's doppelgänger didn't seem to change in the slightest. Even Big Whitney now boasted a pathetic, patchy beard so nobody would notice how alike he and Lauryn's son were. Not that anybody in Elsewhere seemed to notice that sort of thing.

And it was one unspectacular night after Young Whitney promised to have supper with his mom and failed to show up, sending her to tears, that Whitney found himself at the Twilight Manor. He offered to stick around for supper, but she'd asked to be left alone.

"What's the difference between a Westvale whore and a dwarf?" Whitney asked, clothes still stained from a day's work at the Fierstown farm. "One's short, fat, and has a beard. The other lives in the tunnels of the Dragon's Tail."

Hamm, the owner of the place, and all the other men burst into laughter. Whitney joined them, and it was only when the laughter died down that his heart sunk as it sometimes did over the last six years in Elsewhere. It wasn't that Whitney hated being in this Troborough as much as he hated how comfortable he was becoming in this Troborough. His life had been many things, but never before had it been…well… plain. Boring. Like he was any average serf in the Glass Kingdom

A bard by the name of Fabian "Feel Good" Saravia plucked his lute, singing a song about a grimuar. Whitney had never seen the hawk-face beasts in the Pikeback Mountains near Glinthaven. In fact, if he'd not been seated at a tavern in Elsewhere, he'd likely still think them myth, but now, nothing was unbelievable to him.

"My Lord," the barmaiden Alless said, placing another flagon of ale down in front of Whitney.

Whitney's face lit up. Who'd have thought it would take going back in time to the one place he hated more any anywhere else to finally be called 'my Lord?' Sure, his letters patent were gone, and no one but Torsten and Sora remembered him ever becoming Whitney Blisslayer, but that didn't stop him from enjoying the attention.

"Thanks, Alless. Looking good tonight," he said with a wink. Her cheeks turned pink. She dressed modestly, and her strawberry blonde hair was worn long and braided into two pigtails. He'd forgotten how pretty she was back in the day.

"Sure, you don't wanna sit for a spell?" Whitney said.

She looked over her shoulder. "Hamm wouldn't take kindly to that. Lots of folks in here tonight, and all of them looking to be served."

"Chair's always open..." Just as he said it, a lumbering oaf from the north side of town plopped down in it. "Till it's not," Whitney laughed.

She giggled. "I'll have a break soon. I'll find you." She curtsied, then walked away to keep working.

She's old enough to be your mother, Whitney reminded himself. *Oh, and she isn't real.*

There were more than a few times Whitney had considered abandoning his nightly searches, leaving his bed unused, and staying in hers. He'd have to close his eyes and tell himself 'path of least resistance.' Laying with an apparition was the definition of resistance.

"Eyes to yourself, Willis," Hamm said.

"Have you considered some male help then?" Whitney remarked. "An old man. I'm talking saggy and gray."

"I'll think on it." Hamm chuckled. He served someone else while cleaning a mug and continuing the conversation. He was a damn good barkeep in his prime. If Troborough could boast anything, it was that. Best Whitney had ever known save for Tum Tum…

The spell of longing hit Whitney harder this time.

"What's wrong, friend?" Hamm asked. "You look like you've seen a ghost."

"Nothing, I… I'm just tired," he said.

"Old lady Fierstown working you to the bone, is she?"

"That's a word for it."

"It isn't easy work making an honest living, I'll tell you that." Hamm placed his hand on Whitney's shoulder, and Whitney didn't have a chance to respond before the man laughed at the joke building inside his own head. "But that's what taverns are for!"

"Here, here!" a few men down the bar slammed their tankards. The bard took it as recognition for the finishing of a song and began to play louder.

"Truer words never were spoken," Whitney said.

"I'll tell ya, I would have run after Rocco passed, but it's a damn good thing you're doing there," Hamm went on. "Can't tell you how many times I caught that Young Whitney trying to steal from my stores. I don't know how you deal with that little menace."

Whitney wondered if that was how Hamm had viewed him back in the day before saying, "Mostly, I don't see him. Especially after Rocco died. He's got that dirty look plastered on his face every time we run into each other, then he rushes by." All of that was true. Whitney had no love for Troborough, but he never remembered being so angry growing up.

"Well, a boy needs a man around he can respect if he doesn't want to grow up rotten," Hamm said. "And a woman like Lauryn needs a ma…"

Whitney choked on his next sip of ale. "Wait, you don't think…"

"Hey, I ain't one to judge. Rocco's been dead for five years now, and a man from noble stock like you is still around."

Whitney had to cover his mouth to keep from vomiting. "It's nothing like that you horny codger. She just makes a mean pie."

"Damn right she does! Well if you aren't... you wouldn't mind if I asked her to..."

"Please don't finish," Whitney blurted. "But yeah, fine. I'm not her father, why would I care?" The strangeness of this words didn't hit him until after he'd said them. Still, the way Hamm's eyes lit up when he heard Lauryn was available made Whitney feel a bit better. Still disgusted, but this version of his mother deserved some bit of happiness.

Whitney scanned the room. After continually trying to sneak into the Twilight Manor as a young boy, it never stopped being strange to him, drinking side-by-side with the men he'd had thought so old all those years ago. He liked it.

As a child, he never got to hear from all the townsman who'd fought in Liam's wars, who'd had great adventures and then settled down. They weren't all like Rocco who was born on his farm and never left until the day he died. And traders passed through town, even here. Men from Brekliodad and Glinthaven, everywhere. As a child, they'd ignored him, so he'd pick their pockets for trinkets. Now, they'd share grand tales of Pantego, then ride off the next morning along a road Whitney still couldn't travel.

For once, he'd mostly sit back and listen. He couldn't tell any of his stories because they were all in the future—and on a completely different plane. If Lauryn found out he wasn't really a nobleman looking for a simpler life, but a world-renowned thief, he might lose his cushy gig while waiting for Sora.

An odd something in the dark corner of the dining hall tore him from his thoughts. Crouching at the side of the bar, out of the sight of Hamm and the others, was a young Panpingese girl—

only the truth was, she wasn't so young anymore. Over the course of time Whitney had been stuck in Troborough, she'd blossomed into quite the young lady, and Whitney couldn't imagine how foolish he'd been to leave her behind. Growing up every day with her, he'd probably never realized how stunning she was until that fateful day they were reunited.

Presently, he had little relationship with her. From time to time he'd stroll by Wetzel's shack to remind himself of the hope he had for her older version, but talking with her was too complicated, and Elsewhere never let him get close enough to peek inside regardless.

The Sora he knew had always told him of the nights she'd snuck into the Manor to hear the bards play, but he'd assumed she'd been telling tall tales in an attempt to one-up him. They did that sort of thing. Yet there she was, crouching, hidden from all view, a big smile plastered on her face. Upon noticing Whitney eyeballing her, she winced, then retreated into the shadows, but not before placing a finger over her lips in hopes of convincing him not to rat her out.

All these years and she was the one who'd accomplished something he'd never been able to. He couldn't help wonder how she'd gotten in unseen, or why she'd never showed his younger self the way.

He stood, his chair scraping the wood floor. He took a few steps before remembering his ale. Even though it did nothing to make him dizzy and forgetful in this place, it always served to buoy his heart.

"Heading off?" Hamm asked.

"Got to take a piss," he said.

He headed out back to take care of his business, but more so with the intention of looking around the building for where Sora might have gotten in. It was brisk, the late autumn air biting at his cheeks, which meant every window was locked.

"How in Iam's name does she do it?" he asked himself

Hamm guarded the place like a damn golem. He made sure that if anyone was sleeping upstairs, or sleeping with someone sleeping upstairs, they were paying him autlas. He knew every face that entered the hall and expected them all to be drinking or eating if they were taking up space.

"You lost?" The sound of Alless' voice simultaneously startled and excited Whitney.

He turned, and with his back against the wall, said, "No, just getting some fresh air."

She drew herself so close to him their hips were touching. "Fresh air is overrated. It's finally breaktime if you…"

She didn't finish the sentence, but let her fingers finish the implication, crawling up his chest. She leaned in to kiss him, but he ducked under her so that now she was against the wall.

"What's the matter?" she said, smirking, not backing down. "All talk? You do find me… attractive, don't you? Unless it's always someone behind me you're staring at,"

"More than you could possibly…" His voice cracked. He cleared his throat and said, "imagine."

She sauntered toward him again. "Then what's the problem, farmboy?"

Other than how much he hated being called farmboy, that was a great question. It was one he asked himself nightly, and one he figured he'd be asking himself for years to come. The gorgeous barmaid in his hometown that all the young men, including Whitney, only dreamed about growing up. He always told himself that it was because she wasn't the real Alless, but after so long, she was as real as any of the others.

"It's just—"

"You ain't a boy lover, are you?" she interrupted.

"Gods no! I just… I had a lot to drink, and I wouldn't want to take advantage of you."

She smiled. "I didn't have anything to drink. You sure it's me who'd be taken advantage of?"

"You're right," Whitney said, now smiling as well. "What kind of lady are you?"

"A bored one." She wrapped both arms around his neck and pulled herself in close. He could feel the warmth of her breath, real as anything else. "Always the same men asking me out around here since I was a girl. And the traders just want to move on. Why does the man I desire constantly refuse me?"

Whitney slipped her grasp before his heart beat any faster, making sure not to spill his drink, and started off toward the town center. "I'm just waiting for the right time."

She bit her lip in frustration. "Well, I won't be waiting around here forever!"

I will, he thought, then cursed himself for letting it pop into his head. He didn't want to hurt the girl's feelings, real or not, but she just wasn't... Sora. Just as he thought of her, her younger version crept across the darkness ahead, back to Wetzel's shack after her time skulking around the Twilight Manor.

Whitney stopped. "It's been six years, Whitney," he said to himself. "Even if she hasn't forgotten you, she's probably married by now, has kids."

He turned back to the Twilight Manor. Alless remained leaning against the wall, looking as disappointed as every night when Whitney dodged her and promised a future romantic gesture that never came.

"Why do you continue to deny yourself?" Kazimir asked.

Whitney looked toward the origin of the voice and saw the upyr, sitting on the edge of the well in the center of the square, gazing up toward the sky. The sound of the bard's playing echoed soothingly on the air. The ruins of Iam's chapel loomed behind him where Father Fake-Torsten sat, legs folded before a non-existent altar.

"Stupidity probably," Whitney said.

Kazimir cracked a smirk, and Whitney sat beside him. He took a sip of his ale before offering it to Kazimir. In all their time in Troborough, Whitney had never seen Kazimir eat or drink anything save for the bite of duck he'd been force-fed on the night of their arrival. Whitney had also never seen someone so content to simply sit and enjoy the air.

"So, you'll continue your nightly search instead?" Kazimir asked, ignoring the ale.

"It's the best way to keep out of trouble. Good for both of us, no?

"It is. And I'll continue to tell you that you won't be sneaking out of here."

"Kazimir, my friend." He patted him on the back. "If I had a gold autla for every time I've been told that, I'd be rich."

If anyone would have told Whitney six years ago that he'd be sitting in Troborough with the upyr who'd tried to kill him and Sora in Winde Port—or that'd he'd be calling him 'friend'—Whitney would have laughed. Of course, Winde Port seemed a lifetime ago.

They went quiet for a short while as Fabian, the bard, finished up a song.

"You know how many times I've escaped from the Yarrington dungeons?" Whitney said, finally. "There was this one time, some dirty, old man named Reese—"

"I've heard it," Kazimir replied. "Save your breath."

"Youh, well, that was easy. Another time, these giants in the Pikebacks held me—"

Kazimir shot him a sidelong glare that he knew meant he'd heard it. Whitney pursed his lips. He'd been a drifter for so long that he'd never been around someone enough for them to have heard all his stories.

Whitney took a sip of his ale. "When did you decide to be

happy here?" he asked.

"I'm not happy here," Kazimir replied. "But I am here still, and I must accept my fate, as you must."

"Hey, I accept it," Whitney said.

"Your map says otherwise."

"Well, I need something to do besides farm, and you convinced me to play the good guy."

"Is company not enough?" He nodded toward Alless, who'd already headed back inside from her break, shoulders sagging in disappointment. Whitney didn't have a good answer. Six years ago, he probably would have snapped and started a fight with the upyr, but he'd gotten better at not irritating the extremely easy to irritate and only other person in Troborough who knew his plight.

"Six years," Whitney sighed. "Did you imagine you'd be here this long?"

Kazimir looked back to the sky. "Six years for a man who has lived hundreds is like the blink of an eye. The Sanguine Lords will punish me for my failings as they see fit."

"How old are you, anyway?"

"Old enough to have tasted the blood of the first mystics in their fallen Order."

Whitney chuckled. "One day you'll give a real number."

"You misunderstand. I can't. Calendars changed, kingdoms fell—eventually, I stopped keeping count. You will too after enough time here."

Whitney opened his mouth to respond, stopped, then exhaled through his teeth. "It already feels like forever."

"Until it isn't. I've been in this realm many times as you know, and this visit has by far been the most pleasant. For that, you have my thanks. Most times, I spend relative years dodging the wianu. It's been nice being away from the chaos. To stand out in the sun, false as it may be. It's been nice not having to… feed."

It was the first time Kazimir had spoken about that particular affliction since they'd arrived, but Whitney had taken notice. The more time passed, the calmer Kazimir seemed. Whitney still felt things like the need to eat and drink—not hunger or thirst, but the compulsion. Not Kazimir. Whitney wondered what it would be like for all basic instinct to disappear enough to turn a monster willing to murder and drain a man like Tayvada into a stargazer.

"Well, I'm glad my exile is your vacation," Whitney said.

Seeing pangs of regret ripple across Kazimir's face never got normal. "That's not what I meant. Dakel un Ghastrin lives out there, stuck between worlds as all the wianu are, lusting for me as I lusted for your friend, Sora."

"There's more than one?" Whitney asked.

"Many more."

"Then how do you know your squid monster is the same every time?"

"Oh, he's the same," Kazimir assured Whitney. "He knows me, and I, him. Each upyr has one. Just one who will hunt us until the day one of us is destroyed. He knows as well as I do that in this life, its either him or me."

"But you're already dead."

"Not dead. Not alive."

Whitney waved his hands in the air and said, "Woooooo," like he'd seen a ghost, then reached for his ale.

"Make jokes if you will." Kazimir's face betrayed his grave tone. Whitney had always said he was like a fine wine, and the more time together, the more the upyr seemed to appreciate his jokes.

"Okay, fine," Whitney said. "So are you finally going to tell me why this thing gives a hot shog about you? Why are you so special?"

"I'm not special," Kazimir said. "But my power belongs to him. At least that's what he would say if the vile thing could speak. I devoured a piece of him."

Whitney's cheeks went white. "I hate squid."

"It was that or die," Kazimir said, resignedly. "I was young, in love. I refused to leave Pantego until I was ready. Now I can't even remember her face."

"Listen to you, Kazzy in love." Whitney nudged him playfully and earned a glower. The upyr hadn't changed too much, and he hated when Whitney used that nickname.

"Tread carefully."

"Fine, fine. But do you really expect me to feel bad?"

"I expect nothing."

"Well, at least you've got hundreds of years out of it, powers I can't dream of. I'm stuck here forever, according to you, and I'll never see the woman I… I grew up with." Whitney nearly allowed frustration get the better of him, but he took a moment to gather himself. "The truth is, I'm happy you're stuck here. I hope you never get out of Elsewhere to fulfill your dream of drinking Sora's blood."

"Then I will make you a deal." Kazimir stood. He still wore a knife, even though he didn't need it. Whitney winced when Kazimir drew the blade, then the upyr dragged it across his palm and extended the blade to Whitney. "When I return to Pantego with the blessing of my Lords, I will not hunt your friend. And I will indulge in her blood only if she offers it freely."

"No offering," Whitney said. "No blood."

"Don't push me, thief. Should my hunger return, I doubt I could resist. But the blood pact is a sacred oath, more binding than gold or silver. Failing one is the reason I am here, and I do not intend to return soon."

Whitney took the knife, sticking his tongue out as he wiped the blade. "What happens after?"

"You trust me, as Darkings did."

"*You.* An upyr. You're growing on me, but I'm not sure I'm there yet. Here is one thing, but back home?"

"You gave me six years of sunlight and peaceful dreams when you could have turned this place into madness incarnate. You pulled me out of the water when you could have left me for Dakel."

"Six years!" Whitney threw his arms into the air. "Six years I've been waiting for a thank you. Man, was that worth it. Sora, you can let me out now!" he shouted to the sky.

Kazimir wasn't amused. "It is my only offer, thief."

"Ah, screw it." Whitney drew the faintest line of red in the center of his hand. "I've always wondered what it felt like for her anyway." He clasped Kazimir's hand and felt nothing. He wasn't sure why he was expecting some rush of energy.

"That's it?" Whitney asked. "No sacred words or prayers? Torsten had a million."

"The blood says all."

"Well, speaking of wastes of time. I'm going to go see to my map before I do something stupid and ruin your good time." He downed his ale and tossed it into the well, listening as it clanged off the walls then splashed. "Perhaps tonight's the night I get out."

Kazimir nodded to him, then returned to staring up at the night sky. "Perhaps indeed."

"Fare thee well, fair upyr," Whitney hollered. "I hope I never see you again!" He bowed, spun on his heels, and headed down the road. Pillars of smoke rose from all the chimneys in the peaceful little town.

"Goodnight, Father Torsten!" Whitney called out as he passed by the ruined church. The out-of-place priest didn't even acknowledge him.

He said hello to a few more townsfolk on his way home. They were people whose names he'd never even bothered to learn growing up, but now he knew every soul in Troborough. He knew how long they'd been there. Hell, he knew what most of them had in their homes as he'd been invited into plenty. Nothing worth stealing, that was for sure.

He paused by the gate into the Fierstown farm. Lauryn was out front, hanging up some clothes to dry. He wasn't sure why Rocco was always so rude about her weight. Sure, she wasn't a beauty like the Queen of Glass, but she would make this Hamm a lucky man if he ever grew the courage to ask her out.

She acknowledged him, and he her, then he continued on. Around the back of their land stood the small cottage he'd built for himself shortly after Rocco died, when things got too somber for his taste. Lauryn crying, Young Whitney making things worse —Whitney couldn't concentrate on his nighttime activities without quiet.

The cottage was shoddy, slightly crooked, with gaps between every plank. The roof was perfectly set—he'd had plenty of prac-tice—but that was about it. Still, as he opened the creaky door, there was no denying it was one of his favorite possessions he'd ever had, honest or stolen.

The table wilted to one side. He owned only a single chair, and while most of the home was hand-built, he'd admittedly bought it from Lauryn. After the stress of helping construct Rocco's wheeling chair, he was done with chairs. The whole place was one room, though, he never had guests.

"All right, where should we check tonight?" he asked himself as if anyone was listening. He lit a candle, then looked at his pantry which was mysteriously unlocked. He nudged open the doors with his foot. He never kept any food inside, only his map which wasn't there.

"What the..." He placed the candle down and scoured the tiny compartment, looking under shelves. "No...no...no..." He even lifted the loose floorboard he hadn't bothered fixing. "No, don't do this!"

His map was gone.

XXIX

THE MYSTIC

Fading into sleep and waking in a new place was becoming a feeling all too common to Sora. She lay upon something soft and could feel Aquira breathing softly on her lap, her warm body making Sora sweat. Sora guessed she was in her quarters. Her eyelids protested movement, so she stared at their insides, a soft pink glow shining through and no shadows of movement. She was alone.

She'd dreamed of Whitney, of the voice she'd heard in Elsewhere twice now, and was more convinced than ever that he was alive and lost in that realm. She remembered the desperation in his voice, calling out to her. He would have to hold tight until she figured out how to access Elsewhere without sacrificing some poor orphan child.

Stirring slightly, she stopped as she heard two others outside her door speaking in hushed tones. She couldn't see them, but she'd begun to notice a chilling sensation whenever the spectral mystics were around. And despite Aquira's warmth, her feet were cold.

Sora focused on listening to them even though her head was

foggy. "She's not ready," the voice said, unmistakably Madam Aihara Na.

"She summoned fire in a day without blood," Madam Jaya replied. "Healed a fatal wound in herself. Nobody has done that so quickly since—"

"I'm aware. She also couldn't help herself from healing Kai while weakened, when he was in no danger of dying. She could have killed herself, just like..."

"But she didn't. You always say that time is short, that the age of the Glass is coming to an end. We can't rebuild our Order in this state, you know that. We are too weak to instruct through example; our bodies too close to leaving this plane for good."

"Patience, dear Jaya. You preach it to her, and forget it yourself."

"You are wise as always Master, but excuse me for saying this: I think your fading essence has made you blind to see the risks if we are not honest with her. She's headstrong, impetuous. She's already seen and done too much, more than ever we thought she would when she was sent to hiding."

"She asks too many questions, just like someone else I knew."

"And if we hold back, we risk driving her away. Not in my lifetime has there been one so strong in her bond with Elsewhere. She should understand why she is here, who she is—should have the same knowledge as the rest of us."

"You know the risks of showing her the truth. In her past lies clarity, but also the knowledge to open Elsewhere, in which she's displayed far too much curiosity. She's still too considerate. Too stuck on the foolish idea that she can save everyone, and I can see it in her heart, that extends to those who are lost."

"But Ancient One—"

"Enough," Aihara Na said sternly. "We cannot risk a breaching of our realm. Not when there are those so desperate to break free. You heard who Sora saw within, and she is not strong enough to withstand it."

"Then perhaps just something. Not the full truth, but at least who her mother was."

"I will meditate on it, Jaya. For now, continue training her with the bar guai once she is rested. Only when she masters the basic elemental magic held within the runes will I consider showing her the true breadth of her ability."

"Yes, Ancient one."

There were no retreating footsteps, but Sora took the silence to mean that they were gone. It took all her willpower to stay quiet when they mentioned her mother. All of a sudden, everything that had come to pass since she and Whitney left Yarrington felt worth it. She'd wanted to travel to Yaolin City to figure out who she was, and apparently, the real answers were far below her in the Well of Wisdom. And not just that, but the secrets to opening Elsewhere.

All she had to do was stay quiet and train with her new masters until they thought she was ready—masters who'd lived for centuries and grown indifferent to human emotion. It could be years; years of Whitney lost in Elsewhere with Kazimir until he went insane or the upyr killed him, if that was even possible there. The Whitney she knew couldn't very well avoid either for too long.

"Aquira," Sora whispered. "Aquira, wake up."

The wyvern's yellow eyes peeled open from beneath her two sets of eyelids, and she hopped across Sora's chest to lick her face.

"I'm fine, girl," Sora said. She sat up. Moving her head made her woozy. She reached up and didn't feel a bandage, but it was clear she'd hit her head hard. Either her masters couldn't mend the pain within her rattled skull, or they chose to leave it as a reminder of how impulsive Sora had been.

And if they were going to hold back from her, it was time she proved them correct. It was what Whitney would do. If she was going to save him, it was time to do more than just think like him. She needed to start acting like him.

"Aquira, how would you feel about going on another adventure?" Sora asked.

The wyvern screeched.

"Yeah, I know, me too." She tossed the covers and slid her feet off the side of her bed. She had to take a moment to settle her head, then stood. She looked down, pleased that the intrusive mystics hadn't undressed her at the very least. She gathered her belt, and this time hooked her knife to it. Just in case.

Aquira swooped in front of her, landing on the dresser, then released a throaty clicking noise.

"Don't worry, girl. I'm not going to fight them," Sora said. "You heard them; they think I'm special, which means even if they catch me, they won't hurt me... I hope."

Aquira's head and tail drooped.

"I may fit in here, finally, but I have to take the risk. It's the least he deserves." She straightened her kimono and made sure her knife was secure. Her fingertips brushed the bar guai. Madam Jaya had been relatively kind to her and she hated to disappoint anyone. But she'd stood idly and watched after Aihara Na cut Sora's arm open and left her to bleed out, while Aihara Na pretended to sacrifice an orphan simply to make a point.

"Maybe I was meant to be more than some orphan blood mage," Sora said to Aquira. "But if it means becoming like her, maybe I don't want to."

She extended her arm for Aquira, then noticed the bumpy scar running up her wrist from where Aihara cut her. Evidently, she hadn't healed herself enough to get rid of it. Before Aquira hopped up to her shoulder, she decided she'd keep this scar and never feel self-conscious. This one wasn't like the others.

She stopped at the door and glanced up at her friend on her shoulder. "I'm glad you're still with me, Aquira," she said. "Tayvada would have been proud, no matter what they claim he wanted." She nestled her cheek against Aquira, and then they strode out into the hall.

Through the windows along the spiral stairs, she could see the colorful smoke settling over the lake from the all the fireworks during the weeklong Festival of Ghosts. She had figured them magic, but now in the daylight, she realized that they came from boats sitting on the lake, shot out of strange tubes.

Not magic at all.

Above it all, she could see the pale silhouettes of Pantego's moons in the blue sky, inching closer toward covering the sun and reminding Sora of what this night meant in the Glass Kingdom. The Dawning. She'd forgotten that the Gyuan Jie ended at the same time. Forgotten entirely that the Dawning was coming, she'd so lost track of time.

"Ah, Miss Sora."

She whipped around, looking as guilty as one could possibly look even though she only descended stairs. A mystic she hadn't met—or rather whose face she hadn't yet seen from under drawn hoods—stood before her, his face dignified and eyes distant. He appeared far older than Madam Jaya, his cheeks pockmarked from age, and his hair a wispy tuft of gray on top of a pointed skull.

"My apologies for startling you," he said, bowing.

"That's all right, Master…"

"Huyshi," he said. "I am glad to see you are feeling better."

"I am, thank you." She lowered her foot to the next step, and he walked beside her. She kept a brisk pace that didn't appear to tire him in the slightest.

"Training is never easy, but I would not presume to know

what you're going through. It is unique for you as it was for us all."

"Did they stab you?"

"I can't heal. Never could. Even with the bar guai," he pointed to her chest. "I went to drastic measures to try and learn, but it's not for all of us to play with matters of life and death."

He wiggled his sleeve, and out of the corner of her eye, Sora noticed his left arm ended at a stump above his bicep. She slowed. She'd been in such a rush she wasn't sure how she'd missed it.

"They did that to you?" she asked, incredulous.

"Gods no. I cut this limb to pieces trying to find the power, it got infected, and I had to go to a human physician in Yarrington —of all places—to have it properly amputated. Now, I keep it as a reminder that we are not invincible."

"Sometimes it doesn't feel like that."

"I understand that better than most." He stopped at a landing, and Sora found herself stopping with him. He didn't have a kind face, but he did his best to force an unnatural smile. "I didn't find this place and start training until I was sixty years old. It has been a century since, and I remain one of the weakest ever to sit upon the Council. But we are all that remains. Stay the course, Sora. Learn all you can."

He extended his only hand and lay it over Sora's bar guai. She found his presence so comforting that she didn't fight it, and Aquira didn't even growl. He closed his eyes and inhaled. "The gods' Gift is strong in you. I know it is difficult, but you will rule this place. You will help usher in a new age of mystics, and we old, soulless leeches will fade into the mist."

"You truly believe that?" Sora asked.

"The Well of Wisdom shows what has been and what might come to pass. The future is in constant motion, but we have seen great things for you. Great things."

"What if I don't want greatness?"

"Those who reach such heights rarely do." He opened his eyes. "For now, keep growing, learning. Madam Jaya awaits you in the training room. She taught me everything I know about the mystic arts. I resisted too hard because I looked twice her age, but you're in good hands. She has two of them at least." He smiled, then turned and strolled down the hallway onto whatever level of the tower they were on.

His words gave her pause. All her life, she'd felt like she never belonged, yet here, everyone seemed to have been waiting a lifetime for her to arrive. *Can I really just throw that all away?*

"I have to," she said, more to herself than Aquira. "For Whitney."

She continued down the stairs until she reached the common area. The servants were inside preparing supper. She noticed Kai among them, carrying a sack of flour to the back room, in perfect health.

She pressed on before he turned and noticed her watching. She passed by the training room. Madam Jaya sat legs folded in the center, meditating, looking as if she were floating within an all-white sea.

There were no guards to keep her from the glowing door of the Well of Wisdom at the bottom of the stairwell. She peeked around the corner and didn't spot any of the mystics either. They trusted her, or they trusted that their gate could not be breached.

"Okay Aquira, here we go," she said.

The wyvern screeched.

Sora stepped before the great stone doors, large enough to allow a giant passage if one of their kind could even become a mystic. "Aquira, watch the stairs and screech if you spy anyone," Sora said.

The wyvern chirped, then pushed off her shoulder and landed on the railing. She stared intently upward, never letting her sight waver.

Sora tried waving her hand at the door as she'd seen Aihara Na do. As expected, it failed. So, she pressed her palms against the cold stone, hoping to feel something. Nothing.

She looked within as Madam Jaya had taught her, found nothing still. She lay her ear against the surface and heard nothing.

She sighed. "There has to be a way." She started to pace in front of it, thinking about every word the mystics had spoken to her from the moment she met Aihara Na. She knew there had to be a hint somewhere. "Think, Sora. Think."

She ran through the events of the last few days in her mind over and over. Lord Bokeo was the gatekeeper, but that didn't seem to mean this gate, only introduction to the Secret Council itself. Still, she kept going back to him. Tayvada, Aquira, all the things that had been placed in her path to lead her here.

"*Tsu shensughu ywen zhun tahuet feng yaris tsu weyong ywen hou*," she said aloud, her eyes going wide. Those were the first words she'd spoken in Panpingese during the vision Aihara Na gave her. "'The spirit of the gods is found in the one with the will of fire.'"

"Aquira," she spoke with vigor, finding that raging inferno within. At the same time, Aquira returned to her shoulder and stared into her eyes. It broke her concentration, and she was about to tell the wyvern to return to the stairs when she recognized the coincidence.

"Together?" she said. Aquira bobbed her frilly head. "Okay." She spoke the wyvern's name again, louder this time, and the rune in her chest began to glow. The flame danced up her arms, and she extended both palms to focus it into the center of the doors as a stream like liquid, molten lava. She could feel the sweltering heat against her face. Aquira growled, then blew fire into the same spot.

In her mind, she brought herself back to all those memories of fire, both of pain and triumph. She saw herself defeating Redstar, razing Winde Port to the ground, and in the midst of that, saving Torsten from Muskigo's wrath. She saw Troborough on fire, with her too late to save it or Wetzel. And she recalled how it led her back to Whitney.

She didn't just think about those moments, she traveled there. She could literally taste the ash on her tongue; feel it brushing against her shins, great gusts of wind blowing hot against her. And as she did, her chest stung, the pain excruciating. The rune in her bar guai she'd come to understand as fire, grew so bright, that between it and the dual streams of flame, she couldn't see anything when she opened her eyes.

Her legs quaked, but she didn't back down. The bar guai pricked deeper, like it was trying to find its way to her heart. The pain had her screaming, and there was no way the mystics and their servants wouldn't hear her.

The rune on the bar guai suddenly burst into pieces, and the blast sent her to her knees. She kept her arms outstretched, and the fire kept flowing. She wasn't sure how as it seemed that the fire rune was fractured. Once more she felt that familiar pull of Elsewhere. That haunting whisper.

If she was channeling from within, she wasn't sure. But she wouldn't risk it. She accepted the temptation of Elsewhere, keeping one hand raised to continue the blaze and with the other, she drew her knife. Slicing horizontally over her sole scar a few times, she found it no longer hurt her. It was almost pleasurable.

The fire burned brighter and hotter, turning blue now. Aquira's claws dug into her shoulder as her wyvern friend released more fire. Sora sliced her other arm to further fuel the blaze.

Sora could hear Nesilia whispering her name. And not only her, countless voices of Elsewhere mixed and blended, Whitney's among them. When she heard it, she roared, the act making her throat hurt.

Sora released one final blast.

Then there was silence.

Sora was on her hands and knees panting, blood dripping from her arms, surrounded by smoke. She was so exhausted her head felt like stone, but she fought to lift it. A hole had been burned through the thick door, crackling blue at the edges.

"We did it," she rasped, turning to Aquira. The wyvern blinked blearily, took one step, then tumbled off Sora's shoulder into her waiting hands. She was panting, smoke slipping through her flared nostrils.

"It's okay, girl," she whispered. "I've got you." She cradled her against her chest and crawled through the hole. Her muscles were so exhausted she couldn't stand even if she wanted to. Her chest still burned hot, and she noticed a stream of blood running between her breasts from the ruptured rune.

She ignored all the aches and kept crawling. The bubbling pool of blue liquid awaited her, steam rising to meet the stone ceiling. Apart from the preternatural coloring, it was so unassuming, like a natural spring, yet according to her masters contained all the knowledge she could ever want. Sora set Aquira down on the pool's edge.

"Sora, no!"

She glanced back and saw Madam Jaya at the base of the tower stairs. She raised her hand as if to perform a spell, and Sora didn't wait to find out. She pulled herself into the pool headfirst and plunged. She expected to meet the bottom, but the water seemed to descend as deep as an ocean to the heart of the world.

She rolled over, waving with her arms to find the surface. The water was warm but not hot, refreshing. Her fresh wounds didn't sting, but red coalesced with the pristine, blue liquid into beautiful shapes.

She reached the top and gasped for air, and as she did, a rush of thoughts and feelings poured over her like an enormous wave in the Torrential Sea. Colors, shapes, sounds, light, everything all at once.

The shapes and colors began materializing into silhouettes and then full images. Trees, hills, mountains, the vast expanse of Pantego splayed out before her. She could see the harsh, cold lands of Brotlebir and Drav Cra. North even of there, she noted the land of Brekliodad from where the upyr Kazimir hailed. The Dragon's Tail Mountains intersected with the Pikeback like a great **T** upon the land.

Her vision shifted down past Glinthaven and south to the Jarein Gorge and the Walled Lake. She saw Yarrington and Troborough, Winde Port and Bridleton. It was all there, lain before her as if she were looking down upon a living map. As her view drifted across to the Panping Region, she saw a massive army gathered at the western walls of Yaolin City as well as a fleet amassed off the southern shores. The flotilla consisted of ships belonging to both the Glass Kingdom and the Black Sands as if they were allies.

In an instant, she stood amidst the men at the wall, soldiers of the Glass Kingdom. The sounds of them preparing for battle met her ears. Steel sharpening on whetstones, fires crackling while men sang songs of war.

Sora walked, feeling the grass beneath her feet. She'd had an experience like this before when she met Nesilia, but in that vision, she knew where she was—It was Elsewhere, no question. Now, she wasn't sure.

Did she see the past? Were these men huddled just beyond the walls of Yaolin prepared to take it by force?

Then she wondered if she saw the future, the Fourth Panping War, and the army preparing. She thought to look for Torsten, knowing that if she indeed saw the future, he would be there leading his men.

That was when the answer to her question came with certainty. From the slit in a grand tent strode a man no one alive would mistake. King Liam the Conqueror, with his sober expression and eyes a hue of hazel much like amber. His hair was black, the color of youth, long before sickness overtook him enough for Whitney to pluck the Glass Crown from his head. She couldn't help but notice how handsome he was, striking in his bright white and blue armor.

"Men!" he said. "Glory in the name of Holy Iam awaits! Today we prepare to finish that which my father and his father's father could not. But with the furthering of His kingdom in mind, we possess something neither of them had."

The men outside the tent grunted in agreement. They too wore white, and Sora noticed the one standing next to Liam, helmet tucked under his arm. A sinking feeling like she'd swallowed a rock hit her. Relief only came when her mind relaxed and made the distinction between Redstar posing as Uriah and this man, Uriah Davies, the Wearer of White himself.

It was uncanny. Redstar had impersonated Uriah so thoroughly, and if not for this version appearing younger, it would have been impossible to tell the difference.

Liam placed his hand on Uriah's shoulder.

"We attempted this peaceably, did we not?" he asked Uriah who nodded. "I hold no distaste for these fine people, but my mandate is clear. If the salvation of the people requires the blood of their masters, then blood shall run this day!"

Each of the men, who Sora assumed were Liam's highest generals in the King's Shield, roared.

Once they'd settled, he spoke softly. "We occupy and demand the seat of their council. If they attack first, we lay waste to their lands. Spare the women and children unless otherwise necessary.

The mystics are tricksters in true form, and they will not hesitate to throw anything they can summon at us. But we are not Drav Cra savages."

His men nodded and grunted in agreement.

"Get some rest," Liam said. "Uriah, see to it that all preparations are complete. Tomorrow, we march."

Liam turned toward his tent, then stopped halfway. He stared up at the wall of the city in the distance where two women stood, their long robes flapping in the wind. They stared back. Sora couldn't make out who they were, but from their outfits, they appeared to be mystics. One wore the red of the Ancient One, the other yellow.

As Sora took a step to get a closer look, the world frayed to blackness all around her. Footsteps crashed like a thundering herd of zhulong. She panicked. Soldiers formed up, and she expected to be trampled, only they passed right through her, just as she had the mystics so many times before.

She spun. Balls of fire painted the sky orange, filling it with smoke. Bolts of lightning slashed the dirt, and massive vines broke through the earth to restrain Glass soldiers, knocking over even the Panpingese in the effort.

"Forward!" a man shouted. "Iam stands with us!"

"Torsten!" Sora exclaimed. She ran to him, but he didn't notice her. He thrust his sword into the air and raised his shield, painted with the Eye of Iam. He wasn't wearing Shieldsman armor, nor did he wear the white helm, since Uriah was still alive, but he did have on gluruium bracers. He must have been a Shieldsman in training during the siege of Yaolin City.

Soldiers rallied to him nonetheless and charged. A natural leader.

They were through the gates, engaging what remained of the Panping army after years of warfare. Another ball of fire came down, this one slamming into Torsten's shield and knocking him back, but Sir Uriah Davies was there to catch him and continue the charge.

The Glass army was massive, and Sora could see the fear in the Panpingese even as their mystic leaders flung spells of destruction at their enemies. There were Shieldsmen, dwarven and Shesaitju mercenaries, and others, Glintish men and women, skin like Torsten's, and even those from Brekliodad. Everything it took for Liam the Conqueror to vanquish these people of, what he considered, false gods.

Sora ducked out of reflex as Torsten swung at an enemy right over her head. That was when she noticed priests of Iam walking with them into the fray, somehow summoning shields of light to dispel mystic spells as they strolled forward, blind and clutching Eyes of Iam.

"Retreat!" the Panpingese yelled in their language. Their men looked overwhelmed with terror. They turned to flee down the streets of Yaolin when walking toward them came a mystic. They halted at the sight of her. Sora searched through them and felt her heart leap into her throat. It was Aihara Na, flanked on either side by Madam Jaya and Huyshi, but she wasn't wearing red. Another legion of Panpingese soldiers stood behind her. Unlike Liam, Aihara Na didn't look a day younger. The only difference was that her stare wasn't so distant and hollow.

"Stand your ground cowards, or feel our wrath instead," Aihara Na said. She didn't shout, but her words carried on the air with authority. The men stopped, frightened as if trapped between two enemies, invaders and their beloved masters.

Aihara Na and the other mystics joined hands and began a chant. Sora saw the Red Tower standing tall over the rooftops behind them. The ground shook, then a tremendous wave rushed down the street. The water split around the mystics and the army behind them but washed through their own people on route to pushing the Glass army back.

Torsten reached out, and Sora tried to grab his hand before the water carried him away in its strong current. She wasn't moved by it. When the water settled, men of both armies littered the streets, disoriented.

"Kill the Glassmen," Aihara Na ordered to the legion behind her. "Kill them all."

The Panpingese soldiers stared at their people stuck between them and the Glass army, gagging on water, some with their bodies crushed against buildings. They didn't charge.

"Why are we fighting for them?" one at the front said.

"King Liam said any who stood against the mystics would receive mercy," spoke another.

"You think he will show you mercy?" Aihara Na spat. "The liar will slaughter every single one of you. The streets will run red with your blood."

"They already do!"

"Insolent fool!" Aihara Na swung her hand, and the man flew across the street. His back snapped against a column. "This is our city. Defend it, or die!"

One of the Panpingese soldiers glared at her, then tossed his curved blade aside. A few more did the same, until Aihara Na and the other mystics weren't facing the recovering Glass army, but their own people.

"You fools!" she roared. A storm brewed overhead, lower than any storm cloud should naturally be. "Can you not see who the true enemy is?"

"They see, as I do," a deep, basso voice shouted from the gates. King Liam strode in, carrying a sword at his side.

"You!" Aihara Na bellowed. She marched forward, magically pushing all her remaining soldiers out of the way.

"Your people no longer wish to be tools for your profane tests," Liam said. Sir Uriah had recovered from the flood and tried to stop him, but King Liam gestured for him to step aside and unlike Aihara's men, he did so without a fuss. "They no longer wish to suffer as you strive to conquer death."

"And how many of them have died in your quest to rule this world?"

"I gave them the choice to bend the knee," he said solemnly, "to see Iam as their one true savior. It is your kind that denies them peace."

"There can be no peace with the likes of you!" She raised her arms, and a bolt of lightning shot out of the clouds above toward Liam.

"My Lord, no!" Torsten scrambled to his feet and leaped in front of it, but the coruscating stream of light froze right in front of his chest. Torsten hit the ground, clutching his necklace, staring as the bolt vacillated, making the air crackle with energy.

"Enough," spoke a soft voice that, like Aihara Na's, carried. Another Mystic walked out onto the street, more beautiful than any mortal woman Sora had ever seen. She wore the red of the Ancient One, and she stepped in front of Aihara.

"Long have I stood by while we fought back, but for what?" she said.

"Ancient One Sumati, I—" Aihara started, but was cut off by the newcomer.

"No, it is time you listen. I am the eldest on the council, and I will not see any more death. Today, we show them that Iam is with us as well. Perhaps they see no others, but perhaps we see too many."

The woman spun to face King Liam and the Glass soldiers. Sora swore there was something familiar about her, but she wasn't sure what. She was the Ancient One of the time, which meant that she had to be hundreds of years old, but she didn't look a day older than Sora.

Ancient One Sumati fell to her knees and bowed her head. "Let this fighting come to an end, King Liam. Do what you will with us." She gestured back to the Panpingese soldiers. "But spare them."

Liam didn't answer. He merely stared across the smoldering battlefield and into the ageless eyes of the elder mystic. After a few seconds, a smile touched the corner of his lips. What happened next, Sora couldn't see. Again, the world frayed at the edges, and before she knew it, she stood in a dark, candlelit room. An arrowslit window revealed that they were high up in the Red Tower.

Ancient One Sumati lay on a bed wearing nothing but a nightgown, no longer the mystic warrior on the battlefield. Sora considered shielding her eyes, believing she was about to see something meant to be private. She heard screaming, but not pleasurable ones. The woman's swollen belly rose and fell in sharp intervals.

Two others were in the room in addition to the laboring, soon-to-be-mother. Liam Nothhelm sat at the bedside, holding the Ancient One's hand. A handmaiden kneeled by her feet preparing to deliver the child.

Something wasn't right. Sora had seen births in Troborough before, but the mystic seemed to be in even more pain. Sweat drenched every part of her, and the sheets beneath her legs were soaked with blood.

"What's taking so long?" Liam demanded.

"I… she doesn't seem to be able to push. Your Grace," the handmaiden replied.

"Is it blocked?" Sumati grated.

"It doesn't seem…"

"I'm afraid the child will never see the light of this world," Aihara Na said, entering. "Its heart is too weak for this realm. It will not survive the stress and should be dead already."

"What are you talking about, witch?" Liam asked.

"She hasn't told you? Your child should have been stillborn, but Ancient One Sumati has drawn on all her power to keep her breathing.”

Liam squeezed the Ancient One's hand. “What is she talking about?” The woman struggled to speak, and Liam yelled. “Answer me!” Then softer, “Please?”

“Never has a mystic been so skilled in the art of healing, but this is beyond her,” Aihara Na said. “Elsewhere desires the soul it was meant to have, and it will not be denied. Even our power has its limits.”

“Aihara,” Ancient One Sumati wheezed. “I can't… I can't hold on much longer. You must save the child.”

“You are asking me to do something against all that we believe,” Aihara said.

“Please…” Ancient One Sumati said.

“What is this?” Liam hovered over the Ancient One's face. “Why didn't you tell me?”

She stroked his cheek, her hand trembling. “I couldn't bear to see you unhappy.”

Liam took her hand in both of his. He now shook as well. “This is impossible. Iam spoke to me. He told me that this union was destined.”

“Perhaps your savage Queen cursed it,” Aihara Na said. “Her people are known for that.”

“Do not speak of her!” Liam snapped.

“Aihara, please... save our child,” Ancient One Sumati moaned, sweat pouring off her forehead, matting her long black hair. “I know we've had our differences, but you must save her.”

“And risk splitting the veil?” Aihara Na said. “You know what it requires.”

“I can hold Elsewhere at bay. Why else live so long as I have?” She chuckled weakly, then coughed.

“No, Madam. Perhaps you could have, but it is too dangerous now. If you were not in so fragile a state, you would see that.”

"You can save her?" Liam asked, standing.

"Only one of them. The mother, or the child. But it is too—"

"I am your new King," Liam stated.

"And as our new King, you've made it very clear that our magic is outlawed. An act of this magnitude has consequences."

"I know what your people are capable of. You will use any power at your disposal to save them both, is that clear? Queen Oleander has yet to bear me a child. I will not lose my first."

Ancient One Sumati grabbed Liam's hand, groaning in pain from the simple act. Blood had thoroughly saturated the bed by now. "It's okay, Liam," she said. "I've lived a good, long life, rose to the top of the Mystic Order, saw this awful thing called war end peaceably," she paused and stroked his hand, "by finding the peace in you." She rubbed her stomach. "Our child deserves the same chance."

Liam bit his lip. His eyes welled, but he did not weep. A man like him couldn't afford to show weakness, even in a time like this. He leaned over and placed a gentle kiss upon her cheek, then he turned to Aihara Na, his glower hard as glaruium.

"I am your King. I do not ask," he said. "Do what must be done to save the child."

"Ancient One, please," Aihara Na pled. Sora didn't think the woman capable of looking so terrified.

"I can control it." Ancient One Sumati howled in pain and clutched her stomach. "Blessed be the union between our two peoples. Do not fight it."

Liam drew his sword and raised it to Aihara's neck. It was then, as she heard the rasp of another sword drawn from a sheath that Sora noticed Sir Uriah Davies quietly standing guard by the door.

"Listen to her, or I swear to Iam I will burn this tower to the ground," Liam growled. "Prove that it is not just wickedness that springs from this place, and save our innocent child."

Aihara Na swallowed hard. "King Liam," she spoke softly. "Are you asking me to call upon the gods and use their Gift?"

"Do it, Aihara," Liam said. "I won't ask again."

"Do you not care to know the conse—"

"I said, do it!"

Madam Aihara approached Ancient One Sumati. "Move, girl," Aihara ordered the handmaiden.

"But, she—"

"Move!"

Aihara Na flicked her wrist, and the handmaiden slid across the floor and was pinned against the wall by an unseen force. She then placed a hand upon Ancient One Sumati's bulging belly and began to speak low, steady words, multiple languages blending and overlapping. They grew in volume, blanketing the room and making Sora's insides chatter, and then she raised her other hand toward Liam.

"What are you doing?" he questioned.

"Your will." She touched Liam's chest while still leaving her other hand on the mother's stomach as if forming a conduit between them. Ancient One Sumati screamed in agony.

"You're hurting her !" Liam said.

"Then you may want to close your eyes." Aihara Na began to chant louder, and Ancient One Sumati screamed louder. Her body began to stagger, just as Sora's vision did as she shifted within the revelations of the Well of Wisdom. Liam dropped his sword and fell to a knee. He too groaned in torment.

"Unhand the King!" Sir Uriah Davies stormed forward but was thrown back by the aura that pulsed from Aihara Na. Ancient One Sumati's screams grew even louder.

"I can feel the tear," Aihara yelled over the sound of the entire room shaking. "Madam, we must stop."

"No!" Madam Sumati yelled. "I can hold it." Her neck arched, and a stream of dark red smoke forced its way through her eyes.

Sora could hear whispers in a strange, demonic language echoing around her. She could feel the chill of evil even though she wasn't there. "My life I give freely in her name! You will hold no sway over me bastards of Elsewhere."

"What is this place?" a familiar voice muttered. Sora spun in a circle. It undoubtedly belonged to Nesilia, and Sora soon realized that the words were being spoken through Ancient One Sumati's lips. "How long have I been asleep?"

"You will not pass to this realm!" Ancient One Sumati yelled.

"Master, I can't... hold..." Aihara Na could hardly keep her arms up anymore. Liam shouted in pain, now as loud as all the others.

"They have forgotten me?" Nesilia spoke again. "I am buried, not dead, yet they have forgotten me!" A spectral arm extended from Ancient One Sumati's chest which now glowed blue like the Well of Wisdom, like the smoke from Sora's healing. It lashed across the ceiling, rending a large crack.

"Be gone!"

A flash of light—just like the light which Sora had summoned in the Webbed Woods or on the Breklian ship—flung Aihara Na and King Liam against the wall. Even though Sora wasn't physically present, it did the same to her. When she gathered her bearings and ran back to the bed, Ancient One Sumati was gone. Only her clothing and blood remained, and lying in a pool of it in the center of the bed was a crying infant.

Aihara Na panted uncontrollably, unable to stand. Liam scrambled across the room and to the bed. He grasped at the sheets from his knees. "My dearest Sora, don't do this. Come back to me. Please, Iam, hear my prayers."

Sora's eyes went wide. Liam's shoulders shook as he allowed himself to cry. He rubbed the bloody sheets against his face. "May Iam see you suited to walk through the Gate of Light," he sniveled. He raised his quaking hands to circle his eyes in prayer, then squeezed them shut. Sora could see his lips moving as he murmured a prayer to himself. She was too shocked by the name he'd used to hear the words.

As he cried, Aihara Na finally mustered the strength to walk over and lay a hand upon his shoulder.

"You did this!" he roared as he spun on her.

"At your word, I did only what I could to save the child," she replied, not shrinking back at all in the face of the legend. "You, my King, demanded I keep this child alive. Ancient One Sora Sumati, my master, is dead because of you. Your daughter is alive through my hand because she willed it, but her heart is yours."

"My daughter." His gaze snapped back to bed as if he'd forgotten about the infant. He reached out, still shaking, and lifted the crying girl. She sounded healthy, her voice strong. "My daughter." He held her close and kissed her forehead. "She sounds healthy."

"She is, thanks to Sora Sumati. Elsewhere demanded a soul and so the bridge was opened. She risked everything for that child."

"Our child."

"But my master was not alone in sacrifice. The child was not meant for this world, and more sacrifice was needed in defying the fate of the gods. Sora was too weak from preserving your daughter's life for so long in the womb, so the child is alive only by your lifeblood, sharing your heart. As she grows, you will pass from this life. Only in her death can you be free of this bond."

"This cannot be," Liam said, breathless.

"It is. You will gray long before your time. Your mind will become fitful and be filled with unrest, and eventually, you will find yourself present only in body. That is the price you agreed to, my King. A soul for Elsewhere, and a heart for a bastard daughter."

Without even a sound or warning, the world frayed again, and

Sora stood on an unfamiliar street in Yaolin City. It was night, No, not night. Celeste and Loutis covered the sun. The Dawning.

Once again, King Liam stood next to her, surrounded by men wearing the white of the King's Shield.

"Leave us!" the King shouted. His men clomped away, leaving Liam standing beside Aihara Na who now wore a hooded red robe. With Master Sumati's death, it appeared she had taken on the role of eldest in the Mystic Order.

"I only trust you because I trusted her, you know that right?" Liam said.

Aihara Na nodded.

"Do not make me regret it," Liam warned.

"Your trust is well-placed, my King," she said. "If you claim the child publicly, it will only draw questions. She cannot rule in your world as a woman anyway. This is best."

"No one will know?"

"None."

"Send wagons filled with Panpingese war refugees all over the realm. Make it seem like she is any other. Place her with someone you trust to keep her safe, in a place no one cares about at all. Never tell me where she is and I will never ask."

Liam looked down at his daughter, swaddled in a cloth in his arms. She had his amber-hued eyes. He stroked her fine, black wisps of hair. "Daughter or son, you are my first, and I do this to protect you," he whispered. "I fear what I might do as my mind slips should I know where you are, so I mustn't." He held her out so he could look upon her in her entirety.

"So much like your mother," he smiled. "We will never see each other again, but know this; when you are grown, and I pass from this world, I give my heart willingly, as your mother gave hers. Iam saw fit to give you this second chance, born on the Dawning as if you, my Sora, are my light from within. You will find greatness. It is in your blood."

He kissed her on the forehead, and then another gut-wrenching pull made the world fold inward and brought Sora before the Red Tower. Now it was true night.

"Do it now!" King Liam shouted.

Sora turned back to the tower to see all the mystics, hundreds of them, on their knees on the small island beneath the tall, red structure. Each of them was held in place at the tip of a King's Shieldsman's sword. Uriah Davies had his against Aihara Na's neck.

"My King, please do not do this," Aihara Na begged from her knees, her hands cuffed.

"Call it what you will, but your magic is no different from the Drav Cra," Liam said. "I shall let no other share my fate."

"Your Grace, this is what you wanted."

"And I thank you for it. Know that because of your master, I do not do this out hate, but out of love."

"You call this love?" Aihara Na shouted. "We have sealed the tower for good. Cut off our connection to the Well. What else could we possibly do to keep you happy?"

Uriah kneed the small of her back, and she fell to her face. He barked at her to stay quiet. Liam kneeled to whisper in her ear. "Nothing. But so long as any of you know of my daughter, she is not safe. Not from me, not from you."

Liam rose to face his men. "We have tried peace, but Iam has made it clear to me, we cannot possibly coexist with these heathens. Their time presiding over Panping has come to an end. We will not share our rule."

He drew a deep breath, closed his eyes, then looked to his Wearer of White. "Uriah, do it."

It was all he needed to say.

Before most of the mystics could react, they had glaruium blades shoved through their throats. Most of them folded to the ground, dead and covered in the very blood that gave them power.

But Madam Aihara and a few others—Madam Jaya among them, resisted. Aihara Na's chains turned to ice and shattered. She stabbed one of the shards into Uriah's leg and fled onto the lake. The water solidified beneath her every step. A few others killed Shieldsmen to escape, including Madam Jaya.

"Find them and kill them!" Liam demanded. "The Mystic Order is over." His men raced to their boats and set off after the dozen or so escaped mystics. Others fired arrows across the lake. One raced toward Madam Jaya.

Sora yelled out to warn Madam Jaya when the ground suddenly vanished, and Sora felt herself falling. Letters and symbols from every language in Pantego blew past her. She landed with a splash, the familiar scent of boiling flowers in the air. Then she emerged from the Well of Wisdom, gasping for air.

In the present, Aihara Na, Madam Jaya, Master Huyshi, and the four other surviving mystics stood at the edge of the waters looking down at her, faces wracked by concern. "Sora, are you all right?"

She wanted to respond, but couldn't find the words. The truth was almost too much to bear.

XXX

THE KNIGHT

The Queen Mother's white mare was as feisty as she was, but she was as advertised—faster than any horse Torsten had ever ridden. He sat up front on her saddle, snapping the reins as he shouted for the crowd outside Yarrington to part in the name of the Queen Mother.

Faces smeared with luminescent paint were everywhere. The cold didn't matter. All the pious souls of Yarrington and beyond gathered in knots to witness this yearly ritual when they were tested in the darkness. Priests gave sermons on every hillside and promontory. Only they weren't alone. Warlock rituals and sacrifices were scattered amongst them attended by masked cultists while Drav Cra civilians sold furs.

It was a sight Torsten never thought he'd witness, and one he'd make sure he never did again. Allying with the barbarians and heathens of the North was one thing, but inviting them and exiled cultists to participate in this holiest of day, one in which they even didn't believe was another. It was like he'd gone to the dungeons and stepped out into an Elsewhere itself—his own personal exile.

"Would you go faster?" Oleander said. "The Dawning approaches, and whatever my brother plans to show my son, I don't trust him." She sat at Torsten's back, arms wrapped around his waist. It had taken a long time, but Torsten finally felt all those hours catering to her every need was worth it. She was the only ally he had left who saw Redstar for the monster he was.

"I'm trying," Torsten replied. He pulled on the reins to dart around a mob, then nearly toppled over a line of dwarves who'd scurried in front of them. The mare reared back, and Oleander tightened her hold. Torsten and the leader of the dwarven group met gazes momentarily. It was Oathbreaker, Oarbringer—Tosten couldn't remember his name—but he knew it was the construction foreman working to repair the Royal Crypt. The little men darted beneath the horse's belly, and Torsten grabbed Oleander's wrist tight.

"The next fool that gets in our way," Oleander snapped, "plow them over!"

Torsten didn't listen, but he weaved his way to the bottom of the trail leading up the mountain. A warlock and a handful of Drav Cra warriors camped in the path. Two dire wolves lay perched on an outcrop of rock beside them, chewing the meat off the bones of some poor animal. Torsten brought the horse to a halt in front of them.

"Sorry, nobody gets by," the biggest of the warriors said, standing and hefting an axe with both hands. "Orders from the Arch Warlock."

"Do you know who I am?" Oleander questioned.

"Fresh meat?"

"You insolent—"

"Let me handle this." Torsten stopped her from hopping off the horse and doing something stupid. "You speak with the Queen Mother. She wishes to spend the first Dawning after his miracle rebirth with her son."

The warrior sneered. "We're especially not supposed to let her pass."

"I suggest you reconsider. She isn't known for leniency."

"You think we're afraid of the 'Flower of the Drav Cra?' You should try meeting a real Northern woman."

"Stop wasting breath!" Oleander kicked the sides of her horse, and it darted forward. Torsten caught his balance on the reins with one hand and drew his claymore from his back sheath with the other. It slit the warlock's neck as it slipped free, and as the heathen toppled over, fire sprayed from his hand in an explosive blast, blowing back the Drav Cra warriors.

"Get them!" one roared.

The pounding paws and barking that followed were all too familiar sounds. After his trek to the Webbed Woods with Whitney, he hoped never to be caught fleeing dire wolves again, but he'd hoped for much that hadn't come to pass. He spurred Oleander's horse around the first sharp turn on switchbacks.

"You're worse than Fierstown!" Torsten shouted back at Oleander. "Next time warn me."

"It's your sacred duty to know every want and need of your Queen," she replied.

"I'm no longer a Shieldsman."

"You're as much one as I am a Queen."

A snarl made the hair's on Torsten's neck stand on end. Oleander squeezed him harder, and he glanced back to see the two dire wolves bounding after them. Their maws snapped, saliva flinging, and their yellow eyes pierced the white of the snow-coated slope.

They had a lead on the beasts, but the ground was slick, and every time the horse took a turn, the wolves claws allowed them to dig in and take it sharper. Heavy flakes of snow pelted Torsten's face as they ascended higher, and through a break in the clouds, he saw that both moons were now visible, edging ever closer to eclipse the sun.

"Grotesque beast!" Oleander yelped.

Torsten glanced back as they took another corner and saw one of the wolves literally chomping at her heels. Its head was the size of Oleander's torso, and one bite would rip her foot clean off.

"We'll never make it up with them after us!" Torsten yelled.

"I hadn't realized!" She squealed as the wolf snapped at the bottom of her dress and tore off a shred. Torsten grabbed her so the force of the bite wouldn't yank her from the saddle. Then he stretched her hands around him and slotted the reins into her palms.

"I'll handle them," Torsten said. "When I let go, don't stop."

"What? I am your Queen, and I order you to—"

As the horse dug in to make the next turn, Torsten pushed off the side. He flew through the air, slamming into the dire wolf trailing behind which hadn't yet made the turn. He plunged his claymore into its chest, squeezing the handle with all his might. They skidded to a stop at the edge of the rocky path, a hands-length from plummeting together to their doom.

The wolf howled, and its head lilted off to the side, but Torsten's gambit paid off. Wolves were pack animals, and as he stood and slid his blade out of the beast, he saw that the other wolf had stopped in its pursuit of Oleander to face him. Torsten set his feet and tightened his grip. They were a long way up the mountain now, where the slope began to sharpen and grow rocky. The wolf glared down at him from the incline, claws digging into the snow, eyes like ice.

Torsten looked over his shoulder. At his back was certain death, and at his front, a wolf the size of a bovine, with fangs as long as his forearm.

"Come beast!" he bellowed. "I will not be stopped by you."

The horrifying creature prepared to pounce, but just as its hind legs left the ground Oleander's Whitehair's back hooves kicked it in the side. True to its name, the mare was as white as the snow and close to invisible on the trail. The wolf scrambled to find a grip with razor-sharp claws, but the snow was too slick, and it tumbled over the ledge. Bouncing its way down, its whimpers echoed, no doubt drawing the attention of many a pilgrim. Torsten didn't waste time seeing how far it went.

"Must I handle everything?" Oleander called down.

"I told you not to stop!"

"And you promised to kill my brother. Now hurry up, it's freezing."

Torsten stowed Salvation on his back and jogged up to the horse. Oleander didn't slide back to make room for him to take the reins. "She listens better to me," she said. "Keep me warm, knight."

After she likely saved his life, there wasn't much Torsten could say. He pulled himself up behind her, and they took off through the snow and freezing wind.

Up they went until the silence of the mountain grew more unnerving than the snarling wolves. The higher they climbed, the straighter the path became, no longer slicing back and forth but instead was carved around the entire circumference of the mountain. They passed the top entry to the glaruium mine and Torsten could see the glow of the rare element through the cracks. In its natural form, it glimmered in the darkness like stars compressed into stone.

Clouds rolled in, shrouding Pantego in shadow. The sun wasn't yet covered, but the cold was brutal. Every breath was like a chain of icicles down Torsten's throat. He could feel Oleander shivering and wrapped her tighter. The cold was unquestionably getting to her as she'd stopped speaking, and he was used to her sharp tongue no matter the situation. They circled once more around the mountain, and then her horse released a heart-wrenching cry before collapsing to the snow.

Torsten threw his leg over the side of the mare and yanked Oleander off before being crushed beneath the weight of it. He wiped the snow from his face. Off to the side, the horse labored to breathe. He was sure the beast hadn't been in so high an altitude or such cold in all its life. There was good reason people climbed to the summit of Mount Lister earlier in the day or rode mules or stocky Quarter Horses intended for hauling.

"Sora!" Oleander cried out. She scrambled out of Torsten's grip and lay her hand upon the horse's head.

Torsten had seen the Queen be many things, but sympathetic wasn't one of them. As she looked up at him, he swore a tear rolled down her cheek. It froze so quickly it could have easily been a snowflake. "We can't leave her," she shivered.

"We must." Torsten lay his hand on Oleander's shoulder. "Her place is in the Gate of Light now. We're close."

"Then you must end her suffering."

Torsten moved Oleander aside and knelt before the horse.

"Sora," Oleander whispered again.

"Sora," Torsten repeated, the familiarity of the name finally striking him. "I didn't realize that was your horse's name."

"You don't know everything about me, knight."

"It's just a curious name."

"Liam had already named her before she was gifted to me. He said she was as rare as I was. I never asked him the true story of where he got her. I never wanted to know."

"Like I've told you. No matter what was said or done, he loved you, Oleander."

"How could he not?" She stood and turned away. "Now hurry up and get on with it."

"Your Grace?"

"I will not have her suffer. Do what you knights do."

Torsten rubbed the horse's snout and drew Salvation. Of all the things Oleander was, he'd never pegged her for one who'd be unable to watch this mercy. But those Drav Cra warriors were right. She was far from one of them anymore. At that moment, she had more compassion in one of her blonde, nearly silver hairs, than all of them combined.

"Be in the light now," he whispered as he drove the sword straight into Sora's heart. "Suffer no more." He thought he could hear Oleander whimpering, but he showed her the respect of keeping his sympathy to himself. He stood, wrapped his arm around her, and continued up the path.

"Why didn't you carve the fur from those infernal wolves?" she asked.

Torsten smiled, glad to see she hadn't lost all her venom. "My failures abound, Your Grace."He kept her moving the rest of the climb. Oleander's body resisted, but there was no time to rest. To stop under these conditions would mean death. The day had started warmer and brighter, but all that changed. Never in all his life could he remember such a harsh Dawning atop Mount Lister. He couldn't help feeling it was an omen.

The icy wind, for him, was preferable to rotting in the dungeon, breathing in stale air that reeked of shog. His training had prepared him for this. Every Shieldsman was sworn in on the flat top of Mount Lister. He had knelt before Uriah Davies to take the vows as had so many countless others, forced to make the climb alone, with naught but his own two feet.

This was so similar. From a boy, counted out and growing up in squalor, to be raised by Liam Nothhelm to stand as one of his elite soldiers. Now he was an exiled Shieldsman, making the same climb thanks to Liam's widow. It was as if he'd grown close with her, against all odds, just for this moment; for a chance to save the kingdom when so much hung in the balance.

He peered to the right, over Oleander's head, through the fog and snow. She hunched over, breathing into her dress to stay warm, every step a struggle. The edges of the moons were passing across the sun now like a door closing, casting eerie darkness across the kingdom that grew deeper and deeper each second. Eyelids for Iam's world.

Torsten stopped.

"What is it?" Oleander asked softly.

"We're here." Now that it grew darker, he could see the glow of torchlight a short distance above. Indistinguishable voices carried on the wind as he propped Oleander up within a nook that protected against the wind. "Let me go first."

"And miss out on a chance to help end my detestable brother?" she bristled.

"I don't know what's waiting up there, but I do know what he did to you in my chambers. He's been trying some mad ritual to bring his goddess back all this time, and he'll stop at nothing. If I fail, you may be the only one left who can get close enough to him."

Oleander pursed her lips in anger, then her features softened. "Is it wrong that a part of me wants you to fail so that I can have the satisfaction?"

"I would expect nothing less. Stay here." He turned to leave, but she grabbed him.

"Torsten."

"Yes, My Queen."

"Don't let anything happen to my son. Do you hear me? He's all I have left, and after Redstar is gone, I know he'll be fine."

"On my life, the King will come to no harm."

She leaned up to whisper into his ear. "I always knew I could trust you, my dear, loyal Torsten." She pressed her ice-cold lips against his cheek. "I'm so sorry I didn't stand by you after you returned."

"I wouldn't have either." He held her at arm's length, and for the first time in his life, stared into her eyes without a sense of trepidation bubbling up from within. "Liam built this great country for us and for your boy. Today we take it back." He released her and slowly backed away. He'd had his doubts about her for a long time, but here she stood, braving deathly cold for the sake of the Glass. He knew it was likely a prayer, but he couldn't help feeling that after all the madness was over, she might become the Queen Liam always knew she could be, and not the one her people had come to hate and fear.

He believed in her, always had. And as he turned away and their gazes broke, he could tell she believed in him too. That was enough. He drew Salvation and pushed his aching limbs to finish the climb.

XXXI

THE DESERTER

Rand stopped at the corner where Poplar and Newton Streets intersected in South Corner. He followed the spread of a shadow across the dirt, up the wall of an old plaster building, to the moons passing over the sun. A silver glow reflected off the castle's glass spire and cast the city in an unnatural twilight.

The silence was unsettling. Most of Yarrington either sat before the base of Mount Lister, or they had returned home to be with their families to fast before the great feast that would occur when the sun rose the next morning. For a man of the Glass army, there was no more peaceful day, though Rand was usually with his sister by this time every year.

Rand closed his eyes and drew a deep, steadying breath. Remembering where he was and what he was doing, he let out the breath, and his heart plummeted. Torsten was free, and Rand and Codar had made it out of the Royal Crypt without a hitch. But he would never forget the bodies stuffed into graves by greedy dwarves, never to be found again. He'd recited a prayer for Childress and his family, and the others on his way up the construction lift, but he doubted Iam was listening. Not to him. He'd done all he could to rescue Torsten, to finish what he'd started, and now he found himself hoping Iam had turned His Eye away.

"Come, Rand," Codar said. "There is no time to waste."

"I'm just wondering how I got here," Rand said.

"Survival."

Rand opened his eyes and looked upon the callous, mustached man from Brekliodad. Not even his childhood nightmares could've provided such an unexpected situation.

"I don't give a rat's shog about that," Rand said.

"Not yours," Codar replied.

"Buried not dead!" a crazed, masked cultist of Nesilia screamed suddenly as he emerged from seemingly nowhere and raced by. "Buried not dead. Buried not dead!"

Rand spun to watch him, whispering, "What in Iam's name?"

The cultist danced around, continuing his chant, red robe sloshing through the snow, kicking up powder as he twirled and skipped.

A Glass soldier, wearing the mark of the city guard stepped to block the cultist's path. "Off the streets, devil," he ordered. "Just because we have to trust the Drav Cra means nothing for the likes of you."

The cultist stopped, tilting his head, but didn't respond.

"Did you hear me?" the guard questioned. He grabbed the cultist by the collar. "I said, get off the yigging streets. Show so resp—"

The cultist extended his arm, and a knife fell through his sleeve into his waiting hand. It all happened so fast the guard couldn't have done anything. The cultist jammed the knife between the laces of the man's armor. It sank deep into the man's side. "Buried, not dead," the cultist continued as if nothing happened, skipping, dancing, and cackling like a madman.

The guard folded over and clutched the wound. "Seize him!" he shouted to Rand, apparently noticing his armor.

Rand took a step toward the cultist—he couldn't help himself —but Codar tugged him back onto their course toward the gate and their freedom.

"There is nothing you can do," he said. "We must leave, now."

"I'm helping you, aren't I?" Rand bristled. "Valin said nothing about refusing to help othe—" Another cultist appeared from around a corner and drove a second knife into the back of the guard's neck.

"Iam's Light," Rand gasped. He ignored Codar and started off toward the man when, from the opposite direction, two more cultists emerged from an alley and kicked through a door into a shanty-home. The shrill cries of terror of those within gave Rand goosebumps.

Rand didn't think twice. He drew his sword, shoved by Codar, and stormed into the cottage. A cultist had a woman by the hair and dragged her across the floor directly in front of him. Her husband sat on a chair, head drooped back with his throat slit. Children huddled in the corner on the other side of the home, a second cultist bearing down on them.

"Unhand her!" Rand yelled.

The cultist turned his head. His hood was up, and his expressionless porcelain mask with a bloody tear beneath one eye and dark holes for seeing, shimmered with the hearth fire.

"Sacrifice for the Lady," the man hissed, then after a shrill laugh, he raised his knife. Rand darted forward, slicing off the man's arm before he could complete his attack. Rand's own sword found a home, plunging into the cultist's chest.

"My babies!" the woman shrieked.

Rand turned and saw that the other cultist had now cornered the children and was brandishing his dagger. Rand threw a chair out of the way and sprinted, but the cultist turned the dagger on himself and slit his own throat. Blood poured out onto the crying children, and the gargling corpse of the cultist thudded at Rand's feet.

The sight gave Rand pause, but he remembered his training. He recovered quickly and grabbed the children. "Hide in the pantry," he said. "All of you. Hide in there now and don't come out!" He gave a gentle push to get the crying children past their dead father into the arms of their mother.

"Thank you, Shieldsman," she whimpered, but she wasn't looking at Rand. She showered her children with kisses. "Thank you."

"Don't thank me," Rand said. "Just keep them safe."

Bedlam outside drew Rand back to the door where he found Codar already standing on the stack of boards they called a porch.

"You can't help them all, Rand," Codar said. He calmly wiped his dagger on his sleeve, staining it red. Another dead cultist lay a few meters away.

Rand looked past him. With the sun growing dimmer, cultists ran rampant throughout the district. Emboldened by the Drav Cra presence, or invited by Redstar himself, they sowed chaos in South Corner with so few on duty to protect its citizens. South Corner, Dockside, and the rest of Yarrington's poor district were mostly wood and thatch. Thick billows of black smoke hovered over the homes and shops, and a soft, flickering, orange glow painted the abnormally dark sky. The constant snowfall kept the blaze from spreading as it had in Winde Port. The cultists raced around, dozens of them, using the smoke for cover and causing mayhem—flipping parked trading carts, raiding shops for supplies only to dump them all over the streets.

It took Rand a few moments to find his voice. "How could this happen?" he asked.

"How could it not?" Codar said. "You people let a child rule because of his blood and expect peace?"

"This has nothing to do with the King. This is Redstar. I... I told you we needed to stop him first!"

"Is it? Redstar was imprisoned when your King decided to condemn the Caleef. Because of him, the rebels took Winde Port, only to be driven out by Redstar and hand him all the leverage he needed."

Rand didn't have an answer.

"In freeing the Caleef, Mister Tehr will undo the mistake made by lesser men and children," Codar said. "In Brek, it doesn't matter what family you're born into, only what's in here." He pointed to his head.

"There have been many mistakes."

Codar scoffed. "You Shieldsmen... you only ever see what's right in front of you!" He whipped around and flung his dirk right by Rand's head, so close it scraped his pauldron. Rand fell back against the wall of a building and was about to curse the Breklian, when the body of another cultist toppled over, bumping into him. The dirk sticking out from between his eyes caused his mask to crack in half upon impact, revealing the face of an adolescent boy.

"You asked why I'm here. I came to the Glass, sent by my father, to learn from the great Liam the Conqueror. Arrived to find him drooling on himself like a baby." Codar tore the blade out of the boy's skull, his tone agitated.

"Instead, I found Valin, a cripple born from shog," he went on. "And he's more a man than any of your kings or you worthless knights. Now let's go, and no more stopping to play hero. That's not your life anymore. He'll help you be better if you'd open your damn eyes."

Codar hauled Rand to his feet then set off around the building without another word. Rand took one more look at the pandemonium before following. The Breklian was right about one thing—Rand couldn't do anything about this. There was nobody to warn with so much of the city guard off duty, especially in South Corner. Eventually, someone would see the flames and rouse the city guards, but not before the devastation was exhaustive. And if Rand died fighting an unpredictable foe willing to kill themselves to sow terror, his sister would die with him.

He and Codar kept to the alleyways to avoid the brunt of the chaos. They stopped at an opening to a major avenue running along the city wall. "The southern gate is across the way," he said.

"Then let's get this over with." Rand went to move, but Codar grabbed his wrist.

"No, this is where I leave you," Codar said. "Your company awaits in a caravan by the gate. You'll have no trouble getting through, even with the rioting."

"I thought saving the Caleef was heroic since Valin wanted it? Now you run?"

"My face is known to the guards, and so I cannot come. Remember, Valin's role in this affair is one of ignorance. You know what happens to Sigrid should you do anything to change that, or should you fail."

Rand bit back his initial response. He was eager to escape the watchful eye of the heartless Breklian, so willing to wield Rand's sister's name like a weapon. "Tell your boss not to worry. I won't fail," Rand said. "But I have to ask. All this insanity—was it Redstar who inspired it, or was it our mutual friend?"

Rand turned to face Codar, but the Breklian was gone. When he looked back, a cultist stood before the alley staring at him from behind his mask. Rand's hand fell to the grip of his sword.

"Walk away," he warned.

The cultist didn't respond. Instead, he ran a rusty blade across his palm and attempted to use blood magic like a true warlock. The spell backfired, and he wound up setting himself ablaze.

"One for the Lady, one for the Lord!" He screamed as he ran by Rand, flailing his arms. The snow would have easily extinguished him, but he merely let himself burn.

Poor, lost souls...

Rand cringed and averted his gaze. He stepped out of the alley and focused on the summit of Mount Lister where, above it, the two moons had nearly come into alignment in front of the sun. The Dawning had arrived.

"End this madness, Sir Unger," Rand whispered, then set off for the southern gate at a brisk pace. He didn't have to search far to find the men he was looking for. A trading caravan sat before the closed portcullis. A dwarf stood on the back of the cart with a long red beard and eyes which looked two ways at the same time. He had an axe in hand, swinging madly at a group of looters bent upon taking advantage of the riots. Two heavily-armored human mercenaries stood on the street on either side of him, swords at the ready.

"Back ye fiends!" the dwarf shouted. "Ye ain't touchin a blood-soaked thing."

One of the humans swiped at a looter, but they didn't get close enough to attack.

"Do ye plan on helpin?" the dwarf shouted up to the guard tower above the arched gate. Two soldiers were on duty, aiming down over the ramparts with bows but not firing. Only the most inexperienced were put to work on the Dawning, and Rand could see the sweat glistening on their foreheads.

It was time to act like a Shieldsman again. Straightening his shoulders, Rand approached the caravan with his weapon drawn.

"Step back from those traders!" he barked at the looters. "In the name of the King."

The men offered him little regard. "A hand of Iam, come to set us straight," one of them sneered.

"Can't you see?" said another, gesturing toward the covered

sun, then the chaos overrunning the district. "There is no light to judge us now. Iam is gone."

A boom shook the earth as if in response to the man's words, like the quake which had preceded the splitting of the Royal Crypt and Pi's rebirth. Then there was a flash atop Mount Lister, blinding at first, then it appeared more like a vortex. Light and shadow, swirling, distorting all the air around it so even the eclipse wasn't visible.

All the city likely trembled in fear from the sight of the anomaly, but not Rand. He knew what it was: Redstar's dark magic corrupting the world because Torsten had made it out of the Glass Castle to face him down.

I should be at his side, he thought, anger mounting within him. But he'd put himself in this position. He directed that rage toward the looters and took a hard step toward them. They fled like the cowards they were.

"Ye better run!" the dwarf shouted. He hopped down from the back of the cart and approached Rand. "What in the name of Meungor's axe was that up there?"

"A chance to end this lunacy," Rand replied.

"Looks more like the opposite to me. Either way, I be glad we're gettin out of here. You must be the one Valin sent." The dwarf stowed a battle-axe a few sizes too large for him behind his back.

"He did."

"About time." He bowed. "Grint Strongiron at your service, Sir Knight."

Rand thought about correcting him, but he wasn't even sure if he should use his real name.

"That's Zane and Dorblo," Grint continued before Rand could respond. "Fine warriors, but barely got one brain between the two of em."

"Watch it, Grint," Zane said as the two mercenaries moved to the front of the cart where the horse waited. They looked so similar they could've been brothers, perhaps even twins.

Grint set his hands on his broad hips and stared back into the city. Rand joined him. Screams still echoed as the cultists' reign of terror endured. Far down the street, through a brush of smoke, Rand saw a guard chasing one who held what looked like a swaddled infant. Others flung torches through the stained glass windows of a South Corner chapel. Citizens flocked to the streets, sprinting in every direction, faces painted for a Dawning they would never forget.

It was the kind of unholy anarchy Shieldsmen trained for but never imagined they'd see.

"Bastards wouldn't open the gate, even when we were attacked," the dwarf said. "Care to prod them along before we wind up as sacrifices?"

All the screams blended, and in them, Rand could hear those of Tessa and the others he'd hung. All sounding so similar, desperate not to die when all hope seemed lost. Rand felt that familiar aching for a drink swell up in him. Anything to take the edge off; to help him abdicate his sworn duties to the Glass without guilt overwhelming him.

"Move yer arse, Shieldsman." Grint nudged him in the side. "Ain't no good, me dying here and not bein able to spend what Valin's payin."

Rand shook out his head and realized that he wasn't as helpless as he thought. Maybe he couldn't fight the rioters, but he could offer the people of South Corner and Dockside a way out. They were trapped within the walls like chickens in a coup filled with wolves.

"You!" he shouted up to one of the gate guards. "Open up and let these people out!"

"We ain't supposed to!" he replied, voice shaking. "City's on lockdown at night ever since the Caleef got out."

"In the name of the King and the King's Shield, open that gate and let these people out or there will be nobody left to fill this city!"

The guard ducked out of sight, and Rand swore inwardly. He couldn't blame them for not being prepared to handle such a dire situation—he didn't fare much better in his. He was about to climb the gate himself when the portcullis finally stirred, then started to rattle open.

"Well done." Grint slapped Rand on the back and climbed up onto the front of the caravan to take the reins. Either Zane or Dorblo—Rand didn't know one from another—offered to help him up, but he denied the man with a flurry of dwarven curses. "Ye comin?" he shouted back.

"One second." Rand turned back to the city and walked to the center of the snowy road. A cultist tried to scurry past, but Rand grabbed him by the robe and slammed him to the ground. "Flee the city!" he yelled. "Let them take your homes, but never your light! Run!"

All it took was one person to find sense in the pandemonium for Rand's orders to start spreading. "Run for the gate!" a woman cried out. "The gates are open!" shouted another. Then the handful of guards trying to impede rampaging cultists relayed the order.

It wasn't much, but it was the best Rand could do.

He jogged back and kept pace with the caravan as it rolled through the archway. People trickled through around them, out into the frozen farmland where they'd be safe as long as they kept away from the Drav Cra camps outside Yarrington's main entry. If Rand knew anything, it was that structures could be repaired, but horror lived in men forever, scratching away at their sanity, and all these cultists were after was madness. The more people who escaped that, the better off they'd be, homeless or not.

A young woman tripped on a rock on her way by, her baby tumbling from her arms. Rand knelt to pick up the crying infant.

"Rand Langley, the great deserter," someone said. "What is it Valin Tehr's got his hands into this time?"

Rand handed the baby over and helped the women up, then glared at the source of the voice. Captain Henry of the Dockside guard stood before the caravan with a group of Glass soldiers who looked like they might as well belong to Valin's gang as well. Grimy, hawkish, aching for a fight when they should be in the city helping the innocent.

"Dunno what yer talkin about," Grint said. "We be nothin but traders tryin to survive. Ye seen what's going on back th—"

"Shut your filthy mouth, dwarf!" Henry snapped.

The brother mercenaries stood out front of the horse, and their hands fell to the hilts of their swords. "Only we speak to him like that," one said.

"Would you really assault a captain of the Glass army?" Henry asked.

Rand hurried between them before things escalated and faced the guard captain he had served under so many moons ago. "Move aside, or you'll find out."

Henry grinned, half his teeth black and rotten. "You hear that boys? The Queen's hangman has decided to move up from hanging priests and handmaidens." The others laughed with him.

Rand didn't ask politely a second time. He unsheathed his sword and pointed it at the crooked captain. He knew it probably wasn't the smartest move, but the craziness at his back had his adrenaline pumping. "Do not test me. Not today."

Henry didn't back down. "How about you show me what's inside that there cart first?"

"Furs," Grint said.

"Don't have enough of that around here?" Henry nodded

toward the distant glow of Drav Cra campfires by the city's main gates.

"That's why we be leavin with them."

"You think you're smarter than me, half-pint?" Henry spat, stomping forward.

The mercenary brothers drew their weapons as well.

"Now," Henry said, "I ain't gonna ask again. Let me take a gander inside the caravan, and I'll see what we can do about letting you pass. No traders allowed to leave the city without inspection these days, haven't you heard?"

"You know we can't let you," Rand said. "So why don't you go back into the city and help the people you're sworn to?"

"Says the man who took a more sacred oath. Shouldn't you be helping them? No, instead you're here, deserting your people again. I saw those bodies you helped sling over the wall for our whore Queen. One of them was my baby cousin. A rotten scoundrel he was, but blood is blood."

"Step aside, or I'll show you blood," Rand said through clenched teeth.

"You going to make us carve through you? This ought to be good. By Iam, what could Valin possibly have in there? The Glass-yigging-Crown?"

"Like he said, just furs," one of the mercenaries repeated.

"Then what's there to hide? I can keep a secret. I saw Valin take the deserter here in right after he tried to murder the Prime Minister and didn't tell a soul. Just open it up and give us a stake, and we can all move on with our lives."

"One more word and the only person who'll get hurt is you," Rand said.

"I'd like to see you try." Henry stepped closer, not even bothering to reveal his weapon. "You aren't a killer, boy. You weren't when you were a guard, and you aren't now. You're a coward, hanging old men and women for made-up crimes."

He took another step, and Rand flinched without meaning to. The captain's words brought those memories he constantly fought so hard to keep down surging back in full force. The rope creaking, bodies swinging in the wind, Tessa...

"You won't touch a Glass soldier," Henry said. "You don't have the balls. So, move, you cowardly son of a whore, before someone gives you what you deserv—"

"Enough!" Rand screamed. He slashed the man's right leg and sent him to a knee, then kicked him onto his back. The other guards armed themselves and circled him, but Rand held his blade to Henry's neck. His hand quaked, the tip of his swords inches away from taking another Glassman's life. It took every ounce of his willpower not to let rage consume him and drive him to deal the killing blow.

Henry laughed through the pain. "See boys?" He stifled a grimace. "He doesn't have it in him to kill me. I'm not weak enough prey."

"You're plenty weak," Rand said, seething. He steadied his sword and glared up at the circling guards. "I may be done killing Glassman, but my employer isn't. You will go back and help the people of this city, or he'll hear about this." Rand turned his attention back to Henry. "I'm sure his giant would love a word with you."

For the first time, Henry's expression darkened. Rand tried not to show how much it stung him inside to speak those words— to finally claim out loud that no matter what the reason was, he worked for Valin Tehr now.

"Now get up." Rand grabbed Henry by the collar and dragged him out of the way of the caravan.

"Shouldn't we kill them?" Durblo asked quietly. "You know, just in case."

"These men won't say a word," Rand said. "I know cowards

when I see them, I've been one. Now, Captain, go and serve your people the right way while I tend to mine."

Henry's brow furrowed, and Rand realized what his words might sound like, that he'd betrayed the Glass Kingdom and now served a new monarch when really all he meant was Sigrid. Through everything, she was the only constant—the only person he had left. And if acting like a heartless mercenary under Valin's thumb was what it took to win her freedom, he'd become like Codar if he had to.

"Go!" he roared.

Henry's men scampered away. Two stopped to help Henry to his feet. "Valin may have your back now," the captain snarled, limping along. "But if I ever see you again, it'll be the end of you, deserter. I'll hang you off the shogging barrack's tower! You hear me!"

"Well done, knight," Grint said. The two mercenaries agreed.

Rand sheathed his sword while gazing back toward Yarrington. He hadn't noticed, but the strange anomaly atop Mount Lister had subsided, and now only Celeste blocked the sun on its descent behind the mountain. That meant that either Torsten or Redstar had finally claimed the other.

The reddish glow of fire hung over the city itself, pillars of smoke rising here and there. Most of the rioting seemed to keep toward South Corner and Dockside, where the guard presence was due to be lighter, especially with Henry and his men away. More frightened families poured through the southern gate, making Grint's caravan seem like it was just a part of the exodus.

Then Rand turned toward the road. He'd been on it before, but only this time did his heart race. Someone within the carriage pulled the tarp back and startled him. "They're gone, why are we still sitting around?" Bartholomew Darkings asked. He wore the familiar scowl of a nobleman who thought himself superior to everyone around him, like so many who occupied the Glass

Castle. In the back of the carriage, the Caleef sat, dressed in rags like an ordinary Shesaitju peasant. A muzzle covered his mouth, and his arms and legs were bound.

"Ye heard the man." Grint snapped on the reins.

As the rickety, wooden wheels turned, the sound of ropes creaking once again crept into Rand's head along with the desire for a drink. This time, he quickly silenced them. Instead, he pictured his sister's crooked smile, the way she snapped back at handsy drunkards, and more than anything, the way she never gave up on him. Failure to his Order, now a traitor to the Crown—but he refused to desert her.

"For you, Sig," Rand whispered to himself, "and only you," then he set off away from the only home he'd ever known, with a foreign king in tow.

XXXII

THE THIEF

Whitney swept through his cottage, tearing through the cupboards, checking under his hay-filled mattress looking for the map he'd been drawing for years now. He was about to flip the bed over in frustration when he noticed that the back window wasn't closed, rattling from a slight breeze.

He hurried over to it and checked the lock. Busted. He peered outside and saw that the grass leading up to it was disturbed, the barely visible path leading into the forest.

"Still sloppy, you little devil." He left the candle behind and went back outside. He didn't need light to find his old hiding place. "I knew I saw him—er, me—snooping around," he grumbled.

The path of trampled brush led through the forest to the creek, the same spot he and Kazimir had disposed of that thug's body what felt like a lifetime ago. It was the point exactly halfway between Whitney and Sora's homes where they met up nearly every day; where he had hidden so many of his prizes—as if there was anything to call a prize in Troborough.

Whitney saw the candlelight and slowed to a creep. If there was anything he knew he could do, it was sneak up on himself. He sneaked up behind a thick tree trunk and peered over at Young Whitney. Only he wasn't alone. He and Sora kneeled in the dirt side by side, pouring over Big Whitney's map.

"All right, you thieving whelp, give that here!" Whitney jumped out and shouted.

His younger self nearly leaped out of his shoes. Sora flinched, then reached down for the whittling knife strapped to her belt. Only, she had no intention to wield it against Big Whitney. Her hand was exposed, and the candlelight revealed a few pale scars. She hid it behind her back when she noticed hin looking.

So, Wetzel started training her even before I left? Whitney wondered how he'd missed that when they were together so often. Were kids really that oblivious?

"I knew you were a freak, Willis." The name dripped with venom off Young Whitney's lips, as if he somehow didn't realize they looked exactly the same. In fact, Big Whitney had shown no signs of aging in six years, and soon they'd be twins.

Young Whitney tossed the unfurled map onto the ground. It was a hand-drawn plan of Troborough with an amorphous barrier drawn around it. Arrows lined the entire thing with notes scrawled around the edges. Houses had **X**'s over them, the Twilight Manor, Gilly's tailor shop—all places he'd searched ceiling to cellar for a break in Elsewhere's barrier.

He'd grown up thinking Troborough was small, but when every inch had to be covered, it seemed endless. Still, after years there was nary a blank spot on the drawing. His next plan was to start climbing trees and searching higher up on the invisible barrier. Then there was that curious mental block anytime Whitney tried to go near Wetzel's shack as if Elsewhere was determined to keep him away.

"What in the name of the fallen gods is this?" Young Whitney hissed.

Whitney surrendered his position of power without thinking. He fell to his knees and gathered the map. It was only a matter of time before his troublesome younger self ran out of people to rob and turned to him.

"I've always known it was off, you showing up out of the blue one day and never leaving," Young Whitney went on. "What the yig do you want with us?"

"Relax, Whitney," Sora said. "I'm sure there's a perfectly good explanation."

Ever the optimist, Big Whitney thought.

There wasn't one. Even the truth seemed foolish after every conversation with Kazimir reinforced how pointless this project was. Luckily, Whitney had been preparing for just this moment.

"I was a cartographer before I came here," he said. "I do it to pass the time."

"Liar." Young Whitney ripped the map out from under him and held it up, earning a scolding from Sora for being cruel. He ignored her. "Look, right here. It says barrier. There isn't anything natural about that. You're with the Crown, aren't you? They're going to turn this place into a fortress before the Black Sands invade, aren't they?"

"I swear, I just make maps." He extended his hand for it. Young Whitney pulled it back, crumpling the edge.

"C'mon, Whit," Sora implored. "Look at his face. He's being honest."

"That's just because you're bad at reading people," Young Whitney said. "You thought my father was kind."

Big Whitney considered smacking his younger self before realizing he wasn't just doing it for Sora's sake, but for his father's—a man he'd spent a lifetime hating before watching the life drain slowly from his crippled body.

"Just give it back, and I won't tell your mother," Big Whitney said.

"You think I care what you tell her?" Young Whitney retorted.

Now Big Whitney was pushing his tongue against the back of his teeth to keep from shouting at the boy. The truth was, what happened to Rocco had only made Young Whitney more of a brat, unpleasant to be around even in the minimal time Big Whitney spent with him. He wasn't just a scamp, as Big Whitney admittedly was and had been, but he was an angry one. And Lauryn let him get away with pretty much anything... if he even showed his face around the farm, he never helped tend.

"If your father were around—" Big Whitney said.

"He isn't," Young Whitney snapped. "I thought you were protecting me when I was little, but I'm not so stupid now. You were up to something, taking credit like that, getting dad beaten. Now, this?" He raised the map in one hand and picked up his candle with the other. "You're going to tell me the truth, or I'm going to burn it."

"Whitney, you're being ridiculous," Sora said. "All he's done is help."

"And know your name somehow when he first arrived. Maybe you forgot that, but I haven't. If you never showed up that day, maybe they would have just taken it out on me. You weaseled yourself into our home, got rid of my father. Now you live next door. By the gods... have you been trying to get close with my mother, you sick freak?"

"Why does everyone keep thinking that?" Big Whitney said, and immediately wished he hadn't.

Young Whitney's face contorted with rage. It was then that Big Whitney realized this must have been bubbling up in his doppelgänger for years. That mistake his first day in Elsewhere, when he still thought Kazimir's words of caution were foolishness. He'd barely spoken a sentence to Young Whitney in years, hardly seen him, but seeing the map brought it all erupting to the surface.

"Look, I'm telling you the truth," Big Whitney said. "The map is worthless; it's just a hobby. There's no fortress, no plans, and I for sure have no feelings for your mother besides gratitude. I'm practically wedded to Alless from the Manor for Iam's sake!"

Iam's name drew a curious look from Sora. Most of the time, when he wasn't careful with his language in Elsewhere, people stared or repeated themselves on a loop. Not her. She simply looked confused.

"Then you won't mind if I do this?" Young Whitney said. He raised the candle to the corner of the parchment, and the flame took to it. "Too bad. This gods-forsaken place would be better off as a fortress."

"No!" Big Whitney yelped.

"Whitney what are you doing!" Sora shouted. She shoved by him, knocking him onto a pile of sticks. Without thinking, she sliced her palm on the whittling knife, then held it over the burning map. The fire leaped off it and into her palm where it dissipated. A few seconds later, the map lay on the ground, only the corner burned away.

Young Whitney stared at her, then the map, aghast. Big Whitney did the same. It'd been so long since he'd seen her blood magic it caught him off guard.

It took a moment for Sora to grasp what she'd done. "Whitney, I..." she said.

"You can..." Young Whitney said at the same time.

"I can explain."

"Is anyone honest around here?" Young Whitney glowered at Big Whitney one more time, then stormed off into the forest.

"Whitney, wait!" Sora called after him and followed.

Big Whitney kneeled by the map he'd spent so many tireless

hours crafting. Ashes from it brushed against his cheek, carried on the wind.

"What game is this now?" he said. He swore he'd locked his pantry same as any other day. And he'd made the lock, which meant it was far beyond his younger self's skills to pick and it hadn't been broken. A quarter of his hard work, ruined. Months of labor, as if Elsewhere were telling him to stop seeking passage.

He clutched it against his chest. "I'm trying my best," he whispered. "Isn't that enough?" Nothing and nobody answered—not even Kazimir appeared behind him as the wraithlike upyr often did when he lost his way—only silence. All he could be sure of was that his insistence on searching for holes in the barrier had caused Young Whitney to witness Sora's blood magic, something he'd never done until years after leaving Troborough.

What it meant, he wasn't sure. All he could do was brace himself and hope that the history he knew hadn't strayed too far this time.

"Whitney!" Sora shouted again as Young Whitney disappeared into the brush.

Whitney sighed, folded the map and tucked it into his pocket, sighed again, then stood. He lightly jogged after them, knowing he needed to give them a chance to work things out. If he'd seen Sora use blood magic at their age, after all that time knowing he'd been lied to, he would not have been okay.

He shoved his way past sharp branches, swatting them as they poked and scratched at his face and arms, but he continued.

"This part of your game?" Whitney whispered at the sky. "Fallen god bastards. Where's Iam when you need him?"

The terrain dove into a steep slope down a hillside coated in years worth of rotting leaves. Whitney slid a bit, but it was on purpose. Surefooted as a goat, he used stumps and roots to slow his descent.

"Whitney!" Sora shouted up ahead. The boy's head twitched

slightly, almost turning around, but instead, he hopped a few rocks to the other side of the stream. Sora followed.

Little bastard is fast. It was a poor choice of words, what with Rocco's passing.

He wasn't real!

But he was, and that meant Young Whitney was every bit as real as Big Whitney was. This was his world now as much as he resisted it. As he got closer, Sora caught up to Young Whitney. Big Whitney crouched behind some bushes within earshot to give them a bit of privacy—but only a bit.

"Were you planning on telling me you were a gods-damned witch?" Young Whitney asked.

"Witch?" Sora looked hurt. "I'm not a witch. I can do a little blood magic, that's all."

"Right, and old Mrs. Dodson only drinks a little."

"That's not fair, Whitney." Sora pointed her finger. "I would have told you, but I knew you'd act exactly like this."

"Well, aren't you some kind of a genius? You knew that if your best and only friend in the world found out you'd been lying to him for, how long? A year? Two? Ten? You just somehow knew he'd react in a completely normal and rational way. Bravo." Whitney clapped his hands slowly.

"You're a real piece of shog, you know that?" Sora punched Whitney in the arm, and this time it wasn't playful. "It's not like I chose this, you know."

"Oh, someone forced you to cut yourself and throw fireballs?"

"That's not what I meant. You have parents—"

"Had."

Sora growled. "You're insufferable. You know what I meant! My parents died so long ago I don't even know what they looked like. Do you know I don't even know their names? Wetzel is all I've ever had, and he's taught me a few ways to protect myself. Take care of myself."

"It's a good thing he did. If he's *all you ever had*, then I guess I'm not needed anymore. Good luck with your life, Sora."

Sora grabbed hold of his tunic, but he yanked it away then turned around and said, "It's too late. You're the only reason I stuck around in this gods-forsaken town, and even you can't be honest with me."

"Oh, c'mon Whitney, you know that's not what I meant."

"It's all a yigging joke."

"What?"

"Life. My mom won't scream at me no matter what I do or how much she wants to. Her *employee's* a fraud. Everyone remembers my dad as this kind, loyal man, and now you. Nobody's honest, nobody cares. Why should I?"

"Whitney…"

"No, I can't take it anymore." And with that, Whitney took off, scaling the cliffside.

"Whitney, wait!" Sora shrieked, tears welling in the corners of her eyes.

"It's too late, knife-ear. Goodbye."

Hearing that term seemed to stop Sora in her tracks. "Fine, go you selfish child!" Sora screamed. "You think your father was cruel, you're so much worse you're a… a" She threw her hands up in frustration then ran directly toward Big Whitney. She was so distracted she didn't even see him, but he could see the shimmer of tears on her cheeks.

That little shog-faced prick.

As soon as Sora passed, Whitney made his way for the small cliff. His fingertips found a jutting rock, and he started the climb. Fire stirred inside of him. He imagined this was how Sora felt anytime she called upon Elsewhere. It was like molten lava burning a hole in his chest, begging to escape by any means necessary.

The wall was smooth, but he found plenty of hand and

footholds. It would have challenged most, but it was easier than scaling the Whispering Wizards tower, and he'd done that carrying the Splintering Staff in his teeth on the way back down. Close to the top, he felt something pelt his shoulder. Figuring it was just a stone bouncing down from above, disturbed by Young Whitney or an animal, he kept going. Then he felt another and another. The fourth one hit him squarely on the head.

"Hey!" he shouted, looking up to see Young Whitney throwing rocks down at him. "Cut it out!"

"Then leave me alone, freak," Young Whitney yelled back. All his talk of leaving yet he hadn't made it far. "This is none of your business."

"You, have, no…" Whitney huffed, throwing his leg up and rolling onto the clearing, "…idea, how wrong, you are."

"This isn't about you," Young Whitney said. "You can go back to your little house on my farm and finish out your days doing gods-know-what with my mom. I'm done. This place is shog, and I'm through living in it."

He turned to walk away again, and Big Whitney grabbed his shoulder.

"Geez, kid, just stop for a second," he said, still panting. "You're acting like a lunatic."

Young Whitney stopped but didn't turn around. His shoulders heaved like he was holding back rage.

"You don't want to do this," Big Whitney said. "Trust me."

"Why's that?" he barked, whipping back around. There was something about his eyes, something violent and unrestrained.

Big Whitney raised his hands, palms out. "Just calm down, and you'll see reason."

"Reason? I see reason better than ever before. This place is worthless. The people are worthless liars. There's something more out there, and I'm going to find it. Something real."

"I get that," Whitney said. "More than you could ever understand, I get it. But here's the thing… it's going to seem like a good idea for a while. A long while, really. Truthfully, up until right now."

"What are you talking about?"

"Leaving here. The world is amazing. I've seen more than I could fit in a million books. Dwarves, dragons, big, strange octopus-looking things called wianu, giants, giant women."

"What is your point?"

"My point is that nothing in this world is more important than what you have right here, right now."

"Which is what? A mom who's been broken since dad died? I have exactly one friend here, and she's been lying to me for ages. Why shouldn't I leave?"

"You love her," Big Whitney said.

"You'd better yigging take that back."

"Why can't you just admit it?"

Young Whitney, who Big Whitney had to admit wasn't very young anymore, drew his fist back to punch. Whitney had always been fast—that was what being a thief was all about—but farming for so long made him strong as well. His hand snapped up and his fingers closed around Young Whitney's balled fist.

"Stop it," Big Whitney said, but the boy kicked at him instead. Big Whitney scooped under his leg, still holding his fist and lowered him to the ground. Young Whitney thrashed.

"I don't want to hurt you."

"Well, I want to hurt you, home wrecker," Young Whitney said.

"You're out of your mind," Big Whitney said through his teeth as he struggled to hold the boy down. "Mother—your mother is not my type. She's… old."

"She's like your age, shog-breath."

Whitney flipped the boy over onto his stomach and wrenched his arm behind his back, pulling it up with a sharp jab.

Young Whitney screamed.

"If I let you go, will you stop attacking me?" Big Whitney asked.

He didn't respond, but Whitney took it as a 'yes.' Before releasing him, Big Whitney slapped the boy hard in the side of the head. "Don't you ever call her knife-ear again, do you understand me?"

Young Whitney clenched his jaw.

Big Whitney hit him again. "Yes?"

"Yes," Young Whitney said reluctantly.

"Yes, sir?"

"Suck shog."

Big Whitney laughed and let the boy go. He rolled away the moment he was free, then sprung to his feet, defensive.

"You gonna leave me alone now?" Young Whitney asked.

"Not a chance," Big Whitney said.

"What are you really doing here, *Willis*?"

"Clearly, the gods sent me here to make sure you don't make the same mistakes I did and run from here, you worthless piece of shog."

"Gods, huh?" Young Whitney scoffed. "I heard you talking about Iam. No one talks about Iam here. Not even Father Drimmond. So, you show up talking about that evil bastard, you've got a map of our town with **X**'s marked all over it, you kill my dad—"

"I didn't kill your father."

"Whatever," he continued. "He wouldn't have died if you hadn't interfered."

"He wouldn't have died if you didn't steal that crown!"

"Crown? What yigging crown?" Young Whitney asked. "It was a necklace. I knew it, man, you're crazy."

That gave Whitney a reason to pause. Was he crazy? Was he imagining this? At the start of this adventure into death, he'd believed he was dreaming. Was he right and had never woken up?

"You some kind of Shieldsman?" Young Whitney asked.

Whitney laughed harder than he remembered doing since before Sora exiled him. The thought of wearing that ridiculous costume like Torsten. He wiped a tear from his eye and said, "You've got no idea how funny that is."

"Well, your story makes no sense. So either start talking about why you really want me here or I'm walking."

Big Whitney considered telling him everything but worried what might happen if he did.

"Okay, fine." Young Whitney turned to walk away again.

"I'm you!" Big Whitney blurted, forcing the boy to turn back.

Young Whitney's head tilted. All the anger fled his eyes, instead replaced by a blank stare that Whitney found far more chilling. "What does that mean?" his younger self said. "What does that mean?" It wasn't the first time Whitney heard someone in Elsewhere respond on a loop and it rarely, if ever, meant anything good was about to happen. "What does that mean?"

"Not really, I mean," Big Whitney clarified. "I've made the same dumb mistakes you have. I told you I had a friend named Sora. She was more than a friend, way more, and I left her just like you're planning to leave yours."

Young Whitney's head straightened and his eyes refocused. "We aren't like that."

"I've seen how she looks at you." It was true, and Whitney couldn't believe he'd never seen it when he was younger. "Shog, kid, I've seen the way you look at her."

"Like I said, crazy."

"If you don't have feelings for her at all, then go back there and tell her goodbye. For real. Tell her you're going off on some grand adventure to see the world, that you'd rather run away from your problems than face them. Tell her this is for the best. Do it. I dare you."

Young Whitney blew out a breath. "You're a dick." He shook his head and started back on his path to wherever the wind was going to take him.

"You can't. Because it'll hurt too much."

Big Whitney watched for a few seconds. The Elsewhere barrier was just beyond a large tree, and Young Whitney was about to pass through it.

"Coward," he said.

"Liar," Young Whitney replied.

And with that, Young Whitney crossed through the barrier. Whitney watched as light coruscated across the now rippling surface of the transparent wall which he now saw stretched over the whole town like a dome.

As the barrier undulated, Whitney caught a glimpse of something beyond it, darkness unlike any he'd seen before in his life, and then as quickly as it started, it ended, leaving only eerie silence.

He thought about Sora, both Soras. He'd just had to witness one of them experience the same heartache his own must have when he'd been the petulant, selfish child who couldn't even gather enough guts to say a proper goodbye. Sadness—no, not sadness... that word wasn't nearly strong enough. Sorrow filled every pound of him. Six years. It took six years in this shogpile to figure out a lesson as simple as how horrible a human being he had been.

A sudden shift made Whitney's heart leap and his stomach flip. No longer was he surrounded by thick trees and the sound of a bubbling brook, but instead, he found himself on the bank of the Shellnak River. He looked over each of his shoulders in turn, searching for something, anything to tell him what had just happened.

After a moment, he realized he was standing in the same place he and Kazimir had arrived so many years ago, but the remnants of the Ferryman's boat were no longer there.

Did I do it? Did I escape Elsewhere?

Hope flooded over him, enveloping him like a warm blanket. He turned and saw Mount Lister practically sparkling in the distance. Puffy, white clouds frolicked along against a sky painted bright blue. Then, something happened. The blue sky darkened, turning a harsh shade of reddish-purple. The clouds disappeared. Loutis stained the sky alone, pale and pathetic as ever.

"No, no, no," Whitney said, the rush of hope drowned by despair. "No, no, no, no, no, no, no, no, no, no, no, no."

He heard footsteps shuffling behind him. Thinking it to be Kazimir, appearing as usual in the worst moments, he spun. Instead, he saw a small, familiar boy with tawny brown hair, wind-swept and dirty.

"No, no, no, no, no."

"Welcome to Troborough!" the boy exclaimed, his features bright, life not yet turning him into a hateful prick.

"No way," Whitney said. He rushed forward, placed the palm of his hand on Even-Younger-Whitney's head, and shoved him to the side "Out of my way shog-for-brains."

"Excuse me?" the boy said, his voice already far in the distance.

Whitney knew exactly what he needed to do. His map, which he could still feel in his pocket, was covered in marks and Xs, but there was one place he was saving for last. The one place Elsewhere seemed to refuse him access.

Wetzel's shack stood at the base of a tiny hill. Whitney crossed a field of yellow daffodils, small bugs stirring with each step.

"Hey, mister!" Young Whitney shouted. "You don't want to go there!"

"Yeah, I really do, kid," Whitney called back over his shoulder.

"You don't want to go there! You don't want to go there! You don't want to go there!" The boy's word echoed over and over again, and it just kept going as Whitney got closer to the hut.

Again, his body froze outside the shack, every muscle unable to press forward. He fought, but nothing happened. He remembered Kazimir's warning, "You don't carve your own path here."

But Kazimir was wrong. Kazimir had damned himself to this place, Whitney hadn't. Besides, where was the upyr now?

Whitney did the only thing he could think of. He didn't have faith in gods or goddesses; he'd never needed them before. All he knew was all those many years ago he'd made a mistake, and his mistake hurt the only person who'd ever truly mattered to him.

"Sora!" Whitney shouted. "Sora!"

He summoned whatever strength he had in his body, and farming had made him sturdy as an ox. Still, it took every ounce of his energy to lift his left leg. But it moved. Ever so slightly, it moved.

That gave him hope again. He reached deep inside of himself, pushing away all thoughts of Iam or any other god. He thought only of reaching Sora again. His right foot lifted and he placed it down, one step closer.

"Ha!" Whitney shouted loud enough for Yarrington to hear— if there was a Yarrington in Elsewhere. "Suck shog, gods!"

Behind him, he could still hear the boy saying, "You don't want to go there!" on repeat. But Whitney did.

He focused and moved his other foot. He did it, again and again, until he stood right at the threshold of Wetzel's shack. He considered knocking but didn't care. It wasn't even real Wetzel. He'd seen that the barrier of this realm extended all the way across the sky. If there were any connection between Elsewhere and Pantego, it would be in that shack where Sora had grown up. It was the only place he hadn't looked.

He reached down, turned the knob, and the door opened.

Inside, there was nothing at all.

No tables, no chairs, no stacks of strange tomes, no bed, no potions. Nothing at all.

Whitney's chin hit his chest.

"Whitney?" came a voice from behind him.

As he turned, he saw the spectral form of a Panpingese woman, more beautiful and radiant than anything he'd ever seen before. Her long, dark hair fell just past her shoulders, her eyes practically glowed, amber like the sun.

"Sora?" he said. "Sora!"

Whitney tried to move again, but he was stuck. He pushed but still couldn't budge.

"Sora!" he screamed again.

"You could have told me the truth," Sora said, her voice distant, floating on air.

"What? What do you mean? Sora, I knew you didn't forget about me! Oh, gods." He squeezed his eyelids shut, worried he was seeing things. When he opened them again, she remained in front of him. "Sora, I know you didn't mean to do this, but only you can get me out!"

"Did he know?" Sora said.

Whitney looked over his shoulder at Wetzel's shack, not understanding. "Did who know?"

"At least he never lied."

"You're right, I'm sorry. I've lied to about so much. But I want you to know the truth. How I fee—"

"In time?" she interrupted.

"No," Whitney said, "Now. Just get me out, and I'll tell you everything. I'm so sorry." He ran to her and went to embrace her, but his arms passed right through.

"Forgiveness?"

Whitney spun back to her. Her face grew angry and then suddenly, her form disappeared and in its place was just a charred patch of grass. Whitney was suddenly free to move again and fell to his knees, clawing at the ground, tears flowing more freely than he'd ever remembered.

"Why!" he sobbed, staring down. "Sora, come back to me. Sora!" He looked up to the bloodstained sky. "What kind of sick game is this!" he screamed.

He heard the shuffling of feet, expected to see Kazimir, and then Younger Whitney appeared before him. All this bedlam he'd been causing was bound to bring Kazimir around and beg him to stay calm so he can remain on his vacation, but it was clear to Whitney now. That conversation they'd had, and that deal—the upyr only made it because his time in Elsewhere was over. He was gone... free.

The thought of Kazimir getting to leave despite all the awful things he'd done made Whitney even angrier. Sure, they'd moved on from being enemies, he was the only thing he had here, his only connection to the real world. Big Whitney gritted his teeth and began to rise, his head lifting first. He was done playing Elsewhere's games.

"You bring her bac—"

Whitney's words were cut short as he saw the boy, no longer the boy. His face looked as if it were melting like wax under a hot flame. Beneath the pink flesh that had been, there was dark, blood red, scaly hide. Blood poured down his face from two holes in his forehead where horns were growing. He showed his teeth, sharp, long, needle thin.

Whitney fell back on his hands and crab crawled backward until his head slammed against the door of Wetzel's shack.

"Whitney, you stupid man," his deformed doppelgänger said, voice now so deep Whitney could feel it in his bones.

"What… what are you?" he asked as if he didn't already know. Churches of Iam and cults depicted enough demon spirits of Elsewhere for him to take a guess at what one might look like.

"That does not matter anymore. You've been so concerned about what the barrier was keeping in," the demon said, approaching him, "that you've failed to wonder what it might be keeping out. Heragi, God of Misfortune had his fun with you in this realm of mischief, but the will of fire has broken the barrier, and I've had my eyes on you since you fled Troborough. A heartless thief like you deserves torture far worse than this."

Wetzel's shack suddenly exploded from within throwing Whitney into the river. Wood splintered like arrows, some piercing his flesh. A deafening sound so horrific it belonged in nightmares filled the sky, making all other sounds nonexistent. Whitney couldn't even hear himself breath. He rose to his feet, knees shaking.

Demons, hundreds of them, all unique but equally terrifying, poured out of the rupture beneath the shack. They gathered behind the demon that was Young Whitney. One had more eyes than Whitney could count, blinking all at once. A sharp, hooked beak protruded from another's face. And yet another appeared like a goat with ears and tusks like a mammoth.

A blinding light flashed somewhere beyond the town square. Whitney chanced looking away from the horde to see something bright white and in the shape of an Eye of Iam. Dozens of figures moved around within the light, but Whitney couldn't make any of them out.

He tried to speak, but nothing came out. He looked back to the demons.

The one who was Young Whitney smiled, each needle-like tooth digging into its own flesh and producing pinpricks of blood. "Run."

XXXIII

THE MYSTIC

In so many ways, Wetzel hadn't done his job to prepare Sora for the world at large. Sure, she knew there were beasts and evil—but never could she have imagined the kind of evil she'd faced with Whitney and Torsten these last few months. Sora had never been in trouble with the law before Whitney. She hadn't even been in deep trouble with Wetzel other than the time she'd set one of his bookshelves ablaze while practicing blood magic.

Presently, she stood outside a dark room that resembled the one Lord Aran Bokeo had taken her to beneath his bookstore. The mystics had their servants carry her from the Well of Wisdom to the highest floor of the tower, where it tapered to fit only a single, circular room. She was too exhausted to protest, both in mind and body. Summoning enough fire to rupture her bar guai, seeing into the past—it was a struggle just to stay upright, let alone fight.

The servants placed Sora on her feet just within the threshold and dared not go further. She caught Kai's eye as he turned to leave. The gravity of his expression was enough for her to know she was in trouble. He nodded to her as if offering good luck, but said nothing as he and the others left.

Two huge doors slammed shut behind her and startled Sora forward. A bridge led her to a circular dais in the center surrounded by rushing water. Floating, blue torches lit alongside it as she went. When she reached the platform, the bridge disappeared.

Statues of those same creatures Lord Bokeo had called wianu jutted out from the red walls, spitting water from a slit of a mouth. Their two giant eyes, all fashioned from gems more precious than Sora had ever seen, although unmoving, sparkled with the pride of life. She hadn't noticed in the other chamber, likely because the waters didn't rage like this, but tendril-like appendages thrust up from the surface, creating white foam breaks.

Aihara Na, leader of the Secret Council of Mystics, and the most frightening woman Sora had ever met—Queen Bliss included—sat on her throne. Seven others dotted the perimeter of the dais, each with its own yellow-robed mystic seated atop except one. They no longer shrouded their faces with hoods. She recognized Madam Jaya and Master Huyshi, and the others whose names she didn't know. They all looked different, yet had a sameness—an ageless quality, even though some looked no younger or older than Sora and yet others, gray and withered.

Maybe it was their eyes, holding all the wisdom of every mystic come and gone, both calming and terrifying at the same time.

Scary as the Council might've been, Sora refused to cow before them. They'd held back far too much and lied about far more. Even now, she could feel defiance growing once again. She wished she had Aquira with her, wished she could command her little wyvern friend to shoot forth and burn them all to a crisp, but she hadn't seen Aquira since fainting of exhaustion outside the Well of Wisdom.

Aihara Na steepled her fingers, elbows pressed firmly into the fabric of her armrests. Those ageless eyes looked over her over-long fingertips, calculating.

Sora took a deep breath to steady herself for the verbal onslaught she knew was coming.

"Sora of Troborough," Aihara began, "you are brought here before—"

"Why don't you call me by my real name?" she interrupted. She couldn't help herself. Seeing the mystics again now that she'd had time to collect her thoughts caused the words to cascade off her tongue like a waterfall pounding against the rocks with unbridled fury. She was too weary to be coy. "Is it Nothhelm? Sumati?"

"Silence!" Madam Aihara Na bellowed as she stood from her throne and took two steps forward. Each footfall which was previously silent, now sounded like a thunderclap, resonating through Sora's very soul. "You stand here, guilty of willful rebellion against the Secret Council—"

"Rebellion? I don't remember swearing allegiance to anyone."

"If you open your mouth out of turn one more time, I will seal it shut permanently, is that understood? No, don't respond. Just stay silent." Madam Aihara returned to her throne, and this time Sora listened. The Mystic fell into her grand seat and waited a few long, calculating seconds before speaking again. "Your open *rebellion*, disregard for rules, and disrespect of our most sacred ritual place you before us for judgment. How do you plead?"

"Plead?" Sora asked. "I plead taken advantage of. Used by the mystics and lied to for reasons I do not understand."

"You were never lied to," Madam Jaya spoke up. "You simply weren't ready to know."

"It's all the same." Sora almost felt sorry for snapping at the mystic who'd she'd spent so much time training with, but she didn't let it stop her. "I spent my entire life wondering who I was, who my parents were. I... how long were you going to wait to tell me? Until I was over a century old?"

"Half a year ago, who were you?" Aihara continued. "No one. You were little more than some heathen blood mage holed up beneath some backwoods town's crazy healer's shack."

"You know nothing of Wetzel or Troborough."

"Final warning," Aihara said, drawing her fingers across her lips like a zipper.

"The Well of Wisdom is not some trinket to trifle with, yet you treated it as such," Aihara said. "You have opened your mind to the deepest depths, a veritable chasm of knowledge, and you've tainted the waters with your uneducated thoughts and frivolous human attachments like that to this... Whitney Blisslayer who fills your mind."

Sora felt the air flee her lungs. Now, words didn't come to her. She still hadn't told any of them about Whitney.

Madam Aihara paused, her lips tightening to a thin line, yet the corners pulled just barely. "You act surprised?"

"It's just... I..."

"Did you not think Madam Jaya would tell her superior of your dealings with the upyr?"

"I didn't think anything," Sora said, "but I made no mention of anyone but him." She looked to Madam Jaya, her instructor, whose expression betrayed her disappointment.

"Our vision pierces time and flesh," Madam Jaya said. "We've known all along what tethers you, what keeps you from dedicating yourself to this order. You must understand, Sora. Whitney is dead. Forever gone. Nothing you can do will bring him back."

"You're wrong," Sora said, despite the previous two warnings.

"Insolent girl." Aihara raised her hand, swiping it hard in one direction. Even from so great a distance, several meters away,

Sora felt the slap against her face. Her cheeks grew hot as burning embers.

"Death is the nature of Elsewhere," Aihara said. "It is the other side which every living being in this world fights to stay away from until the fight leaves them. It is why only death can bridge the realms."

Sora pushed off the cold stone and returned to her feet. "I don't believe you."

"You dare question the Ancient One?" a mystic she hadn't met snapped.

"No, no. Ghing, let her speak. Perhaps she, in her short time on this world uncovered some great truth we've missed all these *centuries*."

"You said sacrifice was necessary to open Elsewhere, but I've done it without loss," Sora said.

"I've already told you, that was the upyr's doing, not your own, child," Madam Jaya said.

"I didn't tell you the whole truth."

"Tell me then, Sora, what do you think happened?" Madam Jaya said. She didn't even look disappointed anymore. Sora saw pity on the woman's face.

Sora recounted the story aboard Kazimir's ship, how she'd sent both Whitney and Kazimir to Elsewhere before the upyr could kill him.

"You do not call that a sacrifice?" Aihara said. "Come, now, Sora. You've been grasping to willow branches in the middle of the Boiling Waters."

"At least I'm being honest!" Sora yelled. "I didn't kill anyone. Both Kazimir and Whitney still live within that place, I just... I know it."

"It was because of the upyr, Sora," Madam Jaya said.

"You saw them?" Madam Aihara said, ignoring Jaya.

Sora nodded.

"Then they have passed into that gods-forsaken realm," Aihara Na said. "They are gone, Sora, and it is high time you come to terms with it." She steepled her fingers again. "And even if they do live, what makes you so certain the gods would let them return if even they themselves cannot?"

A response died on the tip of Sora's tongue. She hadn't thought much about how to remove them once she'd opened the portal to Elsewhere. Call it blind faith, but she was sure things would come together once the deed was done.

"Many of us have sacrificed deeply for you, Sora Sumati," Aihara Na said. "Even your friend Aquira clings to life in your room after you forced her to nearly drain her body of flame. Without Madam Jaya's healing, she surely would have died."

Sora looked at Madam Jaya. Her teacher hung her head.

"I know what you saw in the Well," Aihara Na said. "How can you not understand how dangerous it is to resist Elsewhere now that you know?"

The news about Aquira caught her off guard, but Sora closed her eyes and tried to focus. She couldn't back down now. "It's different. I was still here, not in Elsewhere."

"Our entire Order crumbled because you were born when Elsewhere should have claimed you!" Aihara's voice made the room quake. "Your mother gave her life in your stead. She opened herself to Elsewhere and in doing so roused a fallen Goddess, inspiring the one called Redstar to cause so much death in the West. Even Liam, the man responsible for our ruin, died for you. An Order of hundreds, and now only seven. We've gone to great stakes to hide you away because my master—your mother— begged us to protect you. You think Wetzel was a stranger to us?"

She'd figured out by now that they knew him, but she had no idea how. "He was a mystic?" Sora asked, hopeful.

"Gods, no." Aihara looked aghast. "He was a student who

outgrew the tower. He was headstrong, broke rules, and tried to take a shortcut with blood magic. We exiled him. Then, after your birth signaled our destruction, we needed someone we could trust. Someone right under Liam's nose where he would never think to look if he decided to end his curse by killing you, and where we wouldn't be tempted to bring you here before you were ready."

"Clearly, we didn't wait long enough," the mystic named Ghing chimed in.

"Or too long," said Huyshi.

"We knew Wetzel would do anything to earn our trust again," Aihara went on. "You see, rule breakers can still receive redemption from the Council."

"He died without knowing he did," Sora said, a harsh edge creeping into her tone. She took a moment to calm herself lest she earn more punishment.

"He continued to pursue blood magic against our wishes, and so, tainted you." Aihara stood.

"Did he know?" Sora asked abruptly.

"About who you are? Of course not." Hearing Aihara scoff in dismissal only served to fuel Sora's frustration. "All he knew was to look after a gifted child and impart what little knowledge he could."

"At least he never lied." She found relief in knowing he was ignorant. She was as close to the old codger as he would let anyone get to him, but he still raised her, opened up her mind. She couldn't bear the thought of being lied to by him as well.

"Sora, you miss the lesson. Wetzel betrayed us as you did, but forgiveness remains for those who atone. Even for you, who stole Madam Sumati, my master, from this world, stole even her name. But life itself was not your choice, and for that, you will not be punished any differently than any other apprentice who once walked these halls."

Sora shook her head. "I saw what happened. You did this. You allowed me to live. You killed Madam Sum—my mother—" Just saying it made her feel strange all over. "You cursed King Liam."

Aihara raised her hand and squeezed her fist. Sora's legs flew out from under her, and she slammed into the ground. Madam Jaya had to look away. The pain made Sora feel the familiar surge of Elsewhere, but along with it, her seared chest. The place where the bar guai rested throbbed. The ruptured fire amulet had left a dark, charred patch of skin between her breasts.

"You will not speak of the atrocities you saw within the Well of Wisdom again," Aihara said. She took several booming steps toward Sora. "You didn't see with eyes of understanding. Your refusal to wait until ready made sure of that. I did not kill your mother. I loved her like any student should their master. She gave her soul up to Elsewhere, siphoning her life away in sacrifice until even this pathetic, spectral form was beyond her."

Aihara extended a hand to grasp Sora's, but it passed right through. She turned her back and drew a long, beleaguered breath.

"Helping my master preserve your life when I knew it was against everything we believe in is my greatest regret," Aihara said, "but it is also why I refuse to give up on you. It is clear to me now that much of the fault in your disobedience lies with us. We should not have rushed you, especially after leaving you with a disobedient former student like Wetzel."

"You could have told me the truth," Sora said. She knew she should fight the anger swelling in her, but she was too tired. Nobody answered her remark. The mystics all remained still and silent except Huyshi who nodded meekly like he agreed with her.

"I tried to teach you the importance of patience," Madam Jaya said after a short while. "I should have tried harder Sora, and that is my failure as well."

"Should you choose the road to forgiveness, vowing to obey

even the smallest command of this Council, to let go of this…
mortal, Whitney, and forsake your endeavors to bring him back,
we will allow you to remain within these walls as a servant. You
will watch, observe and learn what it means to be a member of
this Order. In time, when we think you are ready, you will be
permitted to resume your training in the mystic arts."

"In time?" Sora said, incredulous.

"Yes. We hoped Wetzel would have you more prepared for the
mystic studies, but we were wrong. He led you astray, but at the
very least, he kept you alive and in a time when our allies were
few, that was enough. When you are many years older and wiser,
should your wisdom allow you to make better choices, we will
revisit this council."

"It is a great honor, Sora," Huyshi said. "You are young,
younger than most we ever took on in the golden days of the
Order. Age will refine you. The fault of rushing you lies with us."

"He's right, Sora," Madam Jaya added. "Under your mother,
any who violated the Well of Wisdom would have been exiled,
or worse."

Aihara stopped pacing and stared straight into Sora's eyes.
"Do you accept forgiveness, Sora Sumati?"

Sora's brow furrowed. She stared back at Ancient One Aihara
Na, a thousand different responses bouncing around her head. Her
entire life, she sought a place she could fit in. She hoped more
than anything it could be this tower, once filled with people
touched with the same Gift as her. Now, she felt more alone and
out of place than ever before.

She couldn't help but imagine what Whitney would have said
to people like this, who would have tied him down and kept him
from the world—from adventure.

"Forgiveness?" she said, voice dripping with indignation. "I
don't know why you think I need to receive forgiveness. You

people have access to truth and you horde it away for yourselves. When I got to Yaolin, I wondered why my people seemed so content to live under their conquerors, but I see it now. You think that what I saw in the Well was corrupted, but I think you're wrong. I saw you, forcing our people to fight a war they no longer wanted to, and I saw my mother protecting them."

Aihara bit her lip. "Careful what you say next, girl."

"You've all been here so long and used so much power you've forgotten what it's like to be human. You think that makes you better, but you're wrong, and I think my mother saw it. I think that's why she did what she did that night, knowing how Liam would react. She found love after centuries and saw the need to rebuild the Order because all of you had become so… heartless."

"How dare you speak of her like that!" Aihara roared. She raised her hand and Sora flew back, sliding across the stone and nearly into the rushing waters. Aihara held her there, intense pressure building on all her limbs.

"Aihara, stop!" Madam Jaya shouted.

"No. It is time she learned respect!" Aihara pushed her hand forward, and Sora felt like she was being crushed. She hung over the ledge, further and further. She felt the water beat against her hair. She couldn't breathe or speak—it was the same feeling as when Redstar threatened to kill her, Whitney, and Torsten in the Webbed Woods. His may have been blood magic, but now Sora knew that all magic came from sacrifice, inside or out.

"She just found out who she is," Madam Jaya said. "Of course she's not thinking clearly."

"She just needs time," Huyshi said.

"We have no time," spoke another whom Sora hadn't heard before. "I've seen enough. She is no savior."

"I concur," said Ghing.

Aihara stalked forward, muttering in a mixture of languages.

Elsewhere beckoned Sora as she struggled for air as it had before she stopped Redstar or banished Kazimir, burning in her chest.

No, not Elsewhere.

Sora couldn't move her head, but she turned her eyes downward and saw the bar guai. Each of the remaining five stones glowed as the disc spun, lifting from her chest.

She couldn't scream, but the pain was like nothing she'd ever experienced. Elsewhere called to her, the power begging her to return the call, but with the bar guai there, she couldn't answer. Her body felt like it was tearing in two.

"You *will* remain here without magic," Aihara said. "And you will learn the respect and patience required of a mystic. *My* Sora did not sacrifice her life so you could insult her people! Our visions said you would rebuild this broken Order, so you will serve until you're old and gray and every shred of beauty has left your cheeks if that's what it takes for you to learn. Another fifty years is like a blink of an eye to us."

The bar guai exploded from Sora's body and flew into Aihara's hand. Sora collapsed and gasped for air. She clutched her chest, feeling all the blood, hot and sticky. For a fleeting moment, dread gripped her until she realized something—she could answer Elsewhere's whispers again. She could feel that familiar pull again.

Sora heard Whitney's voice, frantic and desperate. Nesilia's sultry, seductive tones begged her to join her in the red mist. They were distant, but growing louder as more blood leaked from her wound.

Sora got onto all fours. "No," she rasped. "You've let me live a lie my whole life. I wanted answers, I got them."

"You got only what your eyes witnessed, but you fail to see the bigger picture," Aihara said. "You want your mother to have been as rebellious as you are, but it simply isn't true."

"I didn't mean about her."

Sora reached for her knife, but as her fingers closed around the grip, the water churned, the waves reached out and washed the knife into the pool.

Sora turned to see Aihara Na's hand outstretched to the moat. Then she rushed forward and pressed her palm to Sora's chest. The wound inflicted by removing the bar guai began to heal.

"You have no power here," Aihara said. "Now, you will start doing as told. It will take many months to repair the door to the Well of Wisdom. I suggest we start your service there."

Sora's hands balled into fists. "I didn't only use blood magic to open that door," she said, seething. "Or the bar guai." She thought back to her mother on that bed, channeling her power to offer her own life to Elsewhere. Opening that realm so Sora could live when she wasn't intended to.

Aihara removed her hand, revealing Sora's wholly healed chest. Sora closed her eyes and looked inward, focusing on the blood running through her veins, on her heartbeat. Fire crackled at her fingertips, swirling around her hands even though she didn't bleed. They were little more than embers, but they were there.

"What is this?" Aihara Na questioned. "What is she doing, Jaya? She cannot channel."

"'Blood of babe,'" Sora quoted Aihara's own false sacrifice back to her. "'Bone of child...'"

"Stop it. That's not real."

"Bring forth the power of Elsewhere's fire.'"

Sora could barely hear their responses, but the shock on Aihara's face was enough to know she'd figured it out. Their ritual may have been nothing, but in every good lie held specks of truth. Whitney had taught her that, and his insane view of the world often proved correct.

The secret to opening Elsewhere, and all that came with it which the mystics feared so much was the sacrifice of a life. Her own. And she didn't need a knife to sacrifice what was required to open Elsewhere and reach Whitney. She didn't need anything but herself. She knew that now. And even if she never found a way to bring him back, at least she'd be with someone who accepted her.

Every word in the room became distant and removed, obscured by the vague whispers of Elsewhere. Sora wasn't sure how she did it back at the Well, but she had channeled from within like a true mystic. Like her mother, an Ancient One who seemed without equal.

She kept digging within for the answer. Nothing and no one existed except for her own soul, and she offered it willingly, just as her mother had. She couldn't say what channeling her power felt like, but she knew she was doing it. Embers churned around her hands now in a heavy current floating around her eyes. It felt like the energy when she released a stream of fire from her fingertips only it was focused within, rushing through her veins toward her chest.

Aihara used her power to become corporeal and grabbed Sora's face. "Sora, you know not what powers you're flirting with! Control yourself!"

"Let me go!" she roared. Light exploded from her just as it had in the Webbed Woods. Then the room seemed to fade away into a thick reddish haze, the cries of the mystics replaced by foreign shrieks.

Splayed out before her were the kingdoms of the world. She could see it all like in her visions, yet with no detail. A deep, purple sky loomed over everything, and the ground was rent, molten liquid pouring from the fissure. Sora spun when she recognized the feeling of solid ground. She saw sharp, yellow teeth just before they sank into her flesh, only they didn't sink in. They passed through her. Hundreds of the creatures did the same, a cold, empty feeling washing over her as they did. Some had skulls capped by a series of horns, but each one was different. There were faces with large beaks filled with razor-sharp teeth.

Others had a dozen eyes, at least, covering a flat area beneath the facial crests.

Sinewy muscle flexed as they beat the dirt, running on all fours. Their blood red skin glistened, and pockets of pus oozed from what looked like open sores.

"Shog! Shog! Shog!" She heard him before she saw him, but knew without any question—it was Whitney.

His dirty blonde hair bobbed beyond the mass of creatures, red, horned, and scaly beasts, ugly as could be.

"Well done, my child." Sora turned when she heard her. She'd heard that voice before, sensual, intoxicating, euphoric even. "I can feel it. My power, returning from its buried prison after so long."

"Nesilia?" Sora asked. "Where are you?"

The Buried Goddess stood in the distance, towering over a dark figure. Sora could hear indistinct shouting—words spoken with conviction. She closed the gap, and as she did, saw Torsten wrestling with someone clothed in red. At first, she thought it to be one of the mystics. Before she could better assess the scene, she saw Whitney again, running toward her.

No demons followed him this time. She hiked up her kimono and forsook all as she ran toward him.

"Whitney!" she called out.

"Sora!" came a cry from somewhere behind her. She looked over her shoulder at Aihara Na's vacillating form but didn't stop. The old mystic cradled something in her arms and shouted at it. "Stop the sacrifice! There's still a chance to stop!"

Sora continued ignoring her. She saw Torsten, face covered in blood and surrounded by snow, but that didn't matter. She saw a young nobleman wearing a crown, floating in the air, but he didn't matter either. All that mattered was Whitney, and suddenly they were wrapped in each other's arms. Chaos surrounded them, as it always had, but as she looked at him, she felt more at peace than ever before.

"Whit." She was laughing and crying at the same time. "Whitney. I never thought I'd see you again... I... I'm so sorry, I..."

"Shut up," Whitney said as he squeezed her. "You're ruining the moment." His arms were stronger than she remembered. He even had a patchy beard that itched her neck.

Sora laughed again and allowed herself to get lost in his embrace. And it was while she was there, looking over his shoulder, that she noticed where they were. The quaint, wooden homes were unmistakable.

She pulled away, struggling to catch her breath. "Are we in—"

"Troborough," Whitney finished for her. "Welcome home."

She stumbled over what to say next, then settled on her grabbing his face and kissing him deeply, just as she wished she'd done back on that ship in Winde Port before she and her powers ruined everything.

Whitney's eyes went wide, shocked. It wasn't the reaction she expected. She was about to pull back and punch him in his arm when he grabbed her tighter and dragged her to the ground. An axe whizzed by as they hit the dirt. A thunk sounded as it buried into the chest of a King's Shieldsman behind them.

"A Shieldsman?" Whitney said, breathless. Sora wasn't sure if it was due to the kiss or dodging certain death. "How in the world?"

Sora recalled who she'd seen when she entered Elsewhere. "Torsten is here too!" She pointed at the tear in the world she'd passed. She now saw that it was within what appeared like a ruined Church of Iam. The air around it coruscated with energy, but she could see a haze of snow against a backdrop of a black circle surrounded by a ring of fire.

"There, by the church!" They saw him and then he was gone, hidden behind a wall of demons.

"Oh," Whitney said. "That's not really Torsten. Elsewhere is awful."

"No, right there!" she shouted, but a heap of demons obstructed their view.

"Shog in a barrel," Whitney said. "We've gotta get out of here." Whitney started pulling Sora away from the demons and the portal. "Keeps getting better."

Sora looked behind her, the mass of Elsewhere's hounds was already moving away from them, but before them stood two snarling demons. Sora glanced down, then realized her knife remained in the water of the Mystic Council's throne room. She could still hear Aihara Na whispering to her, chanting with the others like they were miles away. She couldn't go back for the weapon now.

"Hold on," Whitney said. He kneeled and pried the sword out of the fallen Shieldsman's gauntleted hands, then pointed it at the beasts.

"Let me." Sora extended her hand for him to cut it, but instead, he sneered.

"Come at me, demon!" he roared. She wasn't sure what he'd been doing for the last weeks, but he didn't seem afraid in the slightest. Almost eager to fight rather than sneak around it.

In response, one of the beasts bounded toward him, but Whitney rolled aside, then came up waving the weapon before him.

"Goooood dog," he said. "Good dog."

The creature snapped at him while the other paced back and forth behind it. The demon rushed at Whitney again. Once more, he attempted to roll out of the way, but this time, the beast was ready for it and thrust its claws out.

They raked Whitney's thigh, drawing three long, bloody lines.

The demon snapped out its arm once more, and as Whitney dodged the swipe, he dove toward the monster. His sword found purchase, digging into the demon's flesh. Whitney pulled hard, dragging the blade across the demon's chest. Blood poured from the chasm as the creature collapsed on top of him.

Whitney let out a groan, and his hand slammed hard against the dirt. His sword was pinned under the massive corpse, making an attack impossible as the second demon pounced. Whitney rolled and used the corpse as a shield. He was flat on his back, unable to tear his arm and weapon free. It snapped its jaws wildly at him as he struggled to hold it back with the other hand.

Sora rushed in. It wasn't a smart move. With her bar guai shattered and no weapon with which to draw blood, she resorted to punching the creature. Its hide was thick as a zhulongs.

"Get off him, vile creature!" Sora shouted as she punched it again and again. The demon momentarily stopped gnashing at Whitney, turned, and regarded Sora with deep-set eyes so red they appeared to bleed. Its right arm snapped out, throwing Sora far and hard. She hit the ground with a grunt but didn't let it stop her.

She rolled and stood, preparing to continue the barrage. As she started, she noticed something red out of the corner of her eye. Her arm was bleeding. The demon must have scratched her with one of its claws.

Focusing, she tried to call forth the fires of Elsewhere, but that familiar feeling wasn't there. Perhaps it was because she was now in Elsewhere, she wasn't sure.

The demon set its focus back on Whitney, snarling gutturally in some demonic tongue. Spit showered Whitney as he scrambled to defend himself.

"A little help?" he shouted.

"I can't!" she shouted.

"Do something!" he cried. "Anything!"

Sora tried again to call upon Elsewhere to bring forth flames.

When there was still no response, she dug down deep to channel like a mystic as she just had when opening Elsewhere. No crackling power raced toward her heart from within, nothing.

"Aquira!" she cried, thrusting her hand out before her. Nothing happened. She shook out her hand, rolled her neck, and took a deep breath, watching as the demon's bite grew ever closer to Whitney's exposed face. He tried relentlessly to stab it, but the angle was all wrong.

"Aquira!" She tried the word that signaled her bar guai, desperate.

Whitney thrashed around.

"It's not working! I... I can't call fire!"

The beast's razor-sharp teeth punctured Whitney's shoulder, and he squealed. Sora conceded to charging it again, hoping to knock it free so she might be able to reach the sword.

"Kaaazaaamiiiiir."

The name of the upyr who'd tried to devour her filled the air, a deep and cavernous bellow. The creature stopped gnawing and looked up, past her. She wasn't sure what terror looked like on the face of such a monster, but she was sure it was there. It unmounted Whitney and scurried away.

"You better run!" Whitney screamed, flipping over and grabbed his sword. Then he too saw whatever was behind Sora and the color fled his cheeks. She almost didn't want to look but did anyway.

Barrelling toward them was a blob of tentacles, rising tall as the Cathedral of Yarrington itself. It whipped a group of demons out of the way, swatting them through the air like flies. More massive tentacles unfurled, revealing a maw filled with thousands of teeth, above which sat two giant eyes, one scarred and calloused. The mere sight of them made Sora's spine tingle.

"What in Iam's name is that?" Sora asked.

"A friend of Kazimir's," Whitney replied. He tried lifting the sword with his good arm, but the wound in his shoulder made him grimace.

"Is he still here?"

"It's complicated."

"What do we do?"

The monster roared, making the very air tremble. One of its tentacles slapped down into the Shellnak, so tremendous it nearly drained the river. A deep furrow cut through the ground, fleeing demons tumbling into it.

"Run!"

Whitney took Sora's hand, and they took off into the town. A tentacle slammed through farmer Branson's house, crushing the roof. They ducked under the flying debris and veered right toward the town center.

"He's not here!" Whitney shouted back at it.

Another tentacle crushed the Twilight Manor and sent them back the other way toward Mrs. Dodson's place. Two more landed with a quake and blocked off the road.

They found themselves cornered into the ruins of the old Troborough Church of Iam. They backed up against what was left of the stone wall behind the altar, nowhere to go. Torsten stood in the center of the aisle, stretching his hand toward a floating child who was within the center of a strange rift in the air that seemed to be following him. His face wracked with pain, he didn't seem to notice them.

"Torsten, watch out!" Whitney shouted just as a tentacle came slithering over the broken walls. Then more.

Sora thought she saw the face of a familiar woman in the rift before the tentacles covered Torsten and it stopped before the altar. The hideous beast drew itself over the roofless church, casting them both in shadow. Sora and Whitney went to grasp each other's hands at the same time.

"I can't believe after all our years here together, Kazimir's going to get me... whatever happens when you die here," Whitney said.

"Years?" Sora asked.

The ground trembled as the beast drew closer, leaning down so she could look into its bulbous eyes. She could smell its rank breath like a graveyard with all the graves turned over.

"Six, in case you lost count. Some nights I worried you'd forgotten me, but that kiss... I'm glad I held out." Whitney laughed nervously. His grip on her hand tightened. He talked when scared. He must have been terrified.

The great, tentacled beast tried to attack, but an invisible field kept it at bay, making its limbs stretch over them as if the bars of a cage.

"What the—"

"I'm here now," she said, ignoring the thing that wanted them dead, not bothering to tell him it'd only been weeks on Pantego. She sandwiched his hands with hers. "I'm so sorry Whitney. I... I'll never leave your side again."

"I'm the one who left you. Besides..." Whitney nodded toward the monster looming over them. "Not really anywhere else for us to run this time."

Sora turned from the monster and their impending doom and stared at him. He looked no older. Messier, yes, but he was still the young, dashing rogue she remembered. It was in his eyes that she saw it, however. That weariness she'd never seen there before. It pained her to think she was responsible for him being stuck for what, to him, felt like years in Elsewhere. All because the mystics decided not to tell her what she was until the time was right.

"I love you, Whitney," Sora blurted out. "I have since the beginning."

"Who wouldn't." She punched him in the arm, he grinned.

Despite all the chaos around them. "I love you, too." He looked to the sky as if seeing something beyond the horrifying monstrosity.

"See, you little whelp? It isn't that hard to admit."

He pulled her close, and she, him. The razor-sharp teeth of the beast above glinted, ready to devour them if not for the barrier. Even still, Sora decided there was no place she'd rather be than here, with Whitney. Everything that had happened, him leaving her, her exiling him—everything. None of it mattered now that they were together at the end.

"For Liam!" Torsten's voice rang out. Then a burst of energy in the aisle sent the beast reeling back, stumbling through the front of the ruined Church. Stone crumbled as its diabolical screams had Sora's eardrums ready to burst.

"You have stopped nothing... nothing... nothing..." the sensuous voice of a woman echoed.

Robed figures circled them as well, mystics and warlocks—denizens of Elsewhere's magic—their chanting like a hymn on the air.

Sora searched from side to side as more of the church crumbled away, the ground too until she and Whitney stood upon blackness.

Torsten appeared again in the center of it all, faint like an apparition, holding onto the boy he'd been reaching for. The rift in the air hung over him again, faded now just like him. Mist rose from the chest of the boy, forming the most beautiful woman Sora had ever seen.

"Uh, Sora... what in Elsewhere is going on?" Whitney walked toward Torsten and waved his hand through him, unable to make contact.

"I... I don't know," she replied.

"Are those mystics?" Whitney turned to her, and a smirk crossed his face. Sora couldn't fathom how much she'd missed that smug look until she saw it. "I knew you'd find them. Whitney and Sora... even Elsewhere can't stop uhh—"

His last word trailed off as the blackness gave way beneath him. The rift that followed Torsten engulfed Whitney now, both the ground and the air, sizzling with energy.

"Whitney!" Sora ran to him and grabbed his hand. She tried to pull him up, but something in the darkness resisted her. Torsten's silhouette was now below them, spectral as Aihara Na and the mystics.

"Sora, what is..." Whitney got his free hand up to try and pull himself free, but an invisible forced yanked him back.

Sora didn't let go. The energy exuding off the strange rift surrounding him grew, so instead, she could feel it tickling her skin. Still, she held on. Then a hand, pale as winter's snow, wrapped around her arm.

"Sora, I've been waiting for you," Nesilia whispered. Her voice was the same as always, sensual but warm.

Sora's stomach turned over. She recalled how she'd felt the last time she'd been in Nesilia's presence and felt every bit the same. She wanted nothing more than to be with her, unendingly, forever. She fought it with all her being, but one of her fingers released Whitney.

"Uh... Sora!" he yelled.

"Why have you kept me waiting all these years?" Nesilia said. "Tell me, are you ready for your destiny?"

"Who the yig are you?" Whitney asked. Sora barely heard him, so enthralled she was by the goddess.

"We are the same, Sora, you and I," Nesilia continued. "Connected since the day of your birth so many Dawnings ago. Can't you feel it?"

The mention of that traumatic night with Sora's mother and Liam snapped her mind back to the moment. She closed her hand tighter around Whitney's and continued pulling.

"No!" Sora said. "I'm through being used."

"We were both forgotten by those who once loved us," Nesilia said. "Tell me it's not true. Abandoned by your own father to live underground. Underground, like me."

"I've dealt with these Elsewhere tricks, Sora," Whitney said. "Ignore her. Let's run while we have the chance!"

Nesilia's hand slid down Sora's arm until it reached Whitney's fingers. She unlatched one, and he yelped in fright.

"No, stop!" Sora shouted.

She unhooked another, and Sora couldn't stop her.

"Don't hurt him!" Sora yelled. "Please, don't hurt him. I'll do anything. Just don't hurt him."

"It's time to let go of what makes you normal, Sora." A smile played at the corners of Nesilia's mouth. She leaned down by Whitney's ear and whispered something Sora couldn't hear. His eyes went wide with horror, then she tore his hand free of Sora's, and Whitney plummeted through the darkness toward Torsten's apparition.

The energy of the rift coruscated with bright lines of distortion. Sora heard his screams grow distant, then stop altogether. The air settled, blackness returning to the ground around Sora, and as she patted it, searching for a way through. Both Whitney and Torsten were nowhere to be found.

"Whitney!" Sora cried out. "What did you do with him!"

"It wasn't yet his time," Nesilia said, softly. "You know that. It was you who put him here because you lost control, but Sora, my love," Nesilia said. "My sweet. Together there is nothing we can't do."

"Come back to us, Sora." Sora heard the distant, familiar voice of Aihara Na again. Then, chanting in a multitude of languages echoed from her, and Madam Jaya, and all the others. She saw them surrounding her again, no warlocks present this time.

"Don't surrender yourself over nothing," Aihara Na went on. "Your future is bright as your fire."

"They would keep you from your destiny!" Nesilia's voice boomed. "Just as the Shieldsman bars me from returning in my own true form. He would keep me buried and forgotten. They would keep you trapped in a tower." Her finger stroked Sora's chin. "But together we can make them all bow."

Another blinding, searing light shone, causing Sora to see nothing but white. A rush of energy made her heart feel like it was going to explode. Then came a tugging sensation. It dragged her backward toward the circling mystics. She clawed at the blackness to try and reach the spot where Whitney vanished.

"No!" Sora screamed. "Not again! Bring me back to him. Whitney!"

More magical chanting enveloped her. Sora tried to grasp onto the ground and tried to crawl forward, but there was nothing but smooth, black. Elsewhere began to tear around her, offering glimpses of the Red Tower throne room and mystics surrounding her.

"Don't be afraid," Nesilia whispered. Sora lost grip with one hand and her legs whipped up into the air. Nesilia kneeled before her, her face a thing of beauty, her eyes completely white and glowing.

"There is nothing for you here any longer," she said. She lay her hand upon Sora's. "It's time to let go."

Sora lost her grip, and everything zoomed past her. Both worlds, all through history, from the days of Liam to her terrible present. She gasped for air, real air, the chamber atop the Red Tower now surrounding her in perfect clarity. Aihara Na was on her knees before her, weak.

"By the gods, she's still alive," the Ancient One of the Secret Mystic Order wheezed.

Sora's head turned from side to side. All the mystics

surrounded her, palms outstretched in her direction, save for Huyshi who had only one. Madam Jaya breathed a sigh of relief.

Sora opened her mouth to speak, but no words came out. Then, out of the corner of her eye, she noticed Wetzel's old knife glinting beneath the calm waters around the platform. A smile spread over her face, going all the way to her eyes.

XXXIV

THE KNIGHT

Torsten lifted one heavy leg after the other up the stairs carved into the mountainside which led up to the summit flattened ages ago in the God Feud. Statues of kings lined the holy walk, each of them leaning on a sword with two hands, eyes closed. At the top, stood an archway fashioned in the shape of the Eye of Iam, made from pure glaruium that would sparkle like glass in the sunlight.

Only now, the sunlight had faded, and an eerie twilight had fallen upon the realm as Pantego's two moons drew closer to one another and threatened to cover the sun completely. Only dim torchlight showed Torsten the way.

No guards stood in his path. His legs were stiff. His lungs burned. He had to close his eyes and focus on every icy breath, so he didn't inhale too vigorously. He'd already drawn Salvation to use as a walking stick, the sound of it scraping across rock drowned out by whistling wind and the distant voices.

Then, after what felt like an eternity, his foot possessed the summit. He opened his eyes. The driving snow dwindled around the clearing as if Iam wanted Torsten to see what waited there—the parting clouds, and the Dawning in all its glory.

Shieldsmen and Drav Cra warriors lined the edge of the plateau, alternating and staring inward. A vast Eye of Iam was etched into the icy surface as always, only this time it wasn't alone. Within the pupil, a triangle, the symbol of Nesilia—her mountainous tomb—large enough for a man to fit inside, was painted in blood. At least two dozen Drav Cra warlocks encircled it, holding hands, faces aimed toward the eclipse. Freydis strolled around them, lighting small basins of fire with her blood magic.

Within that circle stood King Pi wearing half the Glass Crown, Wren the Holy, leaning on his cane with quaking arms, and Redstar, clutching Pi's old orepul, still stained beyond recognition by Bliss' blood. Blood also coated each of their hands as if they'd been the ones to desecrate the summit of Mount Lister with the symbol of Nesilia. Torsten remembered the night before he set off to the Webbed Woods to find Redstar, when he caught Pi, mad and rambling, scribbling bloody symbols upon the walls of his bedroom.

"Redstar!" Torsten bellowed. All eyes snapped toward him. "Enough of this madness."

"Torsten, my friend!" Redstar replied. "I was wondering when you would arrive."

"Do not act unsurprised!" Torsten shoved his sword into the ground.

"Surprised? I knew you wouldn't want to miss this."

"You will unhand the King. Now!"

"The King is here of his own volition."

"We both know that's not true."

"Remove this traitor," Pi ordered. "He is a prisoner now, nothing more." All the Shieldsmen and Drav Cra warriors drew their weapons.

Redstar lay his hand on the boy's shoulder, making sure the

orepul—that seemingly innocuous doll that had been with Pi when he rose from the apparent-dead, which had been there when they slew the monster Bliss—was visible.

"That's all right, Your Grace," Redstar said. "I think he should see. All those who doubt the strength of our unified faith should see."

Pi raised his hand, and the guards took a step back, lowering their weapons. He still commanded respect as King, but it was like Torsten had always feared: Redstar led through him.

Torsten slowly edged forward. "Pi, you must listen to me," he said. "He's using you for... for whatever this madness is. He thinks he can bring his goddess back, but she is gone."

"She helped bring me back," Pi said. "After you allowed me to die!"

"You know in your heart that isn't true! He filled your mind with visions and lies. Now he plays the part of loving uncle. I've seen what he did to your mother just for disobeying her. You cannot trust him."

"My mother refuses to see reason," Pi spat. "She got what she deserved."

Torsten pleaded silently with Iam that Oleander not be within hearing. "Your mother loves you! More than anything."

"My sister is a murdering shrew," Redstar said. "She would see this kingdom and all its inhabitants crumble of her own foolish pride. But we, we seek to raise it beyond even the heights of Liam."

"You dare speak his name!" Torsten lifted his Salvation, the sword wielded by King Liam himself in so many battles, and pointed it at the Arch Warlock. He heard the unified rasp of blades drawn around the circle. He was now surrounded and he hadn't even realized it.

"This profane ritual is nothing but cultish madness," Torsten addressed the Shieldsmen. "You have to see that."

"You are wrong, Torsten," Redstar said. He turned with his hand on Pi's shoulder to face the eclipse. The two moons were nearly kissing now, and soon they would cover the sun in its entirety. "This is the way of the future. Bound in love, our God and Goddess shall be reunited. For He is the light above, and She is below, buried, not dead."

He raised the doll. "Blood of the enemy. Of the Lord and the Lady. Perhaps you weren't as pious as I thought, but this man is, and he stands with us now." He smiled and touched Wren's wrinkled face. The old priest remained hunched over, looking frail as death.

"That is not the Wren I know," Torsten said.

"That is because you refuse to see how your kingdom is changing. Evolving."

"Wren, I know you are in there. Put a stop to this. Tell these Shieldsmen the truth."

Wren raised one hand off his cane. It trembled, more bone and sinew than skin. He reached toward Redstar's neck. For a moment, Torsten thought he saw something in the Arch Warlock's eyes. Fear? But it was gone before Torsten could identify it. Freydis sidled up behind the old man, and his hand fell back to the cane.

"We have lived blindly in our faith for too long. I now see the folly," Wren said. "It is you who are blind, Torsten Unger. The Dawning shall set us free." His head remained sagging. But something else was wrong. Though it was his voice that came out of his mouth, his lips weren't moving. Instead, the warlock Freydis spoke through him, controlled him. Blood stained her face and lips. The sight made Torsten want to vomit, and the moment Wren finished speaking, his entire body fell weak. He fell onto his cane with all his weight just to stay upright.

"Light above," Redstar started, "earth below. Soon all Pantego will know our truth. It is time now for the union of the Dawning."

"I'm ready, uncle," Pi said. "I'm ready to open my eyes."

"Resist him, my King!" Torsten thundered. "Step out from that circle, and I will never let him harm you again. Your mother waits for you, ready to beg forgiveness for all that she's done in your name."

Redstar sighed. "Perhaps our King is right. How many times are you going to go through this, Torsten? My Lady said that no matter what I did you'd be here, but I tire of this. Men, in the name of Pi Nothhelm, the Miracle King, son of Liam Nothhelm, first of his name, and heir to be Dradinengor of the Ruuhar Clan, seize the criminal. Take him alive."

Soldiers closed in, Drav Cra and Shieldsmen alike. Torsten spun to face those who once swore allegiance to him. "I have failed you, men," he said. "I look upon your faces, and I don't recognize them. I should. I should know each and every one of you… as Sir Uriah Davies did. I will pay for that negligence for the rest of my days, but I know your armor. I know what you stand for."

Redstar spoke in Drav Crava, and all at once, the circle of warlocks around him sliced their forearms. They clasped hands, blood flowing down between each of their wrists. In a monotonous roar, they chanted in their language. Redstar did the same, standing between Pi and Wren who remained silent. Pi's orepul lifted into the air. Pi flinched, betraying a bit of the child still beneath the cold exterior, but Redstar took his hand.

"Look inside yourselves and find the light!" Torsten implored. He brandished Salvation now, ready to do whatever necessary.

"There is no light today," hissed a woman, voice like a serpent. With soldiers on either side, Freydis appeared in front of him. Her knees bent in a battle-stance, tossing a dagger playfully between her hands while she licked her bloody lips.

Torsten closed his eyes. "Iam, guide my hand," he whispered, then he charged. An axe swung at his legs, but without his armor, he was nimble, and leaped over it. Then, falling into a roll, he dodged another swipe and brought Salvation crashing toward Freydis' head. She parried left, sliced her palm, and flung a ball of fire at Torsten, but he was ready for it. It flew by his ear and slammed into the chest of a Drav Cra warrior, sending the savage flying back into a few more. Torsten rebuffed the attack of a Shieldsman, then grabbed him and shoved him into even more of the attackers. Torsten winced as an axe grazed his torso and cut his shirt, but he spun, slashing one of the heathens across the chest. A hand grabbed his arm, stopping him mid-backswing. Torsten wasted no time, caught it in turn, and flipped the man over his massive shoulders.

Torsten froze as Salvation drove downward to stab into the assailant. A Shieldsman stared up at him, not afraid, ready to die for what he thought was their cause in serving the King of the Glass Kingdom—Torsten's kingdom. That moment of hesitation allowed Freydis to slide behind Torsten and flay the backs of both his thighs.

He howled as he fell to his knees. An axe knocked Salvation from his grasp, and more hands wrenched his arms between them. He thrashed, but it was no use, like he was back in Winde Port again.

"Release me!" he roared. "Can't you see what he's doing? He'll destroy your King. He'll destroy us all!"

Behind Freydis, tiny droplets of blood trickled out of the floating orepul and began to swirl around it, a web of red lines. Pi's arms were now outstretched, and he too levitated. A spectral presence stretched out from his chest, taking shape like an illuminated wisp of fog.

"Drad Redstar elevates him," Freydis said. She knelt before Torsten and ran her bloody dagger across his cheek. The whites of her eyes shone within the crusting black paint on her brow, freezing off in flakes. "Soon you will see."

Torsten threw his weight at her, but warlocks promptly hauled him back. Though the Drav Cra restrained him without a second thought, the eyes of the Shieldsman present darted nervously between him and the ritual. It was one thing to hear promises of an alliance between gods, but its must have been quite another to see their wicked magic raising their King from the ground; tapping the very light of his soul.

"Look around you men," Torsten whispered. "Is this where you thought you'd find yourselves when you took the oath? Party to the Buried Goddess' blood rituals? If you no longer trust me, I understand. I let hate for anything foreign to us cloud my mind and turn me to rage instead of seeing what was right before me. You, loyal Glassmen. Children of Iam, I should have looked to you and not into the darkness. So, let me pass on, but trust your hearts. Perhaps not all Drav Cra are evil, but that man is."

Chanting in the circle grew louder, Drav Crava filled the air like a brewing storm, and now Pi didn't just float before his orepul, but the air around and between them crackled with energy. Streaks of it distorted the view, and Torsten could see momentary glimpses of somewhere else through them; a small village shrouded in red.

"Drad Redstar says to let you watch," Freydis whispered in Torsten's ear. "But he says nothing about speaking." She grabbed his jaw as he tried to appeal to his men again and held her dagger to his lips.

"Unhand him, witch!"

Torsten peered out of the corner of his eye to see Oleander standing at the top of the stairs, surrounded by the Eye-of-Iam-shaped gate. Sir Austin Mulliner stood at her side, a bow in his hands. A thrum sent an arrow toward the female warlock and sliced her cheek, knocking her back, then continued forward. Torsten turned with her, thinking he knew where it was going to strike until it stabbed into Pi's floating orepul, finally landing on the opposite edge of the summit.

The distortion in the air around Pi suddenly stopped, and the strange wisp of light swirling around him began to diminish. The boy looked from side to side, and for the first time since his reawakening—even for the year before that—he didn't seem emotionless. He was frightened. He continued searching until his gaze fell upon Oleander.

"Mama?" he whimpered.

"Redstar left the wife of Liam Nothhelm to bleed," Austun shouted. "No matter what she has done, no matter who Torsten has killed—we must still protect our own." He drew his sword, and a host of Glass soldiers behind him did the same. "Iam smite me if I am wrong, but this is not the King's Shield to which I swore an oath. Brothers, it is time to take it back!"

He charged, and the men followed him. Drav Cra warriors broke away from Torsten to meet them head-on. The Shieldsmen committed to Redstar were confused. Torsten found himself thrilled that Mulliner saw beyond his hatred enough to do what was right— precisely what Torsten had failed to do.

In the confusion, Torsten broke free of his Shieldsman captor, kicking a downed-Freydis in the face in the process, then ran for the orepul.

"Continue the summoning!" Redstar ordered. "And you." He stopped in front of Wren and laid his stump of a hand over his shoulder. "No more half-measures this time. One for the Lord. A true sacrifice." He drew a dagger and placed it in Wren's hand, then burst through the circle, racing toward the orepul as well.

"The blood of the enemy shall bring rise to her!" Redstar shouted.

"I should have destroyed it when I had the chance!" Torsten cried out. He barreled into him. They tumbled across the snowy surface, stopping just out of reach of the doll. Redstar had no weapon, and in hand to hand combat, Torsten was far more proficient. He pinned the Arch Warlock down and drove fist after fist into his nose. Redstar pawed at Torsten's face with his one hand, clubbing him with his other. The more blood Torsten drew from Redstar's mouth, the more he felt it—fire building within Redstar's palm. The Arch Warlock spread his long fingers, and the heat made Torsten's skin bubble.

"When will you learn to kill me?" Redstar hissed. He squeezed until the pain was too much for Torsten to bear. Torsten fell off him, the imprint of Redstar's hand branded onto his face.

"Perhaps it is time you live like those you bow to," Redstar said. "Like all the Glassmen. Blind."

He stretched his hand across Torsten's eyes. Torsten lashed out, punching Redstar in the ribs, feeling the bone crack beneath his fists, but Redstar held him down. The heat augmented, burning Torsten's eyelids first and then his eyeballs.

"Get off of him!" Oleander shouted. Torsten's eyes were covered, but he heard the soft crunch of a blade stabbing through flesh. Redstar screamed and slid to the side, tumbling off Torsten. Torsten's eyes were so damaged by the magical fire, he could see nothing but shapes, but that was enough. A knife stuck out of the center of Redstar's back, placed there by the Queen Mother.

"Whore Queen!" Redstar snarled. Red-hot fire leaped from his fingertips into Oleander's chest and sent her flying. Then Redstar stood and limped to the orepul. Torsten pawed at the blur of his legs and slowed him, but without sight, Redstar was easily able to kick him away.

Gathering the orepul, Redstar started back toward the blood circle, only to find it compromised. With Sir Mulliner's reinforcements, the Drav Cra warriors were outnumbered. A handful stood with their backs to the circle of warlocks, Freydis at their center. They faced at least a dozen knights and the same amount of Glass soldiers. It seemed that even if they wouldn't fight for their disgraced ex-Wearer, they chose to fight beside their own.

"You fools!" Redstar rasped. "You cannot stop this." He reached behind his back and wrenched out the knife his sister wedged there. With it, he sliced his own wrist, deep, like he didn't care about bleeding out. "Like I told the last of you who thought to rebel, your armor is of the mountain. And what is below the peak, belongs to my Lady."

He lifted his hand and squeezed.

"What the—" one of the Shieldsmen gasped.

"Iam's light!" cried another.

More and more of them shouted in pain as Redstar's arms moved slowly to the side. "Your armor is mine!" Redstar yelled.

Shieldsmen threw themselves into one another without regard. One grabbed a Glass soldier and hurled him over the ridge of the summit, his screams rending the very air.

"Freydis," Redstar shouted, "kill them all!"

She clasped her bloody hands then pulled them apart. The ground split beneath the Glassmen, wide enough for ten abreast to lose their footing. The remaining Drav Cra warriors attacked.

Redstar made his way back into the circle where the warlocks chanted. He raised the orepul, and Pi went from a terrified boy, back to impassive. His body arched and the spirit continued lifting from his chest.

During it all, Torsten dragged himself toward Oleander's body. His vision was still impaired, but it didn't take much to recognize the massive burns coating half of her like a boar left over a hot spit.

"My Queen," Torsten whispered, pawing for her hand in the snow. Finding it, he squeezed.

"T… Torsten," she stuttered. "My sweet, loyal, Torsten."

"Come. I must get you to safety."

He tried to lift her, but she slapped him away. The blow was weak, not like all the countless times she'd done it before, but he got the message. "You made a vow to protect my boy. I... I..." She swallowed back her pain. He could see the red staining her teeth. "I order you to uphold it."

"My Qu... Oleander."

"Redstar thinks he must take his own life. Kill the bastard... for me." Torsten hesitated a moment more, and she pushed him. "Go!"

Staggering forward, still seeing the world only in shapes and contrast of light, Torsten roared, "Redstar!"

The ritual illuminated the entire summit now, and Torsten realized why. The moons and the sun were in complete alignment; the Dawning was upon them. Just a ring of light surrounded them as Iam looked away and allowed his people to find the light within themselves.

Torsten wouldn't ignore the call. He trudged forward, nearly sightless, body battered. Through the circle of warlocks, Redstar eyed him.

"Biding her time, her pain like a flood. Alone in the darkness, she longs for the blood. In the name of the Lady, in the name of the Lord, Shall settle it all with power and sword," Redstar chanted. He lifted his knife, and Wren mimicked his every move with the dagger in his quaking hand. Torsten realized that the poor old man whispered the words along with him as well.

"Then she will arise, in glorious day," Redstar continued. "Through will and through fire, her enemies slain. Forgotten, abandoned, but no longer bound. From Elsewhere and exile, she'll receive her crown." Side by side, Redstar and Wren plunged their blades into their own chests.

Torsten stopped and clutched his own. It stung him deep within to see, even through bleary eyes, the holy leader of his church forced to take his own life—a blasphemy, an abomination unto their God. As they dropped to their knees, the spirit poured out of Pi, taking the shape of a woman whose whispers Torsten heard on the air. It was almost imperceptible, but it was there.

The blood from the orepul fed into it and the very air around them fractured, again revealing a hellish world between worlds. Torsten knew without question what it was. As the fabric of reality had been split in the God Feud when Iam made Elsewhere, now it was being reopened.

"Torsten!" Austun yelled.

Torsten looked right and saw the vague and blurred shape of the Shieldsman on his knees. Freydis had summoned vines from the ice to lash him down. She controlled them with one hand while with the other she stabbed a Glass soldier in the chest repeatedly. Austun tossed something to Torsten. He heard it clatter on the ground and found grip on it. He'd only had King Liam's sword for a short time, but already, Salvation felt at home within his tight grasp.

The space between the circle of warlocks was narrow. Torsten's vision was getting worse, so he closed his eyes and listened only to the laughing of the madmen King Autlas had abandoned in the North so long ago. He drew Salvation overhead, reared back with both hands, and released. In all the chaos, he focused on the thrum as it sliced through the air, pommel over blade, again and again.

It found its place buried within Redstar's chest. Torsten barreled through the warlocks to finish the job, and as he passed their circle toward the rift in the air, he found himself in what seemed to be a new realm. He could see perfectly now, but the world itself had grown red and blurry, darkness tattering the edges. The sounds of battle and the chants of heathens were drowned out by an otherworldly whirr. All that remained was a surface of life upon which Torsten, Wren, Redstar, and Pi remained.

He spun. Around him, he could see countless places—towns,

villages, kingdoms, and plains, but all without focus. He blinked and tried to breathe, then saw something he least expected. Unholy monsters, demons the likes of which Torsten had never seen, chased a man and woman through a village. It all happened so fast, and the vision was unclear, simultaneously all around him and nowhere at all. He spun again and saw a circle of robed figures who looked like the mystics Torsten had fought so long ago by Liam's side. They had their hands outstretched toward a curled-up body.

Between them all, Pi remained affixed in midair, enveloped by what was now the ghastly figure of a beautiful woman.

"Well done, my child," she whispered, voice sensuous, intoxicating. "I can feel it. My power, returning from its buried prison after so long."

The last thing Torsten expected was for Nesilia to look as favorably in reality as Redstar's mural depicted. But behind that beauty were callous, colorless eyes set on devouring the world.

A force pulled at Torsten's ankles as he struggled to move. It seemed to be affecting Redstar as well. His dagger lay before him, and he crawled for it, Salvation skewering his chest. Torsten was able to reach it first and kick it aside.

"You can't stop it," Redstar gurgled. "In killing Bliss, we opened this world to her spirit, but with our sacrifice, the goddess herself may return."

"I can," Torsten replied. In this strange realm, even his own voice echoed, as if a hundred of himself he were whispering from all around. "Today, you die by my hand!" Unseen forces tried to hold him back, but Torsten fought with all his might to grab Salvation's hilt and shove it deeper into Redstar, all the way down to the crossguard.

Redstar cried out in pain, Nesilia's spirit with him. The world flashed, and for a moment, the circle of warlocks and the fighting Shieldsmen were revealed. Then, Torsten was back in what he assumed was Elsewhere. He looked up and saw Pi still in the air.

"I will not fail you," he whispered, although the boy couldn't hear him. He took a step toward Pi when the two people fleeing demons raced by him. For a moment Torsten thought he recognized them, though he couldn't believe his eyes in this other world, then tendrils of darkness closed in around them, coating their faces in shadow as they stopped to kiss. A circle of chanting warlocks halted the darkness, forming a magical shield that glowed red hot. Their screams rang out as the tendrils tore into them, worlds literally colliding.

Torsten ignored it all and extended his hand toward the young King. He could feel Nesilia's power, or perhaps Elsewhere itself pushing him back. The bones of his fingers felt like they were going to snap as they passed through the Buried Goddess' spectral form. His arm pushed forward, and he felt the pain in his forearm, then his elbow.

"Your world is open, and I shall walk it again," Nesilia said. "All those who have forgotten me will be punished!"

"We are the right hand of Iam," Torsten groaned through clenched teeth, desperate to distract himself from both Nesilia's words and the unbearable pain afflicting him. "We are the sword of His justice, and the Shield that guards the light of this world." Her fingers wrapped Pi's skinny arm. "For Liam!" he shouted and yanked backward.

He and Pi fell and slammed into the snow, his arms wrapped around the boy. Above him, the portal stayed open, sizzling in the sky like fat over a flame. Torsten covered Pi's ears and searched his surroundings, his vision impaired again now that he was beyond Elsewhere. Another blurry body soared across the rift. It slammed through a group of warlocks before rolling to a stop.

"You have stopped nothing," Nesilia's voice lingered on the air. "Deny my body this world, but the will of fire is mine..." And with that, she went silent, and the summit along with it. Torsten rolled over and saw with his blurred vision that the moons were now parting, revealing the light of the sun again.

Glass soldiers now surrounded the six remaining warlocks who hadn't been slaughtered by demons, Sir Mulliner at their lead. They looked from side to side, confused, weak. The ritual had melted the paint on the heathens faces, revealing only pale, scared appearances.

A red-stained hand suddenly grasped at Pi. Torsten wrenched it back and pulled the man it belonged to close.

"It's over, Redstar!" he cried over the sound of Elsewhere's veil.

"It can't be…" Redstar choked on blood. "It was her time..."

"It is yours alone."

Torsten wished his eyes worked properly so he could see every ounce of anguish in Redstar's eyes before he rolled over and his last breaths rattled through his lips. His arm fell limp into the bloody snow.

"Drad Redstar!" Freydis abandoned her defense and ran to Redstar's side. She cradled him as blood dripped from his mouth. "Help me with him, you fools!" she hissed at the other warlocks.

"They killed him," one said nervously.

"How could this happen?" asked another.

"Now your time comes to an end, witch." Austun lifted his blade and went at Freydis, but Torsten raised a hand.

"No," he rasped. "Enough have died today."

The warlocks looked to each other, then ran for the stairs. The soldiers let them go. They were all so weakened by the ritual they were no longer any harm to anyone if they even made it down the mountain.

"Cowards!" Freydis shrieked. She pulled Redstar close and whispered to him in Drav Crava. Her lips fell upon his, blood and all. A few guards ignored Torsten's orders and attempted to seize her. She slashed one in the leg, howled like a wild dire wolf, and went to slit her own throat. She was bashed in the back of the head before she could and crumpled atop her master.

"Sir Unger?" a small voice spoke beneath him. Torsten released Pi so he could look upon his face, but his vision was worse than ever as the magical burns Redstar left him with settled. All Torsten could tell was that Pi no longer sounded twice his age.

"You're all right, Your Gra—"

"Mother!" Pi interrupted him.

He squirmed free and ran to his mother, too far for Torsten to see clearly. He could hear the boy crying, shedding love upon Oleander as if the past year had been a nightmare and he'd only then woken. Sir Uriah Davies always spoke of how kind the son of Liam Nothhelm and Oleander Ruuhar was. Now, after all this time, Torsten saw the truth in that.

For a moment, Torsten's heart grew heavy, then he saw that Oleander's chest still rose and fell. He exhaled and rolled onto his back to face the brightening sun, as Loutis moved off and Celeste half-covered her path toward the horizon. His hand brushed against a seemingly harmless little doll a devoted mother had made for her son on the day of his birth. He raised it toward the light.

"You held onto that thing all this time?" The voice that spoke those words sounded familiar but was so overwhelmed by exhaustion it was hard to tell.

Torsten rolled his head to face whoever it was. He could see only splotches and shapes, but that was all he needed to recognize the face. Whitney Blisslayer, formerly the bane of his existence, lay in the trampled snow where the warlocks had been.

Torsten let his head fall back and hoped he was dreaming. When he looked back, his vision was even worse, and Whitney remained.

"I thought I was dreaming too," Whitney said. "But it's really you, isn't it? You're really here."

"Against all odds." Torsten drew a long, deep breath of the cold air.

"That means I'm here…" Whitney patted his own chest. "And she's…"

"Sir, who is this?" Sir Mulliner placed his sword against Whitney's neck. The thief crawled backward until the body of a fallen warlock blocked his way.

"I'm a friend to the Crown," Whitney said, raising his hands. "Lord Blisslayer, the master thief who helped your Wearer steal that doll."

"He isn't Wearer any longer," Mulliner said.

"Seems to be a theme with him."

"Forget the thief," Torsten said. "Get the King and his mother to safety and see to her wounds."

Mulliner hesitated for a second, then sheathed his sword. "You heard him," he said to the soldiers. "Help them and lock up any heathens who still breathe."

"Oh, and Sir Mulliner," Torsten tossed the doll at the Shieldsman's feet. "Burn this."

"After all we went through to get it?" Whitney asked.

"He's right. For Iam's sake, drown the ashes in the Torrential Sea." He let his head fall back into the snow. The loving arms of exhaustion wrapped their proverbial arms around him, and he gave in. Whitney said something, but he didn't hear him.

For the first time in a long time, concern over the future of the kingdom didn't make rest impossible to come by. Neither the impetuous thief nor the cold—nothing could keep him from it.

XXXV

THE THIEF

"Torsten, wake up," Whitney said. "Torsten!"

The big Shieldsman shot upright in his bed. They were in the physician's hall in the Glass Castle, where Torsten had remained resting for the better part of a day. Whitney wasn't exactly sure what had happened to cause so much upheaval since they parted in Winde Port—something about Redstar taking over and Torsten being imprisoned.

Masked Cultists of Nesilia had rioted throughout the city during the Dawning, burning down half of South Corner. Eventually, the city guard put them down, and when the Shieldsmen returned from the mountain, they began rounding up the Drav Cra and sending them out to their tents. Things were safer within the castle, that was for sure.

All Whitney knew was none of it could have been stranger than what he'd gone through. Just breathing the Pantego air again was a thing of beauty, even if the room smelled like stale blood and piss.

"Who is that?" Torsten grumbled. He rolled his head to face Whitney, but a bloody bandage covered his eyes.

"Your very best friend," Whitney replied.

"Whitney? You're still here?"

"You were in rough shape up there. I couldn't just leave you."

"And they let you in here?" Torsten asked, incredulous.

"Wouldn't you know it. One of the Shieldsmen remembered you ennobling me. I always knew that would come in handy."

"What happened… I… the King and Queen."

He tried to slide his legs off the bed, grimaced. Whitney placed a hand on his shoulder to stop him. Whatever had happened, he was fairly beat up beyond being unable to see.

"They say the Queen will live at the cost of her beauty," Whitney said. "Though if you heard her screaming echoing down the hall, you wouldn't think it. And the King is well, talking again."

"I need to speak with them."

"Hold your zhulongs, old friend. If I let you up too soon, they'll never let me back here."

"That's fine because you aren't supposed to be here." Torsten tried to adjust his position, winced in pain some more, then laid back. "How did you get up there anyway?"

"You wouldn't believe me if I told you."

"After what I saw on the mountain, there's nothing I wouldn't believe."

"Honestly? Elsewhere."

"What?"

"I was there for years, trapped by Sora thanks to a spell gone wrong."

Torsten turned over. "C'mon, thief. I said I'd believe anything, but must you always push your stories too far?"

"Hey, I'm serious! There was an upyr, and Barty Darkings, and Troborough wasn't burned down, and… you have no idea how good it feels to be out of that place." He considered telling Torsten that he too was there, as a blind priest, but it seemed like it would only sound like an insult considering his current state. He'd learned a thing or two in Elsewhere about watching his tongue around people that could beat him to death like Kazimir.

"Sounds like a bad dream."

"I hoped so too until I was spat out onto Mount Lister after Sora freed me. Any chance you've seen her?"

Torsten tugged on the bandage over his eyes. "I don't see much of anything now, thief. Besides, as you know, I've been here."

Whitney's head hung. "I just meant... Maybe you'd heard something about a Panpingese woman around here from guards passing through. I don't know." Whitney didn't add that was the real reason he was sticking around. Hoping Sora had been thrown out of the rift between worlds in another direction and was close, and that she wasn't still stuck in Elsewhere with that goddess.

Goddess? You know who that was Whitney.

Torsten turned back. "I haven't heard a thing about anyone except cultists and Drav Cra refusing to be kicked out to their camp. Last I saw Sora was barely a month ago."

"What? Really? How was she?" Whitney asked.

"You tell me. You were there, floating away from Winde Port on a stolen ship after helping me walk right into an ambush thanks to those Darkings traitors."

"A month?" Whitney recoiled. "It's only been a month here?"

He felt sick. He knew it hadn't been six years in Pantego while he was gone. He wasn't stupid. The Prince—or King—didn't appear much older after all and neither did Sora. Six years imagining her face, he would have noticed any extra wrinkles. He'd figured at least one year had passed and he'd arrived at the next Dawning. He couldn't stomach asking any guards on the way down from Mount Lister, but now he knew.

"Whatever really happened to bring you to that mountaintop

did a number on you, didn't it, kid?" Torsten said. "Did Redstar put a spell on you to go after the orepul or something?"

"Something like that… I… look." Whitney slid across the bed to get closer to Torsten's head. "If Sora isn't here, then I think she's in Panping, and she's in trouble. I saw mystics around her, and…" He swallowed the lump forming in his throat. "Nesilia."

"You had a bad dream, Whitney. There are no mystics anymore, and Redstar's attempt at reviving the Buried Goddess failed. He's gone." Whitney could tell the knight didn't even believe his own words.

"Torsten, it wasn't a dream. I was in Elsewhere for six years. You can't make that up."

"Then maybe you'll do a bit of good in your life, so next time you'll reach the Gate of Light."

"You really don't believe me?"

"I'm sorry Redstar's evil got to you, Whitney. I truly am. But it's over now. The madness is finished, and it's time to rebuild this broken kingdom from the inside out. The people have lost trust in the Crown and in Iam. Rebellion still rages in the Black Sands. The King is… I don't know why I'm telling you all this."

"Because we're best friends, like I said."

Torsten groaned. Whitney smiled.

"You're still a stubborn old mule; you know that?" Whitney said.

"And you're still a rotten thief," Torsten replied.

"So, I guess that means you aren't going to help me find Sora? Because I faintly remember there was a bargain struck in Winde Port that if I helped you, you'd help me save her. Considering she saved herself, you still owe me."

Torsten tapped his forehead. "Wouldn't be much help looking for anything now, would I?"

"I suppose not."

A period of silence passed between them. Torsten's expression grew dourer than ever from another reminder of his injury.

"I never had a chance to thank you, Whitney," Torsten said, finally.

"Go on," Whitney said.

"You kept your word in Winde Port when no one else did. Your distraction of Muskigo was exceptional."

"Exceptional, eh?"

"Don't let it go to your head."

"Too late," Whitney joked.

Whitney thought he heard a soft chuckle slip through the Shieldman's lips.

"That's two thank yous in as many days from men I never thought I'd get them from," Whitney said. "All those years in Elsewhere have really improved my influence."

"You're really going to stick with that story?" Torsten said.

"I always tell the truth."

"You're impossible."

"I missed this." Whitney slapped Torsten on the shoulder, forgetting his many injuries. The Shieldsman winced but didn't make a sound. Then Whitney hopped to his feet.

"Well, since you're all right, I guess it's time I head off," he said. "Better get out of this city before something else crazy happens to me."

"Whitney." Torsten grabbed his wrist. "That was you and Sora I saw together when I entered that hellish breach in the world, wasn't it?"

"So, you do believe me!"

"I don't know what I believe anymore, but it seems every time I have all reason to give up hope, your friend Sora is there to make sure I don't."

"She's the best there is."

Torsten nodded. "Whatever happened, I hope you find her

again. I mean it. Even you deserve some sort of happiness in this broken world of ours."

"Torsten Unger, you continue to surprise me."

He scoffed. "Before you go, would you mind getting this thing off me?" He fought through the pain to swing his legs around and sit upright.

"Why?" Whitney said. "You look like one of your priests; it's fitting."

"Whitney."

"I don't want to get into trouble."

"Just do it. I need to know."

Whitney sighed. He sat beside Torsten and began unwinding the bandage covering his eyes. The sight underneath was grizzly. His brown skin was ragged and bubbled across his brow, and his eyelids were nearly burned shut, the lashes seared away. What little of his eyes Whitney could see were gray and calloused.

Torsten turned his head from side to side after the bandage fell free. He looked up, down, then straight toward Whitney. Whitney didn't need the Shieldsman's words for him to know he could see nothing. He'd played the part of blind priest before.

"Anything?" Whitney said anyway.

Torsten shook his head, but he didn't seem saddened by the revelation. "Not even blurs now."

"I'm sorry Torsten."

"Don't be. Thank Iam for letting my vision linger long enough to stop Redstar before he dug this kingdom any deeper into exile." He reached up slowly, one of his arms shaking from the pain. Whitney helped it the rest of the way so that the Shieldsman could circle his worthless eyes in prayer to Iam. He didn't say it, but he nodded to Whitney in thanks for helping him.

"If you don't mind, I'd like to be alone with Him right now," Torsten said.

"Always at his side, just like in Elsewhere," Whitney said.

"I won't even pretend to understand what you're talking about."

"I never do." Whitney stood and took a few long strides toward the exit. He stopped and fell into an exaggerated bow. "Fare thee well, fair knight. Good luck with rebuilding your kingdom. I'm off to find my lady. See you soon—er, until we meet again."

"I have little doubt we will. Goodbye, thief."

At that, Whitney spun on his heel and made his way out the door. He nearly bumped a masked physician on the way out, mumbling his apologies as he sidestepped.

As soon as he was alone his smile faded and his features darkened. He even had to stop for a moment to lean on the wall and breathe. It wasn't just seeing the mighty Shieldsman so vulnerable that affected him. It was everything.

It'd been six years for him since they'd last talked, and he had to act as if no time at all had passed. It was a lie. Maybe Whitney looked the same, but when they traversed the Webbed Woods together, it felt like he was still only a kid. A kid with a crush he refused to recognize that had become so much more.

He drew himself to a window and stared off across the snowy plains. Sora was somewhere out there, and she was in trouble. He wasn't sure how he knew it, but he did. He could never forget that look on her face in Elsewhere right before they were split apart once again. The sheer terror.

Maybe it was the mystics' fault or the Buried Goddess. Perhaps both or something unimaginably worse. It didn't matter. Sora had sought out a people thought to be extinct just to save him, now he was going to do the same for her. Wherever it took him.

XXXVI

THE MYSTIC

Sora heard screams. They weren't the cries of demon spawn in Elsewhere, they were human, and they were horrified. She tried desperately to open her eyes, but she couldn't. The bright light, still searing, still blinding, forced her eyes shut although she fought. It was as if her eyes were controlled by someone, something else. The smell of iron filled her nostrils, a scent she'd become far too familiar with over the course of her lifetime. It was part of her, and she, it.

Blood.

Lots of blood.

"Please, don't." She heard the voice but couldn't see its owner. Even so, she didn't need her eyes to know it was Aihara Na. The voice came from below Sora like she was standing and the other was kneeling. "Together we can start afresh."

"Yes," said a voice, familiar and loud. It belonged to Nesilia. Sora had encountered her enough times to know. And it was loud like it came from within Sora's head.

A sudden flash in Sora's vision revealed the walls of the Red Tower. How had she gotten back there? Was it another vision?

Another flash showed the color red, deep like blood. This time her eyes stayed open and her insides roiled around, gurgling, threatening to make her heave.

Dead mystics littered the floor, Madam Jaya, Huyshi and the others, their blood spattered all over the walls. Red on red. She had no idea they could even bleed, but it was like their spectral forms had been undone. Their blood formed crimson streams, coalescing into one current and pouring into the rushing waters of the chamber of the Secret Council. It frothed beneath the spray of the wianu statues, and Sora could've sworn she saw one of them move.

Her stomach lurched, and she threw up. As she looked down, she saw the bile pooling in front of Aihara Na. The woman was on her knees and didn't flinch as the vomit sprinkled her robes.

That was when Sora realized the blood soaking her shredded kimono and covering her own hands. Wetzel's knife was gripped in one of them.

"Please, Sora, don't do this," Ancient One Aihara Na sniveled, groveling. "I was wrong about you, your power. We can still save Panping and the Order. Together."

"What—what happened?" Sora asked.

Madam Aihara looked scared and confused.

Sora searched the room. Madam Jaya wasn't merely bleeding, she had a gash across her throat left there by a blade. Sora regarded her hands again. She staggered back, the knife slipping through her fingers, landing in the pool of red with a loud clatter.

"You know the truth," came a voice from within, sultry and hypnotic. "No more lies."

"Nesilia?" Sora asked.

From the depths of the waters, vines began to grow, climbing the impossibly high walls and ceiling. Leaves, branches, and thorns congregated together, thick like the Webbed Woods. They weren't just sprouting from the waters. Sora saw them coming from her own hands.

Panic drove Sora to her knees.

"Please, spare me?" Aihara said. The vines wrapped the mystic's calves and throat, slowly squeezing the life from her. Her form was corporeal now as well. "The others they could not see, but I know now this is the form of our saving. Your forgiveness, no? I offer you mine."

She gagged as the vines tightened. Her cheeks went pale. Tears welled in her eyes. A fearless, centuries-old being she no longer seemed, but instead, an old human woman who'd realized she didn't want to die yet. Sora didn't think she could pity the cruel woman, but she did, and the vines stopped tightening. Seeing her fear made her mind drift to Whitney and the way he looked at her before they were split apart.

"Stop fighting." Sora heard the words echoing all around her. Her thoughts were promptly yanked back to her present. The smell of blood gave way to the scent of dirt. "You no longer have to struggle, my love. I will take care of everything." Sora shook like a tall tree amidst a great storm. "Give in!"

Sora's head snapped back, eyes rolling upward. She felt her back straighten, arch, then her feet touched down. It was as if Sora watched herself from within. Not in control. She screamed and begged for answers, but her cries only seemed to fill the formless void she now inhabited, whispers in the dark, like when she used to call upon Elsewhere and heard it responding, but couldn't understand, only now, her mind rumbled with Nesilia's words.

The door to the chamber suddenly creaked, and Sora's body whipped around. Aquira stood in the entry, her big, bright eyes blinking. Sora's hand rose, beyond her control, and the jagged vines extended toward the little creature.

Sora screamed Aquira's name into the darkness. She poured

every ounce of her soul into the word, and the little wyvern's eyes went wide. She screeched, then soared, dodging a snapping vine. She blew fire at another as she twisted back around.

Sora's body turned to watch Aquira spin sideways and zip through one of the tower's narrow, arrowslit windows. She simultaneously felt anger and relief, not sure which emotion belonged to her any longer.

Cloth brushed stone.

"Where are you going, mystic?" said the voice of Nesilia. This time, it came from Sora's own lips. Aihara Na had been crawling away thanks to Aquira's distraction, but the vines rose to wrap her limbs and throat again.

Aihara Na struggled to speak the vines grew so tight. "I'll pledge myself to you," she gagged. "With your power, we could once again rule Panping."

The vines loosened, and Aihara Na collapsed onto her hands and knees, coughing like a mere mortal.

"Why settle for Panping?" Nesilia said. "With this body, together, we can rule it all."

EPILOGUE

S igrid sat silently in a booth on the ground floor of the Vineyard. Valin had let her out of her room, though she wasn't sure why. Screams sounded outside in Dockside, like a war had broken out, some so shrill and filled with terror they made Sigrid wince.

None of it fazed Valin. He sat across from her with his bad leg stretched out on the seat, massaging his knee. With his other hand, he used a fork to enjoy a steak, drenched in gravy, the pieces already cut for him. Two thugs remained so she couldn't do anything but watch him indulge. The rest of the rotten place was empty. Even the few wenches and their regulars who didn't care to honor the Dawning had filed out.

"What do you want?" Sigrid asked meekly. A scream, louder than all the others, made her heart feel like it was going to burst through her chest. What sounded like glass shattering followed it. "What's going on?"

"Progress, my dear," Valin said, chewing on a chunk of meat.

"I don't understand. Can't you help them?"

A flash of orange streaked across a window, accompanied by cheering.

"Save your prayers for your brother," Valin said.

Sigrid slid along the booth toward Valin, but one of the thugs flaunted his cudgel to keep her still.

"Is he out there still?" she asked.

"Not if he cares a lick about you." Sigrid hung her head, and Valin finally glanced over at her. "Relax. I have a good feeling about him. It took some work, but I think I finally got through to him."

The doors swung open, and Codar strode inside. Blood spatter covered half his face, a few spots staining his usually neat, white mustache. Valin sat up at the sight of him. Codar took a moment to gather his breath as if refusing to speak until he collected himself. "They passed through the gates," he said. "I feared Rand might try and come back for her, but it seems he finally sees reason."

"Excellent!" Valin clapped his hands. He stood and waved up to the balcony. Sigrid hadn't noticed before, but one of his thugs had a crossbow perched on the railing aimed at her. The man lowered it and backed away.

A chill ran up Sigrid's spine. Before she could speak, Valin laid his hand on her shoulder. "Just a precaution, my dear," he said, a warmth to his tone that somehow made her feel worse. "I had every faith in him—"

A torch broke through the window of the Vineyard and landed on one of the tables. The dry wood instantly caught fire.

Codar whipped around just before a masked cultist of Nesilia plowed into him. He fended off a fury of stabs and gutted the assailant. Another leaped through the broken window and ran toward the booth where Sigrid sat. He screamed mad, indecipherable words until a crossbow bolt struck him in the chest and knocked him over.

"Yigging savages!" Valin yelled. He slammed his fist on the table, flipping his meal and sending his fork clattering to the ground. "Get this cleaned up. And call for Uhlvark and place him outside on guard. That ought to scare the crazies off."

The two thugs hurried to put out the flames. Valin grabbed his crutch and went to stand, then noticed Sigrid.

"Get her locked up safe upstairs," Valin said. "We wouldn't want anything happening to her."

The thug with the crossbow rushed down the stairs to the booth. "Let's go beautiful," he said. He gave Sigrid's arm a gentle tug despite only just having been prepared to do to her what he'd done to the cultist. Sigrid's gaze darted between Valin as he crutched away and Codar, busy trying to roll the corpse off him.

"I said, let's go, wench!" This time he pulled hard on her arm.

Sigrid instantly recalled the feeling of helplessness when the Drav Cra men tried to rape her. She ripped free and reached under the booth. The thug grabbed her foot and dragged her. She pawed at the floor as she slid until her fingers found the handle of Valin's fork.

The thug yanked her so hard she crashed onto the floor, and when he went to lift her, she stabbed the fork into his eye. His scream made those echoing outside the doors seem tame. Valin stopped by the exit to his office and looked back. Sigrid made eye contact with him, then bolted for the front door.

The crimelord of Dockside didn't seem concerned. "Codar, retrieve her," he groaned, rolling his eyes.

The Breklian pushed the body atop him aside and rolled over. He slashed at Sigrid's legs on her way by, cutting her calf. She fell through the doorway and tumbled down the stairs, but she didn't let it stop her. She hopped back to her feet and limped, glancing back to see Codar leisurely walking after her.

"Get away from me!" she shouted. A crash drew her vision back in front of her. A cart of supplies toppled over, and fish slid from barrels across the snow. Her gaze then rose to see the Dockside church she'd spent many a sermon in over the years entirely consumed by fire. Terrified citizens ran this way and that, some being chased by cultists in their billowing red robes and white masks.

Sigrid slipped and nearly lost her footing. She glanced back to see Codar gaining on her, and when she turned back around, she bumped into a cultist.

"Buried, not dead," the man behind the mask hissed before scurrying away.

Sigrid went to take another step, then her legs went weak, and she fell to a knee. When she looked down, she saw the tip of the cultist's dagger jutting out of her stomach, buried all the way down to the hilt. She'd been so frantic she didn't even feel him stab her.

She grabbed the handle, blood covering her hands.

Codar grabbed her shoulders and gently laid her back upon the street.

"You had to run," he sighed. He inspected the wound, and his expression told Sigrid all she needed to know.

She was going to die.

Sigrid struggled for words, but none came. She didn't feel pain, only a cold sensation spreading within her, a coldness that made the harsh winter air seem warm.

"Rand…" she managed to eke out through quivering lips.

"At least you will die knowing he loved you," Codar said. "You westerners care terribly for being loved." He yanked, removing the blade and stared down into Sigrid's eyes. "Don't worry, girl, it will all be over soon."

He held the blade to her throat, but as he did, his gaze lifted away from her. His face twisted with terror.

"Kazimir?" he said softly.

"Why would you sully such potential with death?" a man said. His voice was nearly as cold as the ground beneath Sigrid. "I can feel the rage within her—power like you never had."

Whoever it was, his presence rendered Codar speechless. Sigrid couldn't speak either, only watch and listen as the numbness spread within her. The newcomer circled them, and the dagger fell from Codar's grasp as he staggered back.

"Grandfather, H… how are you here?" Codar stammered.

"I asked myself that when my eyes finally opened after so many years in Elsewhere and this chaos surrounded me. Now I see. I denied the Sanguine Lords a blood pact owed, and so it is time I offer them a new vessel."

The stranger had silken, white hair just like Codar. But when he knelt before Sigrid, she saw that his face was smooth as a young man despite Codar calling him his grandfather. He kneeled and dragged his finger through Sigrid's blood, then brought it to his lips. His eyes closed, lids flickering like he was in ecstasy.

"How I missed this," he said. Then he stared straight into Sigrid's eyes. His were dark, soulless—the stuff of nightmares, yet she couldn't look away.

"No more a woman than a girl and already your life draws to an abrupt end," he whispered to her. He ran the back of his now bloody hand across her cheek. "Don't be afraid. I'm not here to kill you. Quite the opposite, really."

Sigrid listened but didn't speak—couldn't speak. The stranger leaned down, drawing himself to her ear. She felt no warmth on his breath. She felt nothing.

"Do you not wish to live?" he said. "Do you not wish for more?"

Thank you for reading *Will of Fire*, book three in The Buried Goddess Saga. The story will continue in Buried Goddess Book 4, coming 2019!

Being the new kids on the block is difficult and we could really benefit from your honest reviews on Amazon. It'll only take you a minute but it'll affect the life of this book forever! (Not to mention help feed our families). All you have to do is click here and then scroll down and write a review. HUGE thank you in advance for helping making The Buried Goddess Saga a big hit!

JOIN THE KING'S SHIELD

Sign up to the *free* and exclusive King's Shield Newsletter to receive updates about sequels, conceptual art that breathes life into Pantego, as well as exclusive access to short stories called "Legends of Pantego." Learn more about the characters and the world you love.

ABOUT THE AUTHORS

Jaime lives in Texas with his wife and two kids. He enjoys anything creative, from graphic arts to painting. His office looks like the Avengers threw up on the walls.

Jaime has been writing since elementary school and is a bit of a grammar officer—here to correct and serve.

Rhett is a Sci-fi/Fantasy author currently living in Stamford, Connecticut. His published works include books in the USA Today Bestselling CIRCUIT SERIES (Published by Diversion Books and Podium Audio), THE BURIED GODDESS SAGA and the BASTARDS OF THE RING SERIES (Audible Studios, coming in 2019). He is also one of the founders of the popular science fiction platform, Sci-Fi Bridge.

SPECIAL THANKS TO:

ADAWIA E. ASAD
BARDE PRESS
CALUM BEAULIEU
BEN
BECKY BEWERSDORF
BHAM
TANNER BLOTTER
ALFRED JOSEPH BOHNE IV
CHAD BOWDEN
ERREL BRAUDE
DAMIEN BROUSSARD
CATHERINE BULLINER
JUSTIN BURGESS
MATT BURNS
BERNIE CINKOSKE
MARTIN COOK
ALISTAIR DILWORTH
JAN DRAKE
BRET DULEY
RAY DUNN
ROB EDWARDS
RICHARD EYRES
MARK FERNANDEZ
CHARLES T FINCHER
SYLVIA FOIL
GAZELLE OF CAERBANNOG
DAVID GEARY
MICHEAL GREEN
BRIAN GRIFFIN

EDDIE HALLAHAN
JOSH HAYES
PAT HAYES
BILL HENDERSON
JEFF HOFFMAN
GODFREY HUEN
JOAN QUERALTÓ IBÁÑEZ
JONATHAN JOHNSON
MARCEL DE JONG
KABRINA
PETRI KANERVA
ROBERT KARALASH
VIKTOR KASPERSSON
TESLAN KIERINHAWK
ALEXANDER KIMBALL
JIM KOSMICKI
FRANKLIN KUZENSKI
MEENAZ LODHI
DAVID MACFARLANE
JAMIE MCFARLANE
HENRY MARIN
CRAIG MARTELLE
THOMAS MARTIN
ALAN D. MCDONALD
JAMES MCGLINCHEY
MICHAEL MCMURRAY
CHRISTIAN MEYER
SEBASTIAN MÜLLER
MARK NEWMAN
JULIAN NORTH

KYLE OATHOUT
LILY OMIDI
TROY OSGOOD
GEOFF PARKER
NICHOLAS (BUZ) PENNEY
JASON PENNOCK
THOMAS PETSCHAUER
JENNIFER PRIESTER
RHEL
JUDY ROBERTS
JOHN BEAR ROSS
DONNA SANDERS
FABIAN SARAVIA
TERRY SCHOTT
SCOTT
ALLEN SIMMONS
KEVIN MICHAEL STEPHENS
MICHAEL J. SULLIVAN
PAUL SUMMERHAYES
JOHN TREADWELL
CHRISTOPHER J. VALIN
PHILIP VAN ITALLIE
JAAP VAN POELGEEST
FRANCK VAQUIER
VORTEX
DAVID WALTERS JR
MIKE A. WEBER
PAMELA WICKERT
JON WOODALL
BRUCE YOUNG

www.ingramcontent.com/pod-product-compliance
Lightning Source LLC
Chambersburg PA
CBHW032152180726
48284CB00001B/18